A
PRIVATEER'S
FORTUNE

A
PRIVATEER'S
FORTUNE

BY
ALICE JONES

INTRODUCTION BY
DAN CONLIN

Formac Publishing Company Limited
Halifax

Cover illustration: *Scene in the Bay of Annapolis*, W.H. Bartlett, 1842.

Formac Publishing Company Limited acknowledges the support of the Cultural Affairs Section, Nova Scotia Department of Tourism and Culture. We acknowledge the financial support of the Government of Canada through the Book Publishing Industry Development Program (BPIDP) for our publishing activities.

We acknowledge the support of the Canada Council for the Arts for our publishing program.

National Library of Canada Cataloguing in Publication

Jones, Alice, 1853-1933
[Bubbles we buy]
    A privateer's fortune / Alice Jones.

(Formac fiction treasures)
First published 1903 under title: Bubbles we buy.
ISBN 0-88780-572-8

    I. Title. II. Title: Bubbles we buy. III. Series.

PS8519.O523B82 2002   C813'.52   C2002-903373-X
PR9199.3.J6273B82 2002

Originally published as *Bubbles We Buy* by Herbert B. Turner & Co., Boston, 1903.
Series editor: Gwendolyn Davies

Formac Publishing Company Limited
5502 Atlantic Street
Halifax, Nova Scotia B3H 1G4
www.formac.ca

Printed and bound in Canada

Presenting Formac Fiction Treasures
Series Editor: Gwendolyn Davies

A taste for reading popular fiction expanded in the nineteenth century with the mass marketing of books and magazines. People read rousing adventure stories aloud at night around the fireside; they bought entertaining romances to read while travelling on trains and curled up with the latest serial novel in their leisure moments. Novelists were important cultural figures, with devotees who eagerly awaited their next work.

Among the many successful popular English language novelists of the late 19th and early 20th centuries were a group of Maritimers who found in their own education, travel and sense of history events and characters capable of entertaining readers on both sides of the Atlantic. They emerged from well-established communities which valued education and culture, for women as well as for men. Faced with limited publishing opportunities in the Maritimes, successful writers sought magazine and book publishers in the major cultural centres: New York, Boston, Philadelphia, London, and sometimes Montreal and Toronto. They often enjoyed much success with readers 'at home' but the best of these writers found large audiences across Canada and in the United States and Great Britain.

The Formac Fiction Treasures series is aimed at offering contemporary readers access to books that were successful, often huge bestsellers in their time, but which are now little known and often hard to find. The authors and titles selected are chosen first of all as enjoyable to read, and secondly for the light they shine on historical events and on attitudes and views of the culture from which they emerged. These complete original texts reflect values which are sometimes in conflict with those of today: for example, racism is often evident, and bluntly expressed. This collection of novels is offered as a step towards rediscovering a surprisingly diverse and not nearly well enough known popular cultural heritage of the Maritime provinces and of Canada.

Alice Jones

Introduction

A *Privateer's Fortune* is a story about the conflicts and drama that spring from inheriting wealth from unsavory sources. The two protagonists Gilbert Clinch and Isabel Broderick are both "poor and ambitious" and their attraction to wealth comes with a price. Isabel marries a mentally unstable man she does not love and Gilbert seeks to disinherit others to acquire an ill-gotten fortune. The pursuit of their respective fortunes draws them together and apart and challenges their romantic destinies with difficult questions.

The novel delivers a classic nineteenth-century romance of separated lovers seeking their way between family and wealth in romantic European settings peopled with English lords and Italian counts. While Isabel's tragic marriage with its terrible consequences supplies much of the pathos of the book, it is the murky legacy of privateering that supplies the dramatic interest in Gilbert's discovery of his family's ill-gotten fortune. Revealed in the classic form of a strange treasure discovered in an attic and a secret will, Gilbert's legacy comes from an unknown grandfather, Jonathan Bauer.

Bauer's story emerges in whispers from the shadows — a swashbuckling captain who plundered the

Spanish Main as a privateer, smuggled slaves and later made a killing backing the North in the Civil War. Crafty, ill-tempered, and secretive, he casts a long shadow across the destinies of half the characters in the book with the terms of his conflicting wills. Only a daughter and his second wife manage to defy him.

The real ghost whose shadow haunts the book and clearly inspires the fictional Bauer is the real-life merchant, Enos Collins. This Nova Scotian mariner, privateer and financier was acclaimed on his death in 1871 as the richest man in British North America. Alice Jones effectively mines the little known legends of this colourful Nova Scotian merchant.

Like the imaginary Bauer, Collins came from outside Halifax, from a merchant family in the coastal Nova Scotian entrepôt of Liverpool. He spent his youth in West Indies trading vessels, first for his father, then for himself. He made a few privateering cruises in the West Indies, most notably a six-month cruise in 1799 on the Spanish Main (as the Spanish Mainland colonies were known in the eighteenth century) as first lieutenant in the *Charles Mary Wentworth*. However, unlike Bauer, Collins soon moved ashore, hiring other men and ships to man his commercial empire. Also unlike Bauer, Collins did not die a miserly recluse. He moved to Halifax, married into the local elite, founded one of Canada's first banks and became a member of the Governor's executive council. Collins' marriage to the daughter of Nova Scotia's chief justice seems to have lacked melodrama, although like Bauer he produced only one surviving son (and three daughters) who moved off to England with his fortune when he died.

Although Collins is often associated with privateering, it was in trading and price speculation that he really made his fortune. While Collins was respected for his success, he shared Bauer's grasping and unforgiving reputation in business. He had a pattern of starting equal partnerships and emerging as senior or sole owner. His greed was evident most disgracefully in the Brandy Dispute of 1830: he manipulated duties so that he and other insiders could sell their brandy duty free at severe cost to the public treasury.

Like Bauer, Collins had a reputation for seeing opportunities where others did not. He risked French naval blockades to run supplies, at a handsome profit, to Wellington's army in Spain. He reputedly built such good relations with the revolutionary leaders of Haiti that he enjoyed a monopoly on Haitian coffee exports. Most famously, in 1811 he purchased a small slave smuggling schooner captured by the British navy. Useless for any normal trade Collins bought it for next to nothing, briefly putting her into mail packet service with his hometown under the name *Liverpool Packet*. A year later the long expected War of 1812 broke out and Collins had a perfect vessel, instantly available for privateering on the American coast. Taking over 50 United States' vessels in the war under the capable hands of Liverpool captains, chosen by Collins, the daring captures of this tiny schooner spread fear and anger in American ports.

The exotic trade of privateer is central to Bauer's sinister side in this novel. It was probably influenced by the very first historical research on Nova Scotian

privateers that was presented to meetings of the Royal
Nova Scotia Historical Society in 1900, just about the
time Alice Jones was writing her book. Given the
murky understanding of this unusual trade, it is no
surprise that Jones portrays it as barely legal piracy, a
sort of freelance license to plunder wherever fighting
could be found, all legalized by a letter of marque and
sliding neatly into slave smuggling.

In reality privateering in Atlantic Canada was more
tightly controlled and respected. Privateers were pri-
vately owned warships licensed by the government to
attack specific enemy nations, only in times of war.
They followed the same regulations as the British
Royal Navy (which also depended on the proceeds
from captures to pay naval sailors). Every captured
item had to be scrutinized by a special court in
Halifax that on several occasions gave back captured
ships and their cargoes, with damages, to aggrieved
parties. The British state was anxious to keep neutral
and allied nations happy in their war with Napoleon
and thus kept privateering under a pretty tight rein.
When the Napoleonic Wars ended in 1815, all British
privateering licenses became void and the privateers
of Atlantic Canada quickly switched back to their
peacetime trades.

Of course there is always room for speculation
about what went on in the West Indies, so far from
Halifax. Collins allegedly wrote in later years about his
youthful days in the West Indies, "There were many
things that happened that we don't care to talk
about." While there is no evidence that privateers
were ever involved in smuggling slaves, slavery was

legal during the privateering period and the occasional slave captured was judged as cargo and sold off in the same cold-blooded manner.

There are also some real-life inspirations to one of Bauer's more unseemly acts — robbing from the church. On more than one occasion, privateers did capture objects from the clergy on the Spanish Main. The logbook of the privateer ship *Charles Mary Wentworth* records the chase of a Spanish vessel in July 1799 which ended when the enemy crew and passengers fled into the jungle ashore: "One Priest a Passenger made his Escape on shore & his trunk was left on shore with every article in it and Every thing belonging to him." On another occasion, a Halifax priest writing to his bishop in 1802 reported sardonically, "I am sending you some vestments ... Some privateers from here stole them from some Spaniards, and not knowing what to do with them made them a present to us. You see, my Lord, how the misfortune of some becomes the good fortune of others."

There is even a possible connection to privateering in one of the novel's more bizarre symbols of greed — the ugly and cursed golden statue of the Virgin Mary plundered from a South American cathedral. In Halifax's venerable Saint Paul's Church there are a pair of unhappy blank-eyed gold cherubs staring down at the pious congregation. According to an early history of the church, they were part of a large Spanish pipe organ intended for a cathedral in South America but which fell into the hands of Halifax privateers in the 1750s. The old Spanish organ was replaced in the nineteenth century but the decorative cherubs remained installed on the walls where they still lurk in the back balcony. There is some question about the accuracy of this story, but it is part of the folklore of the church with which Alice Jones would have been familiar.

Although much of the book is set in European social circles, critical early action occurs along the deftly portrayed Lahave River where Gilbert unexpectedly realizes the dream of many Atlantic Canadian exiles of buying the old homestead. Unfortunately his acquisition comes with complications he could not have foreseen. While Jones is clearly much more familiar with the Thames River in England and its social traffic than the LaHave, her portrayal is affectionate and seems inspired by summer visits.

While Jones' romantic story of two lovers separated by family and wealth is a staple nineteenth-century formula, she invests it with some significant early twentieth-century themes. Isabel's influence and success in the art world, albeit mostly in her husband's name, reflect the evolving role of women in the public sphere. There are also ugly racial associations typical of the time in the connotations given to the secret African heritage of Isabel's foe, Margaret. The novel has some subtle reflections of the political tensions of the time. British–American and colonial tensions flare up in several places. There is also foreshadowing of the Boer War with the blows it would deliver to British notions of supremacy, an irony all the more striking for a modern reader aware of the even grimmer tragedy of World War I which would follow. Gilbert's medical specialty as an alienist, the late nineteenth-century term for psychiatrist shows the fascination of the early stages of this science, including its flirtation with eugenic ideas and preoccupation with inherited madness.

In addition to the 'modern' touches Jones injects into her book, it is the classic narrative devices that make it enjoyable for today's reader. She was not afraid to make rousing use of gothic conventions, opening with a dark and stormy night, bringing in an ancient mariner to move things along and springing all manner of dramatic coincidences to advance the plot. Used with unabashed gusto, these devices are part of the novel's charms, fine companions to a mysterious statue and a secret will.

Dan Conlin
Curator of Marine History
Maritime Museum of the Atlantic, Halifax
2002

Biographical note

Alice Jones was raised in Halifax, Nova Scotia, at a time when the colony was firmly established as an economic centre. Fortunes were being made in shipbuilding and trade and the rough edges of the early days of settlement were smoothed over by living standards comparable with any part of the British empire. Born in 1853, to Alfred Gilpin Jones and Margaret Wiseman Stairs, Alice was one of seven children. Evidently they were raised to appreciate art and literature. Her sister Frances Jones Bannerman was a widely respected artist and Alice herself, as evident in A Privateer's Inheritance, had considerable knowledge of the Paris salons and the architectural sites of Europe.

In the 1880s and 1890s Jones travelled quite extensively. She wrote travel sketches and short stories for magazines such as *Dominion Illustrated Monthly* and *The Week*. From her journal it is evident that in the first six months of 1894 she was in Egypt, Rome, Paris, England and Canada.

Jones lived at Menton in the French département of Alpes-Maritime, near the Italian border. Her sister Frances resided nearby, and her brother also had a villa in the area. She died in 1933, leaving behind, in addition to her elegant travel stories, four novels and three unpublished works.

CONTENTS

1	"The Stress of the Storm"	17
2.	Old Friends	27
3.	The Ancient Mariner	35
4.	"In Her Service"	46
5.	The Flowers of Death	56
6.	The Moorings	66
7.	The Lust of Gold	78
8.	The Dead Hand	87
9.	Our Lady of Wrath	95
10.	Isaac Meets an Old Acquaintance	104
11.	Gathering Clouds	113
12.	The Sword of Damocles	120
13.	Separate Paths	128
14.	A Connoisseur	135
15.	In the Days of Her Youth	143
16.	A New Allegiance	150
17.	Clashing Wills	159
18.	Starting Afresh	166
19.	By the Thames	173
20.	Jack	183
21.	Christmas	192
22.	In the Studio	203
23.	In Florence	213
24.	A Wanderer	223
25.	Persephone	232
26.	The Gorgon's Head	242
27.	A Dinner Party	259
28.	The Borderland	268
29.	"Our Hands Have Met"	278

30.	Heathholm	287
31.	"A Day in June"	295
32.	The American Artist	305
33.	Mother and Son	315
34.	The Poison of Asps	324
35.	Sundered Friends	333
36.	Cookham Regatta	341
37.	Jack Goes Soldiering	349
38.	Ellen Sievert Speaks Her Mind	356
39.	In the Day of Temptation	364
40.	At the Shooting-Hut	370
41.	The Power of the Night	378
42.	Release	389
43.	A Forlorn Hope	396
44.	"Homeward Bound"	404

Chapter 1

"The Stress of the Storm"

It was a night when a wild south-easterly storm had swept in from the Atlantic, battering with steady persistency against the walls of a square, white wooden house, bending down the frail saplings of lime and elm planted in front of it, roaring amongst the sturdier native pine and oak in the woods that stretched behind.

It almost seemed as though some power abroad in the darkness had brought an evil force to bear against that human habitation, when the rain was driven against the windows as if flung by an unseen hand.

At any rate, such an idea may have been lurking in the mind of an old man of rough, seafaring aspect, who sat alone smoking, in a room that looked a cross between a scullery and an office, for, at every wild dash of rain or shrill gust of wind, he looked round in a nervous fashion, subsequently making some move to stir the fire that burned in a small stove, or to fuss with his pipe, in seeming excuse for such disquietude.

His small keen eyes peered out in sailor fashion from under the wrinkled eyelids, as if on the watch for some untoward sight, and when the door of the room opened softly, he started violently, and then, to hide the fact, stirred the fire anew.

"What do you mean, woman, by coming creeping in, in that fashion, instead of with an honest bang to the door?" he demanded, wrathfully.

"Indeed, and I thought you'd have your fill of noises to-night, Isaac Neisner. You might fancy yourself off the Jamaica coast in the hurricane season, I'm thinking."

"And I'd just as soon, if not sooner, be there as here, to-night," the man muttered to himself; then, with a sudden purpose, he asked:

"And why did you come away and leave the master's room, when I told you to stay there, even if he should sleep?"

The woman glanced back toward the door before she answered, in a cautious tone:

"And how could I stay when the mistress came herself and sent me away? She said that she had had a long sleep and was quite rested, and that I was to go to bed."

"It would be a brave woman that would go to bed on such a night," was the comment, though whether Isaac referred to the storm or to some other disturbing element, he did not explain. Instead, he went on to ask.

"Was he awake? Did he seem to know that she was there?"

"He seemed asleep," the woman answered, in a whisper; "but as I stood outside, I heard him speak, and thought he called 'Isaac.' I just ventured to open the door a crack and ask if I should send you, but she answered in that quiet voice that gives you a cold shudder down your back, that I was never to mind, for he was just a bit wandering in his head, and that she was going to give him the medicine to soothe him. She was standing with a glass in her hand by the bed. I had nothing to do but come away."

There was a silence between them, only broken by the eldritch shriek of the still rising gale.

They had seated themselves in shabby wooden rocking-chairs, one on each side of the stove, seeming to find a needed moral support in each other's neighbourhood. The man was a rather superior specimen of the long-shore sailor, of about fifty; the woman, a shrewd-faced, kindly-looking country-woman of something the same age. It was she who first broke the silence, saying, with a solemn shake of her head.

"He'll go to-night for sure! Such a storm as this hasn't come for nothing. You know how my old man, who had been on the Spanish Main, used to say that a pirate's soul could only get away in a gale, when there were them abroad in the storm that would not be gainsaid. Go he must before morning," and she looked around her with a shuddering joy in her own flight of imagination.

But the wrath of Isaac Neisner was aroused.

"And who taught you to call the Honourable Jonathan Bauer, member of the Queen's own Council for this country, a pirate, if you please? Keep a civil tongue in your head for your betters."

Ellen Sievert took this admonition quietly.

"You're not the only one who knows things, Isaac. Remember that my old man was more voyages with him than you ever was. I've a good idea that the mistress may know more than any of us. Her eyes are awful tonight. They glitter like the snakes of her own country. I was glad enough not to stay in the room with her."

"Women always know more than any man round, or think they do. For try part, I'm content with what I do know. 'Deed, an' I'm inclined to-night to wish it was less," he added, inconsistently.

On a momentary lull came such a strange tumult of sounds that Ellen started, and asked, nervously: "What's that?"

"Only the wind in that old ventilator. The master wouldn't let me have it mended; said it would cost too much. He has screwed them all down of late."

"Well, she'll soon get the spending of it now."

"That's as it may be. There's no doubt she loves the money to spend, just as much as he does to save. But the son will be the saving kind, I'm thinking."

"He should be here to-night by his father."

"He would be, if she hadn't declared his wife need-ed to see a Boston doctor, and sent them all off."

"As if Nova Scotian doctors weren't good enough. But do you suppose"— here Ellen lowered her voice "that she knew what was coming?"

But Isaac declined to be further drawn. "I don't sup-pose anything. Only, I'm glad them children are not in the house to-night. You and I aren't easily frightened."

All the same, an ashen shade came through the tail of his face, as Ellen sprang up with a low cry. "Some one called! I heard them!"

Sure enough, there sounded a shrill voice in the passage: "Isaac! Isaac!"

But as though it were a summons to the powers of the night, down swept the fierce clamour of the storm in such redoubled force, that one of the tall pine-trees crashed over against the house, which seemed to rock to its foundation.

"The Lord save us!" groaned Isaac, while Ellen clung to his arm in speechless fear. As if before the elemental forces, the door of the room was hastily flung open, revealing a strange figure.

It was a woman of about fifty, whose somewhat unwieldy form was wrapped in an untidily gorgeous red silk tea-gown. Her black hair hung in confusion about the colourless face, from which the dark, shining eyes flared out.

Although the slim hand that held a lighted candle above her head did not shake, the woman was evidently in a state of extreme nervous tension, and there was no pause before she spoke quickly in a shrill voice with a perceptible foreign echo in it.

"Isaac! Ellen! Come quickly! Your master is dead! I had just raised his head and given him his medicine when he fell back with a groan, dead."

Ellen's terrified grasp was still upon Isaac's arm, but he silently shook her off and followed the crimson figure down the long passages and up the big staircase of the silent house to the death-chamber.

Ellen, preferring to follow him, rather than be left alone, went too.

About the halls and staircase were evidences of a certain comfort of furnishing, but in what had so lately been the master's room was only a bareness that was all but sordid.

The faded carpet was worn into holes, the china on the wash-stand was chipped, and of various patterns.

On an uncurtained iron bedstead was stretched out the gaunt, wasted form of a gray-bearded man, evidently over eighty.

In spite of the waste of extreme age, it was to be seen, even now, how strong and powerful had been that frame; how indomitable the will expressed by that heavy jaw and grim mouth; how tenacious the grasp of that bony hand outstretched upon the bed-clothes.

The sight of the corpse seemed to act with steadying power upon both the man and woman servant.

While their mistress stood near the bed, still holding the light, and furtively glancing from them to the dead, Ellen came forward with a professional interest in her face. Many were the dead, old and young, whom her hands had prepared for their long rest.

"You'll need to stir up the kitchen fire, and get the kettles on, Isaac," she said." I'll want all the hot water that I can get to-night."

But Isaac stood unheeding, his eyes never stirring from the death-mask of his old master, his face sphynxlike in its parchment folds.

His mistress watched him as immovably, with as intent a concentration of gaze upon him,

But when, with a grunt of absent-minded assent, "Ay, ay, I suppose so," he turned away, there came over her a visible relaxing of some strain.

The next day the storm was over. The autumn sun shone brightly, and only a few overturned fences and fallen trees told of the night's havoc.

At the Club, and at street corners, men stood and

talked of the life that had passed away with the storm, that of the richest man in the whole Province, old Jonathan Bauer.

It had been so long and so varied a life, that they spoke of it in sections, the earlier parts of it only known to most of them from the talk of their fathers.

Jonathan Bauer had begun life in a small prosperous coast-town, going out as mate in one of the numerous wooden vessels that came and went between the West Indies and Nova Scotia. Salt fish was their cargo out, and sugar, molasses, rum, their homeward-bound freight.

Many were the fortunes built up by the owners in those easy days before steam and telegraphy; many, too, were the chances of private trading open to the crew. At the beginning, as at the close of life, few chances escaped Jonathan Bauer's gray eyes, and soon he was captain of such a vessel, then owner of that and of others. There were troublesome years of revolutions and wars in South America, and other captains sometimes brought home strange tales of privateering doings of "old Bauer's" on the Spanish Main, which seemed to come perilously near the line where privateering ends and piracy begins. However, his own crew always held their tongues, and after each voyage Jonathan reappeared in his native town, more prosperous, more grim and silent and respectable than ever.

When his one daughter married against his wishes, he returned from his next voyage with a beautiful young French wife, whom he announced to belong to "one of the real tip-top old French families who had come out to settle in Martinique."

Then he gave up the sea, went into politics, moved to the capital, where he built for himself in the suburbs the big, white wooden house in which he ended his days.

Then the Civil War brought the great chance of his life, and he grasped it with a firm hand.

There were two possibilities of making a fortune; one in the chances of blockade-running, the other in the fluctuations of the New York Stock Exchange, and of both of these he had made skilful use.

While the men around him lavished their sympathy upon the South, he never doubted the ultimate result of the struggle, meantime, making his profit out of both sides.

The result was wealth, great wealth for those days, and then it began to be evident that shrewdness was, with the approach of old age, developing into miserliness.

His handsome French wife might fret and fume for the splendour after which her soul hankered. He was her master, in his grimly humorous and she knew it, and submitted. She was allowed to entertain, infrequently, and in a dull fashion, the generals and admirals and political big-wigs of the colonial society of the time.

She had one child, a son, who seemed to have inherited neither his mother's looks nor his father's brains.

He grew up plain and dull, a mere puppet in his father's hands, and in the course of time married the plain and dull daughter of a colonel in the English army, branch of a poor and titled Irish house, and had two children, a boy and a girl.

Before this son had hurried home from Boston with his family, the will was read.

It gave two-thirds of the estate to the son, the remaining third to the widow, with absolute disposal of her share.

To his daughter Susan's first child was left the old home near Bridgewater, Isaac Neisner to have the use of it until it should be claimed, Isaac Neisner and Ellen Sievert being each given a small annuity.

It was the evening of the funeral, and Isaac was busying himself rearranging the furniture in the big, bare dining-room, where the company had gathered.

A movement in the room made him look up, and he saw his mistress standing watching him.

Of course her dress was black, but in her Southern fashion she had huddled a red and yellow shawl about her head and neck, which kept up her wonted fantastic air.

"And so, Isaac, you have a home now," she began, as he looked round, "but you will still stay with me, will you, not? I should miss you about me."

The impenetrable gray eyes met the fixed stare of the black ones stolidly, although from the movement of Isaac's hands, it might have seemed that he was nervous.

"Thanking ye kindly, ma'am, but it's the master's orders you see that I go back, and so back I go.

And then, too, I'm thinking that it would make me feel younger again to set a lobster-pot, or take in a net. I don't get enough salt to nourish me here, I think."

"But if I say that I cannot spare you," she persisted.

Isaac wriggled a bit.

"Well, ma'am, there's plenty of time to be talking it over," he compromised.

But the next morning Isaac was gone, not even having communicated his intentions to Ellen, his only intimate, and his mistress was all day in what her servants called "one of her tantrums."

Soon after the old man's death a new era of expenditure began, followed by the removal of the whole family to England. From thence came tales of the great estate purchased on the Thames, of the quantity of servants kept, and the style in which the household was conducted.

Chapter 2

Old Friends

It was a cheerless day of early spring in Boston, and the glow of a wood fire gave its final touch of cosiness to the perfection of Mrs. Broderick's drawing-room. What it was that stamped that room with the ball-mark of success above all other rooms that it was ever compared with, it might have been hard to say.

"Its absence of fussiness," said one.

"Its artistic simplicity," said another.

"Money," was a briefer comment, capped by as brief a one of "Brains."

Certain it was that both brains and money had been freely used in the bringing together of those harmonious tints and costly textures that went to create such a sense of pleasant repose.

It all seemed simple enough, the cheerfulness of the pink and green French silks, the delicate outlines of the Louis Quinze furniture, the one or two Greuze-like crayon heads upon the wall, the few bits of Dresden or Sèvres on the stands.

The cloudy afternoon was dim enough for the flicker of the firelight to be visible in the corners of the room, and to enrich with its glow the silvery folds of Mrs. Broderick's gray silk tea-gown, edged here and there with touches of dark fur.

How was it that a woman of so absolute a simplicity of bearing and aspect bore such a hallmark of fashion, Gilbert Clinch wondered, as he sat opposite to her, studying the woman with reminiscences of the untidy, enthusiastic girl art-student of eight years ago.

Perhaps he was not enough man of the world to appreciate the costliness of the perfect lines of the silk drapery, the finished art in the carelessness of the loose waves of fair hair.

And the serene and dainty bearing of the society woman; perhaps that too had been no less costly an acquisition than the folds of the gown, or the style of hairdressing. But who has ever gauged the cost of that making of a woman?

> "The true gods sigh for the cost and the pain,
>   For the reed that grew, grows never again
>   'Mid the other reeds by the river."

There was something impalpable in the air which told that these two sitting quietly facing each other were not merely engaged in the polite amenities of society.

Isabel Broderick's face had on it the studied calm of a long repression, and her voice was even in its modulations, but in her clear blue-gray eyes there was an unconscious appeal as they rested on her companion's intent face, and her hands moved once or twice to clasp each other nervously.

About the concentration of Gilbert Clinch's interest on the woman before him there could be no mistake, but although there was a certain conquered emotion hinted at, it hardly seemed due to the noon of beauty or to its luxurious setting.

Rather, there was the scientific calm of the naturalist studying some rare specimen; of the man, used, in spite of his youth, to watch the involved workings of the troubled mind; for Gilbert Clinch was already being spoken of, in high medical circles, as a man with a future before him amongst the alienists of the country.

His study of Mrs. Broderick was not, however, that of a possible patient.

Not the most careless eye could scan her without marking the perfect equipoise of her physical and mental balance. She might have been chosen as the type of "the sane mind in the sane body." But it was to her tale, told in a sweet, low voice, that the young doctor had been listening.

"You have done as I asked you to, and had a talk with the two doctors about my husband?" she had asked, after a brief, yet kindly greeting.

Gilbert settled himself back in the deep chair, as he began, gravely:

"Yes, and what they said quite carried out the idea that you had given me. Putting aside technicalities, it is an ordinary case of melancholia, with, I fear, the almost certainty of its increasing into more acute mania. Of course his hereditary record goes against him. There is nothing to be done that I can see, save to follow the advice that they have given you. Let him have as quiet an outdoor life as possible, and above all things keep up his interest in his painting. We need not despair until that goes. It is only a sane person who can work."

Mrs. Broderick's face brightened responsive to his words.

"Oh, his whole heart seems in his work. Of course his subjects are strange; they have always been strange for the matter of that. Have you ever seen any of his things?"

"Only the picture exhibited last year, of the New England witches being taken to death. I thought it very powerful."

"It was. It was also the least mystical of all his subjects. They are almost always of saints and visions, and of late they have grown still more weird and vague. But there is always the same genius in them," she added, with an evident pride.

"And does he show much pleasure in his work?" Gilbert asked. In spite of his familiarity with the tragedies of life, he felt an intense pity for this woman whom he had known as an ardent girl.

Her face shadowed again.

"It is not easy to tell. He has grown so silent, and takes so little notice. But he is always gentle and pathetic. If you saw him often, you would never, I am sure, ask me to consent to putting him under restraint or to leaving him, both of which courses the doctors have suggested."

"Restraint in time is almost always the wisest plan," Gilbert answered, cautiously.

There was a troubling of Mrs. Broderick's surface calm, as she leaned forward with clasped hands.

"Surely not in this case, where I am willing to give myself up altogether to making the days better for him. Surely there is no one who could keep up his interest in his painting as I can, who have always worked with him?"

"Perhaps not," Gilbert acknowledged, willing to bring about gradually her facing of the inevitable. "But you must always remember, there is a point at which self-sacrifice becomes useless folly."

She scarcely seemed to heed his caution as she went on:

"The problem of how to do the best for him had been working in my mind when I heard that you were here in town, and it seemed to me that you were the person for me to appeal to, and that was why I wrote and asked you to come to see me. You know"— here for the first time, a faint flush crossed her face — "you know that money is no question in our plans. There is, in almost any case, more than we need spend. I heard from Doctor Smart of the work that you have done in the Michigan asylum, and of how much is expected of you. He told me, too, that you were ordered a holiday, and outdoor life for a time." She hesitated, as though feeling the difficulty of what she wished to say.

"Is it too much of a sacrifice to ask of you, that you will, at a salary named by Doctor Smart, take complete charge of my husband for the summer? I would leave the choice of locality altogether to you, only asking that it be some place out of the way of ordinary travel, where there will be little chance of meeting familiar faces. I do not mind how simple our surroundings may be, only provided that we are remote from every one and everything we have ever known."

Her voice shook, but she recovered herself, and

went on, more quietly:

"It should be by the sea, too, for once he loved sailing, and it is always possible that he might rouse up to be interested in it again. We can try this for the summer, and then — well, if my plan does not succeed, I promise to do as the doctors wish. Tell me, will you think this over for a few days, and give me your answer?"

Gilbert roused himself from the charm of the low tones.

"It needs no thinking over, and it involves no sacrifice on my part," he said, decisively. "As you say, I am ordered a holiday of outdoor life, but interesting holidays are not such easy things to manage on limited means. Your proposal supplies both the professional interest of the case, and the friendly interest of helping you. Believe me, I am truly gratified that your thoughts should have turned to me in your distress, and I will try to justify your impulse;" then, with a more matter-of-fact tone:

"Tell me, is there any place that you have thought of?"

"No," she said, meditatively. "I had only a vague idea of a fishing village somewhere on the Maine coast. You don't know of any such place, do you?"

"Well, I happened to meet a friend to-day, brown and rugged-looking, and I asked him whence came his offensively outdoor aspect. It turned out that he had been salmon-fishing down on the Nova Scotian coast. It was that put the idea into my head. There seem to be lots of such places as you describe, and getting there by water would be a very simple business."

Mrs. Broderick was apparently lacking in the feminine love of ample discussion.

"Well, there is no hurry, for it can scarcely be weather to get settled comfortably the country for six weeks yet," she said. " Suppose you took a run down there to see, and choose for yourself. I will leave the decision entirely to you. Is that asking too much from you?"

"It is merely asking me to take a pleasure-trip on new ground, and you know of old what a wanderer I am," Gilbert answered.

An afterthought seeming to occur to him, he hesitated, and then plunged boldly into the subject. "I have not asked what you intend doing with your child. You were not planning to take him with you, I suppose?"

As a dog starts on the first note of danger, Mrs. Broderick seemed to be aroused into alertness.

"Why not?" she asked, quickly.

"It can hardly seem advisable to you, I should think," was his quiet answer.

"I could not have the courage for the effort, if I had to part with my child," she broke out, passionately. "You cannot suppose that with the precautions we should take, there would be the slightest danger to him?"

"No," Gilbert admitted. "I must allow that it hardly seems probable. But I am convinced that the early memories of children are more tenacious than we are apt to fancy, and it might be best to keep him apart. However, I can understand how you shrink from the separation, and I trust that we can avoid it. Of course, we must have a strong man-servant trained to the work. With myself, he ought to do. Then you must promise me never to be alone with him."

He looked at her expectantly, but her acquiescence was slow to come.

"I can always soothe him better than any one," she objected

"That power might suddenly fail at the crucial moment. I really must insist on this condition."

His eyes and voice were equally determined, and, after a moment's pause, Mrs. Broderick yielded.

"Very well, it shall be as you wish," she agreed, gently.

Gilbert met her smile with compunction.

"I cannot bear to oppose your slightest wish in the matter," he said. "Believe me, I would not do so if it were not for the responsibility that must rest on me in this affair."

"Oh, yes, I know," she said, hastily, "and I assure you that I do not mean to add to it by any unreasonableness on my part. And you think you can go soon?"

"To-morrow, I hope. There is nothing to detain me here. And so I had better say good-bye now."

They had risen, and as Gilbert stood holding her hand, the old magnetism of her presence swept over him. He rejoiced in his youth and strength that enabled him to serve her, while the man whom she had chosen was a burden upon her hands.

"I hope you know how I would thank you if I could," were her parting words, and the sound of them lingered in his brain as he went out into the cold drizzle of the cheerless streets.

Chapter 3

The Ancient Mariner

Gilbert Clinch's visit to Mrs. Broderick, with its result-
ant compact, had furnished him with a bewildering
amount of food for thought.

Eight years before, he had been the guest of a fel-
low-student in a roomy old farmhouse in the Vermont
hills, occupied for the summer by a hospitable family.
Isabel Steele had come there to visit the daughter,
who studied with her in the art school.

She was then eighteen, badly dressed and angular,
with a manner alternately shy and impulsive, and only
by fits and starts gave a promise of the charm that was
later to make her a well-known society woman.

The bewitching hand of midsummer was laid on
these two impetuous young hearts, and certain sentimental scenes were a foregone conclusion.

But they were both poor and ambitious; both strain-
ing every nerve to conquer the difficulties that barred
their chosen careers. They had both served their
apprenticeship in the school of small daily self-denials
for a dominant purpose.

And so, with the summer their companionship had
ended, each going back to their work choking down a
certain heartache.

The next spring Gilbert had heard of Miss Steele's going abroad, and, within the year, of her marriage to Andrew Broderick, the only son of the millionaire, said to be, on his own account, an artist of much promise.

"Rather an unfair deal of the fates, to have given him the brains that poor men need," Gilbert had commented to himself somewhat bitterly, as he read the glowing accounts of the marriage in the paper.

In the changes of the next few years, that bitterness had all died away, and it was with a kindly interest that he noted the varied statements about Mrs. Broderick's social successes, her dresses, and entertainments, the occasional pictures she had painted and exhibited. And now, to his bewilderment, he found that he had in a measure become her paid retainer. Not that he was really sensitive to the fact, for he knew that the service he was to do her was more than could be rewarded by money. All the same, he would have liked to lay that service at her feet with a lordly generosity.

But such generosity is an expensive thing, and although he had attained to a tolerable certainty as to his daily comforts, he could not feel justified in it. Besides, how could he expect Mrs. Broderick to accept such services save on a business footing? And so he smothered down the feeling, as he had smothered many such results of poverty, with a mental note of combat against that crippling power.

He tried to arouse all his powers of trained beneficence toward the man over whom hovered so hapless a fate. Neither Gilbert nor the authorities with whom he had spoken had any doubt that the course

of a year would see Andrew Broderick a pronounced
maniac. But still, he was not that now, and if his wife
chose to go on fighting a hopeless battle, well, she had
the money that gave her power to do so.

After all, nearly everything in the world is a matter
of money.

And so Gilbert began to meditate on the practical
details of his undertaking. He knew the man whom he
would choose as attendant, quiet, strong, obedient.

He went off at once to look for the fisherman who
had given him the idea of locality, and before he
returned to his room that night, he was supplied with
a full programme of travel. Then he sat down to write
to his widowed mother in her home in a quiet
Canadian town. For Gilbert was a Canadian by birth,
although, like so many of his fellow countrymen, an
American by education.

He told her, with his usual briefness, of this new
undertaking of his, and of the neighbourhood on the
Nova Scotian coast that he was about to visit in search
of summer quarters.

There had never been a habit of familiar confidence between mother and son since Gilbert had out-
grown her narrow creed and austere life.

Her answer reached him at the end of his sea trip to
Halifax.

He was at once struck by some unfamiliar note of
agitation in it.

"It is another of the strange manifestations of the
guiding hand of Providence that have ruled my life,"
she wrote, "that you should, in all ignorance, have
decided to go to the spot where I was born and grew

up, and where your father and I met.

"It was through his wise decision that you were left in this ignorance of our early life. It is possible that you may meet no one who would recognise your name, for it is more than forty years since we left there, and, save my father, I had no near relatives, and but few friends.

"I feel no present tie between me and my old home, nor any wish to see it again. My real home is here, where I spent the happiest years of my life with your father, where many of his congregation still revere his memory.

"I think that there is no need for you to announce your parentage to anyone whom you may meet, but if it should chance that your name is recognised and your family spoken of, you will do wisely to write to me at once as to what you may have heard. I have nothing to conceal, nothing to be ashamed of, although both your father and I agreed that it was unnecessary for you to hear the story of our lives."

Gilbert Clinch sat on the veranda of a country hotel and re-read this letter with an unpleasant sensation. He had often before wondered at his parents' reticence, and had as often put aside the idea that it signified anything beyond a reserved habit of mind. He had gone out into the world so young, and had so immediately become absorbed, in the battle of life, that all these family ways had become unreal to him.

And now, when he was most occupied with other thoughts, these feelings of his youth had suddenly awakened into significance. This letter had reached him at Halifax, had tormented him through the pro-

longed hours of a foggy coasting trip, was tormenting
him on as he sat smoking on the veranda of the little
hotel, on the height above the small town of
Bridgewater.

It had distracted his thoughts a little while before,
when he had strolled in the clear twilight by the beautiful river-banks, to watch the ships loading with lum-
ber in the stream, and the cone of fire that rose
against the sunset from the chimney of the sawdust-
burning furnace at the great lumber-mills above the
town.

Now, with a sudden resolution, he put his mother's
words aside. They probably belonged to that shadow-
land of theological self-tormenting where his parents'
path had lain. He himself had chosen the broad daylight of scientific thought and action. Let him abide
in it, then, and see to his chosen task.

He had taken a fancy to the bright, active little town
on its broad river, but saw that it was not suited to his
purpose. He must get farther, toward the more lonely
places by the sea.

He had already interviewed the landlord and one of
the general business men of small country towns, as to
any such remote seaside dwelling, but they knew of
none, and could only recommend him to go "down
toward the French settlements."

So the next morning, with a pleasant sense of explo-
ration of unknown regions, Gilbert started off in a
buggy, following a road that wound seaward along the
shores of the ever-widening La Have.

It was a sunny morning, and the subtle charm of the
capricious Northern spring lay over the land.

The red tassels of the maple blossoms swayed beside the white clusters of the Indian-pear and wild-cherry blossom. A scent of spruce came from the damp shades; the woods were astir after their long ice and snow captivity.

As he went on, the cheerful little white houses by the river became more scattered, and then gradually ceased, while the dark woods crowded down to the roadside. But there were always the open views tip and down the stately brightness of the river as it broadened out to meet the sea, amongst low islands and long yellow sand-bars. Noonday had passed, and Gilbert had been for some time driving through the solitude of thick spruce woods, with a growing interest in the problem of a possible meal, and rest for himself and his horse.

All at once, the woods fell away to reveal a slope of green fields, down to a cove between which and the open bay ran out a long line of sand. An unpainted gray farmhouse faced the water, with a path rambling down to it between old apple-trees.

There was an ancient gray wharf, and one or two weather-beaten sheds; altogether the place looked as though it might have been of importance in its day, although that day was plainly over.

While old, the house had about it an exact trimness, and there were even signs of a garden along the path leading to the door.

"Now that's a place with possibilities," came in a sudden idea to Gilbert. "At any rate, it's not sordid. Well, let's see if there is food for man and beast to be procured here. Hello, there's an ancient mariner."

The ancient mariner was seated on the door-step, smoking a pipe, and as he looked up, Gilbert saw that he must be over seventy.

A mop of grizzled hair surrounded a face of parchment texture, seamed by the many storms of life, but the small gray eyes were still keen and bright. They were the only sign that he was conscious of Gilbert's approach, as the latter left his horse and walked toward the house.

"Good morning," Gilbert began.

"Mornin'," with an all but imperceptible nod.

"Can you tell me where I can find a house at which to get a meal?"

"There's an inn three miles on, at La Falaise."

This remark was made in the most non-committal fashion, as though to disclaim any personal interest in the traveller's needs.

Gilbert accepted this attitude philosophically.

"That is a village?"

"Yes."

"There are no nearer houses?"

"None."

"You live here alone?"

"Yes, with a boy, a grandson."

"Have you ever let your house?"

The old man made no movement, but his twinkling eyes brightened in interest, as he answered:

"No, can't say that I have as yet. Happen to be looking for one to hire?"

"That's just what I am looking for. I want a place for the summer close to the sea, and not too near any village. Do you happen to know of any such place?"

"Don't know much of other people's houses or affairs. 'Tend to my own. But they're sometimes queer kind of people that are wanting lonely houses near the sea. What might you be meaning to do with it?"

Gilbert, thinking he detected an impulse of parley, answered, conciliatingly:

"I want it for an American lady, who has an invalid husband needing quiet and outdoor life. I am a doctor and I should be with them."

"And you are a Yankee, too?" was the next question.

Gilbert's amusement helped to curb his rising impatience.

"No, I am a Canadian."

"And what might your name be?" was the next query.

Looking into those keen eyes, Gilbert had a sudden strange sense of conjuring with an unknown spell, as he answered:

"My name is Gilbert Clinch, though that can hardly interest you. I thought that perhaps this house might have suited my purpose, but I see that I must go farther."

If he had expected any startling change through recognition of his name, he was certainly disappointed, but at this hint of moving on the old man did stand up, saying with more heartiness:

"No need to be in such a hurry. Who knows that it mightn't suit you after all? At any rate, come in and have a snack, that is, if you can eat sailors' fare, cold pork and hard biscuit. No harm done in talking it over at any rate."

It was with a distinct consciousness of victory that

Gilbert followed him into the square room, half kitchen, half living-room, into which the door opened.

One glance showed him the possibilities of the place. Everything was spotlessly clean, and there were two sunny windows looking out toward the sea.

"The stove taken away, and the fireplace opened up; the floor stained and rugs laid down; a curtain over the door leading into the back kitchen," he summed up rapidly to himself, while the old man bustled over to the cupboard, that bore a great resemblance to a ship's lockers.

About every arrangement of his simple belongings, there was this nautical suggestion. As they began their austere meal, Gilbert was careful to keep from any further reference to business. Instead of which, he spoke of his own seafaring experiences in a yachting trip to the West Indies with a patient, and the bait was immediately taken.

Gilbert now received his first information of the fact he was afterward to have more fully impressed upon him, that to these remote "longshore" folk, the West Indian Islands are "just over the way," places to which if a man has not voyaged himself, his father and brothers and neighbours are likely to have been, and the names of which are of lifelong familiarity to him.

Many a quiet old woman, sitting by her fireside through long Northern winters, can recall the days when, as wife to the captain of a sailing vessel, she felt the glare of the tropic sun over the Caribbean Sea, heard the rustle of the wind in the palm leaves.

His host seemed as familiar with every spot men-

tioned as he must be with the shoals and currents of
the La Have River, and Gilbert observed on the high
mantel, branching sprays of coral and sea-fans, evident spoils of past voyages. Warmed by such reminiscences, the old man became quite garrulous, but
presently Gilbert found that he was harking back to
his former questioning.

"Not been much with your home folks, I guess, as
you're such a young fellow, and been made a doctor,
and then travelling," he suggested.

"Oh, I'm older than I look," Gilbert answered, carelessly. "But, no, I haven't been much at home. If one
has one's way to make in the world, it's best to begin
early, and learn to take the rough with the smooth."

This bit of philosophy apparently passed unheeded,
for it was followed by the brief query:

"Father dead?"

"Yes, my father died when I was eighteen," was the
answer, gives with suitable gravity.

"Then there was just your mother and you?"

Gilbert noticed with that strange quickening of
interest, that the old man was taking it for granted
that he had no brothers or sisters. He looked straight
into the other's eyes as he answered:

"Yes, only my mother and me. She came from somewhere about this neighbourhood, but my father
belonged to Ontario, and they returned there soon
after their marriage."

Under the steady questioning of his gaze, the old
man's eyes shifted uneasily.

"Indeed, indeed," he said, slowly then with a sudden
turn: "Well, now, what of this fancy of yours about the

house? If you were really thinking it might suit you, it wouldn't be a bad idea to take a look at it, would it?"

"An excellent idea," the other agreed, glad to leave surmises for facts.

Chapter 4

"In Her Service"

As Gilbert followed his guide from room to room, he found that the old house was larger than he had thought it.

Off the ground floor was a sort of wing of two rooms which he decided would be suitable for Mr. Broderick and his attendant. Up-stairs the rooms, though low with the slope of the roof, were large, and would supply accommodation for the rest of the party.

"The house would suit me well enough," he announced, presently. "Now the question is, whether you are willing to let it. By the by, I don't know your name yet."

"Neither you do," the other agreed. They were now smoking their pipes in amity upon the doorsteps.

"Isaac, it is," he went on, "Isaac Neisner, and Neisner is as well-known a Dutch name as there is from here to Lunenburg. Well, as to letting the house. Can't say as the idea ever occurred to me before, but come to think of it, don't see why I shouldn't. That's to say, if you don't want me to clear out, but will let me and the boy put up in that little lean-to off the barn over there, so that I come and go with my boat handy, and dig the potatoes, and see to the pig and the chickens. I sha'n't be in your way."

Gilbert had marked the remains of strength in the brawny frame, the shrewd determination in the old face, and he felt that it would be a decided advantage to have such a person about the place. It would add to the force to be counted on in an emergency with his patient.

"I'm sure you wouldn't," he said, heartily.

"And I'm sure you will have no trouble in getting on with Mrs. Broderick. Look here," he went on, with a sudden impulse toward frankness — "I think before we close our bargain, that I ought to tell you that the gentleman is in rather a queer state of mind. Not mad, you know, but melancholy; hardly speaks or takes notice of any one. The doctors want him to have quiet and sea air, and I have promised to look after him. Now you know all about it."

But again Isaac took him by surprise.

"I thought all along it must be something like that," was his comment. "But what I want to know is, are these people friends of yours?"

Gilbert felt thoroughly puzzled by the question, and by the evident importance attached to it, though he was careful to give no sign of his perplexity.

"Yes, they are my friends," was his quiet answer.

"All right then. That settles it. A whole mad-house wouldn't matter to me. I've seen worse than that in my day. We'll call it a bargain then?"

"We had better arrange the terms first," Gilbert objected.

When they came to money matters, he was surprised to observe the indifference that Neisner displayed. He might have been a millionaire, letting a shooting-box to a duke as a matter of courtesy, for all the interest he showed.

However, the sum that Gilbert offered him was liberal enough to have satisfied any one, and booth seemed content with the arrangement. Gilbert told him that he would telegraph Mrs. Broderick for her approval, and would then come down again from Bridgewater to see to the furnishing of the house.

Isaac had grown so friendly that he seemed almost unwilling to let him out of his sight.

Gilbert was sitting in his buggy, all ready to start, and still the old man stood with his hand on the side of the carriage.

"Know your mother's maiden name?" he blurted out, suddenly.

Here it was, this uncanny interest cropping up again, Gilbert said to himself, as he answered, somewhat brusquely:

"Of course I do; why shouldn't I? It was Bauer. Dutch, like yours, I fancy. Do you know any one of that name in the neighbourhood now?"

Again, when it came to the point, the old man seemed to shy away from the subject.

"Used to be some about, but none now that I know of," he said, evasively.

"My mother told me that she thought she had no relations left here," Gilbert agreed.

"Hum! Mother well off?" and again came the furtively questioning glance.

The original Ancient Mariner was a joke to this one, Gilbert thought to himself, while answering, sedately:

"She has always had enough to live comfortably on.

Why do you want to know?"

"Oh, for nothing particular. Old folks like to gossip, you know. It's about all we're good for. But I was never one to talk much, and you won't find me troublesome."

All undertone of wistfulness in the gruff voice touched Gilbert.

"I'm sure not," he said, heartily. "Well, I must be off. You'll hear from me soon," and with a grip of the horny old hand, he went his way.

There was plenty of food for thought as he drove back in the chill yellow twilight.

He felt in curious sympathy with his new friend Isaac Neisner, although he had riot a doubt that the old man was keeping back from him some information as to his knowledge of Gilbert's parents.

What did it mean, this atmosphere of mystery that encircled so prosaic a couple as the minister and his wife must always have been?

"They must have changed their sect, and believed or not believed something, and made a tragedy out of it," he asserted, dogmatically, to himself, with, all the time, all unpleasant underlying sense that there might be some very different reason.

Even prosaic, middle-aged clergymen and their wives have been, ere now, found not exempt from the sins and passions that go to make up the tragedies of life.

While waiting to hear from Mrs. Broderick, Gilbert made himself at home in Bridgewater, with the result of imbibing a good deal of local gossip.

The announcement of his purpose of becoming

Isaac Neisner's tenant brought out a flood of information.

"Old Neisner's down Falaise way? Yes, they call it 'The Pirates' Moorings.' Why? Oh, well, you see there was a rich old man owned it, and left it to Neisner. He died, a grand sort of a person in Halifax, and rich! There wasn't another man in all the Province so rich. But all the same, the country-folk about here have always called him pirate and always will. They say he began to make his money in queer ways, when he was a young man and used to sail to the Spanish Main. You won't easily get any one to go there with you, for the house is said to be haunted by spirits in search of buried treasure. Do I believe the story? Well, no, not exactly. But, still, there's generally some truth under such tales."

Here another lounger broke in with his story that old Isaac Neisner did not own the house, but was merely in charge for some stranger to whom it had been left, but this theory seemed to receive only a small share of popular favour.

However, Gilbert listened to them all impartially. Then came a wire from Mrs. Broderick with directions to take the house, and saying that she was sending down some furniture. With that, Gilbert removed himself to Neisner's, sharing the old man's rough fare, setting a handy man he had brought down, to work at carpentering, tinting walls, staining floors.

Often he joined in the work himself, and old Isaac, catching the contagion, turned to and proved not unskilful in household art.

There were some odds and ends of good old furniture about the rooms, and these were rubbed up, and brought into greater prominence.

"This sideboard must have once belonged to well-to-do folks," Gilbert said, one day, as they set up the rickety structure of pure Chippendale lines in the central living-room.

"Hum! Perhaps it did. Never took much notice of furniture myself. Beds is beds, and chairs is chairs, and we've got to have them both. That's all I know," the old man grunted.

Another time Gilbert unearthed from a rubbish corner, a hanging-lamp, which when rubbed up, proved to be of elaborately embossed copper.

A knowledge of bric-à-brac acquired in the studios of his friends, told him that this lamp must have once been in some Spanish or Italian church.

When he appealed for Isaac's leave to hang it in the centre room, the latter scowled at it doubtfully.

"You've got a great eye for rubbish, mister. Do what you like with it, it's all one to me. I don't know where the thing came from. It's been round the house ever since I've known it. Bought from some Spanish sailor most likely, or perhaps the missus —" Here he checked himself abruptly, going on, "Yes, I've seen the like hanging up in Catholic churches, with the little red light shining in them, and big sailor men down on their knees before them. Perhaps, though," he rambled on, "it made the last taste of the salt water less bitter to them as they went down. Oh, I've seen a good many go down in my time, some with religion and some without. Have you got any religion, young man?" he ended, with one of his sudden turns on Gilbert.

"I have the religion of trying to do my share toward leaving the world better than I found it," the latter answered.

"All, well, you might have a worse one than that," he went off muttering, and Gilbert began to feel sure that this conversational rambling was a trick of the old man's when he wished to head off the conversation in a different direction. But the May days were growing more balmy, and the furniture having arrived from Boston, the old farm-house was looking a more possible habitation for a fashionable woman.

Gilbert felt that he might now go back to Boston to arrange for the Brodericks' journey.

It had been inevitable that of late he had dwelt much in thought of Mrs. Broderick's preferences and comfort. He had put his whole heart into making the old place as artistically dainty for her as possible; reading and re-reading the brief letters in which she had expressed her few wishes.

Now, there was an unconscious quickening of interest in the thought of telling her of his labours, of receiving her approval. Surely she must see how heartily he had strives to do everything possible for her comfort. These thoughts were his companions on the short sea voyage, and sent him without delay to the Brodericks' handsome house.

Once again he stood waiting in the reposeful drawing-room, but this time, instead of the flicker of fire-light, there was the level western sunshine resting on violets and lilies of the valley.

There was a rustle of silk, and, Mrs. Broderick had glided in and greeted him with her usual flushed grace. Was it her elaborate street dress of pale blue, trimmed with black, that made her seem more the woman of society than she had in that soft gray gown by the fireside, or was there really a hardness behind her smile that chilled any manifestation of sympathy?

However it came, the effect was there, and caused Gilbert to feel as though those soft white hands had gently pushed him into a remote outer circle. Smarting with an uncomprehended pain, he strove after the feeling of ten minutes earlier.

"You look better," he began. "I trust things have improved during my absence?"

"Yes, I am better. I suppose I have got my second wind of courage," she smiled, as they seated themselves. "Then there is the comfort of trying to do something definite. And I have remembered what you said about work being the best sign. He has, of late, been more absorbed in it than ever. I have been looking forward to your coming in the hopes that you might detect some improvement. I somehow feel that you understand him better than Doctor Smart does."

It was surely unreasonable in Gilbert to feel hurt at being thought of in his professional capacity, and to fancy that Mrs. Broderick wished to remind him of the work that he had undertaken for her. The only sign, however, that he gave of the feeling was in a rotten of professional mannerism, as he answered, sedately:

"I can hardly hope to compete with Doctor Smart's experience yet awhile. But I am sure you know that the case has my deepest interest, and that I shall spare no effort this summer."

"Oh, I am sure of that," she said, quickly, with a little puzzled glance at him, as though questioning the subtle change.

"But I want to tell you about his work. He has actually begun a large new picture, the best, so far as I can yet tell, of his life. About the time you left, he was always doing studies of flowers and butterflies, though I had not understood what was his idea until he put it into shape on a large canvas. Then I remembered."

She paused, as though feeling the pathos of what she had to tell.

"Have you ever read of poor Guy de Maupassant's last sad days of insanity?" Gilbert silently shook his head. He was again under the spell of eyes and voice, of personality.

"Well, he was surrounded in his visions by flights of butterflies. The white ones were the souls of friends, good spirits, and made him seraphic. The blue and yellow were women he had loved, and the pleasures he had known; but on his gloomy days black butterflies came, and from these he cowered and hid, and called them Death and Pain. I knew his mother," she went on "a grim, old Norman country dame, and she told me of the story. Whether I ever spoke of it to my husband or whether he heard it from others in Paris, I cannot tell now. He has never mentioned it, or breathed a word to show what he is thinking of, but there can be no doubt that is the idea he is working out in this picture. And, oh, it is so beautiful!" she broke off, with sudden fervour.

A remembrance came to Gilbert of times when he had wondered if Isabel Steele had any personality beside the art spirit that inhabited her frame, and now again he wondered which side of her nature life had the most largely developed, the feminine or the artistic.

"I would like you to come to my husband's studio, and see him at his work," Mrs. Broderick said, rising.

"Certainly, if you are sure it won't startle him."

"Oh, no, he never notices any one when he is busy," and she led the way through the house to the studio.

Chapter 5

The Flowers of Death

Gilbert was familiar, through the freemasonry of young men, with several studios, but he could not refrain from an admiring glance at the noble proportions and stately simplicity of this one he now entered. There were indeed two studios, separated from each other by a great sweep of subtle-tinted Indian curtain.

After that one glance around, all his attention was fixed on the man who stood at a big easel.

It was not the first time that he had seen Andrew Broderick, but his renewed impression was of the attractiveness of his appearance. Young and tall and slim, wearing a picturesque brown velveteen painting-coat, he was a pleasing figure as he stood palette in hand, staring intently at his picture, without taking any notice of their entrance.

His hair, of a light blond, was very fine in texture, and worn somewhat longer than usual. The face was of a long oval, and had the pallor that sometimes goes with very fine hair. His eyes were of a prominent blue. No untrained observation would ever have associated his quiet-mannered, hard-working young gentleman with any idea of insanity, and yet to Gilbert's eyes the signs of mental degeneration were clear as written words. He stood in silence, absorbed in this dread fact, for a moment, before turning toward Mrs. Broderick; he saw that her eyes, and apparently her thoughts, were intent on the big canvas on the easel.

His gaze followed the direction of hers, and he suppressed a word of admiration at what he saw. Gilbert knew as much about art as do most intelligent young men nowadays, who live in cities at young men's clubs, among authors, artists, journalists, where such topics are in the air. He knew enough to realise that here before him was one of the masterpieces of American art.

Andrew Broderick must have worked hard during the past weeks, for the canvas was completely covered, and even in parts seemed nearly finished. The picture was longer than it was high, and in one upper end of it, a rising slope caught the evening twilight.

On this slope, stately white lilies grew, and over them, one white butterfly hovered against a radiant opening in soft-tinted clouds. Lower down, halfway up this slope, masses of rich flowers, pink and cream roses and carnations, were fluttered over by blue and yellow and orange butterflies. The foreground lay in blue-gray shadow at the foot of tile slope. Here were ranks of dark red poppies, in their gray-green leaves, while against them showed out one large purple-black butterfly.

The poppies and the black butterfly alone of all the picture had been worked up into the most accurate finish.

But even while Gilbert was admiring the work, he did not fail to mark a sudden restlessness in the artist.

Whether he had only just become aware of their presence or not, he was evidently uneasy at their inspection of his picture, He cast furtive glances from them to his easel, thrust his hair back from his forehead with a troubled gesture, and then dabbled his colours together on his palette in confusion.

Marking these signs, Gilbert turned away to look casually around the room.

His gaze lighted on great boxes of growing poppies ranged in one corner under the shade of a bit of stretched blue-green muslin.

"What wonderful poppies to have been forced indoors at this time of year," he said, in even tones.

Mrs. Broderick looked apprehensively from one man to the other, but her face cleared as her husband answered at once, though with a certain vagueness:

"They are always wonderful; the most wonderful of all flowers; the flowers of sleep and death."

Then having spoken, he filled his brush anew, and became re-absorbed in his work.

Gilbert made no further effort to attract his attention. With a sign to Mrs. Broderick, he withdrew, she following him.

"What do you think of him?" she asked, as they paused in a half conservatory, half passage that connected the house with the studio.

"He may be a trifle better in health than when I saw him before," he admitted; then with more earnestness:

"I saw another easel with a flower study at the other end of the studio. Was it yours or his?"

"Mine. We have always worked in the same studio,"

she answered, as though anticipating an objection.

It came.

"I don't like it," Gilbert said, gravely.

"Why not? His man is generally in the next room or somewhere near. It worries him to have him in sight, and we cannot leave him always alone. Besides, as I say, it has always been our habit, and it used to please him to have me come to work. He sometimes thought that I was neglecting my painting for society or for the child."

"But does it seem to please him now?" Gilbert persisted.

He was smitten with swift compunction as he saw a mist of tears dim her eyes, with her answer:

"No, he does not often notice me."

He held firm to his purpose, however.

"Promise me to give it up," he urged. "It is a needless strain on your nerves, and can do him no good. He would very soon get used to the man."

A quick sob broke from Mrs. Broderick.

"Life seems to have resolved itself into giving up, now! Doesn't it seem cruel that such genius as that should go to waste?" she appealed to him, passionately.

Unconsciously, Gilbert felt a certain exultation to notice that it was for the artist she seemed to be mourning, more than for the man. It gave him a new sense of power to comfort and support her.

"It has not gone to waste yet. He could never have done better work than this," he said, soothingly.

"Come and sit down here," he went on, pointing to a big divan in a palm-shaded recess. "I have had no chance yet to tell you about 'The Moorings,' and my work there. I am thinking of qualifying for a house decorator."

"You have been very good in taking so much trouble," she said, he thought without much real interest.

He persisted, however, in his effort to divert her thoughts.

"I did not tell you in my letter that our residence is supposed to be haunted by an old pirate, otherwise a worthy sea-captain, who made a large fortune, and died in all the odour of respectability. Why he was called a pirate, and why he should be supposed to visit the home of his earlier days were matters of local tradition that I never could master. But it seems certain that it would be hard to get servants there, and that we must take them with us.

"Oh, I would rather do that in any case," she said, hastily; then, with a little shudder: "It sounds rather dreary. I hope it won't have a depressing effect."

"That is only owing to my clumsiness in putting, the worst side first. The place has a wonderfully homelike charm, tucked into its green fields, where they slope down to the water. I am sure that no artist could look at the path twisting between the old apple-trees, or the tumbledown, gray wooden wharf, without their fingers itching to paint them."

"It does sound nice," she acknowledged.

"But I haven't told you the queerest part of the story, which really has a 'shilling shocker' suggestion," and he went on to tell her of his mother's letter, and of Isaac Neisner's mysteries.

"It seems absurd to invent a romance out of such materials, and yet, it *is* strange, isn't it?" he appealed to her.

"It is indeed," she agreed, thoughtfully. "I think that we could do with a little less romance at present. Romance and happiness are seldom synonymous terms."

Gilbert saw that she was not to be aroused from her depression, but as he was about to leave her, a child's voice was heard, and new light shone in her face.

Her very figure lost its languid droop in alertness, as the sturdy, daintily clad figure of a boy of about four appeared, followed by a tall Swedish nurse.

The first thing Gilbert noticed was the child's strong likeness to his mother.

"Mummie's here; was Boyso looking for her?" she said, in a voice like music.

The child ran toward her outstretched hands, but babbled:

"Boyso wants to go to daddy; Boyso wants to see daddy paint."

"No, poor daddy's tired; daddy wants to go to sleep," the mother said, with all the gladness gone out of her voice.

"See, here is the gentleman who is coming with daddy and mummie and Boyso in a big steamer, to a pretty place where Boyso will fish and learn to swim. Ask the gentleman to tell you all about it."

Boyso toddled over and stood by Gilbert's knee, passing him under that crucial test of childish inspection.

"Are there apples there?" he asked, cautiously.

"Yes, plenty of apples," was the rash answer, considering the season.

"And lobsters with big red claws?"

"Oh, yes. There is an old man there who goes out in a boat and catches the big father lobsters, and they are green, until they are put in the pot, and then they come out red."

"I don't like green lobsters," the boy objected.

"Still, if they turn red, s'pose they'll do. And may I go out to catch them?" condescending to eagerness.

"Perhaps so. But I must go now," and with a brief farewell, he left the child and mother together.

The May weather was fine, and their plans were pressed forward.

It was decided that Andrew Broderick must not miss his work, and the most arduous task of the whole affair was getting the big canvas away from him to be packed, without making him too unhappy in the process.

Here his wife's intimate knowledge of his process of thought came in. She began a smaller study of the poppy foreground, into which she put a shadowy figure, raising one hand toward the veil that hid its face.

This figure was merely suggested by some rough brush-work, and seeing the canvas standing there, Broderick began to work on it, becoming so absorbed that he forgot to make any inquiries after his own picture.

"It will be all ready waiting in his barn studio down there, and will, I hope, settle him down at once," Gilbert said.

This matter settled, there came the crisis of getting him away from home without too much distress to him.

He was not too troublesome, but cowered and

shrank pitifully into himself, like a child awed by strange surroundings.

Gilbert noted that seeing him thus helpless and forlorn went farther to convince his wife of Broderick's real condition than any doctor's dicta could have done.

He saw also that it aroused in her that passion of pity which strong women feel for those more helpless than themselves.

In these days Gilbert was driven to acknowledge that no one was so quick to divine what would soothe Broderick's restlessness as his wife; no one so skilful at bringing that power to bear upon him.

Their party was not small, for Gilbert had thought it best to keep the servants with them. These were not numerous, but were picked in quality.

There was a French man-cook, of Norman stalwartness and good humour, who in a large household was always creating confusion by wanting to turn his hand to every task that lay outside of his department. The boy's nurse was a strong, faithful Swedish woman, delighted to be going to a Northern seashore, and Mr. Broderick's attendant had been trained as a houseservant, and would do the waiting.

The farmhouse had no room for more, and Gilbert saw that Mrs. Broderick recognised the fact that, provided they had enough strong men, the fewer people there were about the better.

There had come a haggard, hunted look to Isabel's face by the foggy afternoon that they had reached the Moorings. Gilbert, watching her, anathematised the weather that could not produce one gleam of sunshine to dear her heart. But perhaps the calm of the luminous gray was more really soothing to her wearied spirit.

Before the long spring twilight had darkened, there had come a home aspect over the new household.

Broderick had been soothed into content at finding his big poppy picture standing on its own easel in the part of an old barn which Gilbert had converted into a studio. His paint-box stood open, his brushes and palette ready to his hand, but for the present, it seemed to content him to sit in an armchair opposite it, smoking one cigarette after another, the nervous shrinking fading front face and manner.

Isabel sat in a deep hammock-chair, on the veranda that had been one of Gilbert's improvements.

She was evidently utterly weary, but the terrible strain of the last few days seemed to he already losing its hold. The boy had lost no time in gathering a handful of treasures of stones and shells, chief of these being a great red lobster-claw, the sight of which had filled him with rapture.

"Red lobsters here, not green," he had announced, triumphantly.

He was playing with it now, close to his mother's feet, while the nurse was arranging the room inside. The mother yearning softened Isabel's eyes, as she watched his play and listened to his babble.

But the day had been a long one, and presently, dropping his treasures, the child climbed upon his mother's knee, and nestled to her sleepily.

With a hungry gesture she gathered him into her

arms, and presently rose and carried him indoors, the fine proportions of her figure showing out in the effort.

Chapter 6

The Moorings

Gilbert, smoking his pipe, had watched the group from a distance, his heart thrilled by the familiar home aspect in which he was standing to them. The fog rolled in more thickly, deepening the evening shadows, and he strolled over toward the barn, which had been divided between Broderick's studio and a den for himself, where he could read and write undisturbed, and yet be within hearing of what happened.

This den he had on his first visit made homelike with armchair, writing-table, and his few little belongings, and he now turned toward it with the relief of getting on his own ground.

He was anxious to let Mrs. Broderick see that he did not intend to intrude upon her in any way. As he crossed the grassy space that corresponded with a farmyard, he saw old Isaac fondly contemplating his pigs, and hailed him: "Why, Isaac, I've had hardly a word with you yet. Come over and smoke a pipe with me."

The wrinkled face was stretched into a smile, as the old man hobbled toward him.

"Well, and I was saying to myself that you had your hands full, but that we'd have our talk all in good time," he announced.

This den of Gilbert's was a cosy enough place when his reading-lamp was lit, showing the bright colours of the posters which he had pinned up upon the rough wooden walls, and the archaic patterns of the home-manufactured rugs, purchased from an old woman in the neighbourhood.

"And it's yourself is a handy man to have turned the old barn into this," Isaac said, with an approving glance around; then lowering his voice, "Is he in there?" he asked, with a jerk of his thumb toward the partition.

"No, he seemed tired, and Higgins got him off to bed. Well, this getting here is a good job over, Isaac," he added, somewhat wearily.

"Indeed, you may say so, sir. Many a time I've been wondering how you'd get along. Those mad folk are kittle cattle."

"Please don't call him mad, Isaac; at least to the servants and Mrs. Broderick. It would hurt her to hear it."

"Indeed I wouldn't, poor lady. And what a beauty she is! I feel as though I'd never muster courage to speak to her like to other folks. Well, he had more than us common run to lose, anyway."

As Isaac talked between the puffs of his pipe, his eyes wandered slowly round the room, and presently he got up and strolled over to where Gilbert had pinned up on the wall an old-fashioned photograph of his father and mother, taken together. It had been with the idea of an experiment on Isaac that he had hunted out the half-forgotten picture.

"Humph! Got your parents up here —" he began; then after a pause, going on in a more absent fashion,

"Fine-looking woman your mother — at least, must have been," he corrected himself.

"Say would be about sixty-eight now?"

Gilbert had risen, in the uneasiness which this phase in Isaac always produced.

"That is her exact age. How did you know it? he said, emphatically.

As he expected, Isaac evaded him.

"Oh, well, she looks about that."

"But it is more than ten years since that was taken. Isaac, why won't you say out what you know about my father and mother?"

The two men stood facing each other, the old one obstinately imperturbable, the younger vexed to see that his appeal had been in vain.

"What makes you think as I know anything about them?" was the dogged question.

"How can I help seeing that there's something in your mind and ready to come out twenty times a day?" Gilbert protested.

"But it won't; not until I choose. Wait a bit, there's no hurry. At any rate, I know no harm about them, and I mean no harm to you. That's something, isn't it?" and he laid his great paw on Gilbert's shoulder.

Still vexed, Gilbert laughed in spite of himself.

"There's no doubt that you are a very aggravating old man," he said." Still I suppose that I'll have to put up with you. What is it, Higgins?" for the attendant had presented himself at the door to make his nightly report.

The next day was cheered by sunshine, and all Gilbert's little colony seemed peacefully inclined.

The servants worked busily at unpacking; Broderick

had absorbed himself in his picture, introducing the veiled figure into his larger canvas; Isabel sat on the veranda, stitching away at a strip of embroidery, in which Gilbert noticed she had a trick of becoming absorbed, and, at the same time, keeping an eye upon Boyso, who displayed great energy in fluttering here and there, always attaching himself to Isaac whenever that worthy was in sight.

The old man had won his heart that first morning, by appearing with an offering of lobsters; wicked-looking green ones, still dripping from the water, and snapping their claws and waving their long feelers in a delightfully terrifying fashion, that took all charm from the lifeless red ones of the Boston shops.

"Mr. Lobsterman," Isaac was at once christened, and seemed rather proud of the title.

They were a strange experience to Gilbert, those first meals presided over by Isabel Broderick, with her fixed serenity of manner, her calm which he felt that nothing earthly could break.

For household convenience Boyso had been promoted to table, and sat beside his mother, in a high chair, his prattle a relief to every one. When Broderick did speak, it was in answer to questions of his boy's, some of which Gilbert would have been glad to check.

"Daddy," he demanded, "when you want to paint the angels, do you call them to come?"

The prominent light eyes lost their vagueness as Broderick answered.

"Yes, I call them, and they come."

"But the bad black angels?" the child persisted, in an awed voice.

"Alas, they come without calling," and the pallid face grew wilder and more troubled.

"Isaac caught such a big lobster this morning, and he's not going to take it to the factory until Boyso sees it," Gilbert put in, and at the news Boyso was anxious to be off, and the crisis was past.

Gilbert saw that the another had paled, and when presently they stood on the veranda watching Broderick hastening back to his studio, followed by his attendant, Gilbert said, gravely:

"If he should at any time seem disinclined to come to table with us, I should not urge him."

"You apparently believe in the policy of isolation," she said, bitterly.

Gilbert was pleased to see that she confided enough in him not to care to conceal the jangling of her nerves.

"I wish to avoid any unnecessary risk of excitement," was his soothing answer.

"Yes, I know," she answered, more gently.

"But tell me, you do think that we have got through the journey better than you expected, that being here is good for him?"

Gilbert had served his apprenticeship to those painful questions which doctors must face, so he responded, readily:

"I think that, so far, everything has gone wonderfully well. But I want you to remember that your health and your nerves are an important part of the whole affair, and that you must have change and out-door life. Your husband is safe in the studio with Higgins; will you bring the boy and come up the river

in the sailboat with me? There is one of those ideal
westerly winds which seem to be a summer feature of
this shore."

They went, and the spell of the sweet Northern
spring laid its touch on Isabel's sore spirit. The west
wind was warm and languorous with wood smoke,
through which, every now and then, penetrated the
crisper breath of the sea.

The child babbled happily at her feet, and Gilbert
left her untroubled by conversation. It was pleasure
enough to him to see how the society-woman phase
had been laid aside and replaced by a girlish simplicity.

She looked so delightfully young with her hair
blown about under her sailor hat, with her bare hands
already browning in the sun.

Pleasure enough to hear her laugh ring out naturally, at Boyso's scheme of converting the bottom of
the boat into an aquarium.

"Boyso will turn into a water-baby, and then we'll
keep him in a pool with the crabs and the lobsters,"
she said, gaily.

"But Boyso would have to come back to his own bed,
and to mummie in the dark night?"

"Yes, Boyso shall always stay with mummie in the
dark night," and she drew the child closer to her.

"There, you look a different person for that. You
must come out often," Gilbert said, as they landed.

But as they walked up the path, he saw the shadow
of her self-repression gliding over her face. It is an
awful thing to return to a house that sends its shadows
out to meet us.

After this, it was Isaac who gave them their first

excitement, by going out to set his nets one evening, and managing to get run down by a fishing-schooner. "One of them low Yankee things from Gloucester," as he put it.

His boat was upset, and he was floating about a bit before he managed to right her, and came home very wet and shaky. Gilbert happened to see him land, and got him quickly to bed, with a stiff glass of grog, and a wood fire on the open hearth of his little lean-to.

All the next day the old man seemed dull and chilly, and sat by the fire in his room, but in the evening when Gilbert went to smoke his pipe with him, he appeared restless and talkative.

"I thought it was all over, when I couldn't find that boat last night," he began, "and it did seem cheap work for old Isaac Neisner, who'd been half over the world, to be done for by a Yankee fishing-craft in the La Have — in his own La Have, sir. Tell you what, it wouldn't sound well on a tombstone. I'd be ashamed for the old man to come back and read it. There were other things came into my head then," he rambled on, while Gilbert had the old feeling that this rambling covered some purpose.

"One of them, and that was the worst one, sir, was that if I had went down then, I would have been cheating and robbing you. B'lieve it was that made me find the boat in the dark," he chuckled to himself.

Gilbert was thoroughly aroused now.

"Isaac, you must tell me what such things mean," he said, sternly.

But Isaac, apparently requiring no further urging, went on: "Your mother may refuse what she likes for herself — that's her own affair. But you are a man now, and women, poor souls, aren't fit to do the deciding for men."

But Gilbert's patience had reached its limits.

"Good heavens, man, can't you say what you mean? Have I got another lunatic on my hands?" His protest had apparently a good effect.

Sitting up from the depths of his high-backed chair, and waving his pipe in one hand, old Isaac said, dramatically:

"No, Gilbert Clinch, I'm not crazy or in my second childhood. I tell you that this house and farm belong to you, and I was only in charge until you came."

Gilbert glanced professionally at the old man's flushed face and shining eyes, and said, soothingly:

"Perhaps you had better wait until the morning to tell me about it. I'm afraid you're tired now." He could not have adopted a better method of making Isaac tell his tale, for his obstinacy was aroused by opposition.

"You needn't think I'm getting a fever, or going off my head. It's plain gospel truth that I'm telling you, you mind that, sir!

"Old Jonathan Bauer, that you're so fond of listening to tales about, was your grandfather, though you never saw him, nor he you.

"He knew of you though, for he left this house and farm to you, though your mother was to have the say first as to whether she would take it or not.

"She chose not, for your mother was high-flown, as most good women are, and thought her father's money was soiled by the way it came. As if money could be soiled!"

Here Gilbert in sheer desperation interrupted.

"You don't mean to say that the man they talk about as 'old Pirate Bauer' was my Grandfather?"

"Just what I do mean! I was with him more than one voyage; I was with him the night he died, and who should know if not me?

"That's all old women's tales, calling him a pirate. He was the devil's own for setness, and if he did wild things, it was just when things stood in his way, and he walked over them.

"There's many no better than he, sitting in front pews, in black coats on Sundays. When your mother went off and left him, I thought he felt it more than he let people know. Though I was so much younger, he'd sometimes let me see things that he'd hide from others. It was soon after then, that he brought home his foreign wife from a cruise that I didn't go on — laid up with a broken leg at home, worse luck. There must have been rare doings on that cruise — though that's neither here nor there. She was a handsome young witch then, no older than his daughter, and she always hated him, however he got her."

The deep-seated, jealous resentment of a faithful dog revived in Isaac's voice as he went on:

"She drove me away from his bedside the night that he lay dying. But she didn't know that the day before, when she was out of the way, he had given me a package to go to your mother or you — for he knew of your birth and name, same as he made a point of knowing about everything — when one of you should come back to seek the old house he had left you; not before, for he wasn't one to benefit people against their will. He told me distinct that you weren't to have the papers until you had claimed the house; indeed, I don't know but what I'm disobeying him in telling you about them. Still, perhaps he's changed his mind by now, and anyway —"

He paused meditatively, but, just as Gilbert was about to question him, went on again:

"As I was saying, your mother refused the legacy for herself and her child, but when it was about time for you to come of age, I went to the lawyer in Bridgewater and got him to write again. There was the same old answer, full of Scripture texts, about wages of sin and so forth.

"She needn't have been so down on her poor dead pa, but she was a hard woman, I guess; all the Bauers are. Dare say, too, she was still going by what your pa had said, and parsons —"

In spite of the dull anger growing in his heart, Gilbert checked him.

"Hush, Isaac, you must not speak of them in that way to me. But did my mother refuse like that for me, after I was grown up?"

"Indeed she did, and never let ye know a word of it, I'll be bound. That's just the way with them saints. They'll drive ye in the right way, whether or no, like a pig to market."

Here Gilbert put in: "But tell me, Isaac, was my grandfather really as rich as they say he was?"

Isaac brought his hand down emphatically.

"He was richer far than they ever guessed. He died the richest man in the whole Province, and one of the

Queen's own Council at Halifax, though I never heard of her coming there to be counselled."

"But who has all this now?" came the next question.

"The Frenchwoman has one-third, and that poor stupid son of hers has the other two. Never could have thought that a son of the old man's could have been so wanting in brains and go. His mother used to rule him and his genteel wife, and I expect she does so still. The only thing that he was like his father in, was his love of money, though he'd never have bad the sense to make any for himself. He could save, though, just as well as the old man could, and that was the only thing him and his mother ever differed about."

"But where are these people now? Why, if you are right, he is my uncle."

"He's your uncle, fast enough. And soon after the old man's death, they all went away to England to live. People do say that they live in a house in the country as big as the Queen's, and that they have another in London, too, and that they are both chock-full of servants. 'T would make the old man get up and walk if he knew.

"There's one son and one daughter; little things they were when I last saw them, though the lawyer says that he's a fine young officer now; and I shouldn't wonder but that the girl has been took to make a curtsey to the Queen. Ah, your mother missed a fine chance when she left the old man," and he gave a regretful sigh to the past.

Gilbert sat maze by this picture unrolled to him. Seeing the old man's earnestness, he could scarcely doubt his veracity; besides, were not his wildest statements supported by facts known to his hearer.

But Isaac leant forward, an emphatic hand on Gilbert's knee, his voice hoarse with suspense.

"And now, young man, tell me, what will you do? Will you take the house and the letter, or will you set yourself up to be better than other people, and go on taking care of lunatics?"

There was a silence, on which the wail of the sea-wind sounded at the window. Gilbert rose, and kicked together the brands of the dying fire.

"I can say nothing now. I am bewildered; I must think. I must write to my mother."

Isaac caught at his arm with a grip that made him wince.

"Don't do that! Act for yourself now, if ever you do in your life. She never understood money, and all the good it brings! She never would understand anything save churches and parsons. She's not the kind. If you want to talk, go to the lady out there"— Isaac always spoke reverentially of Isabel Broderick as "the lady."

"By the looks of her, she's got as much sense as women can have in the course of nature," he added.

Gilbert still stood staring into the dying embers, as though reading his fate there. At last he roused himself to say:

"At any rate, I'll go and think it over to-night." Then holding out his hand, "And thank you, Isaac, for what you have told me. I feel sure that you want to be my friend."

"Well, it seems as though the old man's grandson belonged to me in a way," Isaac responded, with an embarrassed sort of heartiness.

Chapter 7

The Lust of Gold

Gilbert went out into the freshness of the summer night, his head buzzing with the conflict of the new line of thought with the old.

The tide was down; there was a nearly full moon, and he took his way out from the shadows of the trees to the firm footing, the air and space of the long sand-bar. Here he could pace with no thought given to his surroundings, and try by action to still the turmoil of his spirit.

There was a dull resentment against the parents who in their self-righteousness had decided his fate for him, when it was the right of his manhood to have spoken for himself. There was a keen curiosity to see these talked-of papers; in fact, he knew in the unexplored recesses of his mind that he could not give up the chance of seeing them. It would have been easier to have renounced a certainty than this wonderful possibility.

The richest man in the Province, and all at once he realised, with a certain shock, the intense desire for wealth that lay in his nature. It must have always been there dormant, as a hereditary feature, or else perhaps created by the self-sacrifices and deprivations of his student life. However it came, there it was, and like Lucifer, the Son of the Morning, it unrolled before him it "the kingdoms of the world and the glory thereof."

He saw himself, freed from the galling bond of being Isabel Broderick's paid retainer; free to devote himself to her service, with as little thought of self as any knight of old; free to be near her under any circumstances, without consideration of his own career.

He had heard her talk of men who led society, who travelled, explored in the wild places of the earth. He could show, her that he, too, given a chance, could take a place among these men, could be good for something beyond medical drudgery.

Gradually, a system of action evolved itself from these confused thoughts, if thoughts they could be really called. He had jumped to the conclusion that these papers must necessarily bring him a chance of wealth, but he compromised on the idea of merely claiming the farm, and reading the papers without deciding to use them. When he had read them, he could write to his mother, for his wrath was already cooling, as he realised that she had acted according to her lights, as a fanatic would act, and that it was irrational to blame her for so doing.

He even went so far as to say to himself that he would do nothing against her wishes, though feeling all the time that the resolution was of frail structure.

There was, of course, the consideration that his mother's secret reason for leaving home may have sprung from so dark a cause that he would have no choice as a man of honour but to abide by it, but this consideration he refused to bring out into the daylight of possibility.

Well, the tide was rising, and unless he wished to return wading, he had better hurry back.

As he went up the path between the apple-trees, he saw a figure sitting on the steps, wrapped in the folds of a long white cloak, and was seized with a sudden compunction.

"Good heavens! I hope that I have not kept you up," he said, hurriedly, as he approached her. "I was stupid enough to forget, when I strolled out, that you did not know where I was. Forgive me."

He almost thought that in the clear moonlight he saw her colour, as she answered:

"Indeed, you were not the cause of my being up late. If I had been tired, I should have gone to bed and left the door open. This summer moonlight seems to arouse one's restlessness. I find that I sleep better if I sit up late."

"How have you been sleeping?" was his quietly solicitous question.

"Oh, fairly well, with ups and downs of course," she answered, carelessly; then turning the subject: "But it seems that the spirit of restlessness has seized upon you as well."

"I had enough to make me restless;" then, with an uncontrollable impulse toward confidence, he began, looking up at her as he sat on a lower step:

"The mystery was settled to-night."

"How?"

He told her Isaac's story. She listened in silence, save when, now and then, she put in a short question, which showed how fully her interest was aroused.

"I am ashamed at my want of stability in being so disturbed by it, but — what do you think of it all?" he appealed to her.

Her answer came with no indecision.

"I think that it may be the one great chance of your life if you seize it firmly. Remember how long and hard your work to get a place in the world was made by poverty. Remember how, in the days when we were both young and poor —" her voice quivered slightly — "we did without all pleasant and cheerful things, just to grind on with doggedness. Think of going out on those early winter mornings after a poor breakfast, and not too warmly clad, to the long day's brain-effort. I sometimes wake up, with a start to those mornings still. Ah, poverty is a cruel, and lovely thing!"

"But the struggle gave us strength," he urged, feeling the subtle pleasure of the "us" that linked them together.

"A hard, bitter strength that darkened our natures," she objected. "Not that natural expanding that comes with ease and space and sunshine. Believe me, I have tasted and I know."

"Then you mean that money is able to give happiness, in spite of what the copy-books say?" he asked, trying to hide the earnestness of the question under carelessness.

She drew a long breath before she answered slowly:

"Happiness being practically an unknown quantity, it is not worth while taking it into account. But content must be far more easily won with all the change and interest that wealth creates around one, with the chances of self-development that it gives. Health and position and career, wealth *can* give; and say that one should be positively unhappy, is not forgetfulness more easily attained in the work that wealth makes easy and interesting? Think," she went on, leaning forward eagerly, "of what your profession might be to you if you had the money to study where and how you liked, instead of, as now, having to consider the earning of your income. You love your work, I know; think of how travel and leisure may help you in it. Think of that before you give up anything. This old man was right. Your mother may be the best of women, and yet not be competent to decide for you in this matter."

"I should not allow her to decide for me," was his quiet answer. "Yes, you are a good pleader, but what if it came too late? What if I had been rich that summer in the Vermont hills!"

The night and his own thoughts were going to his head, but as he looked up at her intently, he saw her wince as if in pain, and the sight sobered him at once.

"Don't!" she breathed quickly, but recovering herself, went on, resolutely: "Nothing comes too late, unless we choose to think it so. I saw somewhere the other day, that 'only the weak have a past,' and I felt its truth."

There was a warning note of self-control in her voice, and, as she rose, Gilbert made no effort to detain her. But she did not turn away at once.

"Promise me," she said, "that in the morning you will satisfy the old man, and get the papers?"

Gilbert did not answer directly.

"If I were rich," he said, "I should always be free to

come when you needed me, to stay near you.

But, after all, what nonsense it is to talk like this about riches, when there is only one small farm in question."

"There is more than the farm in question, I am sure. Take it first, and see what follows. Promise me."

"If you will promise that I may always be your friend," he urged.

"That seems rather an unnecessary ceremony," she tried to jest; then, "but I promise," she added, softly, and let him take her hand for a moment before she moved away.

Gilbert, feeling the uselessness of trying to sleep, forced himself by sheer will-power into steadying his mind with some scientific reading, and then, tired out, slept heavily. In the morning he found, on waking, that what had seemed undecided the night before, was now a fixed course of action in his mind.

He breakfasted early, before Mrs. Broderick had appeared, and then sought out old Isaac, in his hand the letter to the lawyer in Bridgewater, announcing his identity and claiming the farm.

"How would you fancy a sail up to Bridgewater to-day?" he began, and Isaac, glancing from the latent smile on his face, to the letter, took in his meaning at once.

"That's right; you're going to act like the sensible man you are, and get things started right off. Yes, I'll go to Bridgewater, or do anything else you may want me to do. It's the old man's orders as I'm following, and hasn't he given me a roof over my head, this many a day! When shall we set out?" he asked, heartily.

"I'm not going myself, for I don't care to be so long away from here."

Isaac's face fell with open disappointment, but he agreed loyally, with an "All right, sir."

"You know this lawyer, and you can take this letter to him, and tell him who you believe me to be, and how we met. You can find out his opinion as to handing me over the papers."

"But I never told him a word about the papers, and if you'll excuse me, sir, I don't mean to. It was just a matter between me and the old man, without any lawyers meddling! And haven't I the package all ready for you, sir? I got it out of my old sea-chest last night, on purpose."

Gilbert stood thinking for a moment, then he saw clearly that these talked-of documents must be rescued from any air of mystery.

"See here, Isaac," he began, "I know that your object is to benefit me in the matter, and I feel sure that this lawyer of yours had better know about the papers before he hands me over the farm. Some one might, later, try to make out that they were a cooked-up affair between you and me, but if you tell the lawyer about them before you give them to me, it lessens the chances of that being done. Do you understand?"

"Well, I can't quite say as I do," was the dubious answer, "but I'll take your orders on this trip. And you won't even open them and give them a squint over?" wistfully.

Gilbert, too, felt the temptation, though he answered, firmly: "Better not, Isaac, better not. We have plenty of time ahead."

"Very well, sir. I'll be off as soon as possible," and

calling his grandson, the old man hobbled away.

Gilbert stood a moment irresolute. He wanted to go in search of Mrs. Broderick, and yet somehow felt that he would prefer to have an excuse for doing so. Ah, there she was in her white morning-dress, gathering a handful of the honeysuckle that grew by the steps. Boyso stood on the path, looking somewhat tragic, and catching sight of Gilbert, he called out, dolefully:

"Mr. Lobsterman is gone away."

"Ah, but he'll come back. He is gone to fetch me a lobster this time," he said, taking the child's hand and approaching Isabel.

"Good morning," he said. "You see I have been obedient, and despatched Isaac with my letter to this lawyer of his in Bridgewater."

His words and aspect were a continuation of their attitude of the evening before, but were checked against the bright armour of her more formal manner.

"Yes," she smiled, without any show of great interest. "Well, let us hope that your lobster when it comes may be a very big one — how big shall it be, Boyso?" throwing a spray of honeysuckle toward the child.

"Oh, a big, big, grandpa lobster. Don't you hope it will be a grandpa lobster, Mr. Kin?" Boyso crowed, while Gilbert, chilled and disappointed, stood silent.

"Certainly, Boyso, a regular patriarch!" he laughed, shortly.

"Have you seen my husband to-day?" Mrs. Broderick asked, with the little shadowing that always came with his name.

At the simple words Gilbert paled. He chose to

fancy that she was thus reminding him of the reason for his presence, and of his duty.

His manner was all professional, as he answered, with grave politeness:

"I generally prefer to wait until he is settled down in his studio before I see him. But as it is about my usual time now, if you will excuse me, I will go," and with a bow he turned away.

"Mummie, don't squeeze me so tight," the child protested, as his mother sat down on the steps and drew him into her arms.

Chapter 8

The Dead Hand

Sore as he was from his rebuff when he turned away, Gilbert's trained thoughts went at once to his patient, who for the last two days he had been noticing to be more restless.

"What do you think of him this morning, Higgins?" he asked the attendant, outside the door.

The latter shook his head. "Not so quiet, sir, and not so easily pleased. Painting seemed to worry him, so I got him out, and nothing outside seemed to please him, neither. Began to cry because the world was so lovely, and was going to be burned up soon. Told him 'twould make a sight worth painting, but that didn't answer any better. But you'll see for yourself, sir."

Gilbert did see at once that there was no rest or peace in the pathetic face. Instead of working with placid absorption on his beloved picture, Broderick had placed against it a small panel, on which he was sketching out, with his brush, groups of the woeful faces of lost souls, set in wild curves of flame. Gilbert, shuddering, wondered to himself if ever such woe had been put into visible form before.

The thought came to him that insanity must be charged with doubled terrors when joined to the cre-

ative power of artistic imagination. Contrary to his
wont, Broderick turned round to him on his
entrance.

"Do you ever see visions of lost souls?" he asked,
earnestly.

"No, and I think I'd rather not. They can't be pleasant things to see. I don't believe they'd come if you
were out in the fresh air and sunshine. Going for a
stroll this morning?" Gilbert said in studiously matter-
of-fact tones.

A deeper look of perplexed distress came into the
troubled eyes.

"They wouldn't like it if I weren't here;" then, in a
more peevish tone, and with an irritated side glance at
Gilbert, "and they don't like it when people come in
and out, and talk. They want me to put them into
form and shape, so that the living can see their woe -
their woe," he repeated in a dreamy tone.

Seeing that it would be best to leave him undisturbed, Gilbert withdrew.

"There is certainly a change for the worse," he
acknowledged to Higgins. "Still, it is slight, and will, I
fancy, go on very gradually. I think that I shall take my
rod and go after some sea-trout. Keep a careful eye on
him."

He felt that he would do much to avoid meeting
Mrs. Broderick at lunch, and that solitude was the best
medicine for his troubled spirit.

Half an hour ago his heart had been sore and angry
at Isabel's repulse, but now the self-control of his careful mental training resumed its place, and he tried to
think only of the crisis that was coming in her life,

when she should be obliged to consign her husband to what would be a lifelong imprisonment.

What were her feelings toward that husband? What were her feelings toward himself? And with that, his young manhood asserted itself, and he saw her, fair in last night's moonlight, eager in his interest. He saw her next in the morning sunshine, smiling that impenetrable smile, and politely hinting that his affairs were none of her business.

Ah, but they were, and they should be, he vowed, hotly, to himself; and then his last night's desire for riches awoke, riches, to enable him to stand beside her on an equal footing.

They should be no longer the gracious patroness who had bestowed easy and remunerative work upon the clever, struggling young doctor, but man and woman — and what then? his conscience and common sense queried, checking him abruptly, so that, alone as he was, the hot dye of shame rose to his face.

No, he was her loyal friend and servant, and, rich or poor, he would be so still. And who was he to judge her varying shades of manner, he, of all men, who had made his life-study of the subtle action of the distressed spirit upon the body, of the fashion in which tortured nerves can betray themselves? And so, like many another man before him, Gilbert found cairn and courage in Nature's high places, bringing back with him from the shadow of the woods a saner, kinder view of those who made his world. It is a true test of the fibres of our being, whether or not we can go to Nature for new strength and find it.

He had walked far, and lingered through the sunset

time, dear to the heart of the fisherman, so that the world was again flooded in silver when he reached the Moorings.

There was no sign of any one about, and he went off to his own den, where the servants were in the habit of leaving some supper for him if he had been out.

Lighting his lamp, he fell to on the cold meat with the hearty zest of a tired man. As he flung himself back in his hammock-chair and lit his evening pipe, all the self-tormenting thoughts of the day were lost in a general sense of well-being, the result of healthy bodily fatigue.

What a refuge our bodies can be made at times from the wearisome strife of the spirit! He had all but drifted into a doze when his door was pushed slightly open, and Isaac's wrinkled face peered round it. With the sight, Gilbert's wits sprang into sudden wakefulness. Here was the messenger of fate.

"What, Isaac, back already?"

"Yes, the wind was most unusually accommodating. A fair south wind up, that shifted round enough to the west to give us a fair wind down."

"I take it that's a sign of your luck, sir."

"Well, let's hope so. Had some supper? If not, there's plenty on the table. At any rate, sit down and have a pipe."

"Thanking ye heartily, the last's what I'll do. Me and the boy had a mouthful aboard," and Isaac settled himself in a high-backed rush-chair, and proceeded to fill his pipe.

Gilbert watched him in silence, not revealing by word or sign the impatience for tidings that possessed him.

"Well, you'll be wanting to hear what I did."

"In your own good time, my friend." If there were a slightly sarcastic touch in the remark, Isaac failed to see it. He settled to tell his tale, with variations not unbearably lengthy. He had gone to Mr. Scarfe, and recounted Gilbert's first appearance at the farm, and the various questions and proofs by which he had discovered that he was really Jonathan Bauer's grandson.

"Mr. Scarfe thought it all fair sailing, and that when you and he met, he would most likely find that he could hand the farm over to you, — anyways, the delays would just be your getting documents or such from your mother."

"Yes, yes, but how about my grandfather's papers?" Gilbert could not help interrupting.

"That's all right. Mr. Scarfe didn't see no objection to your and me opening them." This was Isaac's method of saying that he had told Mr. Scarfe that the papers were his affair, and that he intended to hand them over to Gilbert, without taking any one else's opinion in the matter.

"And so," Isaac went on, "seeing that that's the case, I just slipped the thing into my pocket as I came over," and here he slowly produced a big sealed envelope, with the dulled tint that years give to paper. With a solemn face, he handed it to Gilbert.

"There it is, sir, and may it bring you good luck."

"Thank you, Isaac," was the warm response, as, with a firm hand, Gilbert took it. The crackling of the seal sounded unnaturally loud in his ears, as he pulled out the one document which the envelope held.

A glance showed it to be a will, short and to the pur-

pose, made by Jonathan Bauer, dividing all his property into thirds, one of which he left to his wife, one
to his only son, one to his daughter Susan's child or
children. The signature was witnessed by Isaac
Neisner and Ellen Sievert.

"You must know something of this, Isaac, for here is
your signature," Gilbert said, with a keen glance at
him. "It is a will of my grandfather's, giving me a third
of his estate."

"The Lord save us! Then it really and truly is that
will that Ellen and me put our names to the week
before he died. The French woman had gone out to
church — it was some saint's day, I think — and he
bade me call Ellen, and shut the door; and he signed
— see, the hand is feeble like — and so did we.

"I heard no more about it till, sitting up with him
two nights before he died, he pulls that envelope out
from under his pillow, and says, 'Keep it for a bit.
You'll understand next week. You're to keep it till
Susan's child comes. She's stiff-necked in her right-
eousness, but perhaps — there, take it; there's some
one listening.' And, sure enough, just as I got it in my
pocket, in comes the French woman, with her snaky
eyes. Well, I never was sure if this were the will that I
had seen or not. Thought the missus might have got
hold of it and destroyed it. But when the years passed,
and I knew that you must be grown up, and you never
came, I began to say to myself that, before I was
bedridden, I must go and look for you. And that's just
what I was pondering over, the morning that the
Powers that be brought you to my door."

And he finished this harangue with a grunt of dramatic solemnity.

"It's all strange enough," Gilbert agreed, when Isaac took up his parable again.

"There's another thing. The old man was never too free with his words. He generally meant every word he said. Now, he left you this house and contents. The contents you saw weren't much; suppose the contents you haven't seen were?"

Staring at him in growing surprise, Gilbert asked, abruptly: "What are you driving at? Do you mean that you know of anything hidden there?"

Isaac shook his head.

"I don't know of anything. 'Twasn't the old man's way. But I've sometimes poked about, with the idea that there might be something, and, though I've found nothing, still, I think it would be worth your while to have a good search."

Gilbert shook his head. "Isaac, you've been reading too many Sunday papers. They are the old abiding-place of buried treasure."

But Isaac stood to his guns.

"Don't you believe it. The old man was a real sailor, and sailors hides things like magpies. It's a way they learn, cramped up aboard ship. Just you believe me."

Gilbert laughed impatiently.

"All right. You're welcome to pull the whole place to bits if it gives you any pleasure, seeing that, but for you, I should never have had anything to do with it. We'll dig up a bag of diamonds in the cellar, and live like fighting-cocks ever afterward, eh?"

But Isaac evidently considered this a flippant way in which to treat a serious subject.

"There's many a true word spoken in jest," was his grave retort, nor could Gilbert get anything more out of him.

Chapter 9

Our Lady of Wrath

The next morning was one of those summer days when, looking out on the world, the soul bids itself rejoice at the fair gift of life.

As usual, Gilbert had breakfasted alone, but when he came out from the shadow of his morning visit to Broderick's studio, he spied the white figures of mother and child out on the sand-bar, and unhesitatingly went down to join them. Isabel was seated on the dry sand in a lazy attitude, but the colour in her face told that she had had a hand in the building of the sand fortress, around which the boy was still hovering, though the tide was sapping its outer walls. Gilbert's first glance into her eyes told him that he need fear no distance-keeping brightness, for those eyes were wistful, almost deprecating.

"This is a morning full of the joy of life," he said, cheerfully. "And I see that you have been at work early."

"And am now sitting watching the coming destruction of my work, and wondering who used the words, 'our life's strong places overthrown,'" she answered, with a languor veiling the hopelessness of her voice. His glance swiftly scanned the drooping curves of her face.

"I'm afraid you are tired," he suggested.

"Yes, I'm tired with the double tiredness of yesterday and to-day. You know that there are mornings when all yesterday's fatigues get up with you."

Yes, he knew well enough, though he only asked:

"How did yesterday go?"

"It seemed somehow a long day," she said, naively. "My husband was restless, and stayed very little in the studio. He wandered about from the shore to the house, and, seeing him, made the boy restless, too. He wanted to follow his father."

"Did you let him?

"Only when I was with him."

Gilbert hesitated before he spoke. "I hate to tell you that you ought to break him of the habit."

Instantly the latent fear awoke in her eyes. "Why?"

"You must know that it will be the best thing for the child to learn to forget him," he said, gently.

She caught her breath before she asked: "You have less hope of recovery, then?"

"Yes."

"You have no hope now?"

"Hardly any. In fact, it is more honest to say that I have none. But you must have been learning the same thing for yourself."

She made no answer, and after those few quietly interchanged sentences there was a silence.

The wavelets of the rising tide broke crisply against the sand wall, and the boy chanted to himself: "The tide comes up, and the walls go down, down."

It was not very long before Isabel's calm voice asked: "Did you have a pleasant day yesterday?"

"I did not want a pleasant day," was the swift answer. "Forgive me for having left you for so long, but I needed the solitude. A tempestuous humour had got stirred up by all the Ancient Mariner's mysteries, and I had to get it settled down a bit. There is nothing like a good tramp for clearing one's brain. Although Isaac arrived with a fresh cargo of wonders last evening, I slept the sleep of the just."

"What are the latest wonders?" and there was now no flimsy pretence at not being interested in his affairs.

Gilbert dug his elbow comfortably into the sand, so that he could lean back and look up at her.

"You were right. I have a chance of riches, though how much that chance is worth remains to be seen."

Then he went on to tell her of the contents of this new will. She listened intently, and then asked: "And have you decided on your next move?"

The wind blew across his hand a long lace scarf that she held in hers, and he caught its edge and carefully smoothed it out on the sand as he answered:

"No, I do not see anything that I can do until I have found out my mother's real reason for renouncing her share of her father's money. It hardly has been a trifle, and I may find that, in common, every-day honesty, it binds me, too."

With an impulsive turn, she caught him by the arm.

"You won't leave me now?" came in an eager whisper.

His brown hand closed over hers. "No," he said, gently.

Presently she drew her hand from under his, and he

did not try to prevent her. Then she spoke in her usual voice again.

"But you must see your mother. It would be selfish in me to try to detain you here. You must wire for another doctor, and leave when he comes."

"Would another doctor take my place with you?" was Gilbert's impetuous question.

There was no answer, and all that he could see was the oval of her cheek, as she sat with her eyes fixed on the boy; but still he seemed to feel that her silence was answer enough.

"Come away from the waves, Boyso," she called presently, in a clear voice, "unless you want to get carried off as a water-baby, and never see mummie any more."

Gilbert stood up, and then spoke, looking down at her:

"I should not in any case, go to my mother at once. I would rather learn a little more from letters first. If our wills were to clash, it would be the less trying process for both of us."

"Do you expect them to clash?" she asked, looking up.

"I should not be surprised if they did. My mother is a determined woman, dominated by a gloomy religion, but she is as just as she is stern. She must see now that I have a right to know what she has kept hidden from me. Then I must choose my own road for myself. But we shall all be turned into water-babies if we stay here much longer. Come, Boyso." Then, as they strolled homeward, he said: "You must have an outing to-day to blow away the shadows. It will be just the afternoon to take you and the boy for a sail."

"That would be nice," she agreed.

And so the hours of another summer day wove their golden link around them.

The next morning a south wind had rolled in the Atlantic fog, chill and dreary with its breath of distant icebergs. Whether it were the influence of the skies or not, there was a corresponding air of gloom over the little group.

Broderick made no effort to paint, but paced the studio like an imprisoned animal. The child was unusually restless and even a little fretful, and Mrs. Broderick looked pale and troubled.

Gilbert, feeling the necessity for some interest, proposed that they should divert the child's attention from his father by exploring a disused garret that ran out over one portion of the house.

"I was only up here once before," he said, "and that was when I kicked against the Spanish lamp that I hung in the hall. Who knows but what we may come on Isaac's mythical hidden treasure! That would be good work for a foggy day, wouldn't it?"

Isabel stood looking round somewhat listlessly on the piles of broken furniture, old feather-beds and pillows that mark such nooks, but, as the boy, seized with the spirit of play, dashed round the brick chimney that rose in the middle of the place, crying, "Catch me, mummie," she stooped in pretended pursuit.

There was a crash from behind the chimney, as of something falling, and Isabel darted after the child.

He was standing unhurt, but dusty and bewildered, by a large square canvas that had fallen to the floor, from where it seemed to have been propped up, painted side inwards, concealing an open hearth in the chimney.

"What's the matter, baby?" was the mother's quick question.

"Nofing, mummie. Boards tumbled down. Look!"

Isabel looked, and her first glance showed her that it was an old painting that lay on the floor. Even through the dust and grime she could see a grave young face looking up at her. Gilbert was now at her side.

"Oh, look," she said, eagerly, "here is an old painting, some saint, I think. Carry it over to the window, please."

Delighted to have aroused her to such interest, Gilbert promptly did so, and, as he held it, Mrs. Broderick knelt on the floor, wiping off the dust with an old wisp of canvas. Gradually, under her touch, the gently tragic face and figure that is familiar to most of us, in galleries, as that of the martyred young Roman officer, St. Lawrence, showed out more clearly from its shadowy background.

"I thought that it was St. Lawrence," she exclaimed, enthusiastically, "and, if I'm not very much mistaken, it is Spanish work of not long after the time of Velasquez."

"How can you tell that?" Gilbert asked.

"I don't know how one can tell it. One feels it more. But this is valuable, I think."

"Strange," he commented, thoughtfully. "That lamp was from some Spanish shrine, and, if this is Spanish, it may have come from the same church. Let us hope that my worthy grandfather did not join the robbing of churches to his other fashions of amassing a fortune."

In spite of the lightness of his words, there was something in them which caused her to glance up uneasily at him, as she protested, "Don't say such things."

"Well, at any rate, Isaac's theory seems to be working itself out. What will you bet on the next treasure-trove?"

His question remained unanswered, for just then, came the child's shout front the dark recesses beyond the chimney.

"Mummie, come and pick up the doll. Too heavy for Boyso. Heavy, dirty doll. Poor dolly in bed in dark."

"What next?" Gilbert said, with an enigmatic smile, as he followed her.

Boyso was half in and half out of the open hearth, and even his protruding legs gave a hint of his grimy condition.

"Come out, Boyso; let Mr. Clinch see," and his mother drew him unwillingly forth.

"Make haste! Get the dolly!" the child cried, dancing with eagerness.

It was only Gilbert's sense of touch that availed him as he groped inside. But there was certainly something there in the inmost corner of the hearts, and at last, used to the darkness, his eyes detected the outlines of an image of between two and three feet long. His hands told him, as well as the weight when he tried to move it, that it was made of metal.

"Here's another saint to match St. Lawrence!" he

said, grimly, as he drew it out and set it upright.

There was something almost like disgust in the way in which he stood looking down at the dark shape of what was evidently intended for the Virgin of the Seven Daggers, but Mrs. Broderick was all delighted curiosity, as she knelt beside it, wiping off the dust as she had done with the St. Lawrence.

Just then a ray of late afternoon sunshine, redly piercing the fog struck in horizontally at the left window.

"It's silver!" she exclaimed with joy.

"'Our Lady born smiling and smart,
    With a pink gauze gown all spangles, and
    Seven swords stuck in her heart.'"

Gilbert quoted, sardonically.

"The 'seven swords' are the only appropriate words, so far," she retorted. "Oh, but look!"

Gilbert, too, had seen the marvellous sight of the line of green fire that answered the ray of sunshine, as her hand passed over the dust on the border of the long robe.

Quickly she brushed over the surface, and then drew back to gaze in amazement. The line of green stones ran right round the robe and up the front, to where its folds were gathered in one hand.

Each hilt of the seven daggers in the breast was of rubies, and over the head hovered an open crown of diamonds. Besides this, it was evident, even to Gilbert, that the workmanship was of the best Renaissance period.

There was no word spoken between them. The only sound was the child's lisp of "Pretty dolly! pretty dolly!" as he twisted one arm around the neck and laid his warm cheek against the cold silver one.

At last Gilbert spoke hoarsely: "They cannot be real!"

The words were neither a question nor an assertion, but merely spoke the bewilderment in his mind.

"They are worth a king's fortune, if they are. And they must be yours. Old Isaac was right."

"I suppose so," he agreed, slowly. "The house and contents did mean something, after all."

The eager interest in her face all at once shadowed over, as she said, piteously:

"Oh, now you will have to leave us at once, and take it and the picture to New York to find out their value. A museum or a millionaire collector would buy the image as it is. It would be such a pity to spoil its beauty."

"You are in a great hurry to decide everything," Gilbert smiled, "but I think that we will take it more leisurely than that. The first thing I must do is to fetch Isaac, and see what he knows about it. I wonder if he has been bamboozling me all along, and meant me to find it for myself," and his air was somewhat stern as he turned away.

Chapter 10

Isaac Meets an Old Acquaintance

He found Isaac, like other heroes before him, absorbed in his cabbages, and hailed him more abruptly than was his wont.

"I wish that you would come up to the garret and see what you think of making another room in the dark north end. It has an open hearth in the chimney, and only needs a skylight in the roof," he found himself improvising. It did not seem so easy to begin at once about the image. Isaac looked up, stretching his bent back, and grunting:

"None there that ever I see."

There, was no furtive inquiry in the ruminating gaze that he turned on Gilbert.

"Something that Boyso knocked down was standing up in front of it. It seems to be an old picture."

Isaac looked more interested.

"That dismal old saint," he said, scornfully.

"Never could make out where it came from among Dutch folk that had ne'er a Papist in their families. The old man had a sort of fancy for it always. He put it there himself the last time that ever he was here. You see, after he went to live in town, and old he'd sometimes take it into his head to come down here for a day or two alone with me, though I never could make out why he did it. He wasn't one to go on about 'the past, and young days,' and all that stuff."

As the old man talked, Gilbert felt his vague suspicions clear from his brain. They had reached the garret, where Mrs. Broderick still sat on an overturned box, gazing at the statue, which seemed to grimly face her and the sunshine. Boyso rushed out to drag Isaac forward by the hand, crying, shrilly: "Mr. Lobstertman, come and see the new doll. Mummie said, it's Mr. Kinch's."

But for once, Isaac paid no heed to the child's touch or voice.

At sight of the silver figure, he almost staggered back, with an alarmed recognition that was unmistakably genuine.

"Great Jehoshaphat! The Virgin of Wrath! Then the old man did really take it. The men always said he did, but I never believed them, and they were none of them able to say what he had done with it. Well, he wasn't scared of Heaven or Hell, he wasn't," and there was something in face and voice, in the very shrinking gesture, which told that the speaker was.

"What should he be scared of?" Gilbert demanded, shortly.

Isaac slowly shook his head, as he answered:

"The natives were every man of them afeard of that Virgin because of her powers. If you went to her alone at midnight with a candle, she'd let you have your wickedest prayer against your enemy! Oh, you needn't laugh, sir. I've known more than one that's tried it, and got their evil will.

"While if you did any slight or disrespect to the image herself, you'd repent it. Now I always thought there was a time when a current of luck seemed to set against the old man. I put it down to the missus's spells, but it's been this as has done it. It stands to reason," he went on, in his argumentative tone, "that no woman so decked out would like to be poked away in a chimney all these years! There! That's better."

With quaint reverence, he lifted the statue and set it on a packing-case, immediately backing away to a certain distance. While Gilbert was below, Mrs. Broderick had been cleaning it still more, and the exquisite modelling of the long, oval face showed out distinctly.

"It is certainly Spanish Renaissance work," she said, laying a gentle touch on its beauty.

"How do you know what image it is, Isaac?" Gilbert demanded.

"Haven't I seen it more times than one, in its own church in Brazil, the pride of the whole countryside? And haven't I heard the men — most of them dead now, but our own folks from round the shore — haven't I heard them tell how the old man cleared out before daylight, after coming on board with a heavy box at midnight; and how they had first yellow fever, and then storms, till no man thought he would ever see the La Have again?

"And didn't they all think that there was some bad luck fallen among them, though 'twasn't till after awhile, when one or two of them had been back there in other ships, that they heard of the story of the vanishing of the famous Virgin, and guessed what had happened. They were scared men then, even to think of it. Ah, I missed a deal by staying ashore with my broken leg that trip."

"But do you mean to say that my grandfather stole that statue out of a church?"

Isaac looked taken aback at the stern voice, but quick to mark how the land lay, he answered, glibly:

"Well, not exactly that, sir. You see, there were wars and revolutions going on, as there always are on those coasts, and the old man, having letters of marque, had a right to have a fist in things.

"In those times out there, everybody helps themselves to every one else's movables, and, of course, if you're a Protestant and aren't afraid of the Church, well, the Church has the most —"

"I see," was Gilbert's comment "And you really think these stones are real?"

"And how could she have been the most famous Virgin in all Brazil if they weren't?" was the indignant demand.

"I suppose not," Gilbert agreed, slowly, then turning his eyes from the silver woman to the live one who faced it, he asked:

"Well, is your desire for the romance of a treasure-trove satisfied?"

Isabel's face had been intense in its watchfulness of him during Isaac's talk, but she now answered with a smile:

"I think it is I who should ask if you are satisfied. But to return to business. Don't you think it would be wise to get your treasure safely stowed away before any of the men about should see it?

It's rather a valuable thing to have in a cottage."

"Tell you what, sir," Isaac put in, "I think my mind would be easier, and perhaps yours, too, if you were to sell it to a church. I fancy she might be in a pleasanter humour toward us, if she were to have a taste of candies and incense again. Dare say, she's been homesick for them long enough. It stands to reason!"

"Well, get your candles. There are plenty downstairs, I suppose. As for incense, Mrs. Broderick has some joss-sticks, I know," was the impatient retort.

"No, sir, you don't catch me burning them heathen Chinese things — I've seen them in Hong Kong — before any Christian woman, be she silver or not, but, if I had a pinch of the real stuff —"

"Oh, Isaac, talk about women — you're worse than twenty old women."

Isaac sniffed in an injured manner, but answered, oracularly:

"Well, sir, I've seen a sight of queer things in my day, and you haven't done with that there Virgin yet, remember!" Which remark seemed to imply that he expected to see some still queerer things shortly.

It was nearly a week later when Isaac appeared one evening in Gilbert's den, with a somewhat sheepish air veiled by an extra solemnity.

"It's a terrible world for gossip," he began, oracularly.

"What's up now?" Gilbert asked.

"Well, I was down to La Falaise to-day to trade at the store, and I finds that the people there had got hold of the story of our finding the Virgin. Terrible interested they were, being mostly French and Catholics. I had a hard time with their questions. Somebody's been making a fool of themselves, and talking."

"That seems evident," Gilbert agreed, with a strong idea as to who the somebody was. He did not show how annoyed he was at the fact.

He was very sensitive at the idea of being a nine days' wonder to these people, who knew more of his family than he did himself.

"The worst of it is," Isaac went on, "that fellow D'Arcy is round the roads again. He held up a man who was taking down the week's pay to the gold mines only a few days ago, this side of Middleton."

Gilbert laughed. "He'd find the lady a pretty solid armful, single-handed, Isaac. She has great passive powers of resistance."

"Don't, sir, don't!" the other entreated, nervously, then going on with his ideas: "Now I was thinking, suppose that you were to sail up with her to Bridgewater, and get her safe in the bank there."

He looked hopefully at Gilbert, who shook his head.

"It is impossible for me to be away for long just now. I will tell you in confidence that I am not at all satisfied with Mr. Broderick's condition. Higgins has just been in to report a more restless day than usual, and the nights have been bad lately. He has not tried to paint now for two or three days, which is the worst sign of all."

Isaac shook his head gloomily.

"She's beginning her work, sir. For the Lord's sake, get her out of here."

"Don't talk nonsense, man. If you want the thing to go, you must take it yourself. Why shouldn't you?"

Isaac's eyes opened in alarm.

"Go up alone in the boat with her? No, thank you, sir."

"Then you want me to do what you are afraid to do yourself. That doesn't sound like you." At this taunt, Isaac looked sheepish, though he persisted: "You don't believe in her. I do."

But Gilbert's patience was exhausted.

"All right. Then her ladyship will have to stay where she is, under my bed," he said, shortly.

Perhaps Isaac's warning had taken greater hold upon his imagination than he knew at the time, for that night he certainly felt disinclined for bed, and at midnight was still smoking, down on his favourite perch of a pile of old boards on the end of the little wharf.

On the breathless stillness of the night, there rang out a sudden clamour of shouts from the direction of the studio, and Gilbert sprang up, alert to face the long-expected crisis.

But even in the clear darkness, he could see that the burly figure that rushed across the garden and leaped the fence was neither that of Broderick nor of his keeper.

But what was that strange white apparition, with apparently high-waving wings, that pursued the fugitive, shouting in a weird, hoarse voice: "I am the Archangel Michael, the Wrath and the Sword of the Lord!"

Gilbert was already close enough now to recognise Broderick in his night-clothes, waving a white sheet in great sweeps over his head.

"He cometh as a thief in the night! Behold I will grind him and scatter him abroad as chaff before the wind," the strange chant went on.

Gilbert was beside him now, though his voice seemed to have none of its usual soothing power and, at the first restraining grasp, he struggled violently, so that it took all the other's strength to hold him. However, the keeper had been in pursuit, and now, coming up from the other side, they soon between them got the poor fellow back to his room, though it was long before he was really quieted down. It seemed that Higgins had been aroused by a noise in the studio, and, going out, startled the intruder, who dropped a lantern and fled.

Broderick must have been awakened, too, and, coming out just in time to intercept the fugitive, had attacked him with a sheet and with verbal weapons.

"Enough to frighten ten robbers away. *He* won't ever come back again," Higgins chuckled, grimly.

But Gilbert looked very grave.

"He's done more harm already than twenty robbers. The first violent fit has come," he said.

"Yes, sir, and others will come, too. An asylum's the best place now," Higgins agreed.

The house had been roused, and, when Gilbert could turn away from his patient, he saw Mrs. Broderick, in long, white dressing-gown, waiting for him on the veranda.

He did his best to reassure her, though he could read in her white face her understanding that another step on the *via dolorosa* had been taken.

With a heartache for her, he turned away, only to find old Isaac leaning against the fence.

"She's waking up, sir; she's waking up. You'd best get her to Bridgewater to-morrow."

"Get her there yourself, if you want to," Gilbert retorted, going off to keep a night-watch by his now sleeping patient.

Chapter 11

Gathering Clouds

The rest of the night passed in quietness, but, when Gilbert returned from his morning bath, it did not need the attendant's gravely significant glance to warn him of Broderick's state.

The change in his face might not be very marked, but it was all the same unmistakable. A sullen gloom, that was not without a touch of fierceness, had replaced the former distressed perplexity. His restlessness had increased, and, seeming to have forgotten his work, he prowled about within a certain distance of the house, only remaining still when there was some one for him to watch.

Mrs. Broderick had been, according to wont, sitting on the veranda, the embroidery which had of late become her more constant companion, in her bands, but, as though the sight of her husband distressed her, she had wandered off across the pasture toward the woods.

The Swedish nurse was sitting sewing down at the shore near where Sam, the old man's grandson, was coopering at his boat; and Boyso played happily near his greatest joy, a little fire of chips lit under the tar-pot.

Smoking his pipe at a distance, Gilbert saw Broderick hovering nearer, as though fascinated by the group, and, at last, seating himself on a log on the bank, with elbows on knees seemed to become absorbed in watching the child's play.

The peacefulness of the scene was dominated by the gloom of that one brooding figure, and to Gilbert the air was heavy with a sense of approaching calamity.

Comfort himself as he might with the sight of Higgins's watchful figure close at hand, with the lusty song of the stalwart French cook, as he gathered vegetables in the garden, he would have now given much to have known Broderick safe in an asylum.

He was beginning to reproach himself bitterly for having yielded too much to Isabel Broderick's wishes in the matter.

"I am going to take you and Boyso out for a sail," he announced to her after lunch, having noted what a mere pretence at eating she had made.

"Have we no choice in the matter?" she asked, with a poor attempt at gaiety that wrung his heart.

"None. You have only to obey."

There was the life of the sea in the south-west wind, and, although she was very silent, Gilbert saw a certain restfulness come over her face, as she leaned back on her cushions with the boy huddled up against her, keeping up the sweet-voiced chatter that reminded him of the daylight sounds from a nestful of birds.

Out toward the open bay they tacked, and, with that sensation of freedom that going seaward always gives, Gilbert felt a mad desire to sail away with her and the child from that trouble that awaited them on the shore.

But no, the wind was getting lighter, and they must turn and run up before it fell with the sunset.

"Going home to daddy! Going home to daddy!" the child sung, gleefully, in unconscious mockery of their forebodings, as the little craft drew in toward the landing.

Gilbert had already sent a comprehensive glance around, but could see nothing of Broderick, of any one, in fact, save Isaac, who was hanging about the boats in his usual casual fashion.

He came forward to help Mrs. Broderick and to lift the boy out, and then, after watching them, as they went hand in hand up the path, he turned to Gilbert.

"There's been trouble up there, sir," he said, jerking his thumb over his shoulder.

"What?" the other asked, sharply, looking up from furling the sail. He was out on the shore in a moment, listening to Isaac's tale.

It seemed that Broderick, after the boat left, had been walking up and down in front of his studio, while Higgins, at a little distance, chatted with Isaac, when he had slipped inside so quietly that it was a few moments before they noticed he was gone. A crash within took Higgins to the studio door, only to see the big picture thrown from its easel, the framework smashed, and the canvas hanging in long strips, at which the artist was still cutting wildly with the one small, dull palette knife that he was allowed to possess.

"It could never really hurt any one; it is so flimsy," Isabel had pleaded; but it was strong enough now to hack and rend the dark fields of poppies, the glowing hillside of lilies.

When Higgins had caught his arm, saying: "wouldn't

do that, sir, if I were you," he had shouted, wildly:

"If I create them, I give them a soul; and, if I give them a soul, and that soul is lost, mine must pay a hundredfold tribute of woe! woe!"

By the time that Isaac had got this far in his story, Gilbert was striding up the bank. He had seen Mrs. Broderick standing in the studio door, and the sight drew him like a magnet.

She looked round silently as he came behind her, and he saw that the slow tears were rolling unchecked down her face,

With a motion of her hand, she drew his attention to the room before them. Scattered over the floor, among the overturned paint-box and palette, were fragments of the canvas that had formed a masterpiece; here and there familiar bits of colour still showing intact in their beauty.

On the sofa at the further end lay Broderick, sleeping peacefully, a shadowy smile on his pale face, the tumbled hair that hung over his eyes giving him a boyish look.

It was a pitiful enough sight, and Gilbert felt a choking in his own throat as he looked.

"The artist is gone, and next the man will go," he heard in a murmur beside him.

He turned and was about to attempt some words of comfort, when, pushing aside Isabel's skirts, Boyso poked his head into the studio.

At the tempestuous aspect of the place, he gave a joyous crow, and, with a sudden rush, was across the room in spite of Gilbert's effort to seize him, shouting:

"Daddy, wake up! Wake up and play with Boyso!"

Isabel rushed forward, but before she could reach the sofa, Broderick had started up, and caught the child in his arms with a wild cry:

"My boy! My boy! Destined to bear all my sin and sorrow! Destined to eternal fire!"

The last words rose to a scream, and the terrified child struggled and added his cries to the tumult.

While Gilbert hesitated as to what to do, Isabel's clear tones made themselves heard:

"Andrew, you had better give him to me. Come, Boyso, come to mummie."

Her spell worked, and, without opposition, her husband let her take the child in her arms and carry him off, soothing him as she went.

Broderick sat staring after her in a pathetically bewildered fashion, and, when Higgins had closed the door upon her, huddled himself together again into the corner of the sofa, a picture of stolid misery.

That night Gilbert took his dinner alone, being told that Mrs. Broderick was having hers in the nursery, but later he found her in her usual seat in the veranda.

"Wouldn't you like to come down on the sand-bar? There always seems more air there," he suggested.

"No, I would rather not go so far. The nurse is sitting with Boyso now, but I told her to call me if he should awake restless or frightened. It took me a little while to soothe him to sleep," was her quiet answer.

This quietness reassured him to go on, though it was with misgivings that he asked:

"Will it worry you to speak of what must be done?

"No, I know," she all but whispered.

"You know that your boy must be sent away at once, either with you or without, as you shall choose."

"Yes," came with a little catch of her breath.

"Will you let me give you the earnest advice that you should go, too?" he said, leaning nearer in his intentness, the words seeming to frame his own doom as he spoke them.

"Then you think that it is coming soon?" and the hitherto concealed horror sounded in her voice.

For the first time, Gilbert realised that, beside her beautiful pity for the man, there could be a personal shrinking from the maniac, and the fact added to his determination to get her away from her husband.

"I think," he said, cautiously, "these two outbursts show that, even with the most careful watching, he is likely at any time to do something that might give the child a severe nervous shock, not to speak of the same danger for yourself."

He paused to let his words take effect, and then made his demand. "Will you let me telegraph for two experienced men, to help me get him back as soon as possible to Boston?

"To the asylum?"

"Yes," he acknowledged, waiting for her decision.

But it was not to come just yet.

"Would he be well enough to understand what you were doing?" was her question.

"Perhaps so, at times. But —"

She interrupted him, following out her own line of thought: "And if I were to send the child home with his nurse, you do not fear danger to any one else here?"

Gilbert saw that he was losing his battle, and, ashamed at the sudden fierce throb of joy in her continued presence, he spoke with grave self-repression: "Not absolute danger, I suppose, if we keep a more careful watch on him, and get another keeper to relieve guard. We are four men here already, you know, counting Isaac, and that Swedish woman is as strong as a man. I saw her turn a boat over by herself, the other day. However, she, of course, would go with Boyso."

"Then I am still free to choose between husband and child?" she asked, with repressed bitterness.

"In one way you may be, though I think it right to warn you that, if only for your child's sake, you have no right to risk the mental and physical harm that such a strain may entail on you, Come," he went on with kindly authoritativeness, "make up your mind that the time has come when you must consider yourself and the child first. You have already done more than one woman out of a hundred would have done —"

"Ah, you do not know! You do not know!" she broke in with a cry of irrepressible pain, that puzzled him with its echo of self-reproach.

Of all wives in the world what could she have to reproach herself with, unless — but he would not put the overpowering thought into form. He only knew that he was her knight-errant, bound to absolutely loyal service. As though repenting her outbreak, she rose, saying quietly: "There can be nothing gained by deciding it tonight. You shall know the first thing in the morning," and without further parting, was gone.

Chapter 12

The Sword of Damocles

The sparkling beauty of the June morning seemed to mock at the restless human misery that it encompassed.

After having kept watch for half the night, Gilbert had gone down early for his swim, getting new energy from the crisp wavelets of the rising tide.

There seemed to be mental as well as physical tonic in the healing waters of the great ocean, for the surging thoughts of passion, against which he had struggled through the hours of darkness, were stilled, and he went back to the house able to bear himself like a man, to fight the good fight for those weaker than himself.

Early as it was, he found Isabel and her boy at breakfast, and one glance at her face, serene through all its traces of past conflict, told him that she too had fought and conquered.

In after years, that picture of her never lost its clearness in his mental vision. He saw the pallor of her face, framed in her loose hair, against the dead white of her duck dress. He saw the shadowy smile that answered the child's prattling, even while her hungry eyes never left his face. It was the hunger in those eyes which revealed to him her decision, even before, the sweet daily intimacy of their meal ended, she came toward him on the veranda. The dewy fragrance from the mignonette in the homely garden, the morning song of the robins amongst the apple blossoms, the flashing sun-track on the water, all told of the joy of nature's high-tide of life. In the woman's face alone was the austere light of renunciation.

"I have decided," she began at once, with that same self-control. "I shall send Boyso off with his nurse in the steamer to-morrow. She shall take him to his grandmother."

She herself would stay, then, was his first thought, crushed down by the remembrance of the harm that doing so might work her.

"And what if I refuse to agree to it?" he asked with a sudden impulse to ensure her safety at any cost.

She smiled securely. "You will not do that. You acknowledged last night that it was possible for me to remain, and I take you at your word."

"It may be possible, but still very undesirable," he persisted. "However, in yielding as to the present possibility, it is with the proviso that any day I should insist on your leaving, you will go, at once. Will you agree to this?"

For a moment her eyes searched his, then, as though content with what they had found there, she said, softly:

"What could I do but obey you, when I trust you so absolutely?"

He could not help it. He took the slim artist hand in his, and pressed his lips to it, then, already ashamed of the impulse, turned away and went down to the shore. Isaac was hovering about his boat, evidently preparing to embark.

"Going fishing?" Gilbert asked, listlessly.

"Just going to have a look at the lobster-pots. Thought I'd take the child along, if you don't object. Looks kind of peeky this morning."

The old man liked to make an excuse that put Boyso's companionship on a charitable basis, evidently considering it a weakness to acknowledge it as a pleasure to himself.

"You'd better not, I think. His mother will want him with her to-day, for she's sending him home to-morrow."

"That's one comfort," Isaac grunted, emphatically. "This ain't no place for a child, with trouble coming thick as a thunder-storm. Tell you what, it's plain to any fool that there ain't no luck in the house, or else, what there is precious bad luck. And for why?" hammering his hand vigorously against the gunwale of the boat. "Because it stands to reason that, with that there Virgin —"

"Look here, Isaac, I'm in no humour to stand any more old wives' tales," Gilbert interrupted, and, deeply offended, the old man shoved off his boat, and paddled down along the shore.

All the morning, Gilbert never went very far out of sight of the studio, where Broderick seemed content to remain. The damage to his painting materials had been repaired, and, for the first time in several days, he seemed to care to work.

"A good sign," Gilbert said, hopefully, to Higgins outside the door.

"I don't know about that, sir. Just take a look at them cheerful kind of things he's paintin'," was the pessimistic retort.

True enough, when Gilbert stood looking over the artist's shoulder, he felt a chill at what he saw.

On the smaller canvas, which had replaced the hapless poppies, were wild streaks of colour seemingly representing clouds, through which peered out lurid, boding heads, faces full of Satanic mockery or rage, and arms outstretched to seize their prey.

Only in one corner of the sketch was any attempt at connected composition, and this, it seemed to Gilbert, was a rough but vigorous suggestion of the sacrifice of Isaac by Abraham. The few touches that represented the victim contained an evident likeness to Boyso, as did the angel hovering above to Isabel.

Pondering deeply over these workings of the disordered mind, Gilbert turned away, leaving Broderick undisturbed.

It was some days since the latter had joined them at their meals, although his place was always kept for him. To-day they had taken their seats, when to the surprise of both, he quietly slipped in and sat down.

"Daddy's come to dinner! Daddy's hungry!" lisped the child, while his mother exchanged a startled glance with Gilbert.

He nodded reassuringly, for he had been quick to see that a calmer spirit had prevailed with Broderick. His blue eyes were again dreamily vague, though, once or twice, Gilbert did notice the side-long glance at the child, that had before now made him uneasy.

He seemed to listen, too, when Boyso spoke, though

otherwise wrapped in his own realm of shadows.

Higgins had followed him in, and waited behind his chair, and, according to his ubiquitous habit, the French cook came and went between the side-board and the neighbouring kitchen.

There was certainly plenty of help at hand, even if Gilbert had not believed there to be a temporary improvement in his condition, and that, for the present, there would be no more trouble.

It was not a cheerful meal, and Isabel gave a quick little sigh of relief when her husband rose and went out as quietly as he had come in.

She looked over appealingly at Gilbert, who hastened to answer her mute question.

"Yes, he is certainly better for the time being. How long it may last I cannot say, but I do not think that we need fear any more trouble for the next few days."

"Thank God for that!" she murmured with tremulous lips, and he saw that the coffee-cup she held shook in her hand.

"You are played out," he said, quickly; "here, let me put this hammock-chair where you will get the breeze, and this cushion under your head, so."

Silently she drooped back, with closed lids, from under which the tears fell one by one.

The child's prattle sounded up from the beach where he played beside his nurse, and they were alone. She let her self-control fall from her as she might have dropped an unnecessary wrap, and Gilbert felt the painful joy that she should trust him in her weakness.

"Will you tell me if you slept last night?" he asked

presently, and she answered him with a silent shake of her head.

"Then won't you try to rest in your darkened room now?" he urged, gently. "See, everything is so quiet and peaceful, and there is nothing to make you anxious. I think you would sleep."

"Nothing!" she echoed, but still she rose obediently, and went up-stairs.

Over indoors and out settled the afternoon quiet, and under its spell Gilbert presently found that he had been dozing in the hammock-chair. He, too, had felt the strain of the past twenty-four hours.

But he shook off the pleasant lassitude, and stood up with a sense of work to be done. Before the evening he must have a letter ready to send over to catch the coach at La Falaise.

He went off to his den, passing Broderick and his keeper sitting on a bench under an apple-tree not far from the house. There he settled himself to write a full professional account of the case to his Boston colleague, asking him to wire back an opinion as to whether the time had not come when they must insist upon the immediate security of an asylum.

The letter was not one to be written in a hurry, as it entailed a frequent reference to his daily notes but it was finished at last, and, leaning back in his high chair, he stretched out his arms lazily, thinking to himself that he would take a survey of his domains, to determine if he might absent himself for an hour's sail. The breeze on the water would blow away this lassitude.

"Judging from the silence, it might be the castle of

the Sleeping Beauty. Even the cocks and hens seem to have forgotten to cackle," he said to himself, as he stood in the open doorway, lighting a pipe.

Even as he said it, the air seemed rent by a long, shrilly piercing scream, — a scream that was the wail of a passing life, and that left behind it the silence of death.

It brought a creeping horror to the roots of his hair, and an icy sweat to his face, as he knew that his worst forebodings were realised.

"Isabel! It will kill her, too!" he heard himself groaning, as, with the instinctive sense of the shore being the scene of action, he rushed past the house. He saw the stalwart Swedish nurse fleeing down the pathway between the apple-trees, and the sight told him that the child had been without her protection.

A wailing cry of "Gilbert" from an up-stairs window only hastened his desperate speed. He must, at any rate, get there before she did.

And then, as the little wharf came in view, the full horror burst upon him. At its very end lay the child on its back, while over it knelt Broderick, one arm raised high, the hand grasping — God! it was one of the sailors' sheath-knives, about which Gilbert had already warned Isaac and his grandson.

But now the nurse had reached Broderick, pinioning him from behind with her strong arms, and a second later, Higgins scrambling up from the beach, they had him securely in their grasp. Then Gilbert, unheeding their struggles, found himself kneeling by that sickeningly limp little figure, whose story was told by the red stream staining the front of the dainty white dress. The first touch, the first look convinced him that life was gone, and yet he still knelt, trying to stanch the blood, feeling the poor little body, that looked so pitifully small, for any last throb of life that might be coaxed back into action. Some subtle consciousness made him raise his head to see the swift rush of Isabel toward him.

"Go back! Go back!" he shouted. "For God's sake keep her back!" but there was no one to do so, and her feet were already on the wharf, as he sprang up to come between her and that still, white figure. He saw her sway forward, with outstretched arms, before she fell her full length toward him, and lay as still as did her child.

Chapter 13

Separate Paths

Few of the passengers by the next weekly boat from Halifax to Boston knew that they carried a child's coffin in one locked cabin, and in another a lunatic, carefully guarded by four men. Lunatics and coffins, not being popular at sea, are generally kept as much in the background as possible.

It being perfect summer weather, when even that treacherous corner of the Atlantic was behaving itself, the passengers did notice the distinguished-looking woman, who sat so still in a secluded corner of the deck, cared for so assiduously by a young man of somewhat haggard aspect.

"Wonder if he's her husband?" said one young woman to another.

"She doesn't treat him over civilly, if he is. She has hardly answered him, or even looked at him once that I've seen. She looks as sulky as a bear."

"And he such a nice-looking fellow, too. But, I tell you what. I think there's something wrong with her mind, or else why should they have that great strong Swedish woman taking care of her.

No, I'm sure she's weak in her head. They must be swells, too," she added, regretfully.

In the distress of those days, Gilbert was almost inclined to the girl's opinion, as each day's duration of her unnatural calm seemed to increase the chance of Isabel's mind never recovering from the awful shock.

It was the night before they were to land, — a moonlight night when the surface of the sea was absolutely calm, rising and falling to the long curves of some far-distant tumult.

Isabel had refused to leave her hammock-chair for her cabin, and, as the hour grew late, and the decks were deserted, Gilbert sat beside her, sharing her vigil. His thoughts were too full of unselfish anxiety on her behalf for him to realise that these were the last hours of their life of daily intimacy. It had grown to seem to him a natural thing that must perforce go on forever.

His one desire now was to make her talk, to break up at any cost that stupefied stillness that might be working such havoc on her brain.

"You will go at once to your own house? I telegraphed to have it got ready, you know," he asked.

For a moment she moved her bare hand mechanically backward and forward on her knee, with that apparent dislike of being spoken to, which he had before noticed, then she answered, in a listless murmur: "I suppose so. It doesn't much matter where."

With a sudden change to startled horror, she turned to him, asking: "He wouldn't be brought there, would he?"

"No, no; you must not think about that. We shall take him direct to the asylum."

He soothed her as he might have done a frightened

child, and, with the reassurance, she shrank back again into herself, staring out intensely along the moonlight track on the water.

"Is there any one, any woman, whom you would like me to send for?" he persisted.

"No one, thank you."

"But your husband's mother will surely come?

Again the startled turn of the head, as she said, quickly: "I hope not. Why should she?"

"She would want to, I think," he said, shrinking from referring more openly to the funeral. Even this seemed to agitate her.

"I am sure that she must hate me," came in distressed tones. "But for my obstinacy, her grandchild would still be left. I wronged her son in marrying him without love, and she always knew it. When we first met in Paris, after I was engaged to him, she warned me against the insanity in the family, and I would not listen to her. She is a hard, honest woman. How could she forgive me now?"

Gilbert, seeing that speech must come to the overburdened heart, went on:

"You must not forget that there is cause for thankfulness in knowing that your child can never share its father's fate."

He had roused her now effectually. With a strange cry and wave of her bands, she broke out: "And so I doubly murdered him, my boy, my own little boy! I gave him that nature, which was a wrong to him! I failed to protect him from the man who was his father! How can I bear to live on, with such a curse upon me!"

Before Gilbert could guess at what she was about to do, she had sprung up, and hovered, with upraised arms, near the rail. Like a flash he was upon her, with his arms wound around her, pressing her struggling figure close to him.

All at once he felt its rigidity relax, felt its weight heavier, and, loosening his grip, saw the helpless head fall back against his shoulder.

In the keen ache of his sympathy, it was almost a relief to see the wan face soften into peace, the weary lids close, and to know that for a time she was unconscious of her sorrow.

For the last hours of their journey, she was like a sweet, sorrowful child, doing what he asked her to do, but otherwise lying still with closed eyelids, through which a slow tear occasionally welled.

The hard, strained look was gone, and Gilbert feared no longer for her mind. All the more, perhaps, was the sense of personal loss heavy upon him, as he stood in the freshness of the June morning, watching the closed carriage that contained Isabel, her maid, and family doctor drive away from the wharf. Henceforth, he knew that he must learn to stand outside her life, though even yet he did not realise how thorough their separation must be. Those long, quiet days of shared anxiety and companionship had made them too much and too little for the continuance of an ordinary friendship. He knew that his wisest course would have been to start at once on a visit to his mother, but he could not tear himself away before the child's funeral, which Isabel was not able to attend.

He hung on the words of the family doctor, who

talked of prostration against which a strong physique was fighting.

"Splendid type, splendid type! Wish there were more American women like her," the old man said, rubbing his hands.

A week passed, a week during which Gilbert received the handsome cheque for his services, which, to his fancy, seemed to put him at a still farther distance. Then, his sense of loss prevailing over sterner wisdom, he wrote her a note, asking if he might see her before going to his mother in Canada.

The answer contained only a few words, saying that she would see him the next day.

The afternoon heat lay heavily upon the city street, but could not reach the cool, shaded room, that he remembered so well in the winter twilight, the early spring sunshine.

There was no scent of flowers there now, and no sunshine; only the soft light from the creamy silk blinds seemed in pity to encompass the tall black figure that rose to receive him.

Something choked him as he looked into the woe-ravaged face, as he held the thin hand in his, but, when she spoke, he knew that there was upon her a force of self-repression that he must not disturb, and that no words of sympathy were to he spoken.

"You are going away?" she asked, almost carelessly.

"Only for a week or two, but I thought that you might be out of town when I return. You are not going to stay on here?"

"No, I am not going to stay on here," she answered, with a little smile, then, as though trying to show an interest in his affairs: "You are going to see your mother about the legacy, are you not?"

"I suppose so," he answered, chilled by her manner.

"And where is Isaac's 'Lady' now?"

"At the bank. Let us hope they are not aware of her bad character," and he laughed, shortly.

He was amazed to see her wince at his words.

"Don't, please! We, at least, have no reason to scoff at her powers of bringing misfortune."

"Forgive me," he answered, with a quick compunction.

"Yes, I am to see Mr. Salmon, the famous collector, to-morrow. I feel that I have a right to find out the value of the thing, to get an idea as to what connoisseurs think of it, before I see my mother. That is all that I can do, for I may, after all, find that there is some real reason against my doing anything about the will."

"Don't be rash!" she warned him. "Remember what I said about money."

"And you still say it?" he asked, thinking only of his own affairs, and with the masculine dislike of hearing his ideal object give utterance to any materialistic sentiment. The effect of his words was alarming. For a moment he thought that she had fainted, as she cowered back into the corner among the cushions, hiding her face in her outstretched arms.

"What an idiotic brute I am!" he ejaculated, savagely, but unheeding him, she moaned: "Oh, no, no! I take back all that I said that day! Better to be a pauper, than to be crushed by the weight of shameful wrongdoing, as I am now."

He could not help it, he was on his knees beside her, holding her hand in his, pouring out protestations that never woman had acted with higher or more unselfish devotion than she had done.

For a moment she did not interrupt him, and then she drew her hand away, the movement recalling him to himself.

"Forgive me!" he stammered, bitterly ashamed of his want of self-control. "I had better go," he added, as they stood facing each other, and her whispered "yes" was hardly audible.

"You will let me come when I return; you will not banish me for this?" he asked, desperately.

"I shall be gone," she said, softly.

"Gone?"

"Yes, I shall be gone before you return," she repeated, with greater confidence. "I am letting the house, going abroad somewhere; it doesn't much matter where; back to the old artist haunts, most likely. Perhaps I can work there; perhaps, in time, forget."

"Not everything?" he urged.

Her eyes met his with sorrowful steadiness. "Yes, everything that I can. It is better so. Now go, please."

He saw her waver, saw that he must be strong both, and, turning, left her.

Chapter 14

A Connoisseur

Although Gilbert had been surprised at Isabel's acknowledgment of superstitious terrors, yet he recognised, with sardonic amusement, a growing respect in his own mind for "Our Lady of Wrath," a respect which would certainly snake him feel more comfortable if the statue were disposed of to a church.

All the same it was with a pleasurable sense of antic-ipation that he sat at the dinner-table of the great col-lector, Mr. Salmon, awaiting their post-prandial dis-cussion.

Everything around him was, in its way, a work of art; the glass on the table was old Venetian, the centre ornaments were exquisitely chased silver models of the craft of Spanish Armada.

The Renaissance was the watchword of Mr. Salmon's life, and although he handled his art treasures as prof-itably as other men do their stocks and shares, yet he always kept the very choicest of them around him to minister to his daily pleasure. The power to do this was one of the joys which his wealth had brought him.

Another, was the statuesque young wife, of the best blond Jewish type, who sat, in serene and beautiful stolidity, at the head of his table, dressed in a Parisian adaptation of the costume of one of Titian's Doges' wives.

Glancing from her to the bloodless-looking, voluble man of sixty, Gilbert's wonder was aroused by the couple. However, after she had left the table, he saw his hostess no more, but was taken to smoke in a wonderful room, part library, part museum, and perfect in every detail.

On a black wooden stand of Venetian carving, under the golden glow of an electric light in the semblance of an apple, stood the silver statue, and Gilbert was conscious of a proud sense of proprietorship as, for the first time, he saw the work of art to full advantage.

As for Mr. Salmon, seating himself in a deep armchair before it, he contemplated it with an air of devout absorption.

"Wonderful! Wonderful!" he murmured.

"There is something in the workmanship that recalls a St. John the Baptist of Donatello's, in Florence. Could it be possible — but no, a work of that value, lost in those times in Florence, would have been heard of down to the present day."

Apparently inspired with a new idea, he leaned forward to fix, with a powerful glass, the wrought bordering to the robe that was set with the emeralds.

"I thought so," he said to himself, then turning sharply upon Gilbert. "Young man, those stones were put in afterwards by an inferior craftsman. The work is quite roughly done. You say that the statue came from South America? Well, it is probable that this masterpiece has been taken out there from Spain or Italy, and subsequently had the jewels added by an ordinary silversmith. What do you say to that?"

"I say that it is quite probable, but that you must have great technical knowledge to be so sure of it," was the answer that brought a pleased flicker to the sharp eyes.

"So-so, only so-so. Life is short at the best. But, if I understood you right, you have not quite decided to sell this statue?"

"To tell you the truth, I have hardly had time to decide on anything since I obtained possession of it. It seems that there are all sorts of old tales as to its powers of bringing down misfortune upon any one who treats it disrespectfully, and — you may laugh, but I have seen such strange things happen lately that I almost feel as though I should like to hedge with Providence, and sell it to some devout millionaire who wished to make an offering to the church."

"There are not many people who would care to make an offering of that value to a church," the older man said, with so inscrutable an air that Gilbert was puzzled as to whether he really wished to become its purchaser or not.

This respectful mention of its value sent a pleasant stir through his pulses, as he asked: "Have you any definite idea, then, as to what it is worth?"

The answer came direct enough. "Well, that I could hardly say, until the stones have been seen by a first-class jewel merchant; however, what I *can* say is that, if the stones are guaranteed as of average quality, I would unhesitatingly offer you fifty thousand dollars."

Fifty thousand dollars! The words sounded like

untold riches to the man who had worked so hard for hundreds.

He was roused from his day-dream by the sharp question, and the sharper accompanying glance.

"I suppose in that case you can give me the facts as to where the statue came from, and through whose hands it has passed?"

A sudden sense of shame came unexpectedly to Gilbert, but he knew that the truth was the only possible thing.

"The whole thing sounds so like a penny-dreadful, that I shouldn't be surprised if you doubted the story, but as far as I know, it was brought from a privateering cruise on the Spanish Main by my grandfather more than seventy-five years ago, and was hidden by him in a garret chimney of an old farmhouse on the Nova Scotian coast. He died a rich and very old man, leaving this farmhouse and its contents to me. I visited the place for the first time this summer, and had hints from an old sailor that he believed there to be hidden hoards about. After all, though, it was quite accidentally, in a rainy day's exploring to amuse a lady and child, that we came upon this statue, and the picture that I told you of. It all sounds improbable enough, I must confess," he ended with.

"Yes, it does," the older man frankly agreed.

"And yet, if anything of that rarity and value had been lost from any church or museum in Europe within the last twenty-five years, I should have known of it."

Gilbert flushed vividly. "You do not mean—" he began.

"I do not mean anything save a few business-like

inquiries," was the soothing answer. "Howard Glenn's letter would make me trust you through any improbable stories. But it is a habit of mine to get at all possible details in every transaction, a habit that has stood me in good stead before now."

"Very well," Gilbert said, swallowing his pride with an effort. "Here is the address of the lawyer in Bridgewater, Nova Scotia, who can corroborate what I have said about my right to it and the farm."

"That's all right," said Mr. Salmon, all the same pocketing the address. "But now tell me, if we should come to a bargain, should I have your leave to publish this story? If I buy this statue, I mean to keep it for my own collection, and half its value would be lost to me unless its history were in my catalogue."

For a moment Gilbert weighed this new question in silence before he spoke. "In any case, I should always prefer that the names should be kept back from the public, but I can settle nothing until I have been to Canada and seen some of my family. Until I return, at any rate. I should wish nothing said about the whole affair."

"You may trust me for that. We collectors do not gossip about our bargains beforehand. But, if you like, you can leave the statue in my strong-room, and I will have it valued for you."

To this the other was glad to agree, and so they parted in amity.

The next morning Gilbert started for the small town in Ontario, where his mother lived.

A smiling little town it was, in that fertile peninsula of the Niagara district where Canada assumes its most southern aspect. Shady streets and bowery gardens surrounded the tidy houses, each set in its own grass-plot.

It was all so trim and bright in its midsummer glow, and yet Gilbert had a half-amused, half-bitter consciousness of the old chill creeping over him, as he paused in front of a prim little brick house, evidently of greater age than its Queen Anne neighbours.

This chill had, from his earliest childhood, accompanied him into the presence of his mother.

He found her, seated in a carefully shaded room in the same old, rigid arm-chair, with the same old, rigid aspect. She was sewing — he had never seen her knit, and had always fancied that she considered it too soothing an occupation — holding an uncompromising-looking white garment, into which she was working buttonholes.

Scarcely was the perfunctory kiss and greeting passed between them, than Gilbert thought that he felt an extra chill of disapproval in her manner.

"And how is Cynthia?" he asked, Cynthia being the young girl whom his mother had brought up.

"Cynthia is well. I believe that she is picking peas in the garden."

"As devoted to her garden as ever?"

"Yes, she persisted in her idea of growing flowers and fruit for sale, and, I must acknowledge, has done well. Still, I can see no necessity for it, and, if she would only have taken up the church work that I was forced to relinquish, she would have had plenty to occupy her."

"Oh, well, I dare say that she likes to feel she earns

her pocket-money," he said, carelessly. He had always had a kindly liking for the girl, but at present his own affairs were of chief interest to him. The cold blue eyes had been watching him narrowly, and had read his preoccupation, and the old woman went straight to the point.

"And so you have accepted your grandfather's legacy?" she said, brusquely. Gilbert answered in a tone of studied impassiveness.

"One can scarcely call that tumble-down, old house much of a legacy, but I took it on account of the papers that went with it. I felt that I must know their contents."

A keen interest showed for a moment in her face, and was immediately repressed. "One step at a time; first the farm, and then this image that you wrote of. After that, there will be some other will-o'-the-wisp to lure you on."

"Mother," he began, more earnestly, "you have not asked what those papers were."

"Why should I ask? Cannot I tell that it is something to entice you away from the path of duty?" was her sombre answer.

"It is a will of my grandfather's, made the week before he died, leaving me a third of his estate. Isaac Neisner has had it in his possession ever since."

It was but natural that he should feel a sense of triumph in the announcement, but if he had expected to arouse even a show of surprise, he was mistaken.

"I was right when I spoke of will-o'-the-wisps. And you will follow this one?" she asked, gloomily.

"I certainly shall, unless you can show me good rea-

son to the contrary," he asserted, his resolution crys-
tallising with his words. His mother leaned forward,
her hands clasped over her sewing.

"And you promise to abide by that reason?"

"How can I, until I am in a position to judge it?
Mother, don't let us be in an antagonistic attitude
now. I might, on my part, complain of the mystery you
had created in our affairs, but all I ask now is to hear
from you the whole story of our family. I have refused
to sell the image without knowing it."

Some softening influence did seem to touch her.

"Your father and I thought to save you from temptation," she said, more gently.

Unwilling to say that he felt they had wronged him,
Gilbert repeated: "I say that I will not blame you for
that, if only you will tell me what concerns me so
deeply now?"

"Very well, you shall have it," she agreed, dryly, and,
during the hours that followed, Gilbert heard for the
first time his family history.

Chapter 15

In the Days of Her Youth

Susan Bauer's girlhood had been spent at the old home on the La Have River, and a dull and laborious girlhood it had been.

Her mother was a fretful invalid, aged before her time by hard work, and the bearing and loss of children. Susan had been the only one of the family who had lived to grow up, and her mother would have liked to have seen her in the enjoyment of some of the little fineries and pleasures of the other girls of the neighbourhood.

But the determined miserliness of Jonathan Bauer had isolated them from the life of the countryside, so that, at last, Mrs. Bauer, ashamed of her shabby garments, ceased to appear even at church gatherings.

To these, however, Susan clung with a pertinacity which she inherited from her German — in local parlance, Dutch — ancestry.

They were both simple, conscientious women, and, believing in the necessity for this strenuous economy, they toiled early and late, asking for no pleasures or change.

The only change came to them in the periodic absences of the head of the house, when they silently relaxed into more restful ways.

Susan was not more than eighteen when her mother died, and her life became truly solitary.

She worked on as before, occasionally shedding furtive tears over her work, and singing a more mournful type of hymn. She also went less to the Lutheran services, and, when her father was away, went as much as possible to a Presbyterian church, presided over by a dyspeptic-looking young divine, whose views as to the eternal arrangements of the universe were as gloomy as his own appearance.

She would sometimes, on Saturdays, lock up the house, and spend the Sunday with an old lady cousin, who lived much nearer this church.

Little as Susan saw of the outside world, she had, during these Sunday visits, heard things said which began to snake her wonder if her father were, if not a rich man, at any rate, not a poor one. Even in her mystical, unworldly nature the thought that hers and her mother's lives had been rendered unnecessarily sordid was beginning to arouse a dull resentment.

She would look down in church at her toil-hardened hands and shabby black dress, and pray that she might be given strength to honour her father.

It was a little more than a year after Mrs. Bauer's death, when her father returned from a cruise of several months in an unwontedly good humour. So comprehensive had this good humour seemed that she had ventured, after their tea, to harness the old white horse and drive up to the weekly prayer-meeting.

On her return she had slipped in quietly from the barn, and, going up-stairs, sat at her window in the dark to live again the pleasure she had experienced in the sound of Mr. Clinch's deep tones, and the exalted sentiments they had aroused in her heart.

She heard the voices of her father and of the mate of one of his vessels, a man whom she instinctively disliked, as they talked just below her on the steps, but she was too wrapt in these pleasant thoughts of hers to heed their words.

Presently a fluttering, gray night-moth blundered against her face, abruptly breaking the thread of her devoutly sentimental meditations. Leaning out in the darkness to brush away the moth, she was not far above the heads of the two talkers.

"Well, the girl will be the gainer by all this money of yours some day, I suppose. There's no one else, to have it, is there?" she heard the mate say.

"No one, save myself, Reuben Stecker, and I mean to have it for many a day yet, so you needn't think you'll get any of it out of me by marrying the girl, for you won't. Besides, what right have you to be saying things like 'all this money of yours' out so loud? There mayn't be so much as you think."

The mate laughed unpleasantly.

"I don't think, I know. I know that you're rolling up money every year, and other folks beside me are beginning to guess it. Look here," and now he did lower his voice, though it was still distinctly audible to Susan, leaning out overhead. "Have you ever thought what would happen if that affair of ours at Mobile last spring were to get blown upon? Have you seen last week's *Citizen?*"

"No, what do you mean?" and through the gruffness

of the question, there was an evident echo of fear.

"Well, here's something I cut out of it for your benefit, and, when you've read it, you just tell me if it doesn't mean us?"

Something was muttered that sounded like an oath, and, peering anxiously down, Susan could see by the light of a match which the mate had struck, that he was handing a strip of newspaper to her father.

Afraid of being discovered, she hastily drew in her head, but all the same she heard her father say: "Do you think me a bat to be able to read in the dark? Here, come inside, and we'll get a light."

Susan knew that her father would light the lamp himself rather than bring her upon the scene, and so sat still, cowering under some new, undefined fear in the darkness. She had never loved her father; in fact, that would have been about as possible as the love of a meek barn-yard chicken for the vigorous old eagle soaring above, but she had been accustomed to look upon him as fulfilling the local ideal of respectability, working hard at his business all the week, sitting in a shiny black coat in the Lutheran church on Sundays, never being known to drink or play cards.

Now this hint of surreptitious riches, and of local gossip over the same, brought the first disquieting thought that these absences of her father's might be the cloak to many an outside element in his life. Her very incapacity to understand his character or circumstances added to this terror of unknown forces in her narrow life.

"Oh, if only mother had lived!" she moaned to herself under her breath.

For an hour or more, the light streamed out from the down-stairs window, and the insistent murmur of low voices went on, while Susan sat in the darkness, a prey to undefined fears.

At last, the dread that her father might discover that she was still undressed drove her to bed, and to troubled snatches of sleep.

Used to early rising as she was, it was half an hour earlier than usual when she was astir the next morning.

She had not enough self-consciousness to look pitifully at her own pale face and heavy eyes in the glass, as would a more modern young woman; she only brushed and twisted up her smooth, abundant masses of flaxen hair into as tight a knot as possible, donned her black-and-white print, and went down. The house, like most of those belonging to the German settlers, was kept immaculately clean, and her trained housewife's eyes caught sight, at once, of a scrap of paper lying at the foot of the stairs.

As she picked it up, and saw that it was a cutting from a newspaper, the whole of the last night's overheard talk flashed back upon her, and she trembled all over as she went, with it in her hand, into the kitchen behind the house.

She sat down in an old wooden rocking-chair, holding but not looking at the paper, which she knew contained the solution of the mystery; her precise conscientiousness still making her hesitate before anything which seemed like prying into her father's affairs.

But the recollection of her own name in the conversation drove away her scruples. She felt that she had, at any rate, a right to protect herself from that hateful mate, with his bold eyes and half-foreign tricks.

The cutting had evidently been an extract from a Boston paper, and told, with great apparent indignation, of a strange outbreak of unlawful slave-trading which had recently come to light in the Southern States. The boldest and most successful of these law-breakers had been a Nova Scotian captain and shipowner, who had, in the preceding spring, brought a cargo of healthy young negroes from the Congo to Mobile, and thence up to a lonely plantation, where they were landed and sold at large the time the story was known, the schooner and her captain were far at sea, but the paper demanded that the repetition of such an outrage should be made impossible.

No American of the 50's could look upon slavery with eyes of the present day, but still, Susan had lately heard a lecture delivered by Mr. Clinch on the horrors of slavery, and her soul had burned within her as she listened. Mr. Clinch had, like so many Canadians, been partly educated in Boston, where he had come under the noble influence of some of the abolitionists of the day, and listened to details of the grim horror that they were fighting.

Her father one of those people held up to moral scorn as a slave-trader! Her father a man who hid his ill-gotten gains away from the light of day, grudging her dead mother every alleviation for her failing health!

If Susan had not been so wretched, she would almost have wondered at the coldly combative strength that awoke in her. It was so new to her to feel anything save meek submission toward the father who ruled her life. She did not yet understand that, not being a woman who would ever think for herself, it was merely a transference of allegiance, and that from henceforth the words "Mr. Clinch said" would take the place in her life that "father said" had hitherto done.

However, even now she extracted her first grains of comfort from the thought that she would consult Mr. Clinch as to what it was her duty to do, for the idea had never come to her that life could move on exactly the same lines as before.

Although she could not have defined it clearly, she knew that something familiar was ended, and something strange was about to take its place. As she rose to open the house-door, the sea fog came in gray and cold, and she shivered, and hastened to light the kitchen fire.

Presently she heard her father's heavy step overhead, but, when it sounded on the stairs, she noticed that it was lingering, and, taking a surreptitious peep into the passage, she saw that he was peering about into corners, as though in search of something.

Instinctively her band went into her pocket to feel that the slip of paper was safely there.

Chapter 16

A New Allegiance

As her father came into the kitchen, where they still ate their meals, she felt that her heart was beating faster, and that her face was pale.

However, Jonathan Bauer had never been in the habit of studying the looks of his women-folk, and, to her great relief, she knew from the first sound of his voice that his humour was still set fair.

"Coffee smells good," he said, rubbing his hands. "Must say you're not a bad housewife, as girls go. There, as I didn't bring you a present, there's a pound for you" — shillings and pounds were still words in use in the Provinces of the '50's — "to buy something smart next time you go to Bridgewater. But be careful of it, be careful of it, for observe, my girl, that it sometimes takes long to earn a pound," and his grudging fingers hovered claw-like around the note that he gave into her hand.

Susan stared in silent amazement at such an unexpected apparition, then, with a sudden movement, she thrust the note back into his hand, and locked her own together firmly.

"I don't want it, thank you, father," she said, the unexplained tears coming into her eyes. "I've got my black merino fresh for Sundays, and I don't need no more."

With the speed of a conjuring trick, the note disappeared in her father's grasp.

"Well, well, I dessay you don't really need it," he agreed, with an unmistakable air of relief. Susan's heart was now hammering so that she hardly heard his words, but under her fright, her newly founded courage held firmly.

"Father," she gasped, "I heard that they're wanting a school-teacher at New Germany, and I thought that if you'd let me go, I'd like to try it."

The effect of her words was not reassuring. The bushy gray eyebrows drew together, and the steel-like eyes were fixed on her face.

"What do you want that for?" was the explosive question.

Her answer came breathlessly.

"It's so lonely here now, and the housework is hard. I could earn my living easier there, anyway."

He laughed with what, if she had had her wits about her, she might have noticed as a growing uneasiness.

"And have a fine time with the young men, hey? But that's all stuff and nonsense. What's to become of me, I'd like to know, with no one to cook or mend for me? There ain't no need either for you to earn your living. I made a good profit on the fish on the last voyage out, and the rum and molasses sold well, too. If you're lonely, you can have a girl to help you in the kitchen; a Dutch girl who'll work hard and not expect meat too often. There, that ought to content ye, and keep you from talking any more nonsense yet awhile."

There was a rough kindness in his voice to which the girl's obstinate fright made her quite impervious.

As her father stood, waiting for some assent to his words, she drew from her pocket her shabby, empty purse, and thrust the newspaper clipping into his hands.

"I found that on the stairs just now. Will you tell me that that ain't the way you got rich?" she gasped, while her father stared at it in bewilderment.

A sudden flare of wrath seemed to raise the heavy gray locks, and bristle the eyebrows, so that he looked like a clamouring eagle as he shouted hoarsely: "What damned tomfoolery is this? Go, and mind your work, and have no more talking! That's what comes of being kind to women! Who told you I got rich, anyway? If I find it's that sneaking parson as brings you gossip, I'll soon put a stop to your churchgoing. 'Spose he thinks if I'm rich he'd like to get a share of it, but he won't."

Susan, shaking under this torrent of speech, felt as though her knees would give way beneath her, but that new force within her held firm.

"Father, if you'll only say that you never made money out of poor wretched slaves, I'll work at home, all you like," she pleaded, even venturing to lay a timid hand upon his arm.

But she had gone too far, and aroused his wrath in earnest. With a grim oath, he struck her down with his clenched fist, and strode away. When Susan presently picked herself up, dizzy and bewildered from her fall, she found with a sense of relief that she was alone.

In years of drudgery, she had acquired the fine stoicism of the working-woman, and, with aching head and trembling hands, now set about making herself a cup of tea.

"He hasn't had a mouthful of breakfast" she said to herself, with a certain sense of guilt at such an untoward event.

Mechanically she got through her morning's tasks, with the ever-present dread of her father's return.

When once these tasks were finished, she peered out timidly at front door and back, then, seeing no sign of life, she ventured more boldly on a tour of inspection in the barn. Satisfied that her father was nowhere about the premises, she went up to her room, and put on her Sunday dress and hat, — poor, shabby black things, but treated by her with all ceremony.

After this it was a simple matter to her to harness the old white horse into the still older buggy, lock up the house, leaving the key in its familiar nook under the door-step, and take the inland road.

Her mind was made up. She must see Mr. Clinch and get his advice on the next step to be taken.

It often happens that to those of resolute mood details lend a helping hand. So now, as Susan and the white horse jogged despondently through the raw damp of the autumn morning, she saw what brought back courage and animation. It was only Mr. Clinch's gaunt sorrel tied up outside the door of the new church that was a recent offshoot from the one in Bridgewater, but the sight made her pull herself upright from the tired droop into which she had fallen, made her face lose its weary downward curves and pallor. She felt sure of help now.

A somewhat strange-looking figure, this gaunt, stiffly dressed parson, of about thirty-five, to be the knight errant of a young girl's fancy, and yet, in his own conventional, narrow way, there was a spark of true knight-errantry in the man's heart, as, busied over accounts in the vestry, he looked up at the sound of a footstep and saw Susan Bauer's tremulous figure, pathetic in its poor clothes, and her distressed face, its blonde colouring all blurred by fatigue and pain. There was no pretence at an ordinary greeting between them.

"What is it?" he said, moving quickly toward her, and taking her appealing hands in his. "I can see that you are in trouble."

As their gaze met, the blue eyes filled with tears which rolled silently down her cheeks, and, all the stiffness and constraint of her shyness gone, a certain charm of youth made itself evident.

For some time Mr. Clinch had been thinking that she would make him a suitably devoted wife, and this moment settled the question in his mind.

"You are tired and agitated. Take this seat and try to tell me what is the matter."

As Susan stilled the one or two sobs that had broken out, and looked up at him obediently, a sudden thought checked her.

It was all very well to tell her own sorrows to Mr. Clinch, but to tell of her father's sin was another matter. The paragraph from the paper had distinctly spoken of broken laws, and the penalty - what if through any words of hers her father should be brought to punishment?

"It is about some one else, too," she faltered, "some one who has done wrong, but, oh, who I wouldn't do harm to."

He saw her point now, and hastened to reassure her, speaking solemnly.

"If you have sin and sorrow to tell me of, you tell it to me in confidence before God. You can trust in me, surely."

"Oh, I do, I do," she repeated, shocked by any doubt on such a point.

Then it was that Susan told her tale, sometimes in confused, disconnected phrases, helped out by discreet questions from her hearer, sometimes with the feverish fluency of unconscious feeling.

When at the end she faltered over the telling of the blow that had struck her down, an indignant pity lightened the austerity of Mr. Clinch's face, and he murmured, gently:

"'Though my father and my mother forsake me, the Lord will take me up.'"

There was a pause while he sat wrapped in deep thought, the girl watching him intently; then, as he looked up and their eyes met, her appeal took shape in words.

"Oh, please tell me what I ought to do; I have no one but you to go to."

Gravely, measuredly, his answer came:

"It seems to me that your own sense of duty has already marked out your path, when you asked your father's leave to earn your living as a school-teacher. You cannot take the wages of sin."

"No, oh, no. But — need I go home again?" she

asked, nervously.

What man with a heart in his breast could have sent the trembling girl back to face her father again?

Mr. Clinch, at any rate, could not.

"Considering that you have already asked his permission, and that you are in fear of further violence, I think that there would be no lack of filial duty in your going to stay with some relative or friend. I myself will take you to old Mrs. Truman, who is a real mother in Israel, and from there you can write and settle matters with your father."

"Oh, how good you are!" Susan sobbed, and the stiff ministerial attitude was somewhat relaxed as he took her hand in his.

"Believe me, you shall never want a friend while I live," he began, and then, in the stilted phrases that sounded beautiful in the girl's ears, he told her how he had been watching the gradual unfolding of her Christian virtues, and deciding that she would be a worthy helpmate in his parochial work.

If St. Peter had suddenly flung open the golden gates, and asked her to take a seat of honour within them, Susan could scarcely have been more overwhelmed at the prospect. To be a minister's wife, to be Mr. Clinch's wife, to see to his comfort, and help him humbly in his work, what could the heart of woman ask more than that?

There was so little uncertainty in either mind as to her answer that I doubt if any answer were really given; but, at any rate, both man and woman were thoroughly content with each other, and, from that day forth, were mutually loyal in word and deed.

For the next few weeks all outward details seemed vague and unreal to Susan beside the great central fact that Mr. Clinch thought her worthy to become his wife. Her stay with her kindly, widowed cousin, her carefully planned letter to her father, which brought no other reply than her little box of clothes, were merely part of these details, and on the day that she stood in Mrs. Truman's best parlour beside Mr. Clinch, the past fell away from her and she was in fact as in name a new creature, Roger Clinch's wife.

With utter unworldliness the two gave no further thought to Jonathan Bauer's money. "He is joined to his idols like Ephraim — let him alone," said the minister, sternly.

But if either of them had had the faintest comprehension of the old man's character, they would, instead of settling down in a cottage in Bridgewater, have gone to make a new home for themselves elsewhere. From the day of his marriage, Mr. Clinch found himself perpetually, and in the most unlikely places, striking against some adverse influence.

Here and there, impalpable but very real, it met him as an opposing force, chilling a friendly greeting, spreading an unfair version of some transaction, Hinting at Susan's unfilial behaviour.

Mr. Clinch was of too reserved a nature to be able to trace and beard this antagonistic force, though even he could see that it came from the seafaring element of the place.

A clergyman and a doctor cannot fight against unpopularity, and at last a friendly deacon came to Mr. Clinch and gave him a word of warning: "The

whole countryside could tell you that Jonathan Bauer
is an ill man to cross. You've crossed him, and you'll
never prosper in this place while he lives. If you take
my advice, you'll look round for a start elsewhere."

Mr. Clinch was shrewd enough to see the wisdom of
the man's words. Without saying anything to Susan,
who had just lost her first child, he wrote to friends,
with the result that in a few months they went to make
their home in what seemed then the very remote
regions of Ontario.

Here they had days of poverty, of sorrow in the loss
of children, but they faced life with the stern fortitude
of their religion.

Chapter 17

Clashing Wills

"And that was all we heard of my father for many a day, for postage cost something in those times, and people didn't write gossiping letters just for nothing," the old lady said. "At last many a year after, came the lawyer's letter telling of his death and of the legacy to me of the old home. He must have guessed that I'd refuse it, for if I did, you were to have the choice when you came of age. It was a short time before your father died, but his faith in me never faltered, and he was as firm as ever against taking the wages of sin. And so we wrote and said we would not take it, and one of your father's dying charges to me was to save you from any part or lot in the evil thing."

Gilbert's was a nature that would have been quick to mark the pathos of the old woman's life story, that life dominated by a single affection and a single purpose, but now in his present humour, he chose only to see the hardness of self-righteous judgment, shutting his eyes to the courageous unworldliness.

"And when I was twenty-one, and the lawyer wrote again, you told him that you knew nothing of my whereabouts, but that I intended refusing the legacy?" he asked, quietly.

Quiet as were the words, his mother was quick to feel that they were out of sympathy with her, and she chilled responsively. The rare expansiveness of a reserved nature is easily driven in on itself. Through all the days of her widowhood, the principal event to which Mrs. Clinch had looked forward had been the telling of her life history to her son, and now he had no word of sympathy to give her.

His thoughts were, it seemed to her, merely set on his own selfish gain. She would not understand the irritation with which a warm-hearted nature finds that it has been kept outside the real life of those nearest to it; she could not see that Gilbert felt that he had been defrauded of something that went to the making of his own identity in the interweaving of family tradition with hereditary instincts.

For the first time now he understood what had caused that blank that had always existed between his mother and himself. She had from the first put him outside the dominant influences of her life.

With an evident desire to justify herself, she looked at him as she answered: "It was that summer when you were camping in the Adirondacks, and I did not know your address. I had also every reason to feel that you would not disregard your father's dying wishes."

At any other time, the subterfuge would have amused him, but now he only commented, bitterly: "Wishes which I never heard."

"Of that your father was the judge," she said, proudly; then with a sudden wistfulness, "And now all our care to save you has come to nothing, unless — Gilbert, my boy, you will not disregard your father's lifelong decision?"

For a moment the thin old hand rested on Gilbert's arm, but it was quickly withdrawn, as he answered, steadily: "Mother, I can promise nothing now. It is my own life, and I must decide it on my own judgment."

"Then you blame us for having kept you in ignorance?" she asked, the weakness of old age sounding in her voice.

A sudden sense of pity distracted Gilbert's thoughts, but he knew that to yield to it might hamper his liberty of action, and so he said, with all possible gentleness: "I certainly think that it was an extreme measure, toward a grown-up son. But there is no use in discussing that now. All I claim is full liberty for the future."

"You will plunge yourself into the uncertainty of a struggle over this new will?" she asked, with the subdued distress of the aged.

"Have I not said that I cannot tell you now, mother?" he said, with a little less patience.

"At least you will assure me that you will not sell this stolen statue?"

"I do not know that it was stolen, and besides, what should I do with it? Do you ask me to try to return it now to the church it came from?"

"That were to encourage idolatry," she answered, with a puzzled air that somehow appealed to him, for he laughed kindly as he said: "You must not worry yourself so, mother. If my grandfather had letters of marque, I can see no reason why I should not sell anything that he took then. I ought to get enough from it to give me a small income, and then I shall go and find out about these unknown relations of ours and the will upon which they acted. I shall be able too to add to your comforts here."

But his mother's face had settled into its well-remembered lines of sternness, and her voice reminded him of the sins of his youth, as she responded: "You have made the purpose of my life but a vain thing, and would you mock at me now? Go, and do not return to this house while that money is in your hands. I hope to die with mine clean."

The sorrow in her voice touched him deeply, and he knew that he could not leave her thus.

"Mother," he said, appealingly, "we cannot part like this. Let me stay one more day with you, and we will leave the whole question alone. I do not think you will really send me away in anger."

He was right, she could not do it.

She yielded enough to say, "Of course you are free to remain if you wish. Perhaps you would like to go and find Cynthia."

As this seemed to supply a peaceful ending to this trying interview, Gilbert willingly assented.

What contrast could be greater, he thought to himself, than that between the colourless, shadowy old woman in the shaded room where musty books, dim portraits, and ornaments spoke of nothing save the past, and this red-haired girl, standing amongst the light green tangle of the rows of peas, the noon-tide light enfolding her as though it knew her to be a child of the sun.

The ready flush that goes with red hair spread over her face at sight of Gilbert, but she reached out a sun-burnt hand, greeting him with frank gaiety.

"I should have been indoors in my best clothes to receive you, if I hadn't got such a noble order from the hotel for my late green peas. But I kept some for you."

Relieved at the change of atmosphere, he answered in the same fashion: "Thank you for the peas, but I don't believe that under any circumstances would you have been found indoors in your best garments on such a day. My mother evidently thinks your love for your garden is a pagan sentiment."

"Yes, I know," with a half-comic glance of compunction. "I'm really sorry, you know, that I hate fusty sick-rooms, and sewing for missions, and all the things she likes best. I really used to try to stand them, and then I found that they made me bad, while out here in the garden I am, in a way, good. And then you know," she went on, more seriously, "it must be right that I should work and earn money for myself, and this is the only thing that I am not stupid at."

"It *is* right that you should work at the thing that your nature teaches you to like. It is the one safe road to walk in," he said, earnestly. "But I do not want you to feel that you must earn money. My mother's home is yours, and there will always be enough for both."

As the girl maintained a cautious silence, a new idea came to him.

"Tell me, Cynthia," he said, quickly, "does she live comfortably, without stint, I mean?"

A half-smile as at the memory of privations cheerfully undergone, curved the girl's lips.

"She is very careful," she admitted, "and in the winter — well, we go to bed pretty early."

A word of annoyance escaped Gilbert's lips.

"And she will take so little from me, always assuring me that she has plenty. But look here! You can do me a real service, if you will."

Would she? What was there that Cynthia Joyce would not have unhesitatingly done at the bidding of Gilbert, the one companion of her dreams, on the memory of whose brief visits she lived.

Utterly ignorant of this element, he went on:

"When I go to-morrow, I will leave some money I will send you some more. Tell me, do you think that you could spend it on some comforts for her without her knowledge?"

The girl shook her head dubiously.

"It wouldn't be easy when she was well," she said. "She watches every cent. But then, if she were sick — she sometimes is sick, you know —"

"Is she?" he asked sadly, looking away over the fertile garden to the sunny fields. In that moment his life seemed a very futile thing. He had failed to help Isabel; must he then fail to help this other, with the closest claim upon him?

"Oh, I am sure that then it would make a difference," she comforted, quick to note his depression.

"And I am probably going away soon to travel," he went on, never noting how at his words all the gladness died out of her face. "And I want you to promise to write to me once a month or so, telling me how she really is, and if she needs anything. That will set my mind more at ease."

"I will be sure to do it," the girl promised simply, "and you may be certain that I will always do my best for her."

"I know you will," he said, kindly. "One could not know you as long as I have, without feeling that one could trust anything to you."

The lightly spoken words were treasured in the girl's heart through many a monotonous day after Gilbert had gone out into the world again.

Chapter 18

Starting Afresh

When Gilbert got back to Boston he found awaiting him a letter from the well-known Colorado heiress, Miss McShane, saying that she had heard through a friend of Mrs. Broderick's, of his desire to sell a costly statue of the Virgin.

She herself was planning to make a memorial offering to a new Roman Catholic cathedral, and would be glad to see him on the subject.

Inexpressibly touched by this proof of Isabel's thought for him, and whimsically sharing her own desire to see the statue safely deposited in a church, Gilbert entered into negotiations with the lady, with the result that the statue became her property for five thousand dollars less than Mr. Salmon was spurred on to offer.

"And after that," he said to himself, as he contemplated the cheque, "I can certainly never lay claim to being an enlightened scientific man. Five thousand dollars thrown away for a superstition which I don't believe in, and the quaintest part of it is that my mind is certainly easier for it."

The feelings of Mr. Salmon were soothed by his becoming the possessor of the St. Lawrence and then, for the first time in his life, Gilbert knew himself to be in possession of a small but secure income independent of the work of his brain.

"I could even afford the luxury of an illness now," he thought.

One of the conditions of both sales had been that the name of the owner should not be made public. Of course Miss McShane's magnificent gift became one of the topics of the day. It was shown in New York, for the benefit of a charity, before being sent westward to its destination, and the papers were full of the mystery of its origin, its artistic beauty, and the intrinsic value of the jewels. More than one hypothetical history of the adventures of the famous Virgin did Gilbert read, histories which accounted for every year during which he knew her to have lain in the shadows of his grandfather's garret chimney.

Sometimes indeed he had to join in speculations on the subject, and when he heard every crime in the calendar raked out to account for the possession of the treasure, he felt heartsick of the whole affair.

A great longing to get away from all familiar things grew upon him, but there was one thing that he must first do. A lingering hope that, in spite of Mrs. Broderick's words, he might still find her in town, took him past her house. No, it was evidently closed.

He sought her business man, with whom he had had frequent communications. Yes, she had sailed for Europe on the very day of his return, with instructions that her address was to be given to no one. But she was surely in a state requiring companionship and care, Gilbert urged, wretchedly.

The answer was that the Swedish nurse, who had proved such a devoted attendant, was with her, and that her physical strength seemed completely restored.

"As clever and capable a business woman as ever, but cold and hard — it seemed as though all feeling had been killed in her," ended the man, who had been her personal friend for years.

"What next?" Gilbert said to himself, as he strolled away from this interview, with a depressed purposelessness upon him. And then in the stale heat of the city streets, he found himself thinking of the westerly breezes on the La Have River; of the sailboat where she had sat opposite to him; of the sand-bar and the veranda with their memories. Should he go there alone and live over again those spring days? But a second manlier thought came to him. Instead of hugging the remnants of a fruitless past, he would try to forget feeling in work. He had the money now to take him abroad, and he would go to Vienna, where some wonderful experiments in his own line of study were being carried on. In this impersonal work his mind would recover its focus, and he would be able to see things in their proper perspective, so that, when ready to go to England, he could rely more upon his own judgment as to his claims to his share of his grandfather's estate.

There was one thing to be done first. He must return to Nova Scotia, and gather some facts about Jonathan Bauer after he became a prominent man, and try to find out whether there seemed any foundation for Isaac's strange tales of the foreign wife. This surely could be no very difficult task in a small provincial city, where tales of old families were likely to be current for a longer space than twenty years.

And so, it was with a well-defined purpose that Gilbert ended one chapter of his life, and turned on to the next.

He was not entirely without acquaintances in the town where the tragic home-bringing of Andrew Broderick had caused him to invoke both legal and medical aid.

It was the jovial, talkative old doctor whom, as an evident mine of past gossip, he chose to start, by mention of the local La Have traditions on the history of the Bauer family.

"Told queer tales about old Jonathan Bauer, did they?" the old gentleman chuckled. "Well, I doubt if there's a saint in heaven that our countrytown loafers couldn't tell queer tales about if they chose, especially when it's some one who got rich by holding his tongue and working while they were talking."

"But they called him a pirate," Gilbert put in.

The doctor gave his jolly laugh. "A pirate! Oh, yes, I dare say they did! There's no doubt that in his young days the old man did a bit of privateering on the Spanish Main, during some of those South American wars. I've heard him myself tell some funny tales of church plundering done then — all fair in war, you know, and he never made any secret of it. But his real fortune — and mind you it was a big one — was made during the Civil War, because, while all the rest of us were going wild over the romantic Southerners, he had the sense to see that the North must win in the end, and speculated accordingly in New York. Ah, if only Providence had given me a head like his!" And the doctor gave a passing sigh to lost opportunities.

"His second wife was a foreigner, I believe?" Gilbert ventured, and the tale was taken up with all an old man's love of recalling the past.

"Yes, yes, a foreigner — French West Indies they said she came from. I was but a boy when I saw her first, a pretty, black-eyed girl, looking more like his daughter than his wife. Quaint, broken English she spoke, then, indeed, always, for the matter of that. Ah, she was a dainty sight in the reds and yellows she loved to wear, and I fancy she might have done damage to some of us young fellows' hearts, if old Bauer hadn't kept a pretty strict hand on her."

"Did he? "Gilbert asked, idly, as though humouring the doctor's talkativeness.

"Strict enough, though always in that grim, humorous way he had, as though after all he had the best of the joke. And he generally had, too! But as he got old, and she lost her looks, and took a sort of witchlike air, I've seen him watch her as though he might be half afraid of her. I'm certain that in his last illness he shrank from her."

The doctor was now speaking meditatively, as though forgetful of his listener, and Gilbert's heart beat faster at this corroboration of old Isaac's words.

"Were you with him when he died?" he asked.

"I was his doctor, but I was not there at the last. It was one of those cases of the last of an iron constitution, when the patient might hang on for weeks, or go out like a snuffed candle; and it proved the latter.

There was a great storm that night, I remember, and when they fetched me to the house, there was a big pine-tree fallen across the door-step."

Gilbert saw that the speaker was under the spell of the past, and forebore to distract him. To his disappointment, however, the thread seemed to have broken, and the doctor shook himself and spoke more vigorously:

"But these are old tales to be bothering you with, and all the family is gone from these parts now. The son was dull and stupid, and married the dull and stupid daughter of an army colonel with good connections, and what with his money and her family, they've managed to become swells in England, bought a big place, and all that. I daresay that their son or daughter may make a titled marriage. And so, you see, even an out-of-the-way corner like this has its share in the evolution of the English aristocracy. There, I've surely bored you enough for to-night."

There were endless more questions that Gilbert would have liked to have put, but he did not wish to arouse the shrewd old man's suspicions as to his interest. What he had already heard had deepened every impression received from Isaac. With a friendly farewell he left the doctor, and the next morning walked past the square white wooden house behind its elm-trees, where some of the story of his race had been enacted.

Eminently respectable and prosaic it looked now in the morning sunshine, and yet his thoughts were on that loveless death-bed, the witch-like figure, the midnight storm, and the fallen tree on the threshold.

For all that, his heart was the lighter for his talk with the doctor.

The more commonplace version made his mother's tale seem all the more the imaginations of a morbidly conscientious mind. He could not but feel that in voluntarily placing their lives under the grim shadow of poverty, his parents had acted unfairly to him. He had not even had the choice of the stern joy of renunciation. All that had been most sordid in his years of early struggle seemed to rise up now to taunt him with its uselessness. Worse than all, was the knowledge that if he had been a prosperous man in the days when he had first met Isabel Steele, there would have been no frustration to their mutual attraction.

But the past was the past, and it remained for him now to make the best of the present. Young and strong, he walked in the light of the sun, with hands and brain trained to noble work.

The world had a thousand interests for one who could see them, and he would fare forth and behold its wonders.

Chapter 19

By the Thames

When fate has put a full stop in our lives the natural
instinct of the healthy mind is to look round for material with which to begin a new sentence. When the
mediaeval knight was disappointed in his lady-love, he
went a-crusading, and when the freebooter found life
hollow he made a tour of the neighbouring high-
roads. Nowadays, the love-lorn housemaid gives warning, the subaltern exchanges to another regiment, the
millionaire gets him a steam-yacht and goes around
the world. It is the old cry, with various translations, of
the Psalmist — "Oh, that I had the wings of a dove,
that I might flee away and be at rest!"

Upon Isabel Broderick, sitting dry-eyed in her desolate home, the yearning was strong, although she
knew that wherever she might go, she would take with
her the same acute sense of loss, the same hunger for
the comfort she might not know.

There would, however, be relief in putting space
between herself and those dread asylum walls which
seemed to come between her and the sunshine. Not
even Gilbert Clinch in the necessary intimacy of those
tragic days had guessed at the abhorrence for her husband which had possessed her ever since she had

gathered her child's limp little body into her arms.

His name — his money — everything that had been his, she longed to cast away from her, and to go out into the world, her own old self once more.

But, even in those first days after her child's funeral, she had the sense to see that the disloyalty of such a course was impossible to her. When Andrew Broderick had been sane, he had given her his best; the ungrudging use of his large income, his well-known family name and social standing, all the advantages of the place which he had made for himself in the art world of Paris and New York.

All this he had given, never concealing the terrible drawback that went with it, and she had accepted his gift with open eyes; what right had she to complain when that one drawback had made her a bankrupt in life's lottery!

Throughout the past terrible year of the gradual development of her husband's insanity Isabel had always kept before her eyes the conviction that she had a debt to pay to him, and it was this conviction that had supplied the fortitude at which Gilbert had so often wondered.

Now, as in those first weeks of solitude, she stood facing a dark abyss of self-despair in which she saw herself indirectly guilty of her child's death, she searched desperately for some means of atonement.

Hers was a nature that must turn to action for relief, and to such natures high thoughts come. Gradually the idea dawned upon her that if she had failed to save the man from his hereditary doom she might at least try to rescue the name of the artist from oblivion.

It was an idea born of the many hours during the past months when, looking at his weird, powerful picture, she had comforted herself with the thought that, if the worst came, it would always be a monument to the artist's memory.

Its destruction had been a blow hard to bear, and this new, wild hope that she herself might attempt its re-creation dazzled her with a fresh purpose in life.

It was wild, but still perhaps not so wild as it seemed. It had always been Broderick's habit to make numerous smaller studies from which he painted his pictures, and she knew that these studies for his last work were all carefully packed in the Boston studio. And she herself had worked for days at similar studies, as an excuse to keep guard over him. From the first he had been her teacher in her work, and now she had followed him with half-conscious imitation until all the technique of the picture had become familiar to her.

Yes, she would attempt it. She would take these studies, and leaving behind all familiar faces and scenes, she would go abroad and concentrate body and soul on the task of reproducing the lost masterpiece.

She fully understood the difficulties of what she was undertaking, but then, in the "impasse" to which her life had come, the tangibleness of those difficulties had supplied a comforting force of resistance.

Wealth helps to make all action prompt and easy, and so, when the full completion of August was ripening into September; Mrs. Broderick inspected and decided on the villa of Heathholm, on the hill above the Thames. Cookham Dene, the postal address, was

a village by right of its church, post-office, and public-
house, but otherwise a mere network of bowery gardens, set amid lanes that rambled up slopes of open
patches of gorse, by plum and apple orchards to the
wide-stretching Berkshire beech woods.

Every here and there through the trees could be
seen a labourer's cottage, sometimes transformed by
the addition of a studio as big as itself into an artist's
abode.

Everything was decidedly up-hill or down-hill in this
region, and Heathholm clung to the steep bank, its
old-fashioned garden sloping down the hill, bordered
by tall hollyhocks and rose-bushes, shaded by a group
of fine walnut-trees.

There was a comfortable air of age about the place,
due to the fact of the house being built on the site of
an old cottage, leaving the garden undisturbed. It had
been built by a man in the first success of art and love,
and he had only lived there two years when, wife and
child dead, he bad broken down in his work and desperately gone abroad in search of a new start in life.
When Isabel first saw Heathholm the hollyhocks had
been still ablaze in the garden, the air heavy with the
scent of ripe fruit in the orchards below, but the rich
sights and scents of the season could as yet bring her
no icy. Day by day the peaceful autumnal beauty deepened in intensity over the riverside meadows and
upland heaths and beech woods, but the great charm
to her of the surrounding world lay in its utter unlike-
ness to that Northern seashore where three months
before her child had played beside her on the sands.

The peace of that quiet English landscape was all

the more to her because it had no key to unlock the inner doors of her soul. It was something apart from her world, the world in which she had been really alive. These thatched roofs showing through the trees, sheltered peasants living much the same lives, thinking much the same thoughts as did their grandparents in the days of the Georges. These winding lanes had been trodden into paths by the bare feet of wandering friars, by the heavy boot of Cromwell's soldiers. These big, fair, plainly dressed men and women who glanced at her curiously as they drove past her on the road in well-appointed carriages were separated from her by nationality and all that it entails. None of these people or things could come near enough to her life to be real.

The very quiet-voiced, deferential English servants who waited upon her had, under their politeness, a chilly air of being on the defensive against any possible eccentricity on the part of their American mistress.

"Not but what she doesn't seem just as much a real lady as any as I've ever lived with," she heard one of them confiding to the butcher boy over the fence — "more than some perhaps, seeing as she never shows no tiresome interest in our affairs, asking if we've been to church and bothering us with that nuisance of a Girl's Friendly. But then, there's the most everyday, civilised things she don't know nothing about, such as when quarter-day is, and what one does on Bank holidays, so she may be queer after all. One never can tell, can one?"

Yes, she was a stranger in a strange land and if she

was desperately, heart-sickeningly lonely, it was with a loneliness that no outside influence could have touched.

There was one friendly presence left to her in Elsa, the Swedish nurse, now her own maid. She had at first intended to leave her behind, but Elsa's stolid determination had been too much for her, backed as it was by the earnest representations of her old business man. Besides she did not wish to be thought any more eccentric than need be, and she knew that it was more seemly for her to have an attendant with her.

Many a time in her new loneliness she was comforted by feeling Elsa's silent, dog-like fidelity near her.

And then she got to work, sparing no detail that could help her, filling the small conservatory with out-of-season bloom from the best London florists, getting over from Paris a model whom she remembered and thought suitable for the half-veiled figure in the picture. She was careful too of her own health, painting in the midday hours of the shortening days, walking or driving on foggy mornings or in afternoon twilight.

At first she had to force herself into a work which seemed like trying to revive the dead, but soon the reward of effort came, and she worked for the joy of creating, the most arduous but the purest joy given to God's children.

This dream-life lasted through the autumn months of fogs and a rare sunshine, and experienced its first interruption on a fine December morning that had all the deceptive spring beauty that makes an English winter endurable.

She had driven herself in her little two-wheeled cart down into the market-town to lay in a supply of magazines at the stationer's in the High Street.

In the shop she noticed a slim girl, smartly dressed in rough red tweeds.

"One of the dwellers behind park gates," she said to herself, with the casually reoccurring sense of amusement that she, Mrs. Broderick, should not know the most desirable people in any neighbourhood. Her errand done, she turned and found herself directly facing the stranger and looking into the eyes of a friend.

Years ago, before her marriage, when she had first gone abroad to study art, Isabel had spent some summer months in a Normandy village, still cheap and unfashionable. In the hotel she had struck up a friendship with a lank, overgrown schoolgirl, sent there with her governess after an attack of scarlet fever.

The governess, being a gloomily selfish creature, the girl, Margaret Nugent-Barr by name, had seemed forlorn and had attached herself to Isabel with that fancy which girls often take to those three or four years older than themselves. She had followed her about, content to sit beside her while she painted, quick to learn when she might chatter and when she must be silent, walking beside her over the cliffs and gathering her great bunches of wild-flowers.

When they had parted Margaret had wept stormy tears, but Isabel had heard nothing more of her until now, when looking down into an oval face of a pale creamy tint, with great dark eyes, she recognised in the smartly dressed young lady the lank little Meg of the Normandy seashore.

Each looked in the other's face in a momentary hesitation, and then, almost simultaneously, came the dawning smile of greeting and the words:

"Miss Steele!"

"Little Meg! Oh, I beg your, pardon, Miss Nugent-Barr!"

"Oh, that doesn't matter! But however did you come to drop down into this little English corner? Perhaps you have married an Englishman?" was the eager response, as Margaret's slim hand grasped the larger one in a cordial pressure.

"No, my husband was an American, and my name is Mrs. Broderick. I have been living up at Cookham Dene — Heathholm is the name of the place — since September," Isabel answered, smiling down into the face that since she had seen it had come into its woman's full inheritance of beauty.

"Since September! It's odd that we have not come across each other before, for we live at Monk's Grange. You know it, I suppose?"

"Oh, yes, is it not all down in Dickens's Guide, and haven't I seen the substantial statue of your ghost on her tomb in the little church! Are you a descendant of hers?"

"No, thank goodness! I don't think she would make a nice ancestress. Though of course it would be much grander to belong to the original old family instead of being newcomers as we are. I must warn you that we are not the genuine ancestral growth of the soil, but only importations on the strength of our money."

Though she laughed as she spoke, something made Isabel guess that the point might be a sore one, so she answered, quickly:

"I think in that case you are likely to be less mouldy. Things don't always improve with age, you know."

"No, I dare say not," the other answered, half-absently. She was debating the phrase "my husband was an American," and wondering if it implied widowhood.

"But tell me about yourself," she went on. "Are you an artist still and have you a lot of people up there with you?"

"I am an artist still, and I live all alone," Isabel answered, quietly, something in her voice that checked further questioning.

Margaret had already noticed that Mrs. Broderick's well-made dress was all of black, and this settled it. If she lived alone at Heathholm she must be a widow comfortably off, and comfortably-off widows are pleasant people to know.

Margaret had that taste for prosperous friends which is such an important factor to success in life.

"Your being alone is all the more reason for my inflicting my society upon you, and I shall bother you just as I did years ago," she said, with ready tact.

Isabel was touched by the girl's friendliness. She knew that when the English foot is on its native heath the English welcome to strangers is not apt to be enthusiastic. "There's a stranger, heave a rock at him," applies in more countries than one.

And so there was gratitude in her face and voice as she answered: "It will indeed be pleasant to have you come. I have been very solitary."

Why had a woman so cut herself off from her friends, Margaret wondered, even as she answered: "Then you mustn't be so any longer. Is that smart little trap at the door yours? Well, then, I think you might offer to give me a lift. I came for a constitutional, but the mud is more than I reckoned on."

Presently they were speeding down the quiet, supernaturally trim and tidy High Street, out over the bridge across the river, rolling dark and full from recent rains, and along the flat bit of road that crossed the meadows.

"Our ancestral domain, at least ancestral in so far that I hope it may go down to my brother Jack," Margaret said, with a light wave of her hand toward the landscape. "By the bye, I'd like you to meet Jack. He's such a downright jolly old dear that you couldn't help liking him. May we ride up to see you tomorrow about tea-time?"

Isabel was a bit startled, for she had not reckoned on more new acquaintances than Margaret, but still it was natural enough that the girl should like to ride with her brother, and after all he seemed to be a mere boy.

"Oh, yes," she said, "if he would care to come, bring him, certainly."

"Oh, he'd love it, I know. Don't bother to drive up the avenue, for my mother's in bed and there's no one else at home. Just let me out at the stile and I'll run up the path. Thanks, until to-morrow, then. Come, Mr. Tomkins," and she and her lively fox-terrier vanished into the bushes.

Chapter 20

Jack

The next day Isabel found that she worked with better heart for the knowledge that the twilight time would bring her some other society than her own.

That twilight hour of lassitude was the one in which she found it hardest to keep memories at bay.

It was pleasant, too, to look around on the costly simplicity of her drawing-room when the western light struggled with the leaping flames, and to feel that her visitors must be favourably impressed with her surroundings.

A door open down into the small conservatory, crowded with bloom, and the scent of lilies and roses stole in like the breath of summer. it was all a suitable setting for the tall woman in her Paris tea-gown of gray velvet, the statuesque folds of which were the work of a master-hand.

Jack Nugent-Barr, home on Christmas leave from Dublin, had grumbled a bit at being taken to call upon an American artist. Still, he had a habit of yielding to Meg's demands in unimportant things, and it was a non-hunting day and so he went, growling amiably the while.

"Your geese are apt to be swans, you know, Meg. I've

seen these women artists, sitting around the banks under umbrellas like toadstools, and I can't say I ever fancied their looks much. Their hair never looked brushed, and they had horrible aprons on."

Meg laughed confidently.

"Wait till you see Mrs. Broderick. She's different. She's an American, you know."

"Well, I've seen lots of Americans," Jack went on in an aggrieved tone. "Girls with snappy black eyes, and what the novels call a 'vivacious' manner, and always wanting you to argue about things, you know. I remember at the Scovills' dance one of them wanted me to discuss England's policy in Egypt."

Again Meg laughed. "Wait and see."

And Jack did see when he stood before that lady, thoroughbred from the top coil of her burnished chestnut hair to the tip of the gray suède slipper showing under her dress.

There was no vivacity or eagerness here, rather, over the graciousness of her welcome there was a film of vagueness as of ever-dominant preoccupation, a vagueness that matched the shadow in her eyes.

Mrs. Broderick read the admiration in the frank, blue eyes, and straightway took a great liking to the big, fair-haired young fellow with that honest touch of shyness over the somewhat stolid reliance of his manner.

Brother and sister could not have belonged to more various types, and yet there was evidently a real comradeship between them. Meg looked at him with pride as she said:

"This is my brother Jack, otherwise Lieutenant

Eustace Nugent-Barr, of Her Majesty's Death or Glory Hussars, and he only condescended to come and pay a visit with his sister because it's an off day for hunting."

"I expect Mrs. Broderick knows you better than to believe all your statements," Jack retorted.

"It's an awful pity," he went on to Isabel, "that Meg hadn't the sense to find you out before. But I dare say you have other friends in the neighbourhood?"

"Not one," she said. "But then I came here for solitude, and I must say that I have had it."

"At any rate, you have a dear place up here," Meg put in, as she nibbled at a little pasty, far beyond the scope of the Monk's Grange cook. "I do wish that the old monks had understood the joy of these heights instead of our aguish meadows and damp cellars."

"Both of which had their uses," said Jack. "The meadows were as convenient for fish-ponds as the cellars were for a tenant backward in his rent."

"You must have been reading 'Ivanhoe' again," Isabel suggested.

"Jolly old books, weren't they?" he said, simply.

Meanwhile Margaret had been taking in the unmistakable signs of wealth. That ebony and ivory cabinet was genuine old Florentine work, she was sure, and that little silver coffer was a gem of chiselling. Really, Mrs. Broderick must have done well for herself in her marriage, and how satisfactory it was. She was like a cat in her love of warm luxurious haunts.

"I don't wonder those mediaeval people were always poisoning and stabbing each other," she put in. "I should do just the same if I didn't live in the sunshine and fresh air. When the evil spirit enters into me,

I ride all over the country until it is driven out."

Isabel smiled at her as one might at a child.

"I hope that doesn't often happen," she said.

"Oh, intermittently," was the careless answer.

"It comes on oftener when I'm with Granny than when I'm at home. When I get to Florence among all those priests and fusty old dowagers, and sometimes can't ride or play golf for a week or so, I feel as though I should scream."

"Try dumb-bells," Jack suggested.

"But why do you go to Florence?" Isabel asked.

"Because Granny chooses to spend her winter there and because Granny seems to have the first right of possession. My parents own me secondly, and I myself come in as a poor third. Granny's in Brighton now, but as soon as she decides to start, she claims me."

"Still, Florence is pleasant enough and I dare say you like the change."

"Of course she does. You never saw any one get bored so quickly without it. And if it weren't for the old lady, she wouldn't be such a smartly got-up young lady as she is."

"Oh, that's because she wants to marry me to an Italian duke. But she's not going to, all the same."

"I'm not so sure about that. Keep a lookout for her conversion in the *World* sometime in Lent, Mrs. Broderick," Jack said, teasingly.

"And you, do you go to Florence?" Isabel asked.

Meg laughed as if at an incongruous vision.

"Not I, thank goodness! Even though I'm toiling at drills in the rain, at the Curragh."

"At drills! Hunting three days a week!"

"And the Lord be praised for the same! But talking of hunting, have you ever tried it?" he said to Isabel. "Do let me find you a horse suitable for the country and take you out," he pleaded.

Isabel had ridden adventurously during a Mexican winter, and the thought of knowing such joy again brought a quick leap of youth to her pulses.

Jack caught the flash in her eyes, and said, joyfully: "You will, I know."

But she shook her head.

"No, I mustn't attempt it. It would take too much of the energy I need for other things. It's delightful to come home tired all over, but that's not the way to do brain-work."

"Brain-work?" Jack asked, puzzled. He could not associate the leisurely elegance of this woman with his idea of brain-work.

"I mean my painting," she explained, with an apparent guess at his perplexity.

"But that's drudgery," he expostulated, "and surely you work for your own pleasure, not for a settled task?"

"I work for my own pleasure and for a settled task both, and I must keep on until it is finished. That is what I came here for."

There was some unknown feeling in her voice which checked his remonstrances, and presently his sister said: "Oh, do tell us what you are painting, and let us see your studio, won't you?"

"Not to-day, I'm afraid. They've been doing some work there, and the place is all upset," Mrs. Broderick answered to the last question, and ignoring the other request.

This was the first of several excuses until they learned to see that they were not intended to ask again.

As Jack Nugent-Barr rode home beside his sister through the bare woodlands, under the wan light of a young moon, his brain was somewhat in a whirl over the vision of a kind face, and a gray figure encircled by the orange light.

What a joy it would be to bring a smile oftener around that grave mouth, to come home tired and sit down by the fire beside such a figure.

At this point Meg broke in with the incongruous remark: "She seems to be a bit of a dark horse, doesn't she?"

"A dark horse! What do you mean by that?"

Unheeding the grimness of his voice, she went on: "Oh, well, you know, being so well off as she seems, and coming here where she doesn't know a soul, for solitude, as she says, and working so hard, and having such smart clothes — "

But at this point Jack's wrath broke out.

"Well, I'm glad I'm not a woman and haven't a feminine idea of loyalty. Here is this lady, who has never made the slightest attempt to look you up, and when you meet her accidentally, and invite yourself to see her and she gives you a charming welcome, you hardly wait until her door is closed before you call her a dark horse! As I said, I'm glad I'm not a woman!"

"Well you may be! But, goodness me, what a tirade all about nothing! I called her a dark horse having a delight in and a keen scent for mysteries, and hoping to have a heroine of romance for a next-door neighbour. It would be such a resource, you know. But, all the same, I think her, as I always did, one of the most delightful women I ever knew. She reminds me of Iseult of Brittany, the Lady of Shalott, and all such mystical creatures. And I tell you what," she went on, with a quick glance to see if Jack's good-humour were restored, "I was thinking that she would be a godsend on Christmas night among all those stupid people. I must impress father with her grandeur so that he won't make any objections."

"That's a good idea," Jack condescended to approve, all unconscious of his sister's mischievous face in the shadows.

"It will be great fun springing such a mysterious beauty on Lord Vernade."

This remark of Meg's failed to meet with the approbation of the last.

"Oh, Vernade," he grunted. "Why doesn't he go back to his excavations in Asia Minor, or the Greek Islands, or wherever it is! I hate to see a man who has it in his power to do anything just fooling about."

"Well, but he had fever, you know."

"Oh, yes, *fever*," and in one of the momentary differences of opinion they rode on their way in silence.

Mr. Nugent-Barr was a "dour" man, of whom his family stood somewhat in awe. His daughter was not without influence over him, though, when she took the trouble to exert it, especially since her social success had led her grandmother to spend more money upon her dress and upon taking her about.

A few remarks casually dropped as to the style of Mrs. Broderick's establishment and Jack's admiration for her were sufficient to arouse his interest.

Like his daughter, he had a taste for the acquaintance of those rich in this world's goods, although there was the great difference that she liked them for the amusement and beauty with which they could surround themselves — he, for the mere sordid neighbourhood of riches.

And so when Mr. Nugent-Barr handed his wife a list of guests whom she was to invite, the first name that she read was Isabel's.

"Mrs. Broderick — you mean Margaret's American friend, my dear?" she asked, in a feebly surprised tone. She was not expected to criticise her husband's choice in the matter.

"I am certainly not aware of any one else of that name. Are you, my dear?" was the chilly reply.

"Oh, no, I suppose not. Only it being Christmas and her being a stranger and an American, it seemed-well, a little unusual, that was all."

"I really cannot see why her being an American should make it unusual to invite her at Christmastime. Having been in Boston, you are probably aware that Americans are Christians?" Mr. Nugent-Barr retorted, with an elaborate air of patience that worked worse confusion in his wife's never over-brilliant wits.

"Oh, of course, I knew that, though when Margaret came home talking so much about this lady I did ask the rector about her and he said that he had never seen her in church, though he was never surprised now at anything that artists did."

"You had better advise the rector to exercise a little Christian charity, my dear."

When Mr. Nugent-Barr brought Christian charity into play it was usually for the benefit of those who did not require any more substantial charity at his hands.

"Yes, but Mrs. Broderick is a widow, and how would you like it if she got hold of Jack?" the mother-hen fluttered, brave for her chicks.

"How would you like it if some actress or music-hall dancer got hold of him, my dear?" This prospect was Mr. Nugent-Barr's constant and most unnecessary dread, his son not being in the least the type that comes to grief in that fashion.

His wife gave a little squeak of dismay.

"Oh, my dear, I hope you don't mean —"

"I mean nothing save that you should write those notes before the second post goes out," and he walked off, leaving the poor lady to recover from the shock in dreams of what Jack's wife should be. She saw in her fancy a nice little pink-and-white English girl, brought up in a rectory or hall, loving to teach in Sunday school, and — fondest hope of all — to make things for bazaars.

Poor mothers, how they dream!

Chapter 21

Christmas

When Isabel received this much-discussed invitation, she, as a matter of course, sat down to decline it, and then a second thought gave her pause with "Why not?"

Too brave a woman to have any weakness for anniversaries, she could not but look forward with dread to the memories that Christmas would bring of her child.

Day and night she heard the silvery voice, calling: "Mummie, mummie, come and see what boofy things Santa Claus brought Boyso!" Day and night she felt the touch of the soft hand on her cheek, felt the warm little body nestling close to her own.

Work as hard as she might, there were times when her powers of concentration failed her. She would try if going among strangers, and having to laugh and talk with them, might not help her to forget.

And so, at the same time that she wrote a large order for toys to be sent to a London hospital, she sent for a black lace dress, the advent of which delighted Elsa.

The party staying at Monk's Grange consisted mostly of cousins, though there were three army youths over from Aldershot, friends of Jack's, and much of the same type, healthily outdoor in their tastes, taking all "the feasting and the fun" that came along, and yet making ready in a matter-of-fact fashion for the baptism of fire that they were so soon to meet on the South African veldt.

Two Nugent girls, cousins, bony and neutral-tinted and aristocratically inane, had been upsetting Margaret's temper for a week. Mrs. Curtis, another cousin, just home with her husband from three years in India, had all her usual characteristics of cheery kindliness emphasised by her delight in being in England again, and in seeing her husband reviving from months of invalidism.

Her sister, ordinarily called Tommy Curtis, with a quaintly pretty face, was just one stage removed from the romping schoolgirl of a year or two earlier. The subs found her delightful, and she and the reddest-haired and most freckled of them had already started a violent but unsentimental flirtation.

The rector and his wife, and Lord Vernade, from his place up the river, represented the local interest. These people were all gathered when Isabel came in, the lustreless black of her dress setting off to perfection her milky skin and shining hair. Through this hair was twisted a string of pearls in a fashion of a Titian portrait, while another string hung low over her dress.

The sensation which her entrance caused was evidenced by the sudden cessation in the hum of talk, and the admiring stares of the youths.

"Good heavens, where did such a woman come

from?" said one of them to the other.

"Those pearls are a fortune if they're real," murmured Mrs. Curtis to the eldest Miss Nugent.

"So this is the surprise you warned me of," said Lord Vernade to Margaret.

"Yes, and she is my own discovery, captive of my bow and spear," she answered, lightly, as she went forward to welcome her friend and lead her to her mother.

All Mrs. Nugent-Barr's motherly misgivings fled before the charm of the newcomer's face, and she made anxious inquiries as to the amount of wraps worn during the drive over the hills, and if she had had a foot-warmer.

The master of the house was groaning in his room with air attack of sciatica, and his absence did not seem to affect the gaiety of the party.

Isabel's attention had been caught by the brilliancy of Margaret's appearance. In a gauzy dress of deep red, wreathed round the shoulders with poppies, and with their half-opened buds crowning her black hair, she seemed a personification of the glow of summer, and yet her friend was conscious of that half-fanciful dread which poppies always gave her now.

"The flowers of death," came to her mind, with an echo of her husband's voice.

"I want to introduce Lord Vernade to you," were Margaret's words that brought her back to reality again.

Turning, she met a pleasant smile on the pale, clear-cut face, and in the light gray eyes of the man whose lazily high-bred aspect she had already noticed.

"I hear that I may claim to be a neighbour," he said.

"It is too bad that I have made the discovery too late for Lady Vernade to call. She has already gone abroad for the winter."

In her life as an unprotected girl in big cities, Isabel had faced such a smile before.

"I fear the limits of the neighbourhood are stretched by Miss Nugent-Barr's charity," she said, somewhat unresponsively.

But Lord Vernade's cordiality was not so easily checked.

"Oh, you have yet to learn our English idea of distances," he answered. "We might have a chance of teaching it to you if we were not scattering so soon."

"Are you going to Rome now?" Meg asked, with interest in her voice. "Oh, no, I couldn't stand a whole winter of Roman society, though my wife never seems to get tired of it. The yacht is at Naples, and I shall take a run out East to see how my man is getting on with his digging. Perhaps I shall find a bracelet of some fair Helen to bring to you in Florence later," he added, in a tone of old comradeship, which in such a man gave Isabel food for reflection. There would have been more if she had guessed how contrary to all his habits was this Christmas in the country.

A proud man was Jack Nugent-Barr when he took his father's seat at the table with Mrs. Broderick at his side.

He had had a struggle to be allowed to take her in, Mrs. Curtis being the daughter of an Honourable, but that lady came good-naturedly to his rescue by asserting that they were mutually tired of each other and wanted a change.

As Isabel looked around the old monks' dining hall on the alien faces around her, a great sense of solitude came over her.

"How do you like our English holly and mistletoe?" Jack asked, as a conversational overture.

"Oh, it's very nice," she answered, absently, not troubling to explain that it had been familiar enough to her across the water.

"I tried," he went on, bending toward her, "to make Meg think of some flower that would remind you of home, but we couldn't hit on anything, and so I got that," and his gesture drew her attention to two crossed sprays of pine before her place.

The green spikes brought a sudden vision of the dusky woods on the hills behind the Moorings, and for a moment she could have cried out with the keen stab of memory.

"It was very good in you," she said, gently, putting out her hand to lay it on the dark aromatic branch. The young fellow's thoughtfulness had touched her keenly.

"I would like to make you feel at home among us," Jack went on, emboldened.

"'I was a stranger and ye took me in,'" she quoted, with a smile.

"I'm sure I might make it pleasanter for you if my leave weren't up so soon. Though I suppose you won't stay on here through the winter?" he asked. He had determined that if he could help it, this radiant vision should not slip away out of his life, and when Jack determined on a thing he usually carried it through.

In former days Isabel would have been quick to note

the feeling she had aroused and to apply an antidote, but now Jack, like the rest, seemed too far away to enter into personal relations with her. So she answered: "I shall stay on until the picture that I am painting is finished. After that — I don't know," she finished, somewhat blankly.

"I suppose you know Paris; all good Americans do, don't they?" put in Major Curtis, on her other side. He thought that Jack had had the best-looking woman in the room to himself for quite long enough.

After dinner, cards were started, and if the master of the house had been on the field there would have been no higher stakes than bonbons. As it was: "Hard cash, ladies and gentlemen," Meg declared, upon which the rector's wife and the elder Miss Nugent said that they preferred to sit by the fire and talk. The rector organised his quiet whist-table — it was before the days of universal bridge — and the bolder spirits launched into poker, out of supposed deference to Mrs. Broderick's American tastes.

"I am a born gambler," was Meg's gay announcement, and Isabel, watching, had no doubt of the fact, as she saw how recklessly she played, never losing a chance of raising the stakes, and abetted by Lord Vernade, who sat next to her, and who had as bad luck as she had good.

The others kept to an average, save Jack, who lost as persistently as did Lord Vernade. It was not that, however, Isabel thought, which caused the increasing gravity in his face, and an occasional almost stern glance across at Meg.

Presently a run of better luck came to Jack, and he

then seized the first chance to stop the game.

"I think that Meg has pillaged her guests quite enough," he said, decidedly. "Eh, Tommy, what do you say? Have you anything left to buy chocolates with?"

But Miss Tommy happened to be a little to the good and was much excited thereat. She also, on principle, opposed any ideas of Jack, whom she knew to have been picked out as a desirable match for her, coming, as she did, of an influential family in army circles, and having a nice little fortune, too, of her own.

"Oh, Jack, don't spoil all our fun by stopping the game now. Meg doesn't want to stop yet, do you?" she appealed.

Meg, with flushed cheeks and shining eyes, looked across at the childish face reflecting the same eagerness, and suddenly sobered down with a half-timid glance at Jack.

"Oh, well, I suppose one can have too much of a good thing. Come, let's count our gains," she said, rightly. "I shall buy a little pig 'porte-viene' with mine to remind me of you all."

"A dance! A dance!" cried Jack, as they rose from the card-table. "Our Christmas country-dance! Mrs. Broderick, you will give it to me? Althea!" to the eldest Miss Nugent, "you'll play us the 'March of the Nugents,' won't you?"

Young and old, they all joined, dancing in the fine old hall where through the tracery of the big window the Christmas moonlight streamed in to rival the lamps. As she moved through the stately dance, the haunting sense of unreality deepened on Isabel.

Was it she, this woman dancing here, who within the

year had lost all that had made her life — no, not all, for did she not still retain her trust in the honour and faith of one — lonely for her sake — who might have made life so fair to her, if only —

"Look at the moonlight!" Meg cried. "The view must be splendid up in the turret with that sprinkling of snow over the country. Now, Mr. Erwin," she called to one of the youths, "this is just the night for your ghost-hunt. Our old lady is said to be particularly active about Christmastime. I challenge you to a run up the turret-stairs, her favourite haunt, you know."

"I'm game, I assure you," Mr. Erwin answered, delighted to respond to any idea of hers.

"Oh, what fun!" Miss Tommy cried. "Meg, I'll go and get some shawls for everybody," and without waiting for an answer she was off.

Isabel shrank back, chilled as she always was by that dark tale of cruelty of an Elizabethan Lady Macbeth.

"Don't let them drag you up there in the cold. I must go to look after them, but you stay here by the fire," Jack said, in a low voice, to her. But Meg called out: "You'll come, Mrs. Broderick, won't you? It's real-ly an eerie sight worth seeing, the old house in the moonlight."

"Oh, yes, I will go," she answered, adding to Jack: "I would like to see the view."

A maid appeared with wraps and they went out — a long procession — along narrow passages and up winding stairs, that for all modern lighting and car-peting, were yet so mediaevally gloomy.

Isabel was just behind Margaret and Lord Vernade, and she heard him say: "This house never seems to me the right setting for you. One of those Italian Renaissance villas is what you should have, all whiteness and sunshine."

"Oh, don't talk to me of Italian villas!" The girl laughed, but with a note of gratified vanity in her voice.

Lord Vernade and Jack carried candles for dark corners, and with their help they climbed the last stair and stood in the small turret-room.

Below them lay the white stretch of snow-sprinkled meadows, through which wound the dark, sinuous line of the river caught here and there by a silver sparkle of moonlight.

"It's a night when you might fancy one of the boats of the Vikings creeping up with a shine of oars on the water. They went as far as Reading, didn't they?" Isabel said, as she thought, to Jack, but it was Lord Vernade who stood beside her.

"I think so," he said, "though, really, I don't quite remember. I fear that our historic sense gets blunted by custom, and is not as fresh as I have noticed it to be with you people from across the sea."

Was there a polite sneer in his words, or was it her prejudice that made her fancy so? At any rate, she turned away, and stood gazing silently down on the stretch of country that her imagination peopled with those who had once come and gone there.

"Has any one seen Tommy and Sutor?" asked Jack, but no one had any answer to give.

"Come, Mr. Erwin," Meg said to the youth who was generally somewhere near her, "there has been no trial of bravery as yet. I am going to start alone down the long gallery and when I call you must come alone, too. You others can wait here."

"Nonsense, Meg, Mrs. Broderick will be frozen," Jack protested.

"Oh, it's only for a second," and Meg started lightly on round the turn and down a gallery that went the full length of the house.

There was the click, click of her heels as she sped over the bare floor, but instead of her gay shout, a sudden wail of terror broke on their startled ears.

Isabel, Jack, Lord Vernade — neither was quicker than the other in their rush into the gallery, though Isabel was ahead when the flying red figure flung itself into her arms, crying: "The ghost, the ghost!"

They had a momentary vision of a hooded white figure, candle in hand, at the farther end of the gallery, and as Jack's indignant voice rang out: "Tommy, how could you play the fool like that!" it resolved itself into that young woman, wrapped in the big folds of a man's white cloth dressing-gown, the hood pushed back to show her disordered hair and dismayed eyes.

"Oh, Meg, Meg, I'm so sorry. Please, please forgive me. I thought you'd know," she protested, earnestly, but Meg still clung with the same convulsive grasp to Mrs. Broderick, who felt the long tremors that ran over her.

"Meg, don't be a coward," said Jack, laying a hand on her shoulder, and at the touch and the quiet command of the voice the girl raised her head though she still clung to her friend's arm.

There was something strangely impressive in her

disordered beauty, and Isabel saw how intent was Lord Vernade's gaze.

Then following on Tommy's footsteps came the sheepish figure of Mr. Sutor.

"Please, Miss Nugent-Barr, put all the blame upon me. It was I who persuaded Miss Curtis to do it." A protesting gasp was on second thoughts stifled by Tommy.

"I know I was an ass, but I never thought—"

"I'm glad you know that much," came from the indignant Erwin, and Jack, forgetting his duties as host, added, severely:

"I supposed that by this time you had got over those fool's tricks of yours at Sandhurst."

The poor youth's humiliation was complete, but it was Meg who came to the rescue. With a quick movement she seemed to shake off her terrors, and, though pale, was her smiling self again.

"Never mind, then, Mr. Sutor, they've no manners at all. I think myself I was the greatest fool of the three. Tommy, you imp of darkness, you look lovely in that gown. It's a good idea for a fancy ball. Come along all of you down-stairs to the fire, but mind, don't tell my mother what a goose I was. It would worry her."

"Come along, everybody," said Jack, "hot punch is what we all need now."

Chapter 22

In the Studio

As Isabel drove home through the pallor of the winter night, her thoughts were busy with the Monk's Grange family.

Jack and his sister's prompt friendliness had roused a very kindly feeling in her, so that any revelation of character was of interest.

And there had been much self-revelation to-night on the part of Meg. Her dress, for Mrs. Broderick was enough of the world to know that when a woman can add a personal poetic touch to the fashion of her dress, she possesses a powerful weapon. Then there were her varying humours. Her excitement over the cards, her wild terror roused by such an easily seen-through trick, and which she had brought upon herself.

And yet what a charm there was about her, with her frank kindness and her warm affection for her brother.

His influence over her was evidently strong, and that it must be all for good, Isabel, remembering the steadfastness of his blue eyes, could not doubt.

Different types, this brother and sister, probably taking after different sides of the house. Ah, well, though they might have their troubles ahead of them, they still had the one supreme gift of youth to make or mar as they would, while she —

It had been good even for that little while to think of some one but herself, but as there was nothing left of real in her life save her work, let her go back to it and immerse herself in it as a swimmer in the waves.

The next morning she was in her studio nearly an hour earlier than usual, and as she stood before the half-finished picture she knew that here lay her best oblivion.

And so when that evening there came a note from Meg saying that they were going to skate the next day on the flooded meadows, and asking her to come down in time for a picnic luncheon, she sent a plea of work as an excuse. For two or three days she saw nothing of them, and then at tea-time they arrived, announcing cheerfully that their guests had left that morning.

"So now we shall have full leisure to devote to rooting you out of your solitude," Meg proclaimed.

"And if you would let me, I could go over early to-morrow to Maidenhead and get you some skates. You really ought to come down and try it in the afternoon," Jack pleaded.

"Well, there is not much clear daylight after three," she yielded.

Jack looked puzzled.

"I mean for painting."

"Oh, then you will come?" Disgust at painting being the first consideration, mingling with delight at her yielding.

And so, for a few days until a thaw came, Isabel

spent her afternoons on the stretch of ice in the Monk's Grange meadows, contrast enough to the forest lake in the Adirondacks where she had last skated.

As Jack walked up through the woods with her in the-twilight, she asked: "Has Lord Vernade gone away?"

"Yes, he went two days after Christmas. Queer fellow, that! He'll lounge about town or Monte Carlo or some such place for months without doing one thing to show that he's any less a fool than the men around him — save that few play as high as he does, but that's in the blood — and then he'll start off to Asia Minor, where he has men regularly at work excavating some remnants of a town, and there he'll stay two or three months at a time, roughing it like the others, mad over some theory about Homer or Troy or something, writing reports to the learned societies, who think no end of him — then he drops it all and is back again, his same old self."

"How strange," she commented. "He is the last man one would imagine to be an archeologist. What does his wife think of it?"

"Oh, I fancy she doesn't care two straws what he does as long as he leaves her to go her own way in a pretty fast lot. It's hard on a man to have a wife like that, you know."

"Yes," she agreed, thoughtfully.

"Well, I'm off for Florence to-morrow," Margaret announced the next day. "Or, rather, I'm off to join Granny in London to buy clothes. I do wish I had you there to help me. Your taste is just perfect."

"Clothes!" Jack scoffed. "If Meg were going to be

tried for murder she would get a regular trousseau. What I like is women who are always perfectly dressed without ever seeming to give it a thought," looking appreciatively at Isabel.

"There's the superior artfulness in that seeming," Meg retorted. "But now to be serious. You'll promise, won't you," to Isabel, "not to spirit yourself away from here without giving me due warning of your address?"

"One really might think I was the flightiest of mortals," Isabel protested, "whereas you will probably find me here when you return. But, yes, I promise, and it is very good in you to care."

And so, with this promise, Margaret went, and her friend really missed the girl who had fallen into the way of running in and out so frequently.

Jack, however, seemed to have mysteriously lengthened his sojourn, and apparently saw no reason in Meg's departure for dropping his visits to Heathholm.

Hitherto Isabel had kept these visits of theirs quite apart from her studio life, and Jack knew nothing of the big nearly completed canvas into which so much of herself had gone. Nothing, that is to say, beyond a vague jealousy of the work that so absorbed her.

The picture was a success, she knew, now that it needed so little to complete it, and with the knowledge some relaxation in the long strain of effort had already come.

It was a hopelessly rainy winter day, and what with the weather and what with the knowledge that Jack had gone up to town, Isabel, expecting no outside interruption, had, as the light dulled, thrown herself upon the studio sofa and fallen asleep.

She was weary with the complete weariness of the satisfied brain-worker. She had looked upon her work and saw that it was good, and mind and body craved for nothing beyond rest.

At sunset a deep red reflection had lit the eastern clouds, filling the room with a lurid glow. Isabel lay among the soft-tinted cushions still in her studio-dress — a loose gown of coarse white woollen material.

The closed lids, the released curves of the mouth, gave her a curiously young and pathetic air.

It was thus that Jack Nugent-Barr, shown in by the servant's mistake, saw her, and stood looking down at her, a deep tenderness in his eyes.

Beyond the wearied figure stood the nearly completed work of the artist with all the light falling upon it, and from the woman his eyes went on to the picture almost with dread, as though there he recognised his worst rival.

It was after all only for a moment that he was free to gaze, for the subtle sense of being watched penetrated through Isabel's armour of fatigue, and, opening her eyes, she looked at him with the slow smile of the half-awakened child. Then once more fully alert to her surroundings, she sat up, pulling herself together in a woman's fashion.

"Oh, have I really been asleep, when I only lay down to rest for a few moments? And I never expected you this rainy day. I thought, too, that you were in town."

"So I was," and the youth had the conscience to blush, "but I came down by the four-thirty train, and as it had stopped raining I thought would stretch my legs by walking back from Maidenhead, and look in

here on the way." It was an audacious excuse, and
must have struck Mrs. Broderick as such if her mind
had not been full of other things.

The red light falling on the field of poppies caught
her eye, and she spoke impulsively.

"Oh, but you shouldn't be in here, you know! I
won't let anybody see my work."

"Surely I am not 'anybody,'" he protested, sturdily,
"and why should you shut me out from what must be
the main interest of your life? You must know that
such an achievement as even I can see this to be could
not make me think you more wonderful than I do
already."

With too late compunction Isabel heard the impetuous words, and realised that he was about to take the
bit between his teeth. Gathering all her wits to regain
her supremacy, she spoke with gentle aloofness.

"Hush, I must send you away if you talk like that.
You shall see any of my other works you like but *this*,"
with a motion of her hand toward the big easel. "It has
been a fancy of mine to keep it to myself. It will be finished next week, and then I shall take it over to Paris
to be framed. But you won't talk about it, will you?"

"I think you can trust me," he said, quietly, a little
paler than he had been.

"Of course I can. I always do," she incautiously reassured him. She could not bear to see that pained look
in his face. She had, however, immediate cause for
repentance in his rejoinder.

"I was thinking of taking a run over to Paris myself
to see some of the early racing. You wouldn't mind if
I were to go about the same time, would you?"

"I shouldn't *mind*, of course, but I should hardly be able to ask you to come and see me, as I should be staying with an American artist and his wife, who live at Passy, and only receive a few artist friends."

Through the politeness of her words Jack saw the hopelessness of his improvised scheme.

"It doesn't sound much of a change for you," he commented, somewhat sulkily.

"Oh, that is just what it will be," was her cheerful answer. "Nothing could be such a change as getting back into the old art life again after being for so long banished from it."

"I fear you must have found us very stupid here," and the smart young hussar looked very like a contumacious schoolboy.

A smile of amusement at his tragic voice flickered on Isabel's face, as she said, kindly: "The only stupidity was in my own dullness. I came here to fulfil a certain task, and now it is nearly done and I am free of its burden. Free!" and she stood up, stretching out her hands before her.

But even as she did so, a sight of the fire in the young fellow's eyes sobered her, and she went on, hastily: "But I was forgetting that I had promised to show you some of my work."

"Oh, no, you are tired now. Another day will do," he protested, sincerely enough, anxious not to have his enthusiasm diverted into the more arid fields of art.

"But I really am rested now," she persisted and he had to content himself with watching the lines of her figure as she held up a canvas to the light, and with the changes that came over her face as she talked of the various subjects.

All these she showed him were familiar scenes, autumn or winter river bits of tawny reeds and swollen gray water, or woodland studies of gray beech-trunks and golden-brown leafage.

Lifting these sketches one after another from a pile that stood against the wall, she took up one at which she looked in silence.

"I did not know that I had brought that with me," she murmured, as if to herself.

It was a slight, sketchy thing, done in the luminous gray of a northern evening, with a hint of the day's labours ended in the net-laden fishing-dory drawn up on the rough skids that ran down near an old wooden wharf and shed, the wood of each being weather-worn into soft gray.

Up the bank was a suggestion of the dark green of distant spruce woods, but elsewhere stretched the opalescent plan of the sleeping sea.

"I did not know that you had been in Norway," Jack said, with a greater show of interest in the new subject.

The gray wooden shed and the dory brought fond reminiscences of conquered salmon.

"It's not Norway. It is Canada, the Nova Scotian coast, you know," she answered, absently, looking at the picture with the intent eyes of a ghost-seer. Truly, for her there were more ghosts than one around that spot.

"Why, those are our native regions," Jack said, now all surprised interest. "We left there when I was ten years old, but I can just remember places like that. I used to think about them in Norway."

Isabel's attention was fully aroused. The associations of the sketch had inspired a train of thought which brought a sudden flash of realisation.

The French grandmother, the avaricious father, the Canadian birth and the English home, the name Bauer disguised into Barr, all showed that these were Gilbert Clinch's cousins.

"But your name is Nugent," she said, following her thoughts aloud.

The young man stared, as well he might.

"I really don't see what that has to do with it," he said, as though apologising for his own dulness.

Recollecting herself, Isabel saw that she had no right to betray any acquaintance with Gilbert Clinch's family affairs.

"My wits must be wandering," she said, with a laugh. "I suppose I meant that to us Americans your double name sounds so English."

It was a lame excuse, but Jack accepted it readily.

"My mother was English, and as she had no brothers, she took the name to please her father. The old gentleman fancied his family no end, you see," he added, simply. "I believe our paternal Barr is German, and was originally Bauer, which does not indicate an aristocratic origin," and though he laughed, he also reddened slightly as though the fact were unpalatable.

Knowing what she did, Isabel felt a warm sympathy for the boy in his pride of youth. How little he must guess of his real family history.

"But your grandmother is French," she suggested, and Jack brightened.

"Oh, yes, her father carried his head out to

Martinique to keep it safe from Madame Guillotine, and when names were changed she tacked on his title 'de Fer-de-Lance' to her own, which with a 'de' before it, made up quite a grand whole. 'Madame de Barre de Fer-de-Lance' looks very well on a card." He laughed, but with visible faith in this family tree.

Isabel, feeling the need to be alone to pull her ideas together, now suggested that it was getting dark for the walk through the woods, and being still answerable to discipline, Jack took his departure.

Chapter 23

In Florence

The early spring was creeping over the Florence hills, bringing out the narcissus in the meadows and the scarlet anemone among the young wheat under the olives.

It brought many a vagabondising instinct to Margaret as she took her first morning peep from her window at the dark curve of Morello beyond Fiesole, at the distant shining Carrara peaks.

Years of habit had never accustomed her to her grandmother's rule never made her resigned to live her life and go the old lady's ways instead of her own.

And certainly the ways of Madame de Barre de Fer-de-Lance were not ones to recommend themselves to a young girl eager to grasp the joy of life with activity.

Dull drives in the big landau up and down the alleys of the Cascine, duller receptions and teas among the most ultra-Catholic element in the Italian society of the town, a life planned to lead up to an Italian marriage for Margaret and a subsequent entrance into the fold of Rome, such had been the routine of Margaret's winters for the last three years.

Was it the thought of Jack's prophecies and gibes that had kept up the girl's powers of passive resistance, or was it the instinctive craving of her nature for a life more suited to her needs?

However it was, she had hitherto held her own against her sacerdotal surroundings, escaping whenever possible to the more outdoor element of her English acquaintances. An occasional excursion among the hills, or an afternoon's golfing would soon brush away the cobwebs gathered in a heated salon, crowded with scented dowagers and smooth-faced ecclesiastics. She had her home alleviations, too, in a whimsical friendship with her grandmother's French companion, poor, scraggy Madame Estivalet, with her quaint antiquarian enthusiasm that compensated her for all her bondage to her grim old mistress.

Then there was Ellen, half-housekeeper, half-ladies' maid, whose protecting, scolding devotion had formed one of Margaret's earliest memories. Ellen, whose sturdy independence held its own even against the old lady's imperious will.

It was Ellen, though, who, in Margaret's occasional fits of rebellion, would coax her into submission.

"She's old now, Miss Meggie, and she mightn't live long, and her with all that money that would make a rich woman of you, and, maybe, after all, she's an easier one to please than your pa, and a woman's got to please somebody — that is, if she isn't a widow with a bit put away — and sure and certain it is that your pa would never have paid all them bills for clothes this last year. No, nor given you that pearl necklace, neither, as you're so proud of. And there's another thing, child," lowering her voice carefully, "there was them at home that called her a witch, and while that may be nonsense, still I never did see those who crossed her have much luck afterwards. In this pagan country, Domenico calls it the evil eye and makes signs behind his back with his fingers whenever he comes near her, but I guess he means the same thing as they did; and so, my dear just you be patient."

But Meg did not always follow this well-meant advice, and at the present she was in deeper disgrace than ever.

Madame de Barre had taken her to a dance given by the American daughter-in-law of a devout countess, and Margaret, instead of modestly accepting the attentions of the Countess Besaglieri's son, had given several dances to a wandering American, and, greatest crime of all in Italian eyes, had even sat out one with him, after which her outraged ancestress had taken her home, and a fine war of words had raged between the two.

"But, Granny, you never minded my sitting out dances in London," the girl had protested, feigning a social ignorance.

"London! that is another matter! Those heavy English are too stupid ever to see or be afraid of harm. But here! when I take you into the best Italian society, when all the Ripamonti family are agog to see what you are like — indeed, the old Count came to town on purpose — you disgrace me and disgust Count Felice."

"That's one comfort, at any rate, and as to disgrace, Granny, if you're so easily disgraced as that you had better let me go home to my mother. Ellen could take me, you know. At any rate, I should like to go to bed now."

As generally happened when Margaret raised the standard of open rebellion, the old lady capitulated, and soothed the angry girl with some phrases almost apologetic, though her wrath burned none the less fiercely below the surface.

She did not intend Margaret to know that the Ripamonti dowager was coming to lunch with her for a cosy little chat over the proposed alliance, and so the next morning she issued her mandate that Margaret and her companion were to improve their minds by a day's sightseeing at Fiesole. Poor Madame Estivalet's face shone with pleasure as she appeared in Margaret's room with the tidings.

"I fear that it will be but a dull day for you, my dear, but still, the weather is lovely," she began, timidly, but was interrupted by Margaret catching her by the arms and whirling her round in an involuntary waltz.

"Dull, my beloved Stivvie, dull! When I expected to be trotted about in the closed landau all the afternoon on a round of dowagerical visits — good word, that, isn't it? And we will get the cook to make us some of your favourite sandwiches and we will lunch on them in the amphitheatre where the maidenhair grows. Then we'll buy some 'dolces' at Doney's on our way to the train. Only mind, now, we play fair. I'll go and gaze at your beloved Etruscan scraps in the museum if you'll promise to sit and do nothing out-of-doors for ever so long."

"Oh, dear child, but you are of an amiable disposition to enjoy going with your poor old friend," and the good creature wiped away a tear of gratitude.

"Don't be a humbug, Stivvie! You know that at heart

we are equal vagabonds!"

Be that as it might, there was certainly enough of a subtle bond between the queerly assorted pair to make them good holiday companions.

The girl who to-morrow might choose to pose as a very up-to-date society lady was to-day in the wildest schoolgirl humour, and, indeed, in her sailor hat and gray tweed, looked little more than a schoolgirl.

The day was one of those perfect March ones of which Florence holds the secret, and Margaret bought from one of the street children at the station a bunch of vivid red anemones and fastened them against the white silk of her blouse.

They had reached their bourn of the Fiesole amphitheatre, with its circling stone seats against the hillside, where once —

"The Monarch and his minions and his dames
     viewed the games."

Below them lay the winding valley that the dark hills closed in upon and hid, and over everything was the peace of the sleeping past.

Margaret lay back with her head at a comfortable angle against a big stone, and, as usual, was not silent for long.

"Condescend, my friend," she said, lazily, "to bring your thoughts into the comparative modernness of the Roman Empire, and tell me if you think the Latin ladies who sat here on these seats on January and February afternoons had the bare arms and those nice little bare toes with gold trimmings that we see in their statues?"

"Perhaps they only had their games in the summer," was the somewhat feeble suggestion.

"I rather fancy they were up to their little games all the year round," Margaret jested. "And then, those wonderful curled head-pieces of theirs! How blown about they must have got if they didn't wear veils, and what guys they must have looked at any time. Now, you wouldn't have caught a Greek woman getting herself up like that. If I were clever and studied things I should want to know all about the Greeks. How would you like to go to Greece, Stivvie?" she asked, tilting her head still farther back to look up at the angular figure perched with stiff incongruity on a great fallen stone.

"Greece! Oh, my dear!" The rapture of the thought was evidently too deep for words.

"Well, I'll tell you what, if ever I'm rich you and I will go to Athens together, and Corinth and Olympia —"

The stream of her idle talk was checked by the sight of two men tourists, who, descending one of the flights of steps of the amphitheatre, seated themselves on the first row of the curving tiers. Here they proceeded to light cigarettes in an evident state of lazy well-being.

Margaret gave a little amused laugh, and said, in cautiously lowered tones: "Do you see the younger one in the felt hat? Well, that's the one Granny and I had the fight over. He's an American, you know, and seemed to take it quite as a matter of course that I should talk to him half the evening. Oh, Stivvie!" she broke off, in a sharp tone of dismay, for a precious fragment of stone from the old Etruscan wall, surreptitiously presented to Madame Estivalet by a workman, and carefully carried by her, had slipped from her grasp, and, rolling from step to step of the amphitheatre, had ended by inflicting a sharp rap between the shoulders of the subject of Margaret's discourse.

The young fellow looked up in such evident amazement that her laugh rang out unchecked. Recognising his partner of the night before, he raised his hat in greeting, and, stone in hand, began to climb toward them.

"Oh, how awful! He must think I did it on purpose. Granny would have a fit," Margaret gasped, choking back her mirth. "Let's go, madame."

"But my Etruscan stone," groaned the other.

It was too late, however, for retreat. The stranger was standing before them, and, with a contagious smile hovering round the corners of his mouth, began: "Excuse me, but, as this seems to be an antiquity, I feel it my duty to restore it, although I cannot guess what I had done to be attacked with such a missile."

Margaret's schoolgirl manner was gone, and she was altogether the society young lady, as she answered, with a frank laugh: "You were right. It is no common weapon, but a precious fragment of the Etruscan wall, and when my friend let it fall from her grasp she had horrible fears that you might confiscate it. She adores the Etruscans, you see."

The elder lady now found courage to murmur, in her broken English: "Oh, monsieur, I am *désolé!* If it should have inflicted a wound!"

Here both the man and the girl laughed out frankly,

the former answering, with a kindly deference: "Fortunately for me, it did not, you see! But I fear I must plead guilty to a rooted distaste for the Etruscans, at least, those I have seen in terracotta in museums. Their smile would lend a fresh horror to the Day of Judgment. I am sure that if I had seen them as a child, those heads would have haunted every dark corner of the room at bedtime."

But Madame Estivalet could not bear to hear her idols thus desecrated.

"Oh, monsieur, but they are so truly antique, so venerable!" she murmured; then, with a sudden recollection of her duties as a chaperon:

"But I fear that we must be thinking of the next train."

Meanwhile, Margaret had been taking a daylight inspection of the man who last night had aroused her interest. He was good-looking, this fair-haired, slim man of about thirty, with the suggestion of a reserve of strength under the quiet of his manner.

What was there about him that reminded her of her brother Jack? She was not quite sure, for his aquiline features were more individualised than that youth's, his observant eyes were of a clear gray instead of the blue of Jack's, and yet with both there was the feeling that they were of those to whom children and dogs would turn unafraid, while a man might fear their anger.

But the second man was coming slowly up the steps.

"Isn't that Mr. Sinnet?" Margaret asked.

"Yes; do you know him?"

"Just to bow to, but Mrs. Sinnet comes to the villa sometimes."

Then, as the tall, thin man, with iron-gray hair and dyspeptic countenance, raised his hat, she said:

"How do you do, Mr. Sinnet? One must come into the wilderness, I see, to meet you aesthetic folk. You don't condescend to teas and such."

The newcomer looked mildly flattered as he answered, in a sepulchral voice:

"Art is long and life is short. We to whom the mission has been given must husband our forces for the doing of our work."

Margaret knew well enough that the doing of this work consisted in the occasional production of some overelaborate essay on North Italian scenery or art, brought out with copious illustrations in "editions de luxe," and she caught a look on the other man's face which told her that he did not take his companion very seriously.

"It must be delightful to go about with so good a guide to Florence as Mr. Sinnet," she said, graciously, to him.

"Yes, indeed, though I fear he finds me a terrible Philistine. I had not time, you see, in early days to attend to the ornamental side of my education," was the frank answer.

"Ah, well, that can always be added on like a piece of lace to a frock. Yes, dear madame, I am ready whenever you are," and, with a bow and a smile which included both men, she turned with her companion to climb toward the entrance.

"What a delightful young man!" Madame Estivalet said, regretfully, as they sat in the shady piazza awaiting the hourly train.

"That's all very well," Margaret laughed, mischievously, "but won't Granny slay us when she hears we have been talking to the enterprising partner of last night?"

Madame Estivalet looked troubled at the anticipation of her report to her tyrant, but presently she spoke, with a fine air of carelessness: "After all, dear child, I see no occasion to disturb your grandmother with the little details of our expedition. She has seemed nervous of late, and easily disturbed."

"Nervous" was the companion's polite expression for what Ellen called "the old lady's tantrums."

"All right, Stivvie, I'm mum," the girl agreed, with an inward sense of amusement.

Chapter 24

A Wanderer

"That's the girl you were asking me about, isn't it?" Mr. Sinnet said, as soon as the ladies were out of hearing.

"Yes, it was strange I couldn't remember her name, for I found her charming company. I rather think the old lady with her didn't fancy her bestowing so much of it on me. She scowled at me fiercely as she left."

"Madame de Barre? Oh, she is an old witch, they say. She keeps mostly to the foreign society of the place, and wants to marry Miss Nugent to an Italian, at least, so I've heard my wife say. I hold aloof from it all, you know. The real Florence lies for me in the nooks and corners that retain the national life, and steep my soul in joy with their contrast to the American crudity from which I escaped as from Sodom and Gomorrah."

"Be sure you don't look backwards, then," his companion said, and then, thinking that, for all his aloofness, Mr. Sinnet seemed fairly well up in the local gossip, he went on: "Miss Nugent seems to have nothing foreign about her except her looks. Her name is Irish, and one often sees Irish girls with that blue-black hair."

"But never with those deep dark eyes, where the

fire, where the passion of this old land slumbers. She is a daughter of the South," Mr. Sinnet declared, enthusiastically.

His friend laughed.

"I didn't know you included young ladies' eyes in your artistic raptures."

"Aesthetic, purely aesthetic! She seemed to personify the freshness of spring among these heavy ruins. But I suppose we must be thinking of getting back in time for dinner. That spaghetti at lunch was only half-cooked, and I was afraid to touch it."

All the same, he had managed a good plateful of it, his friend remembered, but took care not to say so.

Between these two men there was no real friendship or intimacy, though during these days, that delayed him in Florence, Gilbert Clinch had fallen into a habit of taking his walks abroad in the society of the man who, self-absorbed dyspeptic as he was, could rouse into genuine enthusiasm over the beauties of the land he had chosen as a home.

When Gilbert had left America at the end of the previous summer, his first need had been to put a space of travel between himself and the beginning of a new chapter. To let fresh scenes and faces dull the too keen memories and regrets that he took with him. He was not the first to try such a remedy, nor the first to discover its uselessness. He soon found that lounging about among mountains or ruins was not the way to forget. As he watched some little sunset cloud drifting against a mountain peak, his instinct was to call Isabel Broderick's attention to it. When palaces and churches brought new historic ideas to him, he imagined her replies to his theories. The sight of a sad woman's face under a mourning-veil, of a mother's arms around her child — but what was there that did not take, his thoughts flying back to her, true as a homing pigeon?

Then, being in a way a resolute man, he tried a stricter regimen, and went off to Vienna where the man who stood as one of the world's heads to his special line of work was propounding some startling new theories.

The working out of these kept him absorbed as nothing else could have done. Not too absorbed, however, that he did not have time to read the columns of the American society papers, to listen to the chatter of any woman whom he thought might mention the name he hungered to hear. Always he kept before him that in a few weeks, he must go to England and find out more about this uncle of his, find out, too, what were the first steps necessary to the claiming of his inheritance. He had no longer any doubts as to doing that, but he had now what seemed to him like riches, at least enough to free him from sordid cares, and was it not his duty to follow out these experiments to the end? It was, indeed, a great chance for him to be able to do so, but he would go at Christmas. Yes, he certainly would go at Christmas.

But the Fates must have laughed as he said so, for just as Vienna was putting on her festive array — and a very smart array it was — he received a letter from an American doctor in Florence, enclosing a few scrawled lines, hardly legible:

"DEAR OLD BOY: — Heard from some one
you're in Vienna. Here I am — enteric fever up
the Nile — relapse here. Think my time's up.
Could you come and help me settle about the
kids?
"Yours,
"Dick Brindle."

The doctor added his opinion that there was small
chance of the patient rallying from his excessive weakness, and that when conscious he seemed anxious and
depressed about his family affairs. If any friend could
come to him, it would certainly be an advantage.

Now, Dick Brindle had been to Gilbert as a brother
during school and college days. A pluckily fragile little fellow, he had at the age of fifteen seen a luxurious
home go to pieces around him, leaving two baby
brothers more helpless than himself. He scrambled
into a newspaper office and held his own there with a
tenacity of grip, gradually working himself on until he
had done well as a war correspondent up the Nile with
the English troops in the past September.

Gilbert knew that he was on his homeward way and
had been expecting to hear from him, and now he
had heard with a vengeance. There was no doubt in
his mind as to going. Dick had appealed to him, that
was enough.

There was a sigh given to the thought of the week that
he had intended to spend in Paris, for he had cherished
an idea that there, if anywhere, he might find Mrs.
Broderick. True, he must not seek her, but if by any
chance — Well, however that might be, it must wait now.

His trunk was packed and he was off within a few hours of his summons. His reward came when, standing in a small dark bedroom in a Florence hotel, he saw the flicker of a familiarly whimsical smile on a face so pinched and waxy that life seemed to have but little to do with it.

For a few weeks Gilbert's existence was one of those hand-to-hand combats with death which most of us have fought in our time. Then, one day: "You've won, old fellow, though whether you'll find it was worth the trouble is another question," said Brindle, over a bowl of soup. "And how do you mean to celebrate your victory? By an orgie of old masters?"

Gilbert puffed at his pipe, and, lying back in an armchair, contemplated his ghastly treasure-trove with satisfaction.

"By swearing a bit at you now and then when you get fractious. It didn't seem exactly polite to a dying man, you know," he said.

"But I'm afraid I'll get more fractious. That is, people always do when they are getting better, don't they?" was the rueful answer.

"You'd better just wait until you find the use of your legs, then, that's all. Go to sleep now, like the blessed baby you are, while I go for a walk."

This walk took him around by Cook's office, where he made inquiries as to the different northward routes, reading out various items from timetables to his friend that evening. But these anticipations were promptly quenched next day by the well known American doctor, who has been such a good friend to so many of his country-folk in Florence.

"I won't be responsible for him if he leaves here before three weeks or so. You must see yourself," he appealed to Gilbert, "that if he met a cold snap on the journey it might knock him up again, and in that case —" Here he left a silence which his listeners had no difficulty in filling in.

"I suppose you'll get off on Saturday or Monday," Brindle said, with a fine air of carelessness. It was the hour in the day when he was promoted to sit at a window and gaze out on the varied outline of Florentine house-tops and spires, and when Gilbert allowed him to talk most freely.

There had been a ruminative silence between them now while the sunset splendour filled the room.

"Saturday or Monday?" Gilbert made answer, slowly, "no, I think I might as well hang on for a bit longer and see how you get along."

"Look here," came with new energy from Brindle, "I see now that I was a weak coward to send for you at all. I don't think I'd have done it but for those kids, and wanting to make sure that you'd be their guardian." Here he choked for a bit, but in a moment went on, bravely: "I'll do all right by myself now, anyway."

"There's gratitude for you," scoffed Gilbert, cheerfully, "and now will you state your reasons for supposing that I am in such a devil of a hurry?"

"You didn't think that I was listening one day when Baldor spoke of your meeting Doctor Sproules in Paris and you said that you must be in England long before that, and might be detained there on important business. I suppose you meant what you said."

Gilbert laughed shortly.

"You little viper, to trick me like that! Well, were you never glad of an excuse to dodge the beginning of a difficult and unpleasant piece of business? That's the way with me at present. Let me give you your medicine so as to prepare you for a dime-novel romance — pirates, slave-traders hidden treasure, and all the rest."

The room was dark when Gilbert, having finished his tale, asked: "There, what do you think of that?"

"And it is more than six months since you first heard of this will that leaves you a fortune?" his patient demanded, eagerly.

"The chance of a fortune, the disturbing, uncertain chance of a fortune. How can I tell what legal whirlpools and rocks may be between that chance and smooth waters?"

"Man alive, how can you ever find out unless you try? If you want to know what I think, I think that you've been a fool. That is," he added, more slowly, "unless there is something in the affair that I haven't understood." Here his tone became slightly neutral, and he fixed his eyes on the black outline of a turret against the primrose sky. "I think you said that you have told the whole story to no one save Mrs. Broderick?"

Gilbert made a slight movement at the strangeness of hearing the familiar name again.

"She did not hear it all. I — I have not seen her since my mother told it to me," he answered, simply.

"Well, never mind, you've told it to me now, and I want to know what you are going to do next?"

Gilbert laughed.

"What tyrants one's patients become! May I humbly venture to state that when I reach London I intend taking a Boston letter of introduction to a solicitor, telling him my tale and asking his advice."

"You do? Well, then, will you start off on Monday and go and do it?"

"No, I intend to wait for a week or two and hale you off with me."

"That depends, my friend."

Each was determined, and the argument was longer than Gilbert thought good for his patient, but how was he to leave one so helpless to travel alone? At length they came to a compromise that Gilbert should stay on for a bit if he would write at once to the London solicitor, stating his case and asking for advice.

"What I intend to do now, is to get back the use of these legs of mine and cheat you two doctors. You always said I had the obstinacy of a bulldog and I mean to bring it into play."

He did, the next day clamouring to be taken out in a carriage, which feat, being once accomplished, became a daily one, save when a bath-chair took its place. A quaint figure he made, the shrunken young fellow with the handsome head, and the light-hearted, feeble laughter. The old man who dragged his chair, and on whom he experimented gaily in Italian, thought him madder but far more amiable than the generality of the "forestieri," and the flower-sellers learned to track his path and persuade him to heap the bunches of narcissus or red anemones around him, until he announced that he looked like nothing save a legless Bacchus.

"And now we must see the sights that a poor cripple can reach," he said, and Gilbert did all he could to carry out the wish.

Chapter 25

Persephone

Whoever has taken care of an invalid knows what tales may be woven from the slimmest incidents to bring back to the sickroom a bit of the outside world. Gilbert Clinch was by nature a reticent man, but now the little adventure in the Fiesole amphitheatre was spun out to its fullest extent, and Brindle was well up on the subject of the English girl's hair and eyes, even her dress.

"It will be nice to see some smart girls again," he said, "only I'm afraid that in my feeble mental state I shall fall in love with the first one I come across."

"Then you will probably have to fall out of love again," Gilbert retorted.

They were sitting in a sunny nook in the Boboli Gardens, the invalid in a bath-chair, his friend beside him on a bench. Beneath them —

> "White and wide
>   And washed by the morning water-gold
>   Florence lay out on the mountain-side."

Beyond the city domes and spires rose the dark curve of Morello, and away to the south — like the far-off city of the soul — gleamed the white Cararra peaks.

At their feet a great circle of turf was starred with anemones, and sparrows bathed and twittered in the splash of a central fountain. Brindle, looking round on it all with a convalescent's content, drew a deep breath of satisfaction.

"Jove, but it's a good world to be alive in!" he said. "Think of being hidden under the earth on a day like this, under the earth with one's life unlived, like so many of those poor fellows out there on the Nile — like I came so near being myself." He paused for a moment. "Somehow the spring in the air goes to one's head, and one feels as though the old Gods of the land ought to be awakening. And by the whole Olympus of them," with sudden energy, "here comes the very Goddess of Spring herself."

Up the terraced path toward them came a girl in a dress of light gray with big black hat wreathed with spring flowers and carrying in her hands a great cluster of daffodils. The morning light was on her face, and she was laughing at something said by the prim old companion who followed her like a shadow.

"Keep calm," Gilbert said, "this is the girl I told you of."

As Margaret saw him she bowed smilingly, and was apparently about to pass on around the circling path to the flight of steps that led to a higher bank. Was it the sight of the wistful expectancy in a pale young face that checked her and caused her to linger so that Gilbert must needs come forward to greet her?

"What a warm, sunny corner you have chosen," she said, in frank greeting, "but I am sorry to see your friend is ill," with a glance that set the bath-chair quivering.

"Thanks, but I hope he is well on the way to recovery now." Gilbert hesitated and then plunged boldly in. "It would be a great kindness if you would come and talk to him for a bit. He has seen no one save me for weeks."

Margaret laughed. "And is tired of you? I see. Of course we love to play the Good Samaritan, don't we, madame? Come and introduce us, please."

Seldom does a woman show to better advantage than in talking to a sick man, all the latent motherliness rousing in her to help him, if only with a few cheerful words. So now, as with one quick glance, Margaret took in the sight of the blanched, wasted hands lying so listlessly on the rug, the carefully buttoned overcoat, and the deep hollows around the eyes that shone with young love of life, a great gentleness came over her.

Taking a seat on the bench beside the bath-chair, she said: "It must be good to be here in the sunshine, for you have been ill, I hear."

"That can all be a dream of the night now that I sit here like a prince, with such a bit of the kingdoms of the world and the glory of them spread out below me, and with spring coming to me in the hands of Persephone, —

> "'She stepped upon Sicilian grass,
>   Demeter's daughter fresh and fair,'"

the young fellow quoted eagerly.

Margaret gave a little pleased laugh, as she held out her flowers to him to see.

"How nice of you! Did you think of the rest of the verse —

> "'The daffodils were fair to see,
> They nodded lightly on the lea,
> Persephone! Persephone!'

I love to give those dear old outcast phantoms a share of their lost haunts on days like this. But you are sketching?" seeing a little note-book lying on his knee.

Gilbert laughed.

"The sketching is a series of vile caricatures of me. I figure making beef-tea — for I have learned of late to make beef-tea; slumbering in an armchair in the night watches, with my head near a candle, and so forth. There's the gratitude of a patient for you. Hand them over, you sinner," and reaching down, he appropriated the book and held it out with fluttering leaves to Miss Nugent.

But a confidential sketch-book is risky to handle, and the first thing that Margaret came on was a rough sketch outlining the semicircle of the Fiesole amphitheatre, on the top steps of which stood a beautiful, wrathful Bellona aiming a stone at a cowering figure below, with Gilbert's aquiline nose exaggerated into caricature. Behind Bellona a few touches suggested an elderly figure in modern dress.

The corners of Margaret's mouth quivered, as she said, demurely: "You certainly seem to have classical allusions at your finger-tips, Mr. Brindle. First Persephone, then — is it Pallas Athene or Bellona?" and with that the frank laughter broke out.

For a moment the two men looked like school-boys detected in drawing the headmaster; then they too joined in the laugh.

"It was all Clinch's fault," his friend protested.

"He would do nothing all that evening but talk of his surprise at the stone and his pleasure in finding his partner of the night before, so to relieve the black envy of an overcharged heart —"

"You perpetuated an injustice," Margaret interrupted, "for if Mr. Clinch told you the truth, he said that it was not I who dropped the stone, but madame," and she turned and laid her hand on the arm of that worthy lady, who made a little sound of dismay.

"Oh, monsieur, I have been longing to ask if my unfortunate awkwardness caused you any pain or inconvenience," the poor soul fluttered.

"Not at all, madame," he hastened to say, good-naturedly. "It was only told as a joke to entertain a bored and fractious individual."

"It was told with deliberate design to make me envious. I, who for months had only seen the oily beauties of Nubia and the Soudan, and who, as soon as I get back to civilisation, am dumped down like a log in a back bedroom for weeks. But now," — pointing the word with an audacious glance at Margaret, — "I am in that state of Christian beatitude that I can forgive him anything."

"That's just as well, or I might take you home and put you to bed," Gilbert put in.

"Felice would stand my friend. Isn't he a delightfully picturesque ruffian?" Brindle said, nodding toward a tattered being on a bench near by.

"Do you often get out now?" Margaret asked.

"This is the opening scene to a wild career of dissipation," Gilbert said, "We mean to bask in the sunshine like lizards. To-morrow, if it is fine, we shall cab it to San Miniato and spend the morning there. Then I have prospected the sheltered spots about the Viale dei Colli for his benefit. I'm glad now that our quarters are on this side of the river."

"Are they?" Margaret said, with interest. "My grandmother's villa is halfway up the Viale, the pink one at the turn of the road, with a snake on the top of each gate-post — Villa della Biscia the people began to call it, and now even our friends put the name on notes. It's an uncanny crest to have," and she gave a little shudder.

"Is it yours too?" Gilbert asked, with an undefined impulse to keep her to personal topics. The girl had somehow succeeded in arousing his curiosity.

"Oh, no, Granny has it all to herself, I'm happy to say."

Just then the soft swell of the Angelus rose in its daily oblation from the hundred bells of the city below.

"I always think that at twilight one might see the sound spirits going upwards," Margaret said, gently, then as she felt a timid touch on her arm:

"Oh, madame, yes, I know. We shall hardly manage to get home in time for *déjeuner*, and what a fuss there will be. We must say good morning and run away."

"Well," said Brindle, drawing a deep breath as he watched the slim gray figure down the long vista of the path, "that was a piece of luck anyhow."

"Was it?" Gilbert responded, absently. "Perhaps that remains to be seen. I never meet a new person but I wonder what they may bring with them. Good luck or bad."

"And most of them merely bring a pebble to add to the cairn of boredom, which is the gift of man to man."

"And of women?"

"Oh, women! That's a different question. I know that my Persephone brought me a pleasant half-hour, to which may the gods send an encore."

It is hardly to be wondered at that, given the various sunny lounging-places on one side of the winding hill-side boulevard, and the facility with which the pink Villa della Biscia could be identified, the bath-chair was more than once the following week encountered in that neighbourhood by a young woman taking her walks abroad under proper chaperonage. Never had Florence known calmer, sunnier mornings, mornings when it was joy to feel life and youth coming back, and to watch a girl's cheek curving with a smile, to see the quick flash of responsive thought in her eyes, even before the words came.

And Gilbert watched the small idyl with secret misgivings, noting the girl's little outbursts of frank unconventionality and her unvarying kindness to his friend, and remembering how he had heard the Sinnets speak of her as an up-to-date society girl with all the ways of her type. During the past six months which seemed to form a gap between him and the realities of his life he had seen no woman who really aroused his curiosity and had given him any desire to understand her character as much as did this one.

"There are hidden fires there," he said, one night to Brindle, as they sat smoking. "Warring hereditary traits of alien races that change the character as one side or the other gets uppermost."

"I thought it was about time for your hereditary fetich to be trotted out," Brindle grunted. "But all the same you needn't speak as though the girl were a mulatto. How do you know that she is of mixed race?"

"She has an English name and an exotic face and nature."

"She has a sweet face and a kind nature. Not many girls would bother about a wretched cripple as she does," the other protested, vehemently.

"No, she has been charming," Gilbert agreed, a he rose to go and finish the evening at the Sinnets'.

It was after the third of these more or less casual meetings that, on their homeward way, Margaret announced to her companion: "Stivvie, I am sure you must be suffering from an evil conscience."

"My dear, what do you mean?" came with a nervous gasp.

"Mean? Why, what could I mean but that you have forgotten to mention to Granny these two young men whom you have been meeting — let me see, once, twice, thrice —"

"I have been meeting? My dear child, what will you say next?" remonstrated her friend.

"What I am going to say next is that I am going to peach. I shall confess all, Stivvie."

"But I shall be turned out into the world," the poor old lady protested.

"Not a bit of it. I'll see you clear. You leave it to me."
And with a meek sigh madame agreed to this.

Madame de Barre had got through her third rich
dish, and the grimness of her countenance was somewhat relaxed. She had also driven a hard bargain with
a countrywoman that morning for a string of the old
gold and coral beads which are growing rare. She had
a love for collecting all such sorts of trinkets, and now
sat at the table lovingly fingering the beads.

"Granny, do you remember the American man I
danced with at the Della Rovere's?" Margaret asked,
true to her usual bold policy with her venerable ancestress.

Madame Estivalet jumped as though a pin had been
stuck into her, and her tyrant withered her with a bale-
ful glance before she answered, shortly: "I do, certainly. I trust you have not been picking up any more
such acquaintances."

"Well," came the demure answer, "we did meet him
this morning up at San Miniato — you know, Granny,
you said that long walks were so good for my com-
plexion — and there was such a poor desperately ill-
looking young fellow with him that I couldn't help
stopping to say something kind to him —"

"You spoke to these men! If the Marchesa di
Ripamonti should hear of it!" shrieked the old lady,
like an angry cockatoo. "And you, Estivalet –" she was
turning on the trembling companion when Margaret
made her voice heard again:

"It seems that Mr. Clinch is really a doctor —"

"Mr. *who?*" came in a curiously changed voice, like a
child's that hears a dreaded name.

"Mr. Clinch, you know. It seems that he has been delayed here for weeks by the illness of his friend, who had enteric fever up the Nile, when he was war correspondent, and had a relapse on the way home. Such a young fellow he looks."

"Was that why he came here?" the old lady questioned, abruptly.

"Who? Mr. Clinch? Yes, I think so. He seems devoted to his friend. He knows the Sinnets, he says."

"Knows the Sinnets, does he? Well, we must find out who this young man is, who seems to hover about. What did you say his first name was?"

Now Margaret had not said, and she rather wondered that her grandmother should think of asking. However, she answered, demurely: "It begins with G, for I saw that on a letter in his hand."

"Ah, I see," in a less interested voice. "And now, my dear, order the carriage. By the bye, it's Mrs. Sinnet's day and we might as well pay her a visit. I want to ask her about that washerwoman she recommended."

Chapter 26

The Gorgon's Head

"I have been put through my paces on your account to-day. What have you done to arouse such an interest in the Gorgon's breast?" Mrs. Sinnet said to Gilbert, as they sat over a bright little wood fire in her drawing-room the next evening. Mr. Sinnet was taking that absolute repose which he found necessary to his digestion for half an hour after dinner.

"What Gorgon?" Gilbert asked, bewildered.

"Oh, don't you know the name? That's what people call old Madame de Barre. She was here with her pretty granddaughter yesterday and wanted to hear a great deal more about you than I ever knew myself. Have you been making love to the young woman, *par exemple?*"

Gilbert laughed.

"You must blame Brindle, not me," he said.

"His pathetic appearance seems to have stirred her woman's kindness, so that she and the quaint old French lady have once or twice loitered to chat with us in their walks. She seems a fine creature, full of possibilities, doesn't she?" he added, carelessly.

Mrs. Sinnet sent one quick glance over her fire-screen to see if the carelessness were genuine, but observed nothing to confirm the suspicion. She had not thought in the afternoon that Margaret's interest was for the invalid.

"Well, I am under orders to take you to the Villa della Biscia reception tomorrow. Suitable name for the Gorgon's den, isn't it?"

"I haven't seen her. For all I know she may be a much maligned character. But really, I hardly see the good of going there now when I hope to be off in a week or so."

Mrs. Sinnet stared into the fire thoughtfully. Being a lady of vivid imagination, she never brought a man and girl together without foreseeing possibilities.

"Doesn't it seem as though you were bound to go after meeting the girl and talking to her casually?" she suggested.

"Well, just as you like," he agreed. "Will it be a very grand function?"

"There will be a crowd, mostly Italian old ladies and priests, and an assortment of the most fossilised English element. Not many low-down Americans like me."

"And how do you gain admittance?" Gilbert asked, idly.

"Well, you see I have a cousin who married a Roman duke, and that always comes in handy. Besides that, the devout dowagers are under orders to smile upon me and entice me into the right path. There is a charming bishop angling for my soul just now. It is such fun and gives me a glimpse of the old-fashioned Italian society at its best. You know, I am like St. Paul's Athenians and would sell what soul I have for a new sensation. I have only to appear at benediction and a dozen old countesses are after me for the honour and glory of my conversion. And that, you see, is how I come to be admitted to the Gorgon's den."

"It's a great thing to be catholic in your tastes but then perhaps even these dowagers are capable of enjoying a little added spice to their daily gossip. I trust I may prove a credit to you. And now," rising, "I must get back to see to my patient's sleeping draught."

"How is he?"

"Well, doctors differ. I think better of him than Balder does. I sincerely trust I am right. *Au revoir!*"

When Mrs. Sinnet's smart little victoria swept up the carriage drive of the Villa della Biscia there were already several heavy family vehicles at the door

"Why should old ladies' carriages have the same stamp all the world over?" queried Mrs. Sinnet.

That lady was looking very smart in elaborate mauve draperies around which ran outlines of dull sage green and silver.

"Humphry designed it," she said, in answer to Gilbert's expressed admiration. "That's one good, at any rate, in having an aesthetic husband," and it might almost have seemed as though she considers it a lot requiring alleviations.

As they entered, Gilbert looked around with the instinct of one who had often used surroundings as an aid to deciphering character. The first thing that struck him was the curious mixture of really valuable old Italian furniture and stuffs with tawdry modern materials. It suggested to him the palace of some

Eastern potentate, where glass chandeliers from Birmingham hang beside priceless old lamps of inlaid metals.

But to-day the setting lost interest in the groups that filled the vista of the rooms. Awesome-looking old ladies in those black costumes which seem put together from a rag-bag of satins and laces, were throned on sofas and deferentially talked to by gray-haired men with the coloured buttons of various orders against their black coats, while the younger, more fashionably dressed women chattered with officers in the Bersaglieri black and crimson or the cavalry. It was true that the foreign element was the largest, but still there was a sprinkling of smart Americans and comfortable-looking English mammas with their trim half-pay colonels and generals, and big daughters talking loudly of golf and tennis. In fact, there was a little of all the component parts of cosmopolitan society in its staider form.

Gilbert followed in Mrs. Sinnet's wake through the rooms, toward the central point where, enthroned in a high-backed old Florentine chair, sat the hostess.

A weird figure it was, that of this little shapeless old woman, huddled down in the shining folds of her crimson brocade, on which numerous diamond ornaments matched the hawklike brilliancy of the black eyes glowing in the parchment face.

Made a keen observer by his profession, Gilbert felt an insistent spell in the questioning of those eyes, fixed on him as Mrs. Sinnet said: "You see, dear madame, I have brought Mr. Clinch as you so kindly suggested."

"So this is Mr. Gilbert Clinch!" came in the shaky voice of age marked with a foreign accent, "the young gentleman who has been playing knight-errant to my poor Estivalet."

"Indeed it is she and Miss Nugent who have been kind enough to speak a few friendly words to my sick friend."

"I have heard of this friend of yours. It is he who detains you in Florence?" the old lady asked.

"I am waiting for him to be well enough to travel," he said.

"And it was his illness that brought you here? You would not have come otherwise?" she went on, with a strange persistence.

"It is not likely, for I was just finishing up some medical studies in Vienna before starting for London."

"You have never been in England?" and if it had not been so improbable Gilbert would have thought that she attached some importance to the question, and seemed relieved when he said no.

"Ah, you had better not be in too great a hurry to forsake our Florence spring. They tell me your friend is able to sit in a bath-chair in the sunshine. Perhaps you would like to bring him to my terrace some morning. It is sheltered and warm. Come to-morrow if it is fine. And now you will want to go and speak to my granddaughter, I know," and with a wave of a bony, much-ringed hand she dismissed him.

Gilbert, although he could hardly have given any reason for it, had rather the sensation of having passed through an ordeal.

While he was being put through his paces, he had

been keenly conscious that Miss Nugent, dressed in pale green, was watching his reception from under a curtained archway.

"Why didn't you come to my rescue?" he asked, as she held out her hand in greeting.

"I thought you would do better without me. And really, you must have bewitched Granny! I haven't seen her so smiling for an age."

He wondered with a sense of awe what her unamiable side might be like, but did not reveal the sentiment.

"She very kindly told me to bring Brindle tomorrow to sit on your terrace. That will delight him," he said.

Margaret stared in amazement.

"Well, I can only repeat that you must have bewitched her. And after her making all that fuss about my sitting out two dances with you —" she checked herself, with a slight blush.

"Did she?" Gilbert laughed. "It must be that, since then, she has discovered my harmless character. If you only knew how old and cynical yours and Brindle's youthful talk makes me feel."

The soft dark eyes were raised to his.

"I'm sure you are not cynical," she said, gently.

"Hullo! in the absence of Brindle the siren is trying her wiles on me," Gilbert said to himself, all the while noting, with a certain pleasure, the narrow white hand that toyed with a cluster of red anemones in the front of her dress.

"You keep up your character of Persephone, I see," he said, bringing a ready smile to her face.

"Poor Mr. Brindle! Will you take him one or two from me?" she asked.

"Not I! such a gift would be bad for his tranquillity, both mental and physical," he protested, half in jest and half in earnest.

"What a poor creature you think me," she said, and he was surprised to see that he had somehow wounded her.

"Ah, no, indeed! I think you a wonder of kindness," he asserted.

But Margaret was looking anxiously across the room to where a stout, much-ornamented dowager and an old gentleman with waxed gray moustache were advancing.

"Oh, take me quick into the next room for a cup of tea! There are Mamma and Papa Ripamonti bearing down upon me. They are trying to marry me to the son, you know."

Gilbert's American chivalry was astir at the first word of a girl's marriage being arranged by any one but herself.

"But you won't have to marry an Italian, will you?" he asked, directly they were safe in a corner of the next room.

Margaret looked pleased at his earnestness.

"I'm afraid I can hardly pose as a persecuted heroine, for I sha'n't have to marry any one unless I choose. If Granny got too much for me, — and she sometimes does, I must confess," she said, with a touch of gravity, — "I have only to call in my brother Jack to the rescue. He wouldn't stand any nonsense."

"You have one brother?" Gilbert asked.

"Yes, only one. And you, have you any brothers or sisters?"

"None! I am a solitary being. But tell me, how did your grandmother know my Christian name?"

"She didn't. She asked me yesterday if I had heard it and I said I knew it began with G. I had seen it on that book you had."

"Well, she called me Mr. Gilbert Clinch just now."

"Mrs. Sinnet must have told her, then. But I must go back. You will come to-morrow morning, won't you?"

Her friendly little appeal was very pleasant, and as Gilbert left her to find Mrs. Sinnet he had to make an effort to revive the siren theory.

"I've brought you some bonbons from the party, you young sinner," was Gilbert's way of announcing to Brindle the treat that was in store for him, and the idiotic fashion in which that youth behaved justified him in having kept back his news until the last moment.

"Was there ever such a disgusting lot of neckties beheld by human eyes?" he said, ruefully, contemplating his small supply. "Say, Clinch, don't you think you could go out and get me something better?"

"Well, if you want to spend all the morning dressing —" Gilbert began, and the other cut him short with:

"Of course I don't. This navy blue one will do. What o'clock is it now? Ten? Surely Felice ought to be here soon. Poke your head out and see, there's a good fellow!"

"Keep cool. He'll come up to help you down, you know."

They were pathetic enough, these struggles between the self-will of young manhood and the helplessness of weakness, but a certain whimsicality of Brindle's

made them easier for both. There was something in
the fashion in which he scoffed at his various afflic-
tions that reminded Clinch of the much loved
Stevenson.

It was still early enough when the patient Felice
pulled the bath-chair up toward the Villa della Biscia.

"Supposing there's no one in the garden, will you
ring at the door?" asked Brindle, with the mingled
fussiness of an invalid and an amorous man.

"I'll dump you in the window if you say much
more," Gilbert threatened. "There, do you see that
flower-wreathed hat beyond the cypress hedge? Now
you're content, I hope?"

Yes, Brindle was thoroughly content when a white
serge-clad figure was seen coming down the path to
meet them.

"I've been picking out a nice warm corner for you,
Mr. Brindle, and Madame Estivalet is dragging out
rugs and cushions for your benefit," Margaret said in
greeting, smiling out beneath the shade of her broad
hat, over the brim of which hung clusters of red flowers against her hair.

No one who has not been in Italy can know the joy
of terraces — terraces to farmhouses where the pep-
pers and pumpkins are dried, terraces to villas and
palaces haunted by the shades of old pleasures and
old sins.

It so happened that when this spick and span modern villa had been built, it had fallen heir to one of
these red-tiled farmhouse terraces, clinging to the
hillside and overlooking the fair valley of the Arno
and the city spires.

Sheltered by one end of the house, it was a pleasant spot even in winter and now on this spring morning it was a joy indeed. There were heavy rugs spread over the red tiles, and a group of chairs — one especially deep and cushioned.

Margaret looked dubiously from the bath-chair to the terrace.

"Would you rather not come up the steps —" she began, when Brindle said, eagerly:

"Oh, please let me get out of this thing that's so like a coffin. Clinch, you'll give me an arm up?"

As Felice and Gilbert helped him up the steps, Margaret turned her eyes away in pity, while Madame Estivalet fluttered above like a benevolent stork.

Margaret had stooped to the beds of many-coloured anemones and tulips, and now came toward Brindle with a cluster in her hand.

"Here are your flowers," she said. "I know people who have been ill love to hold and handle them."

He took the flowers with the single word "Persephone!" in which sounded the tribute of thanks and admiration.

"I'm not sure on second thoughts that I like the name. There's a creepy feeling of the dark king looming up in the background," Margaret said, as she settled into one of the basket chairs. "But tell me, did you bring the Soudan sketches you promised to show me?"

"I have brought photos which are better. I don't do illustrating work, you know. My sketches are just a matter between myself and my —"

"Conscience," put in Gilbert. "Here are the photos,"

pulling a small package out of his pocket.

These were as grimly interesting as are all war photos, and in the morning beauty they looked long at pictures of men sore wounded, or being carried to their graves under the desert sands. More cheerful ones showed groups of shirt-sleeved men cooking, eating, resting.

"This is our correspondents' mess, and here am I cooking some bacon — Ah, that bacon! It was truly an oasis in the desert."

"What a horrible, uncomfortable, dirty thing war must be!" Margaret said, as she laid the photos down.

Gilbert was a bit surprised, having expected the usual young lady cheap heroisms on the subject. The girl had certainly a curious streak of sincerity in her.

"How did you, an American, come to be up the Nile as a war correspondent, instead of out in the Philippines?" Margaret asked.

"We go whither we are sent; besides is there any place in the world where you will not meet a Jew or an American, the oldest and the newest products of civilisation? The American journalist is ubiquitous in every city of Europe, like the American artist for the matter of that."

"Do you know many American artists?" she went on.

Gilbert laughed.

"He is the special patron saint of artists. You should see the pretty little articles he has written about their various colonies such as Grez, Concarneau, Newlyn, Broadway. They make him touching offerings of sketches to secure his favour."

"Don't play the fool," Brindle interrupted; then with

a mellifluous change of voice to Margaret:

"Can I place any of my acquired knowledge at your service?"

"Oh, I was only going to ask if you happened to know Mrs. Broderick, who is an artist?"

What is it makes us aware that we have unwittingly cast a bombshell into the conversational circle, even though there is no outward sign of the fact? Whatever it may be, this knowledge came to Margaret in the pause that followed her remark.

Brindle gave one quick inquiring glance at Gilbert and then began to carefully sort out his loose photographs.

Gilbert, who was seated on the stone steps, gave no sign of having heard the question save for a certain troubled pallor that showed itself in his face.

Seeing that he was not going to take the answer on himself, Brindle spoke.

"Oh, Mrs. Broderick dwells in more exalted regions than the Bohemian circles haunted by me. I have seen her, of course, and have written about her pictures and her dress, and her parties, but I have only spoken to her once, I think. You know her, Clinch, don't you?"

"Yes, I think that I may say that we are old friends," Gilbert answered, in even tones. "And you, Miss Nugent, know her, I suppose?" Their eyes met and Margaret saw the hungry yearning that underlay his composed manner.

"Yes, I knew her years ago in France, at the seaside when I was a schoolgirl and before she was married. I adored her then, as little girls do adore such women, and I was overjoyed when she turned up in our neighbourhood at home last autumn."

"In your neighbourhood — that means?"

"On the Thames, near Maidenhead. She took a house and settled down to paint there."

"And she lives there still?" and now there was no mistaking the eager light in Gilbert's eyes.

"She did when I last heard, and I think I should have had a wail from my brother Jack if she had left, or else have heard of him on his travels. He promptly fell down and worshipped at her shrine, did that young man. And she is a great friend of yours, Mr. Clinch?" she asked, with suspicious innocence.

"We have known each other for a long time," he said, quietly. "But after — when she was first in mourning, she had a fancy to leave home without letting her friends know her whereabouts. I am glad to hear about her again. Did she — does she seem strong and well?" he asked, wistfully.

"Oh, she gives one the idea of perfect health. I'm sure she couldn't toil at her painting as she does if she weren't strong," she said, lightly. "But I have some little odds and ends of scribbles of hers that I stole in her studio the other day, in my writing-case over there. Would you care to see them?"

Would he care to see the sunshine and breathe the fresh air? Gilbert was never quite sure what he had said, or if he had said anything, when he held a sheet or two of drawing-paper in his hand, all scribbled over in the dear familiar fashion.

"I saved that one because it had such a good thing of Jack on it," he heard the girl say, and his jealous eyes sought the sketch.

Yes, there it was, only a few pencil outlines, but giving such a vivid suggestion of a stalwart young fellow in riding-dress holding up a biscuit to a begging Irish terrier.

"And it's so good of Mr. Tomkins, too," Meg went on, with a little nervous haste, as Brindle noticed. "I think I must have it framed."

Gilbert was looking closely into the medley that covered the paper like written thoughts. Ah! here was something to show that her mind had not forsaken the past. Flight of butterflies hovering over a row of poppies. He well knew what that meant.

"You say that Mrs. Broderick was painting regularly," he said, looking up abruptly at Margaret.

There was something almost like a flash of anger in her eyes, as she answered:

"Yes, she worked steadily for most of the day, though she never would show us what she was doing."

Ah, she had kept those new friends out of her real, her inner brain-life then! The comfort that he drew from this thought was shattered by Margaret's next speech.

"She dined with us on Christmas night, looking oh, just splendid in the country-dance! And we had some jolly days skating on the meadows before I left. Jack is something a bit out of the common on skates, and they looked so well together."

"Look out, Clinch, those photos will be scattered to the four winds. Give them to me and I'll put them in their case," Brindle said, with a great appearance of concern.

"My dear fellow, you're growing as fussy as an old woman," Gilbert said, rising to hand him the photos. "And now don't you think you've been hung out to air long enough, and had better be conveyed to your own quarters?" Brindle was beginning a protest when a look at Gilbert's face stopped him.

"Perhaps it's best not to overdo it," he said, meekly, and heroically rejecting offers of beef-tea or wine, allowed Gilbert to get him into his chair and to start Felice on the road.

There were few words between them until Brindle had been got to his room and settled down and fed. Then Gilbert said:

"Somehow, the spirit of unrest is on me to-day. If you don't mind, I'll start out into the country, and have a bite at any *trattoria* I come across."

"Off you go; you do look bilious, now that I come to think of it. Just shove the writing things up to me before you go, and I'll try to finish that boy's story. Must keep the pot boiling, you know," Brindle answered, cheerfully.

But when Gilbert was gone, the boy's story remained untouched, and the invalid sat glooming at a highly coloured picture of Victor Emanuele at the battle of San Martino on the opposite wall, as though he owed it a mortal grudge.

"Her kindness to me is all done for his benefit," he said to himself, as though summing up the matter, "while he is thinking of nothing save that wandering 'Lady of Sorrows' of his. I wonder if she saw that he had pocketed that smaller sheet of paper. Well it's the unpleasant way of the world, but Brindle, my good fel-

low, you can play the man even without the use of
your legs, I suppose, and what you have to do is to get
that use back again as quickly as possible. And meantime get this story finished up with ten followers of the
Mahdi killed, and the two English boys rescued — so
here goes."

Meantime Gilbert had taken a steam-tram out into
the country, and when it stopped had wandered up
hillside paths among the olive groves, where here and
there an almond-tree was outlined in pink blossom.

He had the uncomfortably stripped feeling of one
whose dream-life is suddenly overthrown by a rude
touch of reality. Day by day, Isabel Broderick in her
lonely life of work and sorrow had been near to him;
now a curious new sense of isolation came with this
different picture of her. Isabel dancing, skating, amusing herself with strangers, how hard it seemed to
imagine. Had she learnt to depend on this young fellow as once she had depended upon him?

He paused in his stride, struck with a sudden
thought. He had been content to stay away from her,
to let their lives run in different grooves, because he
had felt it necessary for her peace of mind, guessing
that she had morbidly blamed herself for some of
those summer hours by the La Have, but now, if she
could give to another that close companionship that
had been at once his joy and his temptation, did not
the fact free him from the obligation of his self-
imposed exile?

Was he not now free to go and at least enjoy her
comradeship again? It would not content him, he
knew, he had got too far for that, and he knew too

that he should suffer the torments of jealousy, but in his present mood any active unhappiness seemed better than the cold neutrality of separation.

In this new sense of loss, all ambition fell away from him. What would be the use of his fighting for money he did not need, when it was not to be shared with her?

His life would henceforth be one of work, but first, as soon as he could leave Brindle, he would find his way to that English village where she had hidden herself, and would see her face again. That was all at present, just to bear her voice, look into those steadfast eyes again.

Sitting at a table at a wayside inn, after a meal of macaroni and Barola wine, he scanned every line in that sheet of drawing-paper, finding a certain consolation in a vague outline of a net-laden fishing-dory, such as they used to see on the La Have.

Chapter 27

A Dinner Party

When the two young men had left the villa, Margaret
had given them a general invitation to return again,
and on two more mornings they had come, and finding her on the terrace had spent an hour or so in idle
talk.

On the last of these, Margaret had seemed in high
spirits, which she explained by saying: "I'm going to
have a treat to-day, a long, vagabondising afternoon's
ride. Lord Vernade, a neighbour of ours at home, has
brought his horses on from Rome, where he has been
hunting this winter, and when he comes I always get
about the country a lot. It *is* such a change from driving with Granny. By the bye, Mr. Clinch, he met Mrs.
Broderick at our house on Christmas night, and
admired her very much," and she looked at him with
a smile which somehow seemed to-day harder and
more brilliant.

Gilbert immediately of course included Lord
Vernade in the hatred which he felt for the unknown
Jack.

"I am sure he would," he said, evenly, and again
Brindle interposed another topic.

"There's a cold north wind. I think you had better

stay in to-day," Gilbert said one morning, when they had planned to go to the villa. But Brindle was so persistent that Gilbert yielded — after all, his friend was so much better that it could hardly hurt him. There was no broad-brimmed hat to be seen on the terrace, and presently the Italian butler brought out a little three-cornered note addressed to Gilbert.

"We are going for an early ride, and if I am not back by the time you come, please give me a little grace and wait for me, making yourselves quite at home."

"Mademoiselle has found more amusing company," he said, grimly, as he passed the note to his friend.

"And the fine weather is over," the other said, somewhat inconsequently. "See how the laurels are twisting in the wind. Those who can ride and arm their blood have the best of it to-day. A bath-chair is not an exhilarating steed." There was dreariness under the whimsicality of his voice, and again Gilbert urged the prudence of a retreat, but Brindle put him off, until presently, with a little shudder, he said:

"I feel as though the eye of the unseen Gorgon were piercing my back from some window. Let's get home."

The treacherous wind met them in the sunless street, and before night Brindle was in a high fever, and for the next few days all Gilbert's energies were thrown into the old grim fight.

"He'll never have the strength to pull through," he said, on the second day, to the Florentine doctor, but that optimistic person answered with his usual undaunted self-reliance: "Oh, we'll manage it somehow or other."

There were times when the patient's tongue was

loosened by fever, and then he would ask: "Has she written to know where we are?" and one night he kept calling out that she was riding, riding away from him and that he was left alone in the desert to die, and again there were rambling words, of Persephone being carried off to the realms of shadows, which Gilbert could easily interpret.

These worst days were fought down, and now there was nothing but the extreme weakness to be conquered. "Nothing!" Gilbert said, bitterly, as his cheerful colleague announced this opinion.

Frail indeed looked the boyish head against the pillows, all life seeming concentrated in the big eyes.

"Any news of Persephone?" he asked, with a feeble jauntiness that was widely different from the pathos of delirium.

"There's a precious effusion that has just come," Gilbert, said, tossing a note down on the bed. He chose somewhat unreasonably to consider Miss Nugent to blame. The note was from her, saying that she supposed the stormy weather was the cause of their absence from the garden, and giving a message from Madame de Barre to ask Gilbert to dine with them a few days later.

"I am going to send Felice with a refusal when he comes to do the errands," Gilbert said, but straightway his patient waxed excitable, insisting that he would not have his friend stay at home for him, that he must think him about to die or he would accept the chance of bringing him news of the out-side world. He must be soothed down at any cost.

"All right, my dear fellow, I'll go. Yes, you'll be quite

fit by then to leave with the sister. She can't snore your head off in that time. See, I've written to accept. Will that content you? Now shut up and go to sleep."

And Gilbert himself felt rather relieved at being forced into a meeting that might bring him some further tidings of Isabel.

That afternoon he took his usual constitutional through the Cascine, where he met Mrs. Sinnet's carriage. She stopped to speak to him, asking after the invalid and condoling with him on their bad luck.

"You look somewhat ghastly yourself," she commented. "I met Miss Nugent yesterday, and she was asking what had become of you."

"I believe the whole thing was her fault," Gilbert grumbled; "if she hadn't turned his head, he would never have bothered me into letting him sit out that cold morning, and then my lady went off amusing herself elsewhere."

"With Lord Vernade?"

"Yes."

"I declare it is incomprehensible to me —" Mrs. Sinnet was beginning, with energy, when she checked herself, saying, "There they are now."

Down a cross avenue ahead, clearly seen through the young leaf-tips, came a couple, riding. The animation in Margaret's face and voice, the beauty of the horses, the air of quiet distinction about the slim, pale man who bent toward her with such an evident absorption, all made them a noticeable sight.

They passed without even looking round, and Gilbert commented: "So that's Lord Vernade, is it? But I beg your pardon, you were saying?"

"I was merely going to say that I don't see how any decent people can let a girl go about with such a man. Of course, I suppose the excuse that is made for him is that his wife is worse than he is, but that is no reason why Miss Nugent should be seen with him. He's rather a favourite in society, I believe, but I can't bear him. I happened to know a pretty little fool of a woman from home who was bitten with a society craze, and left her husband toiling out there in his office. We both came over in the same steamer with Lord Vernade and — well, in a month or two she went off with him in his yacht. He left her alone and friendless in Naples, and her poor husband had her found and taken home to her mother. And lots of people know that story," she ended, darkly.

"Pretty bad!" Gilbert commented. "I suppose he will be at the dinner on Thursday?"

"Sure to! You're going, are you? Well, I'll see you there, then. *Au revoir!*"

It was into a pretty interior of shaded lights, masses of flowers, and deep-tinted brocades that Gilbert was shown on Thursday evening. His hostess, in purple velvet and amethysts, looked more like an old begum than ever. She sat in her usual armchair by the fire, and the new arrivals went up to and made their greeting to her. There was Lady Vernade, short and somewhat stout, a triumph of art in her masses of golden hair, her blackened eyes, her red lips, her marvellous Parisian gown. Beside her Margaret, in white satin, looked like a school-girl.

There were an old English general and his wife, with a painfully overgrown daughter, the Sinnets, a swarthy, twinkling little Irish priest, and a big cavalry officer in the beautiful blue and silver uniform, whom Gilbert had no difficulty in identifying as the Conte di Ripamonti, and lastly, lazily observant, there was Lord Vernade.

"What mischief can Miss Nugent be up to, to look so demure?" Mrs. Sinnet said to Gilbert. "It can't be much, as I am to take her in," he answered.

"Well, I trust that you are content with your fate?" the girl said to him, as they settled in their places.

"I am more. I am immensely flattered."

"Oh, you needn't think that you were my choice. I never have any voice in the matter. It was Granny's mandate."

"Well, then, I may repeat your own remark and hope that you are content."

"I'll decide that after I see how you treat me. But tell me, how is Mr. Brindle?"

"He has been at death's door since I saw you last," was his sombre answer.

A beautiful light of pity softened her face.

"Oh, I did not know. I never guessed from your note that it had been as bad as that. Tell me how it all happened?"

In spite of her appealing eyes, Gilbert was pitiless.

"It all happened because a certain young fool, having had his head turned by a lovely siren, would go out in a cold wind, and when he was disappointed in finding her, would wait on in the hopes that she might come — that's how it all happened."

There was no answer, and he turned his head to see the dark velvety eyes brimming with tears.

The sight checked him.

"Pardon me, if I have been too bold," he said.

The tears were brushed away with feminine skill.

"You have been too hard, I think," she said, somewhat proudly. "If I tried to be kind to your friend it was merely because I was sorry for him. How could I have any idea that he would make more of it?"

"You are right. How could you? But you see I am rather a bull in the social china-shop. You must forgive my awkwardness."

"You said what you thought, but I would like you to think better of me. Won't you promise to try to believe that I meant no harm?"

Gilbert was conquered by the frankness of her words.

"What is more, I will believe it on the spot," he answered, with a smile. "You must forgive me, for too much sickroom has made me grumpy, though I trust that we are over the worst now. But tell me about yourself. You have been riding a good deal, haven't you? I saw you one day in the Cascine."

"Did you? Yes, it is a bit of a holiday for me when Lord Vernade comes, and the fun of it is that these rides of ours have quite upset the Ripamonti faction. My matrimonial prospects are down to zero," and she laughed as though she found the fact an exhilarating one.

"Against Italian etiquette, I suppose? But I wonder that, in that case, your grandmother has not put her foot down."

"No, the queer thing is," and here she lowered her voice, "that Granny seems rather off the idea. Now a month ago, if he hadn't taken me in to dinner, he would have been placed well in view of my charms, whereas now I have to strain my neck around the corner to see him flirting with Lady Vernade. He is evidently delighted with her."

"He must be fond of art, then," Gilbert said, dryly. "But he's a big, handsome fellow."

"He's just my idea of a Roman gladiator," she said, and Gilbert looked down the table to note the appositeness of the comparison. Here Lady Ogilvie, the English general's wife, turned to him, saying: "I believe that you are an American?"

"I fear that I must plead guilty," he answered, with a smile that puzzled that lady. She did not know that her tone had been that of one graciously condoning an error.

"I have passed several years in the West Indies when my husband was a colonel," she announced, and I must say that I grew very fond of the life."

"Some day I mean to go all around the West Indies. Granny —" Margaret began, in a slightly raised voice.

Gilbert saw the bent head of the hostess turn with a bright glance from under the heavy eyelids, and the sign for the ladies to leave the table was given.

He had noticed once or twice through the evening that the sharp eyes of the little Irish priest sitting opposite had seemed to be studying him, and now the latter lost no time in beginning a conversation.

Starting with a casual remark on the beauties of Florence, Gilbert found himself being led on to tell of his friend's illness, the delay in their departure, and his earlier studies in Vienna.

"It is some time then since you left America?" Father Kehoe asked.

"Only last August, although it seems much longer," he answered, half to himself.

"And your summers are so hot that I suppose you had not been in Boston then?"

"Oh, we workers have to stand the heat as best we can. But as it happens I spent the early summer on the Nova Scotian coast in charge of a patient. I am an alienist, you know," Gilbert found himself saying.

"Ah, a sad and yet an interesting work. And your patient recovered?"

"No, I regret to say that I was obliged to get him back to an asylum. It was an unusually sad case." His desire to close the subject was evident, and his questioner acknowledged it.

"And perhaps I have disturbed you by leading you to speak of it. Pardon me. And now, gentlemen, I am charged by our hostess to shepherd you into the drawing-room."

Gilbert had a certainty that the reverend father had been pumping him, though he could not imagine why. But it did not seem to matter at all. Old women of both sexes are often inquisitive with strangers.

Chapter 28

The Borderland

After dinner Gilbert was standing talking to Mrs.
Sinnet when Margaret crossed the room toward him,
followed by Lord Vernade.

"Lord Vernade would like to know you, Mr. Clinch,"
she said.

There was no doubt that the man's quiet smile was
attractive when he chose it to be so.

"Miss Nugent tells me that you come from across
the water," he began. "I was A. D. C. in Ottawa in my
young days, and used often to run down to
Washington to see a cousin there, so I know a little
more of the country than most Englishmen do. But
what I like best are the Rockies, where I've been once
or twice shooting."

"I have never been farther west than Michigan,"
Gilbert answered, in a non-committal fashion, unwilling to establish any bond of interest by acknowledging
himself to be a Canadian.

"Miss Nugent tells me that you are a friend of Mrs.
Broderick's," Lord Vernade began again. "Charming
woman. Can't understand her staying in that damp
hole all winter. She is rich, isn't she?"

Gilbert flushed angrily at the careless question.

"I believe that she is comfortably off," he answered, stiffly.

"She looks it," turning to the girl, "I must get Lady Vernade to call and persuade her to give us a week's end in the spring. Such a dark horse would create a sensation amongst a party from town, eh?"

Margaret laughed, and Gilbert caught a mocking gleam in her eyes.

"You will be stirring up Jack's evil passions," she said.

"Master Jack must be content with his share," was the retort, and Gilbert turned away to stand for a moment contemplating the party with profound disgust. A stir of departure relieved him, but as he said his good-night, he was detained by his hostess.

"Your patient's relapse will detain you longer in Florence, I hear," she said, fixing her beady eyes on him.

"Not much longer, I hope," he answered, with sudden resolution. "If he goes on improving I shall leave him with a nurse under Doctor Balder's charge."

The old lady shook her head and scowled.

"You ought to stay here and enjoy the spring-time. I will get you invitations to the after-Easter balls if you like."

"You are very good," he said, making his escape, bewildered by this uncalled-for amiability.

"Queer enough people!" he said to himself, as he emerged into the soft starlit night to walk home. Yes, he was determined, he would see Isabel Broderick before any of those other people got back to form a circle around her.

Two or three days later, while these plans were still

unspoken, he returned from a walk to find Brindle
looking unusually excited.

He hardly waited for Gilbert to close the door
before beginning.

"Balder has been here and I've stolen a march on
you. He says that considering the lateness of the season, and the creditable fashion in which I've pulled
up, he sees no risk in taking the journey through to
Paris. A night train, a Pullman, and no stoppages, he
recommends. What do you say to that?"

"I say that you are both crazy," was the answer, but
after more or less of discussion and a little delay, the
plan was carried through, and Gilbert felt a weight off
his mind when he saw his friend safely settled in quiet
sunny rooms overlooking the Luxembourg gardens.
When he had gone to leave a farewell card at the Villa
della Biscia he had not been admitted, and Brindle
had shown no desire for any further communication.

And so the episode seemed closed.

Just before leaving Florence Gilbert had had a letter
from the London solicitor promising to procure him
information as to his uncle's family and fashion of life,
but warning him that any contest over the estate
might entail a costly expenditure. "A will signed during the last days of illness, unknown to nearest relatives, might be open to a strong suspicion of undue
influence," he said, going on to advise the establishment of friendly relations with his kinsfolk.

"There's a sample of English caution for you,"
Brindle said, contemptuously, after reading the letter;
"take my advice and have nothing to do with any
Englishman in the matter. Whatever you do, do it

from your own side of the water."

"I don't feel much like doing anything at present."

"That's the trouble," Brindle grumbled, taking care, however, to make no sign as to what subject he supposed to be monopolising his friend's mind.

Paris was full of friends and comrades of hot men, and as they flocked to Brindle's room, smoking and exchanging yarns until Gilbert turned them out, Brindle ungratefully said:

"Florentine sunshine is all very well, but this is living instead of vegetating. The very air of Paris stirs up one's brains like an egg-beater."

"Rather disastrous to the gray matter, I should think," Gilbert commented.

It was the season when, from all over France, from seacoast and woodland villages where they have been toiling at their pictures, the artists flock to Paris to receive their meed of success or failure from their peers, for France is of all countries in the world that in which an intellectual effort is most judged by the inner circles of its craft. Many of these men were Americans, and Gilbert and Brindle were welcomed in studios up on the Clichy heights, or in their own Luxembourg quarter. And amid all the talk Gilbert kept careful watch for the sound of one name, for any hint of one presence in the swarming city. Of course there were many hours spent in the salons, in an inspection of pictures that did not overtask Brindle's strength, and in long talks over "bocks" and cigarettes in the restaurant.

One of these days, Gilbert, having deposited Brindle in a comfortable seat, went for a later tour of the rooms with a quiet Boston artist, a man to whom success had come after his whole nature had been hopelessly depressed by long striving.

"I suppose you've seen one of our American successes, 'The Borderland'?" the artist asked.

"Not that I remember."

"There it is," said the other, and as Gilbert looked across the room, he could have sworn that he was the victim of an hallucination, for there on the wall, its colours palpitating in the clear light, was the mystic picture that he had watched growing under the hands of a maniac, the picture that he had seen lying in shreds on the floor of the country barn studio.

Some instinct of caution, following on his first amazement, made him check the word of surprise on his lips.

As he stood, staring in utter bewilderment, he heard his friend's voice going on: "By the bye, I think that you knew him and his wife — Andrew Broderick, I mean. Sad story, wasn't it? They say he had just finished it before he had to be taken to the asylum."

Still Gilbert stared in silence.

"Come over to it. I want to look at it close," he said, and crossing the room, he peered intently into the work. No, it was in some places painted thinly enough to show the warp of the canvas, and there was no trace of any join or repairs. It could not by any possibility be the same picture that he had seen stabbed and trampled upon.

The name was signed in small printed scarlet letters such as he had often noticed on some finished pictures in Broderick's studio, and the date was that of the past year. What did it possibly mean!

"Let's see your catalogue," he said, turning to the other man, who was watching him in a somewhat perplexed fashion.

It was apparently all simple enough.

"Le Pays des Rêves" was the French title, to which the English one of "The Borderland" did not literally correspond. The artist's name was given, "Andrew Broderick, American, pupil of Carolus Duran," address a well-known London picture-dealer.

With a strong effort at the commonplace, Gilbert said: "Yes, I often saw him working at this picture, but I did not know that he had quite finished it. You have not heard, I suppose, of any recent recovery?"

"No, and I fancy if there had been I should have known of it, for this picture has been one of the art topics of the day. But look here, Brindle will be waiting in the restaurant. Shall we go?"

"If you will go and help him to a cab, I think I'll stay here and prowl among the pictures for a bit longer," he answered, gladly hailing the chance of solitude.

When his friend left him, Gilbert seated himself on a bench in front of "The Borderland" and gave himself up to its contemplation.

There was all the brilliancy of technique and the force of the destroyed picture, and yet the longer he looked, the more persuaded Gilbert felt that it was not the work of the same hand. Especially in the figure in the corner of the foreground, that stood raising its veil with one hand, was here a mystical touch which had been absent in the other.

And then he recalled the history of that figure, how

it had at first formed no part of Broderick's composition, but painted by Isabel on a smaller canvas had been copied into his own work by her husband.

Did it really mean that Isabel, a woman broken down under the shock of a hastly tragedy, had had the courage and power to paint this virile masterpiece? It seemed a hardly possible idea, and yet the longer he thought, the more he felt that it was the only explanation.

Absorbed in the picture and the thought it caused, he paid small attention to the increasing crowd, until a familiar voice beside him broke in on his reverie.

"I thought it was Gilbert Clinch when I saw what you were studying so earnestly." Turning, he saw the grizzled hair and shrewd, kindly face of the Brodericks' doctor.

"What, are you holiday-making like all the world?" he said, as they shook hands.

"Yes, only as you see, I don't find it so easy to get away from the affairs of my patients. A sort of father confessor, a family doctor. But of course in this case you are behind the scenes too?"

And he directed his words with a wave of his hand and a glance toward the picture.

Gilbert had sometimes wondered how much those shrewd eyes had noted of the intimacy between himself and Mrs. Broderick on that tragical homecoming, and he now walked warily.

"If you mean the Brodericks' affairs, I have heard nothing about them since I left home last August," he said, quietly "I have been grinding in Vienna all winter, you know, and seem to have got out of touch with home news. Still, though I cannot claim to be behind the scenes, I will acknowledge to you that this picture has filled me with amazement. I saw its duplicate that Andrew Broderick had painted, torn into shreds by him in his first fit of violent mania — would to God that I had taken the warning in time. I know that in all probability he could never have recovered sufficiently to have painted this one, and yet here I see it before me, as splendid a piece of work as Broderick could ever have turned out. Who painted it? The only possible answer seems to me too improbable, and I give it up."

Doctor Slater's twinkling eyes looked into his with a concentrated extract of meaning in them.

"If a theory is utterly and palpably improbable, then you may be sure it is the correct solution," was his oracular comment.

"Then you really think that she painted it?" Gilbert said, as though answering a spoken word.

"I don't think, I know that she did; though, mind you, she has never said so to me in words, and I would let no one save you know it. I never dreamt of your not guessing it at once."

"I did guess it, though not at once. But it seemed too wonderful."

"You may well say that. The strain upon her nerves for weeks must have been something like sitting day by day painting her dead. And yet to-day she is a stronger and more serene woman for having done it. The work has somehow satisfied a need of her conscience or heart."

Gilbert left the last sentence unheeded.

"To-day?" he stammered. "You don't mean —" and paused.

"Didn't you know that she is in Paris?" The quiet words steadied him. For her sake he must not reveal the tumult of his spirit, even to this old seer of household tragedies.

"I only came from Florence a day or two ago, you know," he said. "But if you will give me her address I should like to go and see her."

"You'd like to? Poor wretch! You won't know one happy moment until you do," the old doctor commented inwardly. His spoken words were more commonplace: "The Stacys have lent her their house, 'Passage Lamartine, Rue de la Pompe, Passy;' you will find her there most evenings, I fancy."

"Thanks. And Broderick — what news have you of him?"

The doctor shook his head.

"He is — as you predicted — a gloomy and dangerous maniac, encircled with as many precautions as any poor wretch in the place. In his worst moments he thinks he is kept down in hell-fire by demons with whom he struggles while his strength lasts, and then sinks back into coma."

"The same leading idea. That's what comes from an ancestry of Calvinist divines," Gilbert commented; then, hesitating a moment, asked: "Does Howard think him likely to live?"

The doctor's eyes were intent on a strikingly dressed Parisienne as he answered.

"I asked him that just before I sailed, in case she — And it's the same old thing: no reason he shouldn't live as long as any of us. But really, that's more in your line than mine. Well, I must be off. See you to-night at the minister's, perhaps."

"Perhaps," Gilbert answered, and the doctor first chuckled to himself and then sighed as he walked away.

Chapter 29

"Our Hands Have Met"

The broad, quiet Passy street in the yellow evening light, a passage where a row of bright little houses looked across at the blossoming fruit-trees in a convent garden, an upstairs drawing-room, and a gray figure rising from a seat by the window, while a voice that set Gilbert's heart leaping madly, said: "It is you, then?"

All he could think of to say as he held her hand was: "You got my *petit bleu*?" The low laugh he had loved to hear, greeted this.

"Naturally, as I answered it. But come, sit down by the window and talk."

"But I can't see you in this twilight," he objected.

"Ah, surely you don't want to shut out the evening! You shall have lights by and by." But all the same she moved her chair enough for the yellow glow to fall on the dear familiar face, showing Gilbert that the old shadow of suppressed dread was gone from her eyes, which, though sad, were serene.

"You have done your hair differently," he criticised. Truly this was hardly the manner of a hopeless lover or a dignified professional man.

"That might be expected in all but a year's time. But

surely you have something more interesting to say than that?" she smiled back.

"Forgive me. I am bewildered by all that I would say." Then in a graver note, "I was at the Salon to-day, and saw the 'Pays des Rêves.' I like that name better than 'The Borderland.'"

"So do I. And you understood? You did not blame me for the deception?" Her voice was low and troubled.

"Blame you! I thought it the most magnificent feat woman ever accomplished. I thought I understood that it was done as the last of all the help you had given him, the help to complete his career."

"You always understand what I mean," she said, restfully.

Conquering his great desire to take her in his arms, he went on: "And it did not injure your health? You had no one to care for that while you were going through such an ordeal?"

"I think being alone made me stronger, and if I were tired it was only with the healthy tiredness of work done. There was the satisfaction of being able to do it, you know," she said, simply.

"Yes, I can understand that. I have so hungered to know how it was faring with you, and never until a-few weeks ago in Florence have I heard even your name."

"You heard of me? I thought no one knew?" she asked in surprise.

"And that was from strangers whom you had not kept at a distance as you did your friends. It was Miss Nugent who told me of your English home and the life you led there."

Isabel leaned forward in her deep chair.

"Do you mean Margaret Nugent, who lives in Florence with her grandmother?" she asked.

"Madame de Barre? Yes, I dined with them."

"And you don't know who they are?" It was Gilbert's turn to be surprised now.

"I know that the grandmother is an old hag who is trying to marry the girl to a big ox-like Italian officer, and that the girl would have a fine nature if it got a chance. She seems devoted to you."

He could not see how pale the calm face had grown as she went on: "And you don't know that that girl is your cousin, Margaret Nugent-Barr, and the old woman is the West Indian wife whom old Isaac used to talk about."

Gilbert sat for a moment assimilating this fact.

"Good heavens! what a fool I was not to take it in sooner. And I had a letter yesterday from my uncle, Mr. Nugent-Barr of Monk's Grange, and even then I never saw it. But — why do they have all this fantastic dividing up of names?" he said, irritably.

"It's simple enough, the way Jack explained it to me one day," she said, unheeding the arrow she planted in Gilbert's breast. "They took the mother's maiden name of Nugent to please her father, as he had no sons. The German Bauer was softened down into Barr when they went to live in England. Then the old lady, reverting with her Continental life to her old French ways, branched out into Madame de Barre de Fer-de-Lance."

"It's as fantastic as a comic opera," Gilbert insisted. "And why, if the family is Nugent-Barr in England, was the girl called Miss Nugent in Florence?"

"Just accident, I think. She told me that the people there never had got into the way of using the double name. Jack and she always laugh at it a bit."

Again that familiar mention of a stranger.

"You like this brother and sister, don't you?" he asked, gloomily.

"Yes, they went out of the way from the first to be kind to me, and when I was tired their coming seemed to bring a breeze of young life that blew away the cobwebs. I was very solitary when they found me out."

"You need not have been. It was your own choice that made you dependent on the kindness of strangers," he broke out, in irrepressible reproach.

"Sometimes strangers are the easiest to begin again with," she said, gently, "though now they are not strangers but friends."

"I see."

"And you, you have written to their father, you say?"

"Yes, and I have just had a cordial enough answer, inviting me to come and stay with them. Strange to say, he makes no mention of my meeting them in Florence, and yet now that I think of it I'm sure the old lady knew who I was, and would naturally have written to her son."

"What makes you think that?"

"Well, even her granddaughter noticed the queer sort of interest she seemed to take in me, and Mrs. Sinnet told me that she had been pumping her about me. Yes, it all fits in. She called me Mr. Gilbert Clinch one day when I couldn't imagine how she had got hold of it. Then at dinner a little priest, who seemed

a tame cat of the house, asked me a lot of questions —
yes, and she gave me the girl to take in —"

He checked himself, following out the recollection
of how Margaret had said that her grandmother had
suddenly lost interest in the Ripamonti match.

"Well, at any rate, if the old lady is up to any
schemes, her granddaughter is ignorant of them," he
said, decisively.

"I am sure that she would always be what is honest
and frank," Isabel agreed, while a little quickly caught
sigh told of the last hope wrecked. Yes, it would be better, surely be better that he should marry his cousin
and thus come peaceably into his inheritance, and yet
—"

"And you will go among them and make friends with
these new kinsfolk of yours?" she asked, presently.

"I want to try to make friends with them, but I don't
feel as though I should care to stay in their house. The
obligations of the salt, you know. If afterward it should
come to a fight —"

"Then you have decided nothing as yet?"

"No," he said, uneasily. "I never was supposed to
lack decision before, and yet somehow I feel myself a
weak, vacillating creature in this. It seems a cold-
blooded sort of business, to attack what people have
enjoyed for fifteen years or so, when one doesn't really need the money, and has no one but oneself. You
see the sale of the treasure-trove gave me enough to
free me from drudgery, and for an occasional holiday.
The rest I can earn for myself. Of course, I can't say
that this mood is permanent, but then I do feel that
way at present. Tell me," he went on, leaning forward

earnestly, "it would pain you to see these friends of yours losing some of their pretty surroundings, wouldn't it?"

"Yes, I think I should be sorry, for them, but still that is no reason —"

"Oh, yes, it is," he interrupted, recklessly, "if you like, I will make you a promise now and settle the matter —"

"No, no," she checked him, "you shall make no such promise to me. You may feel sometime that it is best to claim your rights. Leave the question open."

"Well, remember that it is your doing!" he said.

"And now tell me, I should like to go and stay somewhere in your neighbourhood where I could get to know these new relations and yet keep my independence. Do you know of any country inn or lodgings near you, where Brindle and I could put up? He needs some quiet country life before he goes back to work again. The plan is of course subject to your approval. We shouldn't bother you, should we?"

Unheeding the wistfulness in his words, she felt rather hurt at their doubt, but only said, quietly: "That's hardly likely, is it? Yes, I think it is a very good plan, and I know just the place for you. A little cottage quite near my house, with a nice old woman used to boating men and artists. She will delight in feeding up your friend, and the air is high and pure."

As she spoke, she was seeing quick mind-pictures of long summer twilights together again, and then the pictures broke away like a shattered mirror before the thought of Margaret's young smile. It would be best for him.

"I'm sending a note home to-night, and if you like, I'll tell them to engage the rooms for you," she added.

"Thank you so much. In ten days we should be there. And you? You will be at home by then?"

"Oh, I go back at the end of the week, and shall be waiting to greet you."

"No greeting could be as good as that," he said, forgetting his role of resignation.

There was a silence save for the distant street noises, and dreamy waltz music from a neighbouring window.

"Well, I suppose I must go and see if Brindle's all right," Gilbert said, unwillingly. "But mightn't we have a gleam of light before I go?" he urged.

"How pertinacious you are!" and she reached out her hand to touch the button that flooded the room with a soft glow.

They had both risen, and as Gilbert stood looking into her face he almost thought that he saw a blush pass over it.

He could not help it, he must strike a more personal note before he left her.

"You do not mind my coming? You are glad that we have met?" he said, impulsively.

A mist of tears came over her eyes as she said: "Oh, how could I but be glad to see the truest, best friend woman ever had? You must always, whatever happens, be sure of that."

The "whatever happens" struck cold on his heart. Did it mean that even if in a happier future she were to marry Jack she would always be his friend? With a husky "God bless you" he left her, to walk for more than an hour the Paris streets.

Twice again they met before Isabel left Paris, once at a crowded reception at the American minister's, when it was a case of –

"Maud in all her splendour."

It was years since he had seen her thus, in the glow of white satin and pearls, observed among groups of fashionable women and well-known men, and, save for the half-hour she kept for him, he was content to stand and watch her as a beautiful apparition.

Their second meeting was an afternoon which they spent together among the young greenery of the St. Cloud woods, with the garlic blossoms shining white on the ground, and the mysterious call of the cuckoo echoing from the forest depths.

By mutual consent they avoided all topics that might be painful, Gilbert telling her of his studies in Vienna, while she spoke of her long effort of work, of having brought the picture to Paris in March, and of its immediate success.

"And now that the habit of steady work has taken hold of me, I could never be an idler again. I have a dozen projects ahead, for when I get home."

"Ah, but you must spare me some lazy hours," he urged.

They were standing at her door to say good night.

"As many as you will want, I expect," she answered, with a wistful smile, and before he could quite understand what she meant, she added: "Good-bye now, or rather *au revoir* until the fifteenth."

He watched her into the house and up the stairs

before he turned away, a passion of useless longing at his heart. Oh, if only she were free he would not let this Jack, or any other man, take her from him without a struggle.

Chapter 30

Heathholm

Mrs. Broderick was at home at Heathholm again, enjoying the blossoming time of her little kingdom, trying to keep down troublesome thoughts by a system of steady work.

The sight of the Paris Salon, the art talk in the air, had stirred her creative faculties, and the very day after her arrival she began to paint. Every morning she drove down to a certain reed-fringed meadow, where, on the river-bank, she posed a favourite, flaxen-haired, lanky, sixteen-year-old model. In a loose dress of blue-gray muslin, with bare feet overhanging the water, a long green reed in her hand, the girl, in the bucolic calm of her stupidity, gave a fair enough idea of the mystic stream-maiden, Undine. Stupidity often looks as though it were evolving the soul it does not possess.

She usually took her lunch with her, returning in time to dress before tea. It was a perfect afternoon, and she had had tea taken out under the shade of a walnut-tree in the garden, where she could sit in a deep hammock-chair and look down at the sea of white cherry and plum blossoms on the hill-side below.

"Only two more days to the fifteenth, and how Gilbert will enjoy it all," she thought to herself, the air sleepy with the droning of a big bee.

The stillness was broken by the sounds of wheels, the yapping of a terrier, the click of the gate, and the sound of footsteps.

Lazily raising her head, she saw the very smart apparition of Margaret, dressed in the latest Parisian arrangement of pale green and black, and waving a red sunshade toward her, as she called out:

"Here is your own bad penny back again, you see! Don't look so amazed. Didn't you know I was coming?"

"Now, how could I? I went to call on your mother the other day, but she —"

"Had neuralgia, of course," put in Meg.

"But I am glad to see you, and how smart you are!"

"I thought I'd give you a treat before I fell back on shirts and tweed skirts again. You yourself aren't amiss," with an appreciative glance at Isabel's white serge. "And then it seems I'm not likely to get much chance of wearing my smart town clothes this year. Granny is laid up with gout at Aix with no chance, the doctor says, of getting away for two months or so, and my father says he won't foot the bills, so farewell to my London season."

"Are you disappointed?"

"Well, I don't exactly fancy dropping out of the swim, you know. The waters so soon close over one's head. For the matter of that, I suppose I'll come in for odds and ends with various people. But it all seems queer, somehow. Granny was in such a desperate hurry to get to England a month earlier than usual, and then, when she got laid up, she was in a great stew; nothing would content her but packing me off home with a maid, and, now that I am here, they want me to do nothing but poke about at home, instead of every one making a fuss about my prospects for the season. I don't understand it, and I hate things I don't understand," she ended.

Isabel was used to soothing the girl's little humours.

"I dare say it is simple enough. They would probably rather not have you go out with strangers, and think that you have had a good deal of variety," she said.

"My father ought to take a town-house like other people. I tell you what," with sudden vehemence, "I believe it's this friend of yours, the new-found cousin, that has upset them so."

The eyes of the two women met, both eager to read the other's thoughts, while defending their own. Isabel was the first to speak.

"What fantastic ideas you do get! Why should poor Mr. Clinch upset any one?" she said, as lightly as possible.

"That's just the question. It struck me that 'poor Mr. Clinch' was very well able to take care of himself. He snubbed me dreadfully in Florence. But, tell me, he's a great friend of yours, isn't he?"

"Never woman had a better one," Isabel answered, out of the loyalty of her heart.

"And were you surprised to hear that he was our cousin?" came the question.

"Not altogether. Something your brother said after you left me made me think it possible."

"I wonder you didn't tell him then."

Isabel had a queer feeling of being on her trial, and laughed it off with: "What a cross-examiner you would make. I thought it best not to interfere in Mr. Clinch's affairs. And now tell me about your Florence winter. You're not engaged to that Italian marquis yet?"

Margaret laughed gleefully.

"No, and Granny had such a lovely spider-web of plans for an alliance with the Ripamonti — old Piedmontese nobility with actually pots of money behind them. The man himself looked like a prize-fighter, but that didn't seem to count. Granny and Mamma Ripamonti had their heads together for weeks, and then all of a sudden the whole thing dropped. I never found out the reason, whether they were shocked at my riding all about the country with Lord Vernade, or whether — She hesitated a moment. "Do you know, I sometimes think the cousin upset that, too," she ended, flushing vividly.

Isabel did her best to hide that she was startled, as she asked: "How could that be, if neither he nor you knew?"

"I have thought since that Granny knew, she was so queer. Still," looking half-defiantly at her friend, "she could hardly want me to marry an American doctor." For an instant their eyes met, and Isabel, feeling the stab of jealousy, had guessed the girl's secret. Yes, it was all working out toward the suitable ending, and who was she to wish it otherwise?

Paling a little, she said, with a smile: "Thank you. You see we, who know no better, are apt to consider an American doctor good enough for most people."

"Oh, you know what I mean. Granny's ideas of a grand snatch, and all that. And how soon is the cousin to appear, do you know?" and again Isabel felt that new hostile element in her glance.

"He asked me to engage his rooms for the fifteenth," she said.

"Oh, and Jack will be here at the end of the week, so it will be a gathering of the clans. He told me to be sure to get you to come up to Hurley on Sunday. We shall have the cousin and his friend, I suppose, and Tommy Curtis is with us, had down for Jack's benefit, so that makes six. You remember the little wretch on Christmas night? And, by the bye, I promised to get back early for a game of tennis, so farewell," and the young woman was off, leaving Isabel much to think about.

"There is nothing left to me save my dignity. Whatever comes, I must not lose that," she murmured to herself, presently.

The first chill of the evening dew seemed in the air, and, rising with a shiver, she went into the studio, where she stood long in contemplation of her day's work.

"I could not have done it a year ago, and surely that is something," she thought.

It seemed as though she had need to call in all her forces for the fight.

"The bovine calm of the English meadows is already stealing over my spirit. I feel as though, a little more of it, and I would stand and chew the cud like those big red-brown beasts," Brindle said, as the Great

Western train took the two friends through the quiet riverside country.

"Well, a little more stolidity would do your character no harm," Gilbert retorted. "And look here, I hope you won't make a fool of yourself over that young woman any more."

There was a touch of real anxiety in his voice which Brindle took very lightly.

"Persephone? No, she may go to — Hades for me. Not that I sha'n't flirt with her if I get the chance — I always do that on principle — but surely I know my duty better to the *jeune première* when the *jeune première* is round. I should expect to die in the second act if I didn't."

"I wish you'd get over that silly habit of talking as though all the world were a stage —"

"Well, we have the immortal bard's authority for it, anyway. But to revert to that little temporary weakness of mine for Persephone — can't you see that it was a phase of the illness, like the eruption of measles?"

"Well, have it so, then," Gilbert answered, half-convinced.

The next two days were momentous ones in his life. Every place and action were of interest; the drive up steep hillsides to the cottage among the fruit-trees; the kind old landlady's voluble account of how "the lady" had said that the gentlemen must have this or that; that the evening's sight of Isabel in the harmonious of her own home, recalling his visit to her in Boston; the next day's walk through the woods and across the meadows and park walls of Monk's Grange, "that slurred the sunshine half a mile."

"I felt like a small boy had up for apple stealing," he said, later, when over a pipe he told the tale of the day to Brindle. "The whole place was as severe as a prison. The butler took me into custody and handed me over to his master in a mouldy-aired study. The man did his best to greet me properly, but there wasn't an ounce of warmth in him — a shrivelled, neutral-tinted, peevish, fishy sort of a man —"

"Save a few epithets, anyway."

"He evidently knew very little about my mother, or his father's earlier days; said Madame de Barre would remember this or that, and it was a pity she was not here. He had heard of our having met in Florence. All through I had an impression that he was somehow afraid of committing himself, and was acting under orders. I suspect that the old Gorgon is really the ruling spirit all round. After he had done the civil for a bit, he made a move to take me into the drawing-room, and there was the mother, an amiable nonentity huddled in a shawl, and your Persephone with the air of a convent schoolgirl. Every now and then she made polite little remarks, when I felt as though she were making fun of me. She thawed, though, when just before lunch the brother came in. Jove, that's a fine young fellow! The best type of the man who hasn't had a struggle for existence. It makes one think what our own lives might have been without the early grimness."

"Haven't I thought, when I've seen the manliness of those gilded youths up the Nile! I used to console myself by thinking we mightn't have had so much grit but for the struggle. Well, how did he treat you?"

"Frankly and honestly, with an open curiosity that had nothing offensive in it. I felt at once the blood tie with him."

"And not with Persephone?"

"Well, yes, perhaps after a bit, when we were sitting outside, just the brother and sister and I. They are very jolly together, the two."

"Better not feel that blood tie too strongly. It might stand in your way if you decided to make a fight of it, and then if you did the other thing, it might stand in your way even more."

"I wish something stood in the way of your being an ass."

"Such criticism is always the fate of the Greek chorus, I fancy. And now," as Gilbert rose, "I suppose you are off to report at Heathholm?"

"Yes, will you come?"

"No, thank you," with commendable dulness. "I shall toil at my sanguinary yarns. There seems a good demand for them just now."

"Oh, I forgot" — lingering, — "they want us to spend Sunday on the river with them. Mrs. Broderick will be going. I shall get a canoe to-morrow."

"All right, my son." Then, as Gilbert left the room: "The plot thickens!"

Chapter 31

"A Day in June"

When six people, three couples, are to spend a day in boats or carriages, it is evident that not every one can attain to their ideal position.

Perhaps on this perfect Sunday morning when they all started for Hurley, the brother and sister had, as old inhabitants and organisers of the feast, the best chance of carrying out their wishes.

Certainly Jack in his double-scull skiff looked very handsome and happy, rowing stroke with Mrs. Broderick steering opposite him, while Miss Tommy Curtis plied the bow oar, with Brindle behind her.

"An invalided man has no place in the scheme of creation," the latter said, gloomily, as he watched the rhythm of her arms, but he soon cheered up under her bubbling stream of chatter.

Gilbert had at first nourished hopes of getting Isabel to himself in the canoe, but those hopes withered when, on paddling up to the Monk's Grange landing, he found her already installed in Jack's boat, while that youth hailed him with a cheerful demand that he should deposit Brindle in the bow of the skiff and take Margaret in the canoe. The latter settled down on the cushions, a mass of flowered muslins, tilting a lace parasol between her and the sun.

Gilbert chuckled grimly.

"Look at Brindle's wistful face. I wish I could have taken him in here."

"Oh, you couldn't do that. Tommy must have somebody to talk to, and Jack wouldn't hear a word she said, *now*," was her comment.

Well, if his cousin chose to scorch his wings in an unattainable flame it was no business of his, Gilbert thought to himself, while Margaret went on: "Now you look your natural self again. I don't know which had the most priggish and uncomfortable air the other day, you or my father."

"I seemed to have that effect upon you all," he said, somewhat bitterly.

"Oh, no, *please* don't think us horrid. Jack took a great fancy to you, and said no end of nice things about you that night at dinner," she urged.

"And did you play the part of devil's advocate?" he asked, more amiably.

"Not if it is anything that isn't pleasant. Really, you understand that Jack and I want to be friends with you, don't you?"

"Yes, thanks, I do feel sure of that. Then your father didn't fancy me much?"

"I think it was the story of the jewelled image that upset him," she answered, frankly; then with childish glee, "And, oh, won't it set Granny frantic?"

"Are they so fond of money then?"

"Well, I suppose most people are. I am, I know. Not to save up, but to spend on all the pretty things I see. Oh, dear, I hope Granny will soon come back and pay my bills. My father would have a fit if he saw them, but Granny never minds."

Gilbert was silent, meditating on this novel view of the girl's character.

"There," she said, "do you see that big house above the weir? That's Lord Vernade's. They have a lot of people down for Sunday and sent over this morning to get me to go up to Henley in the launch, but of course I wouldn't leave our cosy little party," with an upward glance from under the parasol.

"That's very amiable of you. I hope you don't repent."

"Oh, I dare say it would have been fun, but then somehow Jack's not overfond of the Vernades – thinks them a bit rapid, you know," mischievously.

"I don't wonder," was his energetic answer. "If you were my sister I should have very strong opinions on the subject."

A soft little laugh greeted this statement.

"But then I'm not your sister, you see," she said, and something in the eyes and voice rather dazzled him.

"How quietly and quickly you paddle," she said, and after a pause. "You don't look like the other people here do. You kneel upright and hardly raise your paddle. Is that the American way?"

"It is the way I learnt from Indians on the St. Lawrence. I certainly never saw *them* lie back against cushions and wave their paddles, like, a spoon helping porridge. I suppose that's the English way."

"Don't be supercilious! How could we be expected to paddle like Indians!" she retorted.

"No, the English mind is hardly imaginative enough

to grasp the fact that if the Indian evolved the canoe, he is most likely to understand the best way of getting it along."

"Do leave us poor English alone!" she pleaded.

"'Us' poor English? I thought you were a Canadian!"

"An English Canadian, the same as you are an American Canadian. Betwixt us two there is a great gulf fixed."

Gilbert was silent, realising how much more of a gulf there was between them than she guessed — the blood of the Martinique brown woman, and all that it implied.

"You didn't mind my saying that?" came a timid voice. "You look so grave."

"You set me thinking on some pet theories of mine on race and nationality, that was all. And here is the lock and there is your brother shouting to us to hurry in."

As the canoe glided in under the shadow of the masonry, Gilbert brought it close to Mrs. Broderick's side.

"How do you like canoeing on the Thames? Is it as good as the little Adirondack lake?" she asked, smiling.

"Not as good as *that,*" he answered, in a low voice, in which sounded a deep regret for those lost days of youth.

Presently the two craft were gliding into the still green world of Hurley backwater; above, a network of green branches between them and the sky; below them, that network reflected in calm water. In those winding ways there were the number of boats usual to a fine June Sunday, but once find an unoccupied flat meadow bank and one or two willow-trees, and the other boats and their occupants matter nothing.

The picnic was much as other picnics. Margaret and her cousin Tommy devoted themselves to piling up cushions for Brindle's benefit, until that youth was overwhelmed by mingled delight and disgust.

"If any one does anything more for me, I shall just roll to the bank and into the stream, which will bear me away like Ophelia," he threatened.

"And before it bears you away, you are likely to find yourself prodded all over with boat-hooks. A hero will spring from the shadow of every tree and you will be 'butchered to make a Hurley holiday,'" Meg retorted. She had immediately joined Brindle and Miss Tommy, leaving Isabel to her two knights errant.

Did Mrs. Broderick ever look more lovely than to-day, the adoring Jack wondered, in her favourite white serge with one knot of deep purple velvet at her neck, and a wreath of dark pansies around her hat. Jack had hardly as yet taken in the full extent of the intimacy between her and Gilbert, and even if he had, his innate sense of fair play would have kept him from showing any jealousy.

"Perhaps you and Gilbert have had picnics together before now in America," he said, as they sat around the white table-cloth, over which the slim tracery of the willow leaves danced in light and shade, Gilbert on one side of her, he on the other.

Involuntarily the man and woman turned toward each other, their meeting eyes telling of the same memories: a dark pine-fringed lake in the days of that long-ago first summer; a yellow sand-bar against which the blue ocean crooned, while the child played at their feet.

Attributing all the pain in her eyes to this last fact, Gilbert answered, quickly: "Yes, we have broiled a trout over the ashes, and gathered our quart of blueberries, in our day. To think of your being Canadians and not having known the joy of picking blueberries!"

"Ah, but we're going out there some day salmon fishing, Jack and I," put in Meg, who had been listening. "Perhaps, Gilbert, you'll come and play the host to us at that place of yours, 'The Moorings'?"

If Margaret's keen eyes saw Isabel's nervous start at the word so long unheard, Gilbert marked it, too.

"You must be more enterprising than that and have a camp up one of the rivers, in the woods. That would teach you what mosquitoes were like," he said, quickly.

"Perhaps we may really do it, some day," said Jack, "though it may be a good while first if I get the staff appointment I am trying for." The simplicity and downrightness of the young fellow showed in every word, and Gilbert felt strongly drawn to him.

"Do you want foreign service?" he asked.

"Yes, one ought to see something of the world. I've the best chance for South Africa, I think."

"Wouldn't you rather get to India?"

"Yes, but there'd be big game in South Africa, too."

There was to be bigger game than Jack or any one else thought before many months were over.

"Don't you people want to come over and see the boats at the lock?" demanded Margaret. "There's a perfect stream of launches already, and the theatrical people will all be about just now."

"You're an utter cockney, Meg," Jack protested, but still he rose and offered a hand to Isabel.

"I had better stay with Mr. Brindle," she said, hesitating.

"I'll take care of him and see that he doesn't do anything desperate," piped up Miss Tommy.

Jack looked at her quizzically.

"The tender mercies of the wicked are cruel," he said; then in a lower voice to Isabel: "Do come."

She yielded with less restraint in her manner. If he were going abroad so soon, a stern hand might not be needed after all.

The two couples, Gilbert and Meg ahead, strolled across the meadow where the strange effect might be seen of the upper parts of boats or launches gliding swiftly on, apparently over the grass, in reality along the hidden canal that led to the lock.

"You'll see a little of everything here on a June Sunday," Meg said, and it was true enough. It was a side stream from the great current of London life that poured past that country field.

Electric launches crowded with overdressed Bayswater Jews, or groups from some of the many foreign colonies of London; noisy theatrical folk making the most of their one holiday; boats-full by the dozen and hundred, of young men, at their best in the equalising boating flannels; habitual river-folk in punts or canoes, and occasionally a small smart launch party, evidently from a country-house.

Meg was at once in her element, picking out some

notoriety, a statesman, a peer or lady fresh from the divorce court or a card scandal, and commenting on them with a frankness that rather amazed Gilbert.

The lock had filled and emptied, and now as the downstream craft flocked in, the launches with the right of way were led by a perfectly appointed electric one, which held a small party of ultra-fashionable people.

"Oh, Jack, here are the Vernades, now!" Meg said, moving forward to the edge of the lock, while her brother followed less eagerly.

Lord Vernade, who had been lounging in a deep wicker chair, beside a much-painted lady who seemed to be doing her best to entertain him, sprang up, and before the level of the water had begun to lower, jumped up beside them.

"I have been on the lookout for you all day, only to nearly miss you at last," he said taking Margaret's hand. "Why, this is a regular gathering; the new cousin — I congratulate you on it, Mr. Clinch — and I am glad to see that Mrs. Broderick is still a neighbour," with a pleasantly deferential how to her. "I mustn't stay to talk, or I'll be stranded high and dry, but won't you all follow us down and have tea on the lawn? I'm sure that Mrs. Broderick will forgive the informality of Lady Vernade not having yet called, You'll come, won't you?" and his eyes dwelt insistently on Margaret, who, flushed and smiling, looked all readiness.

"I don't know, what do you think, Jack?" she appealed.

Jack, who had taken one long, steady glance over

the smart people in the launch, recognising, although he was not as familiar with the London world as his sister, a recent divorcée and another lady scarcely less notorious, answered, with quiet decision:

"Thanks, but I think that we had better stick to our plans. I promised Mrs. Broderick a quiet day, and Clinch has an invalid in charge."

The excuse was flimsy, but neither Gilbert nor Isabel, after looking into Jack's face, made any protest against standing in their way. Lord Vernade's face hardened somewhat as he turned to Margaret: "Might I venture to suggest carrying you off in the launch?" he said.

It was Jack's voice answered: "You wouldn't want to leave your guests, Meg."

Gilbert, watching, saw that her face had paled and her eyes dilated curiously, though she answered, with a laugh: "Oh, certainly not. You see I'm under orders, Lord Vernade."

The launch was sinking with the lowering water in the lock.

"I must be off. I'm sorry," he said, letting himself lightly down. He was greeted with a remark from one of the women which raised a general laugh, and as Meg turned away from the lock there was a red spot on each cheek.

Gilbert kept beside her across the grass, with much the same feeling of indulgent pity as one has for an unreasonable child.

"I am sorry you were disappointed," he said simply.

"Oh, no, you weren't. You and Mrs. Broderick think Jack is right in not wanting me to know amusing people.

How am I going to be a success if I stick among the frumps, I should like to know?" she flashed out.

"Thanks," he said with a laugh of frank amusement, which in a moment she echoed, saying:

"There, I won't be cross any more."

After all she was very like a wilful, attractive child.

"Just look at Tommy and Mr. Brindle gazing into each other's eyes," Meg went on, as they came back to the scene of their encampment. The shadow was gone, and when, between the evening opalescence of sky and water, they drifted down with the current, Meg was at her gayest and most seductive, so that Gilbert could not but feel his heart warmed by this new sense of kinship, a sense that had hitherto been so singularly lacking in his life.

Chapter 32

The American Artist

It was one of the languorous afternoons that June brings to the Thames valley, and Margaret was lounging in a deep chair under the trees, well in view of the river, a becoming hat tilted over her eyes, a soft-tinted pink cushion behind her head, a pile of illustrated papers her ostensible study. Tommy Curtis had betaken herself to her favourite amusement of fishing, and peace reigned.

At first Meg had given her papers but a small share of her attention, allowing it to stray after each interesting-looking craft that passed, or even to the vagaries of a swan family giving the young ones an airing.

But presently, in lazily turning over a page, she spied something that so interested her, that boats and swans were allowed to pursue their course unregarded.

It was a reproduction of the picture "The Borderland," and the name of the artist caught her eye. "Mrs. Andrew Broderick" was an address that she had seen more than once on papers or parcels at Heathholm — indeed, was it not on her friend's visiting-card?

She turned over to the letter-press. Yes, here was the paragraph headed, "An Artist's Sad Story."

It told how "The Borderland," one of the most successful American pictures of the Paris Salon, had been painted last summer, just before the artist had become hopelessly insane. It had been brought to Paris by his wife, also an artist, after the unhappy man had been confined to an asylum.

Besides its artistic merit an interest had been given to the picture for Parisians, by the fact of the subject having evidently been evolved in his troubled brain through some remembrance of the illusions of poor Guy de Maupassant's first days of insanity, when he was haunted by good and evil spirits in the form of butterflies. The paragraph ended by saying that there was no doubt that, but for the artist's tragic condition, this picture would have earned him a "mention," or even a second medal.

Margaret turned the page to gaze intently at the weird composition, and only looked up as Jack came toward her in riding-dress.

"Look here," she began, almost before he reached her. "Here's such a queer thing — a picture in Paris painted by an Andrew Broderick last summer, just before he went mad. Now I've often seen her name, Mrs. Andrew —"

"Let's look," Jack interrupted, taking the paper from her hand. As he scanned it, his sister sat staring up at him, realising that nothing she might say would attract his attention.

When he raised his eyes from the page, she saw that his face was very set and still, with a look that she had only seen there once or twice throughout his boyhood.

"Dare say it's a brother-in-law or cousin," was his brief comment.

Margaret checked the obvious retort, that brothers and cousins did not generally possess the same Christian name, but as Jack turned away, she called after him: "Give me my paper."

"I want it," came back over his shoulder.

"Aren't you going to have some tea?"

"No."

Margaret sat staring after the retreating figure.

"So that's it, is it?" she said to herself. "The Lady of Shalot is a grass widow, and my poor Jack —" and she breathed a very genuine sigh. "And he has gone to have it out with her now, too. Well, it won't do him any good for me to sit here and think about it, so I might as well go for a paddle." Then on a sudden came the thought that if Isabel could not marry Jack, neither could she marry Gilbert, and her heart leaped with a fierce joy.

Margaret was right. Jack had gone to have it out with her, riding up through the beech woods with an unfamiliar look of pain on his young face.

He had not yet, however, quite accepted the fact of Mrs. Broderick's having a living husband. He felt morally certain that she herself must have painted the picture which he had seen unfinished in her studio, and tried to convince himself that the mystery in which she had enwrapped it was merely some artistic trick to secure its success.

Women certainly wrote books under the name of men, and might do the same with pictures, for all he knew to the contrary. The weaving of these fine theories brought no relief to the tension of his mind, and when he pulled up at Heathholm gate, his horse bore signs of harder work than usual on the long up-hill stretch.

Yes, there she was down the garden path, sitting before her easel at this unusually late hour of the afternoon. Jack was not the one to understand that it was the luminous gray that had tempted her into making a study of a bank of azaleas in a blue twilight caused by the overhanging trees. At sound of his footsteps, Isabel looked up with her smile of friendly welcome.

"Is Meg with you?" she asked, and then paused, checked by some unusual element in his face.

"No, I came alone. I hope you don't mind my interrupting your work, but there is something that I must ask you."

"Yes?" She had instinctively risen, and stood facing him, her eyes nearly on a level with his own, the long folds of her plainly made dress of light gray giving her the shadowy air of a mediaeval saint in a modern picture.

From his pocket, Jack pulled the roughly folded sheets that contained "The Borderland" and its descriptive letter-press.

"Will you look at this?" he asked, quietly. "I fear that I must disobey your wishes not to speak of the subject, but this is the picture that I saw here, in your studio, is it not?"

There was the slightly startled air in Isabel's bearing, which is aroused in any one, by an abrupt intrusion into their personal affairs, but that was all, as after glancing at the paper she answered, "Yes."

"I cannot pretend not to know that you painted it."

At his expectant pause, she bowed her head acqui-escently.

"Then if you are Andrew Broderick, what does this account of the artist mean? "

This almost stern demand was met by a silence when her eyes met his steadily.

He answered the look as though it had been spoken words.

"You mean have I a right to ask that? You know that I have. I will tell you presently what that right is. Is there really such a man as this artist whom they call Andrew Broderick, and if so, what is he to you?"

"My husband," came the words, low yet distinct.

"Alive?"

"Yes, or as it says, in the living death of an asylum."

The quiet words struck home, and the boy's face set-tled into the lines of manhood's enduring sorrow.

"But why should you paint the picture in his name?" he said, vaguely, as though his mind were still occu-pied with the details of the story, while the one tragic central fact was not yet fully realised.

"He had painted a great masterpiece, and destroyed it in his frenzy. With the help of his studies, I repro-duced it. I could not have done so if I had not worked with him so much, and seen him paint it. He was a great artist, and I have saved his name," she said, with a strange pride.

"Good God, how you must have loved him!" Jack broke out, fiercely.

The mask was down from her studious self-control,

and with a strange outward wave of her hands, as though putting from her a long-carried burden, Isabel spoke: "Loved him, no! I doubt if I ever did that, even at the first! I admired the artist, I was grateful to the man for what he gave me. Then all at once it changed to hate, such hate that his name, his money, were a burden to me until I had repaid something of my debt to him. It is done now, for it is I who have made his name famous."

"You hated him?" Jack gasped, forgetting his own trouble in the face of these hinted-at tragic forces.

"I hated him, yes, for what in my darkest moments I have felt to be more my fault than his. For when his mind began to be clouded, my one thought was to act as a wife would have done who had married him for love, not to fail in one effort to save him. Against the doctor's wishes, I took him away — Gilbert Clinch came in charge of him — to that little Canadian fishing-place you saw in my sketch. I was determined that he should not lose one day's sunshine and free air that I could give him; that he should have his liberty to the last. And my reward" — here her hands fell and her voice dropped to a dulled tone — "my reward was to see my child, my one hope in life, lying dead at his father's feet, his blood running down from the knife held above him!"

"Your child! My God!" Jack gasped, feeling himself and his passion put off at a great distance by the tragedy of her fate.

"Can you wonder that I am different from other women?" she went on, more dreamily. "Can you wonder that I crept away, here to the solitude of a distant country to hide myself? It was a strange chance that brought me in contact with my old acquaintance, Meg. You and she have been, oh, so good to me, and led me back into the serener ways of life. Believe me, I am grateful to you, and would be pained to give you trouble —" she ended, with a wistful look at him.

Jack hesitated, his honest soul rent between the passion of pity evoked by her words, and his own certainty of the wrong that her silence had done him.

"I suppose," he began, after a moment, "the way was — perhaps it was natural enough — that you never thought how hard it would come on me, leaving me in ignorance. You weren't to know, of course, that I should make such a fool of myself" — then his pain mastering his compunction — "but oh, if you only could have guessed what you have grown to be to me, what it will be to live without seeing you!"

She twisted her hands together with a little movement of pain.

"It hurts so to have to hurt you," she whispered.

"But we seemed such ages apart, you with everything bright ahead of you, and me a poor bruised, battered creature in whom all feeling should be dead."

He turned on her quickly.

"And is it really dead? Is there no one else can wake it up?"

For a breathless moment she stared into his eyes, and then a crimson flush passed slowly across her face. Silently she shook her head, but Jack spoke, very gently: "Ah, I see. Forgive me, I should not have said that. Well, it is good-bye now. I go back to Dublin next week anyway, and think I'll do the rest of my leave in town. I'm sorry I bothered you and made a fool of myself. Good-bye," and just touching the hand that hung by her side he turned and was gone.

Jack was not again visible to his friends until he appeared late at the dinner-table; and then, after one quick glance at his face, his sister did not look at him again, but kept up a stream of talk as best she might, enticing her mother on to discourse upon a bazaar, and her father to point out at length his views as to the mistakes committed by the present government, all the while keeping an eye on Tommy Curtis, in case she should tease Jack.

The meal was nearly over when Jack broke his silence, and Meg started nervously at something unfamiliar in his voice.

"Ellen will be able to commence one of her favourite house-cleaning sprees in my room to-morrow, mother, for I think that I'll be off in the morning to Cowes. I've only a week's more leave, you know, and Dick Loring writes that he is just taking his yacht out and will land me at Kingston. Don't you wish you were coming, Meg?"

"That I do," she answered, not looking up from an elaborate pattern of strawberry stalks on her plate.

"Whatever is up, Meg?" said Tommy, taking her arm as they went out into the clear darkness of the summer night. "You look as though you had just had a legacy that you must keep dark, and Jack suggests nothing but a toothache. And yet you generally hunt in couples. Can the lovely widow have refused him? What fun!" For if Tommy was ever vindictive to any one, it was to Jack, who for years had been held before her in the light of a desirable husband.

Meg felt a pang of shame that her joy should be Jack's sorrow. But there was no time to be lost in getting that lively young woman out of the sufferer's way.

"Look here, Tommy, go in like a dear, for I want to speak to Jack presently. Go and play something, not gay and not sad — something dull and neutral."

"That's a large order," Tommy commented, as she obeyed, and apparently found it impossible of solution, for no music sounded from the windows.

Presently Jack's cigar showed a red point in the doorway, and knowing that the light was on her white skirts, Meg waited to see if he would come to her.

"You there, Meg? Where's Tommy?" came the cautious question.

"She's indoors. She won't come out."

"That's right. My father has just been suggesting that she and I pledge our troth before I go, and I said 'No, thank you,' civilly. One comfort, she'd never have me," and he laughed dismally. "But look here, you know that thing you showed me in the paper today? Well, I wouldn't say anything to Mrs. Broderick about it if I were you."

"No, I won't."

"It was her husband, you see, and the poor fellow's mad, and she doesn't like talking about him, you know."

This was delivered with a fine air of carelessness which caused Meg's eyes to grow dim.

"I dare say not," was her mechanical reply.

"She's had a lot of trouble — dreadful trouble — and — you'll be kind to her always when you can, won't you?" came in more muffled tones through the darkness.

All their childhood's loyal comradeship rose up in that moment to fight down the fierce jealousy in Meg's heart, that kept repeating, "And yet she can make every man care for her; why must she take every one?"

There was an indignation, too, for Jack's hurt, but the old loyalty asserted itself in her words:

"Of course I will, Jack, but — must you go to-morrow?"

"I might as well. And look here, don't bother to be up early. I must be off to send some wires and pack now. Bye-bye, Meg," and with a quick farewell kiss he marched away, while Meg choked back a sob and gave a vindictive thought to the friend she had a little while ago considered perfection.

Chapter 33

Mother and Son

For the next few days Margaret kept as much to herself as possible, brooding over poor Jack's tragedy,
and the parts played in it by the different actors.

The longer she brooded, the stronger became the
impression that there must have been something
more than accident in Gilbert Clinch's reticence as to
Mrs. Broderick's history. It must have been by her
orders, she said to herself, bitterly, only for what
cause?

"Well, that's what I mean to find out," she decided,
and putting on a very, smart red and white boating-dress
she summoned Tommy Curtis to an afternoon in the
punt. Meg knew that she never looked so tall and slim
as when reaching up to grasp the long punting-pole.

When dwellers on the Thames want to see their
acquaintances, they go out on the water, as dwellers in
villages walk down the High Street.

"I wonder if Mr. Clinch is out in his canoe today? I
haven't seen him since Jack left," she remarked, carelessly, and Tommy answered, with the tranquil innocence of a two-year-old:

"They generally do go up-stream about four o'clock,
I think."

Her information proved correct, for presently, when the long pole had securely wedged the punt in among the sweet-scented reeds under an old willow, and that destroyer of peace, the spirit-lamp, had been started, the canoe came gliding in toward them, Gilbert paddling and Brindle stretched lazily out.

"You're like the swans, and scent the tea-basket from afar," Tommy said. "Come, Mr. Brindle, sit on these cushions and draw me pictures."

"I don't see why cushions and myself always seem to be associated in the feminine mind," Brindle lamented, though he made the change to the larger quarters with great alacrity.

Gilbert sat still in the canoe, one hand lightly holding by the punt. His head was bare, his hair slightly disordered, and to Margaret he seemed to have a younger, brighter aspect, which she highly approved.

"You *are* like Jack," she said, suddenly. "I never saw it so strongly before."

"I'm glad you think so, for I know that must be an open door to your favour," he said, cheerfully, and the girl blushed with a new sense of shame.

"But I'm very sorry he had to go off in such a hurry. I should have liked to have seen him first," he went on.

A sudden purpose came to Margaret. The two at the other end of the boat were absorbed, and she and Gilbert were practically alone, their voices covered by the sound of the weir.

"It was the best thing he could do, he was so worried and upset — I never saw Jack looking so upset before," she said, pathetically; then looking up at

Gilbert with the full force of her big dark eyes: "Why did neither you nor Mrs. Broderick ever tell us that her husband was alive?"

His face set, as does a strong man's to meet a sudden attack.

"If she chose to be silent, it was not for me to speak," he said, gravely; then questioned, almost sternly: "But why do you ask me that now?"

Her answer was a triumph of pathos.

"Only because I cannot help thinking so much of them. It might have saved him — and her — from a lifelong sorrow if you had been more frank."

Gilbert paled under his bronze at the certainty given by her words that Isabel shared Jack's feelings, but he had long ago learnt the lesson of self-control, and only answered, with quiet reserve: "I think that if you knew more of the circumstances you would see that I could not have acted differently."

Her arrow was planted; it was no part of Margaret's plan to estrange Gilbert.

"Forgive me if I seem intrusive, but you know what Jack is to me, and Mrs. Broderick has been my ideal since I was a long-legged tomboy. I haven't the courage to go and see her grieving, when I can do nothing for her. Have you seen her since —" she paused.

"I saw her yesterday," he said, his mind meantime anxiously recalling each little sign that had made him think her overworked and depressed.

"Tea is ready," sung out Tommy, from the other end of the punt, and as soon as possible afterward Gilbert took his departure.

"Change partners, and down the middle," said Brindle, as they drifted down, "the fair Persephone never vouchsafes me a glance nowadays."

"You don't give her much chance, it seems to me," Gilbert said, rousing himself from his abstraction. "And do you think you need devote yourself quite so violently to the little Curtis girl? I understand she is a bit of an heiress, and is destined for my cousin Jack."

"They neither of them seem in much of a hurry then. My dear fellow, don't you know that when a nice little girl shows that she wants me to amuse her, I do my best at it? I hate that cold-blooded English way of accepting their attentions," Brindle retorted.

"Well, don't go making a fool of yourself, that's all," Gilbert cautioned.

At the same time Tommy was saying:

"I do think that American men take so much more trouble to amuse girls than Englishmen do, don't you, Meg?"

"Perhaps so. They are different, certainly," Meg agreed.

Meetings like this one took place frequently, and every day Gilbert's feeling of interest in Margaret grew stronger, as well as his resolve never to put himself in a position of an enemy to the brother and sister who had given him this new sense of kinship.

Isabel had immersed herself in her work, making excuses whenever Gilbert tried to persuade her to go out on the water with them. And so they remained a quartette, until one day when Mr. Nugent-Barr, taking a walk along the towing-path, spied Tommy and Brindle drifting about in the canoe, evidently absorbed in each other, while the punt was nowhere in sight. He went home, meditating, and making no comments, wrote that evening a letter which two days later brought one summoning Tommy back to her family the next day, on plea of a coming dance.

"You'll say good-bye to Mr. Brindle for me, Meg," she said, dolorously.

"I won't do anything of the kind, and I think it is rather a good thing you are going back to Selina. She'll keep you in order," announced Meg, who had made up her mind to do all in her power to get Tommy married to Jack.

"We'll see about that," was the stout answer, and that evening there was a little note slipped into the village post-box which would have shocked Meg.

Tommy had at last found something original to suit her tastes, and she did not mean to let it slip in a hurry.

Things were not cheerful at Monk's Grange. Mr. Nugent-Barr was more peevishly restless than ever, perpetually questioning Margaret as to what Gilbert had told her of his life and prospects. When his nephew came to the house, he seemed constrained and uneasy in his presence, and yet if he failed to appear at the usual time he worried at his absence.

There was a decided tone of relief in his voice when one morning at breakfast he looked up from a letter to say to Margaret:

"Your grandmother is on her way home, coming straight through from Aix."

"Granny!" Meg said, with a little gasp of dismay, "why, I thought the doctor had her safe at Aix for the whole summer!"

"I trust that she is safe, wherever she is, was the prim retort. "But, yes, from what Madame Estivalet says, she certainly does seem to be acting against their wishes."

"Whatever is she in such a hurry for?" asked Meg.

"The wish to get home is natural enough."

Meg had her own thoughts, but held her tongue, and she had further opportunities of discretion, when her grandmother arrived, horribly fractious, and evidently suffering in mind and body.

Madame Estivalet immediately retired to bed with an attack of nerves, and Ellen Sievert confided to the housekeeper that she wouldn't go through that journey again for a hundred pounds.

The master of the house alone seemed pleased at his mother's arrival, and was closeted with her early the next morning.

An awesome sight was the old woman, sitting bolstered up with many cushions in bed, head and shoulders swathed in a red silk shawl, her hands, as usual, loaded with rings.

Hardly was the door closed before she demanded:

"Well, have you found out what he wants?"

"What he wants? You mean Gilbert Clinch?"

"Who else could I mean? Hasn't he showed his hand yet? Has he done nothing?"

Her son shook his head, and answered, with the slowness that always stirred her impatience: "Nothing save come and go, as any other neighbour might. The young people and he made friends, but I thought it best not to drop any hints."

"No, you never could manage Margaret. Leave her to me. And you think she likes him?"

Mr. Nugent-Barr tried his best to look dignified, as he asked: "And what does it matter whether she likes him or not?" Then breaking down into an appeal, "Mother, you must tell me why you make so much of this?"

But unheeding his words, the old woman was muttering to herself, and he paused to listen: "Old Isaac! Old Isaac! That most pig-headed of all pig-headed Dutchmen! I always knew that it would come through him! Why did I ever let him —" even in the outpouring of her rage she checked herself here, with a furtive glance at her son, who asked, uneasily:

"*What* would come through him?"

She leaned forward and clutched his arm in her bony grasp.

"I always thought that your father wanted to make another will. At the last I felt sure that he had made it, and if so, old Isaac knew of it. What if that is the reason of his coming now?"

Her listener glanced around with an uneasy laugh.

"Hush, mother, better not talk about such things. Even an old fool of a fisherman wouldn't keep a will hidden away for nearly twenty years and then produce it."

"Well, what is this man coming here for if not to find out about something that Isaac Neisner has told him of?" she hissed, in an angry whisper.

"What could he find out? There is no one here to tell him anything."

"There is Ellen Sievert."

The son stared at his mother with a growing fear in his eyes, as though of some coming revelation.

"What is there for her to tell him?" he asked, in a

more authoritative tone than he had often used to her.

"Nothing, of course, nothing. What could there be? Only — you know that she and Isaac helped me to nurse your father at the end, and if there were any such last attempt at a will she may have known of it. She had known that daughter of his when they were girls."

"Ellen is not likely at this time of day to risk her good home for a man she has never seen," he answered, his very want of imagination dulling his suspicions. "All the same I cannot understand your fear of this man. Mother, what was the true story of this half-sister of mine?"

"That's what he never would tell me," the old woman answered, in low, intense tones. "I knew from Ellen that he had kept her and her mother living like working women and that, after her mother's death, the girl quarrelled with him, and left home to marry this minister of some American sect, and her father never saw her again. I never wondered that she quarrelled with him, but who knows what shame or crime may have been hidden — who knows?" she crooned to herself, as though forgetting her listener in the shadows of her past. With a start she roused herself, though still seeming vague.

"It was that look in his face that frightened me when he came in Florence — the look of Jonathan Bauer, who all his life got what he wanted at whatever cost." Then in a brisker tone, "But it's no use talking about the past; we must get things in hand now. I sent you the letter in answer to my inquiries, the letter that shows that this Mrs. Broderick must have come here to spy out the land beforehand for him. Whether he's a tool of hers, or she of his, remains to he seen. Anyway, we must try through Margaret to detach him from her, so that if the worst comes to the worst —" she paused, as though swallowing a, bitter pill, and then broke out:

"My pretty Margaret! My dainty Margaret! Of whom I meant to make a *grande dame* — a *grande dame!*" and again the senile vagueness came over her.

Her son sat looking at her with a new awe of the barrier that was coming between them, realising his own weakness without her. There could be no doubt but that Madame de Barre was aging fast.

"Where's Meg?" she asked, with one of her sudden starts into keenness, "I must have a talk with her soon. You haven't told her anything of this story of his being Mrs. Broderick's old love? No? That's right. We mustn't set her against him yet, until we see how things go. Leave me now to rest."

Chapter 34

The Poison of Asps

Margaret had been spending a long solitary afternoon on the river, looking over at the closed shutters of the Vernade house and giving a sigh to their London gaieties, wondering with uneasy jealousy if Gilbert were with Mrs. Broderick, and generally feeling at odds with her world.

It was late when she left the punt at the steps and strolled up toward the house, its gray walls, dark against the sunset, seeming to reach out their shadow to draw her away from the evening peace and beauty.

She looked up at them with all her old distaste.

"I don't know when you look darkest and dreariest," she apostrophised them, vengefully, "on a fine summer evening or a dreary winter day. Other old houses don't look such a concentrated essence of dead sins as you do. Why can't you look cheerfully respectable as a decent house should?"

But the old walls stared back at her as though they knew a very good reason for looking the contrary.

Her own room was a cheerful place enough, with its yellow and white furnishing, and its western sunshine through a gap in the heavy trees.

Cheerful too from long affectionate habit was the

appearance of the old woman with shrewd, kindly face who knocked and entered, saying in the half-scolding, half-welcoming tone of nursery days: "You're very late to-day, Miss Meggie. Your grandmother's been fussing this hour past."

"Fussing for any reason, or just because she felt like fussing?" Meg asked, as she took off her hat before the glass.

"Well, she does seem to have something on her mind like — has had all the time we've been in Aix, for the matter of that. But she quieted down a bit after she had her tea, so you'd better go to her now and get what she has to say over, ha'n't you, my dear?"

"All right,"— then turning suddenly from the glass to face the servant, — "Lennie, do you know if it's about my cousin, Gilbert Clinch? Didn't Granny tell you that we had known him in Florence?"

The name seemed to act like a spell on the old woman, who jumped as though she had had a pin stuck in her.

"Susan's child!" she said, in shrill tones. "The Lord's sakes! Is he here? Sure enough it's been him that's put the old lady in such tantrums for a month and more!"

Margaret's face reflected that uncomprehended fear that she saw before her.

"Why should it?" she demanded.

"I don't know, child. I don't want to know, and don't you either. It's the best way," was the hurried answer. It brought a light of determination to the girl's eyes.

"I *will* know. I *will* find out. I'm going to her now," she said, throwing her hat on the bed and moving to the door.

The nurse laid a detaining grasp on her arm.

"Miss Meg — my little Meggie — don't ask *her* any-thing. Don't make her angry. No one ever prospers that does. If there's anything you want to know — though I says it again, don't you know it if you can help it — come to your old nurse who loves you true."

"It's all right, Lennie, don't worry yourself," Margaret said, looking down with a smile at the bent form beside her. "You know that I'm never the least bit afraid of her. I leave that to my father. I've seen her angry before now, and it didn't hurt me; besides, I can't think what on earth she has to be angry at. Anyway, I'm going to find out. Bye-bye, Lennie," and with a laugh she was gone.

For all her brave bearing, Margaret felt a curious chill upon her as she opened the door of her grand-mother's sitting-room. A stately room it was, once the withdrawing-room of an imprisoned princess, and in its great oriel window, that looked down a reach of the river to the little town, sat Madame de Barre, huddled in her usual fashion in bright shawls.

The melancholy charm of the summer night had apparently no interest for her, for instead of sitting idly reminiscent under its spell, as is the wont of nice old ladies, she was trifling with a small tray of bric-à-brac set on the table beside her. There were bits of clumsy jewelry set with rough turquoises and garnets, such as the Florentine women used to wear; there were the heavy coral or gold necklaces of the Roman peasants, as well as some Swiss ornaments and strings of bright amethyst and cornelian beads.

Madame Estivalet was apparently sorting out a box

of the same kind of treasures, and one glance told Margaret that she wore her most cowed and dispirited air.

The heavy air of the room with windows closed, and great bunches of heliotrope about it; the fantastic figure of her grandmother, all, used as she was to it, increased the girl's vague sense of uneasiness.

She had expected to be greeted on her entrance with a voluble outburst of wrath, instead of which the old lady looked up and nodded with a smile which might have frightened a child into fits, but to which Margaret was accustomed.

"Ellen said that you wanted me, Granny," she began.

"Ah, yes, I was asking for you awhile ago. We old folks find the days long when we don't know what is going on. Estivalet and I have taken to toys like children. You can go now, and write or whatever it is you bemoan yourself in," she said, with a vicious snarl at the scared companion, who hastened to avail herself of the permission.

With a weird return to her honeyed manner, the old lady resumed: "And now, come and sit down cosily, and tell me what you have been doing since I have seen you. I fear it's dull for you here. We must see about your getting to Cowes in a week or two. There are plenty of people would be glad to have you."

"The Curtises want me to go up for their dance and a lot of things next week, but I would need some new clothes," Meg said, striking while the iron was hot.

"Well, well, we must see about it. But tell me now, how have you been getting on with this new cousin? Jack liked him, I hear?"

Meg, intending to keep her schemes and hopes to herself, felt the black eyes boring her through like gimlets.

"Oh, Jack would like any one that Mrs. Broderick ordered him to. He is just a sheet of blotting-paper to that lady at present. He's taken himself off in the sulks because he finds that she has a live husband, even if he is a mad one," she said, the soreness of her heart coming out in petulance against her ally.

"Well, well, Jack never had your head, my dear. No, it is you who should have been the man and had the bigger share of the money. I shall see that you have it too, if you get a fitting husband."

"I only want my share," Meg protested, while, even with the words, a dazzling new possibility stirred her heart with the love of gold.

"And so this American lady has got Jack under her thumb, has she? It's a little way of hers, from what I hear. She took advantage of Gilbert Clinch's poverty to make him a sort of upper servant, paying him for going about with them to look after her husband, and when, as soon as he got any money and got away from her, she followed him to Europe, and knowing that he meant to come and claim our relationship, settled herself here first and made a mouthful of our poor, soft Jack. You were rather rash about her, I must say, my dear, for you should have seen enough of the world to be able to class such women."

This honeyed flow of malevolent words bewildered Margaret with their horrible plausibility, the old truth holding good:

"A lie that is half a truth is a harder matter to
    fight."

"How do you know this, Granny?" she asked.

"It was easy enough to make inquiries when I knew
that they had spent last summer at the Moorings.
These facts were well known to our agent. I only got
the letter last week." Then with a change to a more
wheedling voice, "But you know, my dear, we mustn't
be too hard on your cousin, who seems to have done
his best to sever the connection. Who knows but what
it may all have originated in ambition on his part? A
great deal lies in your power in exerting a better influence over him. I cannot believe that my pretty girl
could fail to influence any one she wished to," and the
old woman ended with an unsavoury leer.

Meg sat gazing out upon the dark masses of the park
trees, a sick disillusionment with life at her heart. Was
there no one left true and good in this world? Were
Jack and Gilbert both weak tools in the designing
hands of a woman? She could read through her
grandmother's wiles easily enough, and saw that she
was under orders to do her best to make her cousin
fall in love with her, and these orders filled her with
an uneasy fear. Why should her grandmother feel
such a desire to get a hold on this apparently unimportant American cousin unless there was some harm
that he was in a position to do them?

Well, at any rate, her grandmother's schemes
seemed to march with her own at present, she said to
herself with a new recklessness. But there was one
question more she must ask: "Under the circum-

stances I can hardly understand his coming here to claim our friendship. Can you, Granny?"

The old woman sent a long keen glance after her, before she played her next card.

"Some motive he must have, my dear, and that remains for us to find out. After all, I cannot but feel a hearty sympathy for the boy when I think that he is most likely ignorant of the doubtfulness of his mother's marriage or his own parentage. That there was some such cause for my husband's anger with his daughter I have good reason to know. But of all that, this poor young fellow is probably ignorant. His little legacy was left to him by name, you know. I should like to treat him as my husband's grandchild."

Even with the smarting pain at her heart these noble sentiments on her grandmother's lips struck Margaret's quick sense of humour, so that a hard little laugh came.

"All right, Granny, I understand. I am to kill the fatted calf for the one sinner and shake the dust off my feet with the other. That's the way of the world, isn't it? I shall wear my little white pongee, as a suitable robe of innocence when the prodigal comes to dinner to-night. And by the bye, may I write to Clementine to-day about a new ball-dress? I have such a good idea — the palest, palest yellow with yards and yards of daisy and buttercup edgings. I want to dress the part, you know. And I suppose I may have a garden-party dress, too? Thanks, ever so much," then pausing at the door, "and perhaps, Granny, it would be just as well not to let Jack get hold of these pretty stories of his Dulcinea, or he will come charging over — a regular Don

Quixote — and likely upset the apple-cart."

With this mixture of metaphors she was gone, and the old woman sat shaking her head.

"She is clever. She understands and feels more than she will show. Thinking to fool me with her daisies and buttercups," she chuckled to herself.

With an instinctive craving after a healthier atmosphere, Meg went off and sought her mother in her sitting-room, where the light-coloured chintzes formed such a contrast to the tawdry splendours of Madame de Barre's rooms.

That lady, placidly dozing over her lace-making, looked up in surprise at her daughter's advent.

"Have you been with your grandmother, dear? I hope she is feeling less fidgety now?"

Meg laughed drearily.

"Oh, yes, I think her temper is settling down. She has promised me some smart gowns if I go up to town next week. You wouldn't miss me, mother, would you?" she added, wistfully.

That lady seemed rather at a loss.

"Of course we always miss you, dear, but I suppose that your grandmother wants you to go?"

"I suppose so," and then to her own, and her mother's astonishment, a few impetuous sobs broke out.

"Oh, mother, I wish you and I could just settle things for ourselves like other mothers and daughters."

A touch of maternal tenderness showed in the lymphatic lady, as she soothed the excited girl.

"There, dear, there! I always wished it might be so, but your father would be angry if he heard us. You must try to be patient if she is worrying, and perhaps some day —" but finding herself about to indulge in an unchristian wish for the speedy end of her life's tyrant, she checked herself. "There, dear, it's time to dress for dinner. Run away and get ready."

Margaret took herself off, having learnt the lesson that the weak can give no help.

Chapter 35

Sundered Friends

Margaret sat on the lawn at Hurlingham in great content with her surroundings. She had been driven down on the much-coveted box seat of Lord Vernade's coach to one of the smartest polo-matches of the season; greetings on her return to Vanity Fair had been cordial; and she had seen many an admiring or envious feminine glance sent after the daring combination of her white and black and cherry-coloured dress. Lord Vernade had seldom left her side that day, and she knew that his presence gave her more success in other women's eyes than any Parisian toilette.

It was restoring, to at least her vanity, to know that he would not have left her for Mrs. Broderick or any one else.

Their chairs were a little apart from the group of their friends, and they could talk freely.

"Are you all still under the rule of the fascinating American widow?" he asked, idly, watching Margaret's colour deepen as she answered:

"I don't know about being under her rule, but, as it happens, she turns out to be only a grass widow after all."

"Ah, that explains many things."

"What do you mean?"

"Well, for one thing, it explains why the newly found cousin has not-married the moneyed lady instead of — well, taking lodgings near her. My man, who is an inveterate gossip, tells me that the morals of the neighbourhood are much exercised thereby."

Margaret's heart gave a great leap and then went dizzily down. She sat staring at a rush of horsemen across the dazzling green of the field, her one thought being not to show that the blow had gone home. Her grandmother's virulence she was used to mentally softening down, but here was a man hinting, from another point of view, at the same facts.

"But Mr. Brindle shares his lodgings," she said, rather helplessly, and her plea was greeted with light laughter.

"As a chaperon? I fear even your charity must abandon that excuse, for I happened to pass that youth in a music-hall last evening, and heard him say that his holiday was over and that he was doing London correspondence for American papers. So your dear relative has lost that moral shield, you see."

"Yes, I see," she agreed, listlessly; then, with a little laugh:

"Granny has already been expounding the same theory to me, only she takes the view of Gilbert being the victim of feminine wiles, whom we in charity should rescue and reclaim. She appears to look upon me as the chosen instrument in my dear cousin's conversion."

A steely light flashed in Lord Vernade's gray eyes, though his voice was as deliberately soft as ever, as he said: "I think that if Jack were here he would advise you to have as little to do with this Gilbert Clinch as possible. That, I am sure, would be a man's view, and in such matters, a man judges better than a woman."

The animation in Meg's face answered his words. It was such a relief to have her dark hidden feelings justified to herself.

"I am sure you are right," she said; then, with a sudden dispirited relapse, "but Granny is set on my keeping friends with him, you see. It seems so strange that his coming should have upset them so."

She looked at him appealingly, and Lord Vernade assented: "It does seem queer," and tried to keep any significance out of his voice. His private opinion of the elders of the family was of the most uncomplimentary character, and no queer revelation about them or their riches would have surprised him. He himself had not a doubt that this new cousin had come on a blackmailing expedition, against which the old lady was hedging. Gilbert's influence over Margaret had not been unobserved by him, and he was swift to seize the chance of undermining it, even with a tale invented on the spur of the moment.

"You mustn't let these people worry you too much," he said, gently. "You ought to stay up in town now as long as you can, and leave them to show their true colours by themselves. Their sort always do. Now, try to forget all about them and enjoy yourself, won't you?"

Through a mist of tears the girl smiled at him, and when presently they strolled across the grass side by side, Lord Vernade had a sense of purpose achieved in that half-hour's talk.

Through the following ten days' London whirl, Margaret had a half-alarmed, half-vindictive consciousness of the trouble ahead when she should return home and kick over the traces of her grandmother's driving.

While afraid of the mischief she might work, all her pride, all that was best in her, was up in arms at the idea of lowering herself to win over Gilbert even while ostracising Mrs. Brodcrick. Perhaps such feelings were strengthened by the knowledge of the difficulty of the task.

Twice she was summoned home and made excuses, but her ready money was slipping away, and as she knew she would get no more, she went off heavy-hearted. As the time came nearer she doubted her own courage to oppose the fierce old woman who ruled the whole family.

There were no doubts or misgivings, though, when at Paddington, her maid, having picked out a carriage in which sat only one lady and turning to call the porter, left her looking up into Isabel Broderick's quiet eyes. A dawning wistful smile showed on the latter's face, and she almost timidly leant forward with the word: "Meg!"

She had been keenly wounded by the way in which Margaret had ignored her since Jack's departure, but she would do what she could now for a reconciliation.

The smile, the appeal, added fuel to Meg's wrath. In a blind fury, such as of old had driven her savage ancestors to stab and spare not, she turned away, saying, in vibrant tones: "Never mind, Toovy. Here is an empty carriage further down."

The hour of travel that followed through the sun-shiny country was not a pleasant one to either woman.

Outraged affection and sense of personal dignity at first cost Isabel a few bitter tears, but before that hour was ended, her face was firm again in its lines of composure, and she knew what she meant to do.

Margaret was thankful for two river acquaintances who got in at the last moment, and kept her from thinking what was to happen next. They were to get out at Taplow, the station before Mrs. Broderick's, while she herself would go on for one or two more to get to the other side of the circle made by the river.

"Now if it were a slow train, I might have to change at Maidenhead, and meet her on the platform. As it is, I'll just lean back till she's gone," she said to herself, not reckoning with Mrs. Broderick's moral courage that always took her to meet a difficulty.

Taplow! Her friends went cheerfully off.

Maidenhead! She sank back in her corner, her eyes fixed on a fashion paper — the carriage door opened, but still she did not look up.

"Margaret, I have come to know what it all means. What have I done to be so treated?" Mrs. Broderick stood at the steps, in gray travelling dress and hat, her face a little pale and set, her steady eyes fixed on Margaret.

For a moment the sweetness and sincerity of her words asserted their power over the girl, and then — all the fiercer for the reaction — she broke out in the passionate invective of a lower race.

"What have you done? Wasn't it enough to come here to spy out the land for your lover, before he arrived to try to foist his illegitimacy on an honest family? What does he want to blackmail us for, I wonder? And you must pretend to be so fond of me, and try to break my poor Jack's heart —" her voice choked with passion, and Isabel spoke gravely and almost pityingly.

"God knows I have done none of these things. Margaret, my poor child, whoever has influenced you like this has done an evil work."

The guard was banging the open doors and Isabel turned away, feeling that this was not the place to say more.

Nothing could have so intensified Margaret's wrath as her attitude of sad, almost pitying, calm, and the allusion to influence seemed the last straw.

There was no more compunction or doubt in her attitude toward these two who had once been her friends.

As Isabel drove homeward, she let her pony walk up the long climb of the hillside, and thought over the whole incident, beginning to realise that the girl's taunts were something more than an outburst of temper.

"Gilbert her lover, for whom she was a spy! Gilbert illegitimate, blackmailing his relations!" The shameful words brought a hot glow to her cheeks even while she was searching her mind for their origin and reason. And then the word "blackmail," striking so evidently a note of fear, suggested an answer. From that moment she never doubted that the old lady, if not her son, had cause to fear and hate Gilbert. Even while outraged by Margaret's treatment, she felt a deep pity for the nature that could allow itself to be thus swayed, and thinking that Gilbert's best chance of happiness lay in a marriage with Margaret, hoped that, even yet, it might not come to a quarrel between them.

Perhaps what hurt her the most, was the sense of shame with which she thought of her own imprudence in letting Gilbert settle so near her. It had been her weakness in craving his presence which, she told herself, had wrought the harm. She should not have returned here from Paris in the spring. She would go away now, at once, only it would seem like a confession of guilt. That evening when she was sitting in the twilight of the studio, Gilbert came, as was his habit, and sat idly talking.

Isabel was surprised to find that she was glad of the shadows to hide a new shyness, the reflex action of those cruel words.

"I am in more need than usual of the restfulness of your presence," he said, and how grateful were such words to her, "for I have undergone one of those awesome inspections of my venerable step-grandmother's."

"Inspections?" she asked, absently, her mind harping back to the same old words.

"I can call them nothing else. Her poor old companion writes a little note demanding my presence, and I go and sit spellbound under a series of artful questions and reminiscences arranged to draw out mine, and when she stops to breathe her son takes it up. What do they want, I wonder?"

"I expect they are trying to find out what *you* want," Isabel guessed, going very near the truth.

"Well, I shall soon show them that I want nothing. I feel sure it would be folly to waste my time and money in a sordid struggle for more than I need. These people have, in their own way, treated me well. Let them keep what they have always had. My share shall be the Moorings and its treasure-trove. I can see now that the very thought of the thing has taken the life out of my work. I must put it all aside and go home and get into harness again."

An involuntary joy took possession of Isabel, to be immediately shadowed by the thought of parting. She was silent for fear of betraying either feeling, or of telling him what she had resolved to keep to herself.

"All that I mind is the leaving you behind," Gilbert said, in a strained tone, that might have told any woman she was loved. "Is there no chance of your coming home soon?"

"I cannot! I cannot!" she almost whispered. Then in a quieter fashion, "I shall give up this place in September. It served my purpose for solitary work, but now I need more of an art atmosphere. I shall spend the winter in Paris. I ought to be very thankful that the wish to work has come back. I must not let it go again. If is all I have."

It was not often that she spoke of her own desolate life, and with the words a silence of endured renunciation fell upon them both.

Presently Gilbert roused himself from it to say: "I shall leave here in a day or two. To-morrow is Cookham Regatta: come with me in the canoe for a last day on this English river. Who knows when we shall have another together?"

"I should like to go," Isabel answered, gently, claiming that one day from the Fates, and yet with an inward misgiving lest Margaret should be there.

Chapter 36

Cookham Regatta

The next day was still and gray with a premonition of the early English autumn in the damp air. It was the breaking of a long drought, and the tawny stretches of field and the yellowing foliage showed its results. The riverbanks alone were green and luxuriant.

The quiet perfection of Mrs. Broderick's gray cloth dress and black hat would have caught any woman's eye, though a man's might have noticed a pale intensity that gave force to her beauty. She had left the paddling to Gilbert and, seated low in the canoe, could look at him as they talked. What did they talk of, she wondered afterward, for through all speech "the last time, the last time" was repeating itself in her brain.

They had not started until after lunch, and reaching the course when the regatta was in full swing, had to draw hastily aside up against an electric launch to make room for a race.

"How the colours vibrate under this gray sky," Isabel said, with all an artist's pleasure in the sight.

No answer coming from him, she looked up to see him pulling off his cap with a friendly smile up at the launch just above them.

Her gaze following his took in a background of gaily

dressed lively groups and, seated on the deck just
above Gilbert's shoulder with Lord Vernade lounging
beside her, the figure of Margaret in her favourite
white and red colours.

Watching for what was coming, she saw Gilbert's
smile fade before the hard stare of his cousin's hostile
eyes, saw the angry flush in her face as Lord Vernade
said something in a low voice, at which she laughed
contemptuously.

Gilbert was now looking before him down the
course with a fixed and grim expression, his kneeling
figure tense with the strain he was putting on himself.

On one of these silences of the crowd that marks
the waiting for a race, came the familiar sound of
Margaret's voice: "As Granny says, one can never tell
with Americans. In any case, I am not responsible for
Jack's taste."

Gilbert looked down into Mrs. Broderick's face, his
sternness softened by anxiety.

"I think that in a moment I can move on and find
you a pleasanter place," he said, in even tones.

As the race swept by, he followed, without any sign
of haste, guiding the canoe onward through the phan-
tasmagoric pageant of flower-decked houseboats,
launches, and boats full of gay dresses and gayer blaz-
ers, and multi-coloured parasols.

Presently they were beyond the thickest throng of
craft, and Gilbert checked the canoe by an overhanging bank.

"You shall have tea here in the quiet. I cannot bear
to think that I should have taken you in the way of
such insult," he said, with troubled eyes.

Even now Isabel did not see that his thought was for her alone, and tried to soothe the hurt Margaret had given him.

"It does not matter for me, only — I am so sorry for *her*. She has too much good in her to be so influenced by some lower nature. I thought it was that dreadful old woman, but now I am afraid it is Lord Vernade. Oh, Gilbert, can nothing be done to win her back again?"

His face did not soften under her appeal.

"I do not care who has influenced her. After the way in which she has treated you I never wish to see her again," he said, bluntly.

His words were sweet to her, though she still thought it was only his chivalry that was aroused.

"You must not say that. I could not bear to know that you two had been separated through me!" she protested, her eyes filling with helpless tears.

"Separated!" He was leaning forward, his face gray with the strain of repressed passion. "Isabel, isn't that a cruel word to use to me? Can it have any meaning to us, save where you and I are concerned? Haven't I tasted the full bitterness of the cup? Am not I going into exile again, and yet you talk to me of separation from her."

She sat looking up at him with dilated eyes, and as his full meaning came to her, a beautiful light dawned upon her face.

"I thought you had forgotten, Gilbert," she whispered.

"Forgotten! And I suppose you were glad it should be so, when this English boy took my place with you!"

he said, bitterly, all unselfish restraint lost in elemental passion.

"The English boy? Jack Nugent-Barr, you mean? He never took your place. There was never any one save you, Gilbert." Her words had the candour, the conviction of those spoken at life's end, when nothing remains save the realities.

For a time they sat looking into each other's faces, satisfying their long heart-hunger, then Isabel's eyes grew wistful.

"It is still separation," she murmured, deprecatingly.

"You are not to think of that now. To-day is the gift of the gods, and we are rich," was Gilbert's brave answer. "Let us get out and sit on the bank. There, can you step now?"

How long they sat in a little grassy patch among the willow bushes, as alone, for all the passing craft, as Adam and Eve in Paradise, neither could have told. At first they talked but little, content with each other's presence.

"Nothing matters so much now, does it?" she asked, at length. "I mean things like this afternoon?" As she spoke she saw the lines of Gilbert's mouth harden.

"Some things matter more," he said, decisively.

"Such as the way you were treated just now. Last night you said you would stay on over here, but now you must see that I cannot leave you here alone. You must be where I can look after you."

He was lying stretched on the grass, propped on one elbow to look up at her, as she sat leaning against a tree-trunk.

There was an appeal under the resolution of his

words, and the pain in her voice answered it.

"All the more I must stay behind. Can't you see that distance is the easiest thing that separates us? To be near each other would be too hard."

"And must it always be so? When we grow old and we are lonely —" he said, hoarsely.

"Believe me, it is better to wait and hope, apart."

"See how near every-day life was to estranging us," she pleaded.

"Never estranging, though that girl made me believe you had acknowledged you cared for her brother. But," he persisted, "at least come out home a few weeks later than I do. We need not be in the same city, but still we should be within reach of each other."

She shook her head.

"There is one reason alone that would make me stay on here now." A painful colour stained her face, and she clasped her hands nervously. "Gilbert, I didn't mean to tell you, but I see that you must know now. I understand the reason of Margaret's behaviour to-day." Bravely and simply she told him the story of the day before, ending with, "You see how all this follows on the old woman's arrival. She must have some good cause for hating you so."

"She shall have more cause yet before she is done with me," he said, with a calm more portentous than any anger.

"You understand what this inevitably leads to?" he asked, then seeing her puzzled look, "I mean that now I have no choice but to do my best for my mother's sake, for yours, to prove the later will. I shall write to my uncle to-night, giving him warning of what I mean to do. Then I shall start at once to go and try to prove the will in Halifax. There will be a big fight, I suppose, but I shall spend every penny of my treasure-trove before I am beaten. I have no doubts as to the right now. Only I cannot bear to leave you here alone."

"No one can hurt me," she said, with a brave attempt at a laugh; then, "Don't you see that I must stay on after you go and live down their story? Do you know," with a sudden intuition, "I believe it was Lord Vernade who started it to set Margaret against me, while the old woman told her that about your mother."

"A pretty pair," he commented, grimly.

"A pretty pair to have an influence over a young girl," she said, sadly. "And she has such a warm-heart-ed, open nature when she has a chance. I cannot be angry with the poor girl, I am so sorry for her."

"Well, you may be sorry for her if you like, as long as you don't bestow too much sympathy on her brother," he said.

"Poor Jack! He will be going to South Africa soon, I suppose."

"Lucky for him to get away from such relations! No, I can feel no Christian charity for any of them to-day. But, good heavens, I have forgotten all about making your tea, and there is the sun setting, and the paddle up-stream will take an hour or so. What a fool I am!"

Isabel laughed out in a fashion he had not heard since her child's death.

"Never mind, there is no mist to-night and we needn't hurry. We'll make it now."

Like two children they picnicked in the evening gray, regardless of coming separation and strife, paddling home afterward through a wonderful blue-green world lit with fiery rays of Japanese lanterns and coloured lights, the end of the regatta festivity.

"Let me write the letter to my uncle here, and then you can read it," Gilbert said, after their late supper that evening. And Isabel sat watching the lamplight on his head as he wrote it.

"Yes, I think that is all you can say," she said, thoughtfully, after reading it.

Through all that day of revived trust, he had scarcely even held her hand longer than usual, but now, as they stood face to face to say good-night, he whitened with passion.

"Must I go?" he said, hoarsely.

She too was pale, and her breath came quickly.

"Yes, yes, go! Oh, please go!" she cried, in distress.

Carried out of all self-control, he seized her in his arms, pressing her to him with hot kisses.

For a space she yielded, and then, shoving him off with her two hands on his chest, she panted: "Gilbert, will you do one thing out of your love for me?"

"What is it?"

"Say good-bye now. We have had our one day. We must not have more. Say good-bye now, and go to London in the morning. You can write me all there is to say, but — we must not be together now."

One long look showed him her firmness.

"Yes, I'll go. Perhaps it's best. But you must make me a promise. If — if *he* should die, you will let me know at once that I may come."

"Yes, I promise. Oh, my love, my love!" and she

clung to him sobbing.

"Go now," she said, presently, loosening his hold with her hands, and he turned and went.

Chapter 37

Jack Goes Soldiering

Home seemed gloomier than ever when Margaret returned there fresh from London gaieties. She had no intention of telling any one of her quarrel with Isabel, but all the same, she had an uncomfortable conviction that it would leak out sooner or later and get her into a scrape.

She found her mother sitting over a fire, the usual fancy-work in her hands.

"There is to be a bazaar to buy a reredos for Hugh Stayner's church, and I promised to send him a box," she announced, after greeting her daughter.

Showing no interest in this important piece of news, Margaret said: "Barnes told me that Granny is ill. What is the matter?"

"I'm sure I can't tell," her mother said, with the aggrieved air of the family invalid with encroached-upon rights. "She is nervous and fretful enough for anything. She has sent Madame Estivalet on a visit to her sister and will hardly let Ellen Sievert out of her sight. I can get no use of her at all."

Even this feeble complaint showed that the reins held so long by the family tyrant were slipping from her grasp.

But the habit of years still proved strong enough her mother to say, nervously: "You had better go up and see her now. She won't like it if she hears you are with me."

With reluctant steps the girl went, feeling as though those sharp eyes would read the secret of her disobedience to her implied orders.

She was not experienced enough to note the new feebleness in the huddled figure, the something like fear in the eyes that followed her about the room. There was the same old delight though in the account of Margaret's social successes, the same keen questioning as to what she had done.

"Gilbert Clinch will be glad that you are back. He was here yesterday and seemed dull. You must get some people together for him. Tennis or picnics or something. There's Cookham Regatta to-morrow. I suppose you're going to that? Why not take him?"

"The Vernades are coming down for it with a party. Their launch calls for me on the way to meet them at Taplow. I couldn't very well ask them to take a stranger," Margaret pleaded, thankful for the excuse.

"You could manage it fast enough if you chose. Well, then, you must do something for him the next day. And listen, Meg," leaning forward to lay a bony grasp on her arm, "the solicitor is coming down to-morrow to see about altering my will for you — but mind you don't tell your father," she added, in a whisper.

"All right, Granny. Just as you like," Meg agreed, disquieted by her own satisfaction in the news. That night she was startled from sleep by sounds like distant sobs and groans, which aroused a latent element of imaginative terrors. She lay for some time afraid to strike a light, chilled with fear, though healthy fatigue at last conquered, and she slept long and heavily.

She awoke to find the cheerful daylight streaming in, and Ellen Sievert's comfortable face looking down upon her.

"Bless me, child, but you slept late," that worthy said.

"I don't wonder," stretching her arms above her head. "Oh, Ellen, there were such strange noises last night! I was sure the wicked old ghost must be walking about. Did you hear anything?"

"Hush, child, hush!" Ellen said, nervously.

"Don't talk about ghosts! Yes, I heard the noises all right. It was your grandma, who's taken to having queer fits at night, waking up moaning and screaming like a child. She won't be left alone, keeping me up half the night sometimes. It's very wearing."

"It's very unpleasant," Margaret agreed.

The next day, however, the old lady roused into something of her former keenness with the appearance of the fat little London solicitor.

"Has she said nothing to you, nothing at all about what she is doing?" Mr. Nugent-Barr asked his daughter, at frequent intervals through the day, but every time she presented the same front of serene ignorance. She was far too astute to let fall any hint of her grandmother's promises.

These promises had settled themselves in her mind, and she had now dropped any mental pretence of not desiring the riches they might bring her.

But she had not reckoned on a telegram from Jack

to say that he had obtained the promised staff appointment at Cape Town and, as he was to sail at once, would have little more than a day with his family.

Jack going abroad for an indefinite time, and she almost relieved at his absence in her consciousness of disloyalty! No wonder she was pale and restless, and went off for a long solitary ramble.

And when Jack arrived, it was to find the whole household in a commotion over Gilbert's letter announcing the second will.

Mr. Nugent-Barr fumed and fretted with the helpless anger of the weak. His mother raved at Margaret, whom she guessed to be keeping something to herself bearing on the affair, but getting nothing out of her, worked herself up into a state that she had to be quieted with a soothing draught.

Margaret paid little attention to either of them, being absorbed in the fighting instinct aroused in her by the first threat to the money that she now knew she loved. She had wanted Gilbert Clinch to think well of her, to idealise her, had suffered in his liegemanship to Mrs. Broderick, had hated him with the hatred of futile jealousy, but now all these feelings were merged in the frank enmity of greed.

Jack, full of his new life, brought a breath of the healthy outside world into the disturbed household. At first sight of his familiar face, Meg felt all evil thoughts fall away in the joy of his presence — the old brother and sister comradeship that can survive so much. She saw that the boyishness was gone, though the manhood was as frankly and sturdily honest as ever. The new gravity sat well on his sunburnt face as he listened quietly to his father's excited story.

"It certainly doesn't seem what I would have expected of him," Jack said, the letter in his hand, "to come to us and be treated as a relation and then all of a sudden to fire this bomb at us in a distinctly hostile fashion. And you say that he was here to dinner two or three days ago? Well, I'm disappointed in him.

"He'll learn that advancing claims is a different matter to getting the money. He cannot have the capital for a long fight such as, if the worst came, we should make of it."

"Unless he has some one backing him up," Meg put in. Jack gave her a quick glance, but said nothing.

"Look here, Meg, what did you mean by that about some one backing Gilbert up?" Jack asked, when presently they were alone together on the terrace.

"Oh, I don't know, it was just a guess," she answered, evasively. She had already repented the speech.

"I was afraid — though you could have hardly meant Mrs. Broderick," he said, jerking an idle pebble toward a swan among the reeds.

"Oh, no," she agreed, hastily. She felt that whatever happened she must part good friends with Jack, but how she hated the woman whom she felt to be in some measure the cause of his going.

"Have you seen anything of her lately?" he asked, still intent on the swans.

"No, not lately. You see, I've been in town for a fortnight and — well, I had a feeling as though she didn't want me to come much. She always seemed to be busy and — perhaps it was this thing that made a difference."

"Why should it?" was his brusque question.

"Oh, well, you know they are old friends." She had no courage to imply more.

"Well, I don't understand it at all," he said, moodily. "I could have sworn that he was an honest man, and I'm half inclined to believe him so still. I shall try to get my father to have a meeting with him in town before he goes to America. You see, Meg," he went on, slowly, "if that second will should chance to be genuine we have no right to fight him down through sheer power of money."

Meg felt like a child who sees its shining toys being withdrawn from its grasp.

"But it would be a third of all that we have," she protested.

"What does that matter if we had no right to it? We should even then have plenty left. Let's try, Meg, never to get like my father and the old woman. And look here," he went on, very soberly, "when I'm gone be friends if you can with Mrs. Broderick — it would make me happier, Meg."

"Yes, Jack," Meg sobbed, for the moment completely under his influence.

"That's a good girl," and Jack patted her on the head, and strode away to hide his own feelings.

Meg never knew what passed between father and son, or whether Jack saw Mrs. Broderick that day.

The next morning he went, and once free from the magnetism of his presence, Meg had the old harrowing mixed sensations of regret and relief.

There had been none of the shadow of coming war over the parting, for though in those days there was already talk of a few troops going out to over-awe the troublesome Transvaal politicians, no one dreamt that for more than two years Englishwomen were to watch their men go forth, so many to their death.

Chapter 38

Ellen Sievert Speaks Her Mind

The weeks went by and life was dull at Monk's Grange, though the season ended and shooting begun, had brought neighbours back from town.

Margaret went about as much as possible, often staying away on short visits, glad to escape from home, where her father went up and down to frequent interviews with his town solicitors, returning to be closeted for hours with the old lady, hours which left them both very fractious.

About this legal business they had both become very mysterious to Margaret, a course which intensely provoked her curiosity and also worried her with a sense of mistrust.

She had found out, through the servants, that Mrs. Broderick was still at Heathholm, though since that encounter at the station they had never met each other.

Jack's first letter had not cheered her in its undertone of implied reproach.

"I am hoping when my home letters arrive," he wrote, "to hear that my father has come to some arrangement with Gilbert Clinch. It is surely just that he should have a share of his grandfather's money."

And then he went on to say, "I think, Meg, how solitary you are at home, and I should be glad to know that you were much with Mrs. Broderick, who would be so good a friend to you."

"And twist me round her finger as she did him! I wonder what she has said or written to him about me!" she said to herself, bitterly, and then, with a desire to shake off her gloomy thoughts, she started out for a ramble up through the beech woods.

Leaving the highroad, she struck off by a stile into meadows that were part of the Vernade lands. The corn was in most places cut, and a deep peace brooded over the empty fields under the western sunshine and the long blue-gray shadows of the waning day. She was on comparatively high land and every now and then could look down on some shining reach of the river.

Why would it remind her of that Sunday in June, and their cheerful group? Was even her old friend the river going to recall estranged friends!

It was with a pleased sense of coming companionship that she saw Lord Vernade approaching with gun and dogs, evidently returning from shooting. How slim and alert he looked in his country dress! Something that was almost proprietary pride warmed her heart as she watched him. However cynical and lazy his manner might be, she knew that nowhere else did she ever find such subtle intuition into her moods, such power of adaptation to them. When with him she always felt that sense of being understood which puts one at one's best.

As she went along Margaret had gathered sprays of

the fluffy gray clematis, with deep-tinted trails of brambles, that now hung loosely from her grasp.

"Welcome, Ophelia! Only not away to seek a watery death in the backwater, I trust?" he began.

"I am only taking an aimless stroll," she said, and at the first sound of her voice he gave a keen glance of inquiry into her face.

"Then you might be very nice, and turn now and walk back with me. You must turn sooner or later, you know."

"I suppose so," she agreed, and they paced on for a moment in silence, even the sound of his regular footstep giving her a sense of companionship.

"I only came down yesterday and meant to look you up to-morrow. And now it seems to me that you have a dispirited air. What is it?" he said.

"Times are dull at Monk's Grange since Jack left. Granny is ill, and her humours are so fantastic that even I am half afraid of her, and I never was that, you know. And then she and my father are in an awful stew over business."

"Nothing wrong, I hope?" he asked with interest. It was a part of his scheme of things that Margaret should be a rich woman.

"It's the cousin," she said with a short laugh. "You were right that he wanted something. He has produced a later will of my grandfather's which would give him a third of the estate."

"That's modest!" Lord Vernade commented. "But your father will fight it of course?"

"Oh, yes, and really the lawyers don't seem to think much of it. He claims that an old sailor, who was about the house when my grandfather died, produced this will which he had hidden away for eighteen years or so.

"What a cock-and-bull story! And are Mr.Clinch and his patron saint still dwelling on the hilltops?"

"No. That is, she is at Heathholm, I believe, but he must have gone away a day or so after we met them at Cookham. I have been so worried about it I haven't told any one — but wouldn't it be dreadful if my making him angry had started all this?"

"Why, it must all have been a put up thing long before either of them ever came here," he said with conviction.

"I'm so glad you think so. I didn't venture to tell any one at home," she said, wistfully.

This appealing attitude in the girl usually so lazily self-reliant was rousing dangerous forces in him. He found it momentarily harder to keep his eyes from the curve of her cheek, the loose hair that hung about her ear, the line of the neck and shoulder under her tight-fitting jacket, and when she turned her languorous eyes to him the hot blood leaped in his veins.

"Poor little one," he said, very gently, "you should be taken away from all this into the brighter life that belongs to you. Think if only we were yachting in the Mediterranean now. Would you come if I got up a party and made Estelle ask you?"

Her face had flashed round to him transformed into radiancy, but what she read in his eyes caused her head to droop. They had instinctively paused by a stile that led into the highroad. He did not wait for her answer to his question, but went on: "I always like to think of you with sumptuous surroundings, the *grande dame* that you should be. The other day, when I was down at Saxhurst, I was haunted by visions of what the house might be with another kind of mistress. I seemed to see you in the state drawing-rooms, on the stairs receiving royalty —"

His voice had grown hoarse, as though each word forced itself out, and somehow her hand was in his, the leaves fallen to the path. She felt under a spell, as if being swept on by a great wind, until the strain that had held her broke.

"Oh, don't," she cried, wildly, pulling her hand away. "Oh, you must never speak to me like that again, please! You must let me go now. We are here at the lodge, and I want to speak to Mrs. Cox about her chickens."

In silence he helped her over the stile, and it was only when at the door of the lodge that he said, with grim self-repression: "I would not interrupt such an important mission for worlds. Good day," and raising his hat, went off down the road.

Margaret stood for a moment at the cottage gate to recover her equanimity. In the tumult of various feelings that possessed her that of which she was most conscious was the fact of having pained him. She could not help it; virtuous indignation would not come to her aid. His admiration, and something which she had read in his eyes that was stronger than admiration, had aroused unknown feelings in her before which everything seemed petty and mean. If Jack and Gilbert set a stranger before her, there was still some one with whom she counted first, she said to herself, with a new exultation.

It was a striking change of scene to go in upon Ellen Sievert having a friendly cup of tea with plump Mrs. Cox by her cosy fireside. The latter lady's principal boast in life was the large family she had produced and partly sent out into the world.

It was a great thing to have a listener to tales of this girl's welfare in service, or that son's doings in the army, and Ellen made the best of listeners because she had no desire to narrate her own experiences. She had, after a short time in England, decided to keep her Canadian origin a secret, and called herself Scotch, not considering it likely that she would fall in with any of that nationality, and remembering that her mother had been of Scotch origin.

"Them English always turns up their noses at any one who's seen more of the world than they have, and as far as I can tell, they don't seem to know the difference between me and a Yankee anyway," she had said to herself, veiling her respectable past with a secrecy usually reserved for a more varied one.

The ample form of the hostess fluttered a greeting, but the absence of a smile on Ellen's face reminded Margaret that the window where the two cronies were sitting looked down the field-path by which she had come. Was it possible that she had a sense of shame under her nurse's gaze?

"Don't disturb yourselves when you are having a cosy chat!" she said, airily. "I am sure that Mrs. Sievert needs a little cheering up, Mrs. Cox, after the time she has had lately nursing my grandmother. I just ran in to ask you when you can let us have those chickens. My mother was talking about them this morning."

"'Deed and, miss, the housekeeper sent down for them three days ago," Mrs. Cox protested, and Ellen's inexorable eye seemed to rend her excuse to tatters, and ask what she had to do with the household larder.

"Oh, well, then, I won't disturb you any longer," she said, but she was not destined to get off without a chaperon.

"I must be getting along home myself, miss, for I promised Sarah the housemaid as I wouldn't be more than an hour, and I guess it's near that now, and, poor silly thing, she always gets nervous when she's sitting alone in the old lady's dressing-room, though why she should — well, at any rate, miss, if you don't mind, I'll come along with you," said Ellen, somewhat stiffly.

"All right, nurse," Margaret replied, feeling much as she did when, as a child, she had inked her pinafore, and knew she would be scolded for it.

"When I first sees you coming down through the fields, miss," Ellen began, in a mildly conversational tone, "I thought as how I wished the gentleman with you might be your cousin instead of that Lord Vernade."

Ignoring the disapproving accent on "that," Margaret answered, sharply: "Didn't Granny tell you that Mr. Clinch had gone back to America? She would have, if she had known how much interest you took in him."

"And why shouldn't I take an interest in him, when I played and went to school with his mother away off there by the La Have, that maybe I'll never see again, and nobody to be sorry neither," came with a sniff that sounded tearful, "but dead or alive, Miss Meg, indeed

I'd never be happy to be knowing you to be walking round the country with them as isn't fit company for no decent girl, lady or no lady. Just listen to me, my dear, while I tell you what happened —" In her earnestness she laid a tremulous hand on the arm of the girl, who shook it off in a gust of passion.

"There's your way to the house," Margaret said, pointing to the path that led to the servants' entrance, "I shall take this one," and she hurried off, leaving the old woman shedding the few slow tears of age.

Chapter 39

In the Day of Temptation

The autumn and the war had come, and Meg was in a panic of an unfamiliar dread. She would start up at night with visions of dark hillsides on which lay motionless figures, one motionless figure; visions of hospital tents and a white face turned up toward a rough attendant. Imagination at such times is a woman's worst foe, and of imagination poor Meg had plenty.

Living under such a strain, her visits to her grandmother's room became daily a greater ordeal. She never could tell what irrelevantly keen question might not pierce her armour.

One day the old lady was especially maddening. "Jack was always unlucky, he will be sure to get wounded. When he was a boy and fell from a tree, he always broke an arm or leg," she soliloquised, "and when he is wounded"— Meg could have screamed — "I wonder if that American woman will go out and nurse him. Do you know if she has followed him out there?" she asked, imperiously.

"No, Granny, why should she?" came the listless answer.

"Why should she? Because she knows he is a fool

and, if she told him to, would give up everything to his cousin. But he hasn't got it to give," she chuckled. "He tried the wrong person when he tried to make my son loosen his grip on money. Meg!"

"Yes, Granny?"

"Promise me that when I die, and you have my money, you won't let Jack have any of it, or he'll give it to that son of Susan Bauer's. Promise me!"

"I can't promise not to give anything to Jack."

"You must! You shall! Or I'll leave it all to your father! He won't give any of it away. Meg, if this man takes away all our money you will be sorry you did not try to marry him. Oh, I know you didn't try, and that you offended him and made him angry!"

"What makes you say so, Granny?" came in a feeble protest.

"Oh, I know things. I sit here and piece them together like a puzzle until they come out clear. But listen now," and a tragic eagerness came into the weird figure, "we made a mistake in letting the Ripamonti marriage fall through. We'll send for Estivalet and she can write to the mother. They don't really want so big a 'dot.' And then there's Jack — he can be provided for by marrying Tommy Curtis."

In spite of her growing uneasiness, Meg gave a cynical laugh.

"Tommy Curtis has electrified her family by announcing her intention of providing for Mr. Brindle. He sailed for South Africa yesterday, and it seems that they were secretly married the day before. Father had an explosive letter this morning saying that it was all our fault."

"Fools! That will be a nice dose for their family pride!" the old woman snapped, vindictively. She had always hated her daughter-in-law's aristocratic relations. "But now go over to the table and write to Estivalet to come home and start this Ripamonti business again."

"No, Granny, I won't," Meg said, decisively. "I would never marry that great big prize-fighter of a man. And why should I? What is it you are afraid of? It looks as though you knew that this will must be genuine —"

A fierce cry from her grandmother interrupted her.

"How dare you say I am afraid of him, you wicked girl! If you knew more of the world you would understand what a misfortune to a family the flimsiest claims boldly pushed can be. Look at the Tichbourne family, all but ruined years ago by an Australian butcher. No, your grandfather was a tyrant, but never a fool to go making confusion with wills. But old Isaac, and the wind that night —" her voice rose into a scream, and Ellen appeared at the door with a warning glance at the girl.

"Better let her be quiet and go away to your ma now, child. It's more healthy company for you."

Margaret lost no time in leaving the room, but some reluctant attraction made her pause in the dressing-room and seat herself in a high-backed armchair that stood turned from the door near an open window. The south wind blew in softly from the river, and the distant sound of a railway whistle, the measured clank of oars soothed her with the consciousness of a saner, brighter world outside.

Within the bedroom her grandmother's wails were

gradually yielding to Ellen's soothing, as might those
of a frightened child.

"There now, there," she heard Ellen saying, "let me
put some cologne on your head, that'll make you feel
better, and just take a little sip of this. You don't want
to go to sleep, and you want to talk, do you? I'll talk,
if you like. I've only been a poor working woman this
many a day since my brother-in-law went and lost my
husband's savings in that plaguey gold mine, but I
come of just as good old Lunenburg stock as the
Barrs, and have known them all my life. I knew the old
man, and I knew Susan, and I never knew either of
them to yield in a thing that they had once made up
their minds to, and is it likely now that this boy will?
Lord knows you've got more than you know what to
do with, you and the master between you, so why can't
you give him a share of his grandpa's money without
going to law over it? It's a bad thing for them as has
old secrets they don't want known, to begin going to
law —"

Here came a fierce murmur, and then the low,
steady stream of talk went on.

"Oh, yes, I know what I'm talking about, and I don't
mean to forget my place, but I've made up my mind
to speak out once for all, and when the time comes I
shall, too. You're old, and the days of your life must
soon be ended. Now wouldn't it be better to try and
straighten things up a bit before you go? Tell your son
the things you've never told him yet and get him to
help you. Tell him that ye were nothing better than a
brown Martinique girl, who the master won one night
at cards and took away with him the next day — tell

him how your sort have queer poisons the doctors
know nothing of, and use them — oh, yes, I know. My
old man was on that cruise and he told me wild things
when his end came, and the fear of death took him —
and the rest, Isaac Neisner and I guessed for ourselves. What do you suppose he went off home for so
sudden if he wasn't afraid of following his master to
the grave too soon?"

Here the hoarse, inarticulate sounds which had
made themselves heard throughout the woman's
speech took form in words.

"Go away, go away, ungrateful, lying creature, and
never let me see your face again! I will tell your master to have you turned out of the house!"

"Oh, no, you won't; you'd be afraid to," came the
even tones again. "I'm going to stay with my little
Meg, and her poor mother, same as I've always done.
And besides that, I'm going to take care of you, and
see that you don't die the death that the old master
did, with your soul carried off in the storm! Perhaps
there'll be a tree crash down here, too! No, you and I
are used to each other, and I don't mean you any
harm if you'll only be fair to Susan's boy —"

"Ellen, listen!" and again the hoarse, feeble voice
made itself dominant, "you say you care for Meg, and I'll
tell you what I haven't told any of them. I've left everything to her, and if only you'll hold your tongue —"

"Oh, yes, I care for her, and if you hadn't set her
against her cousin —"

Once or twice Margaret had made an effort to rise,
with the impulse of going to her grandmother's aid, the
instinct of race and of class making this relentless

upbraiding of the old woman too repulsive, but the spell of that smooth stream of words bringing out horror upon horror held her bound helpless. She must hear, she must know what other shame rested upon her.

She felt as if something that went to the making of her own identity were falling away, leaving all her personality beggared of dignity.

Her own instincts, her mother's and grandmother's teaching had given her an intense pride of birth. She had believed in the legend of the noble French family fleeing from the Revolution to Martinique, as she had believed in the greatness of her mother's titled Irish relations, whose stately, dilapidated castle she had seen.

"A brown girl — that means a slave," she supposed — won at a game of cards and taken away in a vessel; one who knew strange poisons, and had, on some occasion that she dared not think of, used them — could such a creature be a blood-relation of hers, existing side by side with this luxurious, upper-class English life, which she had sometimes grumbled at as humdrum, but which at the moment seemed to her such a secure refuge from those outside lawless elements? Why, the very servants who waited upon them so deferentially would shrink in horror from such a person. And if they were-ever to know, if all her world were to hear the story, what would become of her?

A horror of learning more took the place of the morbid curiosity that had held her, and she slipped noiselessly away, drawing a long breath of relief as she gained the outer air.

Chapter 40

At the Shooting-Hut

A day of still gray autumn beauty was drawing to a close, and as Margaret, after hastily ordering her horse, rode through the yellowing woods, by heaths rich with heather, and brown harvest fields, the rapid movement and open air soothed her jangled nerves into lassitude.

At first she had ridden fast, but the habit of caring for her horse was too strong for her to forget it even now, and after taking a long turn she was going along at a walk, her face set homewards.

It was not a highroad, indeed little more than a cart track across a heath, and as it turned to lead down-hill into a lane between high wooded banks, she saw Lord Vernade standing by a gate into a field, his gun on his shoulder.

She remembered now that near the gate stood a little hut, used in winter as a lunching-place for the shooters. She had sometimes come with Lady Vernade to meet them there. Was it joy or fear, the keen throb that shook her as he came forward into the road and laid a hand upon her horse's neck? Was there relief or disappointment in noting that his manner, his voice, even the look in his blue-gray eyes, were marked by nothing more than their usual quiet friendliness?

"This is unexpected luck," he said. "I was just arguing the point with myself whether it would be unsportsmanlike self-indulgence to go to the hut and light the fire and make a cup of tea. The fact of entertaining a tired wayfarer would remove all my scruples, so you won't have the heart to refuse me."

The words were a humble request, but the manner took it for granted, and Margaret allowed him to lift her down from her saddle in a light but lingering grasp.

"It would be nice," was all she said, as she followed him into the field. The hut was small and rough, but comfortable, with one or two fold-up chairs. A fire of logs and brushwood was ready built on the hearth, some plain tea-things stood on a deal table. A match to the wood sent a red glow through the room, and Meg sank into a chair before it with a sigh of relaxation. It was the getting away that she had wanted.

"Shall I cut the bread and butter?" she asked, as she watched him hanging the kettle above the flames.

"No, you are to sit still and let me minister to you. Why do you so doubt my capacity? Don't you know that all sportsmen are handy men?"

The work of preparing their little picnic seemed to fully occupy his attention, and it was not until the tea had been poured out and the bread and butter cut that he seated himself opposite her.

"Did you ever observe what an atmosphere of conventional virtue surrounds such articles as a brown earthenware teapot and thick bread and butter? Now, if one could only found a sanitarium for imbibing

virtue by such outward means" — then abruptly dropping the nonsense he had been talking — "Aren't you
going to tell me what has been troubling you?" he
said, quietly.

She had been saying to herself as she sat there that
she must not tell him what she had heard to-day, but
all instincts of prudence went, before the influence of
his steady eyes, and that craving for sympathy, which is
always such a weak spot for women. Perhaps it was
because he was the one of all others in whose eyes she
most dreaded to lose her prestige, that she proceeded
to recklessly lay bare the dark story.

"I am feeling rather bewildered, like a poor doll
might whose card-house had fallen to bits on its
head."

"Has yours?"

"Yes, I fear that I shall never be able to believe in
card-houses again," and the attempt of her laugh
ended somewhat tremulously.

"Build more durable ones," he suggested, humouring the parable.

"Oh, nothing will ever be worth doing any more,"
she broke out.

"That's a large order, in your twenties. Tell me about
it. Here, make a footstool of this log of wood and let
me put this coat behind you," and as he did so, his
hand touched the back of her neck, brushing the
loose curls into place, and answered almost as in
words by the flush that rose on the clear skin.

"Now tell me," he said, going back to the seat that
seemed to have edged itself round the corner of the
table.

It was a relief for the tumult of her spirit to find vent in words.

"I know you think it's only some girl's quarrel or nonsense," she began, "but if you knew what I heard to-day! How would you feel if you had found out that your grandmother had been a West Indian slave girl, won at cards, and that her own servants supposed her to have poisoned her husband who had been something very like a pirate? Why, it is as though one had done it oneself!"

A restraining hand was laid upon hers clasped upon the table, and even through the power of those terrible facts as she first put into words, that touch came as a new force into her life. So did the voice, that, masterful for all its calm, broke in upon her speech.

"Hush, my poor child! Try to be calm! It's been upsetting for you, no doubt, but you'll soon see how little those old sins have to do with you. It is what a woman *is,* that matters, not what her grandmother has been."

As he thus waved aside all modern theories of heredity, he withdrew his hand, and, leaning in his chair, went on, in a more matter-of-fact tone.

"And when once you think of it, most of the British aristocracy is in the same boat. Weren't the forefathers of all the oldest families Norman freebooters or Danish pirates, and as for the modern ones, what great fortune has ever been made with clean hands? Then in regard to the ladies, how many English families have been founded by royal favourites, and in later days how many actresses have supplied the needed brains and beauty? Don't you think that you might see it in that light?" and Meg knew without looking up, that the half-cynical, half-indulgent smile was bent upon her.

"Yes, one knows all that, but one's own people always seem different," she murmured, with a new shyness.

"But why should they?" was the cheerful retort. "It's only a matter of habit, after all. Now, if I had ever taken to heart the sins of my grandfather, George IV's Lord Vernade, and his excessively lively French wife, I should have had a nice subject of meditation."

"Are you half French? I'm glad," Margaret said, with sudden animation.

"Yes? Why?"

"Oh, I don't know. I suppose because I always liked the idea that I had some French blood in me," and the first hint of a smile crossed her face, though it darkened into a new anxiety.

"You don't think I look one least little bit like a black person?" she asked, with girlish solemnity.

The man laughed out heartily. Both he and the girl were too thoroughly European to have any comprehension of what the taint of another race would have meant to one reared on the other side of the Atlantic. If the skin were white it never occurred to them that the nature could be shadowed.

"You ridiculous child! Do you want me to tell you what I think you look like?" and again her head dropped under the meaning of his eyes and voice.

There was a pregnant silence, while the brushwood fire crackled loudly, and Vernade's long brown hand lay on the table, as though kept from moving forward

by a strong will. When he began to speak again his
voice sounded more forced: "You can comfort yourself, too, in the fact that a woman is never so deep-
rooted in her own family as a man. In a few years you
will have another name, probably that of some great
house, and you will have a position of your own in the
world. And how you will fill it! Oh!" — his voice deepened into the hoarse, intense tones that had thrilled
through her the other day — "if only things had been
different with me —"

His hand was on hers now, but Margaret roused into
a last effort of resistance — the effort that fights
against the weakness of one's own desires, and she
sprang up, saying, quickly: "Don't, please don't! I
must go if you do!"

But her hand was still in that firm grasp, and,
though he made no movement to draw here nearer,
he would not let her go.

"No, you must listen to me now, for I have made up
my mind to speak. Meg, you know well enough what
my wife is, and you guess perhaps what she has made
me, but before God, I would be an honest man to a
woman who trusted me. *You* could trust me, Meg!"

She stood very still beside him now, with a look on
her face as though it were fate that held her in its
grasp.

"I feel certain," he went on, "that she would like
nothing better than to have a chance to divorce me;
that she has reason to believe that Martingdale would
marry her, and would probably have gone off with
him before now, if she had been sure of my divorcing
her. So, you see, if you had the courage to come away

with me, it would only be a sharp, short ordeal, and then, dearest, then —"

With an impetuous movement, Meg had shaken off his grasp.

"Oh, never, never," she cried, wildly. "Think of my mother and Jack! They are good, at any rate!"

The man showed no signs of a rebuff, but went on with the same self-contained strenuousness, standing now beside her.

"Perhaps so, if goodness is not merely neutrality. But Jack, as you have told me, is a weak tool in the hands of Mrs. Broderick, and, through her, of this cousin of yours. As for your mother, well, you know that if she has her doctor, her parson, and a bazaar to work for, nothing else matters much. Are they two worth weighing in the balance against what I give you? I never guessed that it was in me to care as I care for you!"

There was no answering flash of passion, as Margaret stood before him, chilled by doubts and fears.

"Oh, dear! How hard life is," she sighed.

He was too set upon conquering her by force of will to weaken into pity.

"No, it is easy enough to grasp its chances firmly. It is only to the wavering that it is hard. Meg," both her hands were now in his, "for both our sakes, don't be weak now! Remember it is my chance as well as yours! Face it now and settle the matter."

"I can't do that," came low with an accent of decision, before which his face grew grimmer.

"Then promise me to think it over well before you decide against me. I have to run up North to-morrow on a few days' business. Promise me to have decided when I come back," he persisted.

"I will promise anything if you will only let me go now. I must go," she sobbed; then looking up at him with a new fear, "but if I find that I can't do it, you won't be angry with me? I sha'n't lose you as a friend?"

He saw his advantage and pressed it home.

"I couldn't stay on as your friend now. You must know that we've got past that. We've been talked about, too, and that would make it harder for you. I should probably spend the next six months in India or South Africa after big game."

As the heavy tears rolled silently down her cheeks, a light of exultation shone in his eyes, and drawing her closer by the hands he held, their lips met.

It was a moment before she freed herself, pleading: "Let me go! Let me go!"

"Yes, you shall go now," he agreed, and hand in hand they went out into the gathering autumn twilight to where her horse was waiting.

When he had put her up he kissed her bare hand, saying, softly: "Next week!"

She made no answer, but he could hear that she was sobbing as she rode away into the darkness.

Chapter 41

The Power of the Night

October had come, bringing with it tidings of the first battle of the war, tidings that were to strike all England with a blank amazement, a sick mistrust. At the same time as his news, came Jack's letters to Meg, full of a new serious purposefulness, a wistful affection that frightened as much as it moved her.

"Although every man feels sure that he is going to come through it, still, fighting ahead is a fact that straightens out one's perspective," he wrote. "Some things look all at once so big, and some so small. Truth and honour, these are the things that, whatever else a man loses, he must keep. I have written again to my father, asking him to try that at whatever cost we treat Gilbert Clinch with justice and fairness. If anything should happen to me, dear Meg, I hope that you will always remember this is my earnest wish —"

Margaret flung down the letter in an outbreak of bitter weeping. All at once the knowledge of Jack would think of the way in which she had of late been drifting, came over her with a new cowardice. She did her best to shake it off saying to herself that at any rate she would be no hypocrite like that hateful woman in whom nothing seemed to shake Jack's belief. Perhaps some day — and then, even in thought, she shrank away from what that "some day" might be bringing.

How it rained in those late October days! The steel-gray stretch of the river under the low sky seemed day by day to widen, until, at last, it was over the banks, and the low-lying meadows were turned into great sheets of water, the trim new brick villas that skirted the town standing up disconsolate like old ladies in their best clothes in a mud-puddle. The waters were out over the high-road, and Monk's Grange's communication with the outside world was carried on by means of punts.

In these days the interest of the gloomy house centred round the sickroom where old Madame de Barre was evidently making ready to set out on a journey which floods would not prevent. Day by day the intervals when she roused into full consciousness became less frequent, the periods of heavy torpor longer.

"She's slipping away peacefully, if it'll only go on to the end," said Ellen Sievert, with an evident conviction that it would not.

Then one grim day, when the southwest wind drove the sheets of rain against the windows, the conscious times were replaced by a dull monotone of rambling, rising now and then in shrill cries on which Ellen, if possible, shut the door to every one. When the doctor appeared in a punt, he said, briefly, after one glance at the patient: "I think that you had better send over to the town for a priest."

"There is a telegraph-boy crossing now. We can send a man back with him," said Meg, who was standing in one of the windows that over-looked the river.

In a few moments more Mr. Nugent-Barr was reading out in tones of incredulous horror, such a telegram as was soon to bring woe to so many English homes.

"Your son, Captain Eustace John Nugent-Barr, killed leading a charge against the Boers at Elandslagte."

Meg heard the words as one under a spell, and while her mother sobbed and screamed in hysterics, she left her to the ministrations of her maid, crouching with strained, pallid face, like a frightened child, in the corner of a big sofa.

Only when old Ellen came, the tears streaming down her face, and laying a tender hand upon her head, said: "Miss Meg, my little Miss Meggie, speak to me," did a quiver pass over her face and a few slow tears fall.

Since the day when they had walked home together from the lodge, the friendly intercourse between the two had been in abeyance, but now Meg clung to her old nurse with all the abandonment of her childish days.

"Oh, nurse," she sobbed, "if only he and I could be children together again."

But Ellen could not be spared from the dying to mourn the dead.

"Please, Mrs. Sievert, Sarah says she can't keep the old lady quiet no longer without you," said a frightened-looking servant, and as Ellen went, Meg clung to her and followed her with an apparent dread of being left alone. Mrs. Nugent-Barr had been put to bed with a soothing draught, and her father was pacing the corridor outside of his mother's room.

The cause of the patient's restlessness was soon made known.

"The priest! Send for the priest at once!" clamoured a shrill voice with that strange new strength which nurses learn to know as a sign of numbered hours, while a clawlike hand grasped Ellen's arm.

The latter soothed her with professional serenity.

"And isn't it more than an hour since Jenkins went over to the town, and shouldn't they have been back before now but for the current bein' so cruel strong! But, sure and certain, they must be here in ten minutes at the very outsidest, so try and lie easy and keep your mind clear for the time when Father Staunton comes, that's a dear soul," and Ellen patted her as benevolently as if she believed her old mistress destined to a heavenly harp and crown.

Her spell worked for a moment, and then with a long wail of the still rising storm the old woman started fearfully.

"What's that? The wind?" came in a hoarse whisper that shook even Ellen's calm.

"Lord save us, yes! What else should it be?" she stammered.

"Where is my son? He should stay by me now," the patient wailed to herself.

"I am here, mother," came an answer from the doorway, and out of the shadows appeared the haggard face of the unhappy master of the house. The nurse drew back, searching with an anxious glance the corners of the dimly lit room for the girl for whose sorrow her heart was aching.

Not finding her, she passed on into the dressing room, where the light burned brighter, and there, seated on the floor, her hands clasped round her raised knees, on which her chin rested, staring into the shadows with sombre, unseeing eyes, she found her. She had not even drawn near to the comfort of the fire, but, held in a mental and physical tension, awaited the next stroke of Fate as a child might await a blow.

"My poor precious girlie! Are you here by your lone, grieving?" the old woman cried, hurrying toward her with an outstretched hand, but something in the dark eyes turned upon her from the unmoving face, staying her steps.

"Well, you have got your wish!" came in a fierce whisper. "Are you *glad* now that the Messenger has come in the storm?"

"For the Lord's sake, Miss Meggie, what do you mean?" the poor old soul stammered, drawing back in dismay.

"I heard you when you threatened her! You, whom I used to think were kind and good!"

This was too much, even for Ellen's sense of pity. "Well, then, and I'm sure, poor sinners though we all are, as you've no cause to say otherwise —" she began, volubly, when a cry so wild rang out from the next room that her words quavered and stopped.

"The priest! The priest!" came the wail as of a lost spirit. "Will no one stir to fetch him, and save a poor old woman's soul? Something, some one is calling and I must go! Howard, you are my son, I did it for you! I knew that your father wanted to make a new will! I gave him the medicine to stop it! Oh, those medicines we used to make long ago in the hot sunshine — hear the palms rustle — Meg, my little Meg, at least I have

loved you — Meg, come to me before I go — oh, they
are calling me —" The broken words died in a long
wail as both women reached the bed, and the raised
head dropped back among the pillows with a lifeless
thud.

Outside a fearful gust beat and tore at the windows,
and the responsive crash of a falling tree rang against
the house.

Meg was now flat upon the floor as though beaten
down by the storm, her face hidden, her hands over
her ears, all the hereditary quailing before the unseen
powers of darkness of a savage people dominant in
her soul.

She did not know how long it was before her
father's hand drew down hers with a new gentleness
of touch.

"My poor child, there is nothing to be frightened of.
She is gone," he said, wearily.

"Gone where?" She was now sitting looking up at
him, and, unimaginative man as he was, he was
checked by some unfamiliar element in voice and attitude, as though a restraining force of civilisation had
been cast off by a carefully trained barbarian.

"Gone where?" she cried. "Oh, father, father, what
curse is it on us that crushes us down? I know now that
I have felt it, guessed it always, but never as I do to-
night. If you know what it is, I implore you now to do
your best to atone for it!"

Over the man's wearied face came the cold anger
which any opposition was wont to arouse in his narrow
nature.

"Are you off your head," he began, "as your grandmother has been for weeks past? Surely you never were so foolish as to attach any importance to her ravings? But there, God knows we neither of us are fit to talk any more to-night! Get to bed, child."

Forgetting his wrath, he sighed for the fateful day past, but neither his pity nor his anger turned his daughter from the impulse that swayed her, and her voice went on, rising and thrilling with that unfamiliar exotic echo in it.

"Father, by our two dead, both perhaps lying unburied to-night, will you promise me to do your best, and find out what is right to do, as Jack asked you to? If you will only promise me that, I will not trouble you any more."

"You had better not, for I have had too much of this nonsense. One would think that good taste if not good feeling would keep you from it at such a time. I have surely enough to bear to-night," was her father's icy retort, after which, ignoring her, he turned to whisper with Ellen.

In silence Margaret got on her feet and went away to her own room.

In the household confusion the lights were unlit, the shutters still unclosed, letting in a flood of white light from a full moon, now shining triumphant through a wild tumult of clouds, now lost in the darkness of their impetus.

She flung up the window, letting a rush of cool damp air beat on her as she crouched on the deep window-seat. The refreshment of the air and the darkness and silence were all she thought of first, as she listened to the hoarse roar of the river over the weir, wetting her hands with the raindrops on the ivy and pressing them against forehead. But one of the last scattered showers that end a big storm, swept up in a dark, menacing cloud like a great clutching hand, over the moon. With its darkness and with the rising gust that accompanied it, that unaccountable horror came over her again, and in a panic of fear she closed the window and shutters and lit the light on her table. She had that keen vision for trifles which is said by some to be one of the marks of a low type, and even in the tumult of her spirit her eyes did not fail to see a note laid on the stand for letters.

She knew that minute cramped writing, too, and saw that there was no postmark.

> "I got back this morning," the note ran, "and am here alone in the house waiting — You know for what. The yacht is all ready at Marseilles for us. It is too late to hesitate now. Ah, be brave, and make up your mind to come to me! Who else is there who wants you as I do? VERNADE."

Who else? No, there was no one now. Save Jack, there never had been any one good and true, and he was dead and would never be grieved to hear what she had done. If churchgoing and prayers could veil such lives as her grandmother's and her father's, should their shadow have power to spoil her happiness?

She would be happy! She would, she would! she found herself gasping as she stared into the glass at her flushed cheeks and distended eyes.

Even her own image seemed company in the solitude of the death-hushed house.

But the resolution once taken steadied her nerves and drove away her fears of the unseen world.

There was some one waiting for her, and she must get to him without delay. There was no thought, no compunction for those she was leaving; only that hysterical impulse to get away at any cost.

One of those matter-of-fact instincts of her strangely mixed nature came to remind her that she was now in all probability a rich woman. She knew that her grandmother's will had been made in her favour; she knew that. She was her father's heir without any power on his part to disinherit her; and a knowledge that however completely she might fling her destiny into Lord Vernade's hands, she would always be financially independent of him, helped to decide her. The impulse that had made her urge her father to cast off the weight of an evil inheritance was past, with all that was softer and weaker in her nature. She was a creature now of fiery passions, fierce to grasp at and keep what she wanted.

In the confusion of the past day, she still wore a walking-dress of thick serge, and the boots in which she had at midday made her way to the stables.

There only remained to take down a rough coat and hat, and she was ready. She was not of the type of the heroine of "To Leeward," who, eloping, took with her a box of hairpins and a bottle of cologne. Down the quiet passage and stairs, with a furtive glance back toward the death-chamber, out through a side door into the outside space of the moonlit night. The terrace around the house was dry, but a little canal that edged it, remnant of a former moat, had spread out into a shining sheet of water.

Here, at the foot of the terrace-steps, a punt was moored, that had been used through the day by messengers. Margaret knew the outline of the country so well that she understood exactly how she could take advantage of the shallow water that would be out over the park meadows, avoiding the heavy current of the river in flood, and coming round behind the weir to her destination.

If there had been any one abroad in the night, it might have started strange legends, the sight of that slim girlish figure, forcing her punt on with practised strokes, through the swiftly changing spaces of light and darkness, the hoarse sound of many waters around her.

Lord Vernade sat in his library, a room with big windows opening like doors on to the lawn, and, according to his usual fancy, these windows were unshuttered. He was a restless, outdoor being, and liked, even on a winter night, to step out on to the paved path for a few quiet turns.

He had been busy tearing up letters, filing away bills, making preparations for a possibly lengthy absence, but looking up thoughtfully, a bright burst of moonlight drew him to the window, which he flung open to stand watching the still writhing trees, the expanse of water above the weir.

Heavens! what was this coming toward him across the submerged lawn, this long black propelled by the woman's figure, silhouetted the shining waters beyond?

For a moment, childish recollections of a much-feared legend of a darkly veiled lady who came down the river to bring tidings of doom to his race chilled his heart. The next, his face aflame with gratified passion, he had sprung for reach the punt.

"I knew that you would be your own brave self," he said, triumphantly, as he drew her into the house.

Chapter 42

Release

Early in September, learning that she could have her friend's house at Passy for the winter, Isabel closed Heathholm and settled herself in Paris, warmly greeted by her artist friends.

"I have come to sit at your feet," she said to Edward Clarke, the apostle of a certain set of rising men.

"You need sit at no man's feet," he said, pointing to the Undine studies which she had just been showing him; "work and concentration, that is all you need to make a great picture out of that material. But," with one of his keen glances from under grizzled eyebrows, "it is not your work, but yourself that is my wonder. What fountain of youth have you discovered since last spring? You look ten years younger. Of course," with an abrupt little bow, "you were always charming, but then you were August, to-day you are June."

With that rare evanescent blush dyeing her face, she put up her hands in protest.

"Take care! If I were once to betray the fact that you could pay such compliments, your influence as a prophet would be gone."

"Influence is a thing that must take care of itself. I don't waste compliments on many people. But work,

work now!" he admonished, as he left her.

"If that poor crazy wretch were to die, I shouldn't be surprised if the old cynic, Edward Clarke, were to make a fool of himself," he muttered, as he walked down the street.

The elixir of life which Isabel had found had been the old simple draught of happiness. A happiness which, though she had not seen Gilbert since that night when they parted at Heathholm, had quenched the fever and fret of her thirst.

Gilbert had never wavered in his love, his care for her, and for his sake it was joy to be young and fair and strong, to be praised by her peers for work that but few women could do, and thus cheer him with the knowledge that her life was no poor maimed thing.

And so she began on her large picture of Undine, to be painted from her summer studies, for next year's Salon; visited her friends and entertained them, using her wealth to surround herself with all beautiful and artistic things.

And every week came Gilbert's letters, telling of his first legal steps toward proving the will, and speaking hopefully of the result; and every week she wrote him long tales of the daily current of her life, and both his and her letters had occasional phrases and self-revelations on which two souls lived.

Never had work seemed so easy to her as now, and Edward Clarke's critical approval drove her on. "Stick to it. It goes," he said, watching her work. "I have almost left off predicting anything for clever-woman work, but still I'll venture so far as to say that if you choose you have a future before you."

"Of course I choose," she retorted, her eyes still on her easel. "But why have you washed your hands of poor women-folk?"

"Why?" warming to a favourite subject, "because I've known such dozens of hard-working 'female girls,' as poor Morris calls them, and when I've asked about them a few years later, one had married a parson and only did children's portraits; another had overworked or underfed herself into nervous prostration; a third had gone to the Fiji Islands to look after her brother's orphan children, and each one of them was conspicuous by absence from the year's catalogues."

Isabel laughed idly at this diatribe.

"Well, you can except me from all those cases," she said. "I could not, if I wished to, marry again; I have a most healthy appetite, and no brothers or sisters to leave me their orphans, so don't you think you can count on me as an artist?"

"There's no foretelling the disturbing force, where women are concerned," he answered, darkly.

Isabel remembered these words, when that day she encountered a disturbing force in the person of the little Tommy Curtis whom she had seen with the Nugent-Barrs.

They met on the stairs of one of the English banks, and the round, childish face changed from thoughtfulness to smiles at sight of her.

"Mrs. Broderick! Oh, I'm so glad to see you! You remind me of the dear river! May I talk to you for a bit?"

"Certainly, my dear Miss Curtis. I was just going to take a solitary turn in the Bois, and should be delighted to have your company."

Then, with a blush and a smile, the truth came out.
"Oh, you didn't hear, then? You see I'm Mrs. Brindle,
not Miss Curtis, now. Dick and I were engaged, just
without any one knowing, and then he had a good
offer to go to South Africa, and I felt as though if I let
him go I might never see him again and — well, I was
of age and I haven't any father or mother. Just troublesome brothers, and uncles and aunts. So, the day
before he left, I slipped out and we were quietly married, and then went back and told my uncle and aunt,
and wasn't there a row!"

As the words poured out, Isabel stood looking into
the childish face in mingled amusement and respect
for the woman who had known what she wanted and
got it.

The amusement conquered in a frank laugh.

"Why, what a little wretch you were," she said, and
then, seeing a wistfulness in the eyes, she added:
"Though it was rash, I don't think it was foolish. Mr.
Brindle is an honest, kindly fellow, who, I am sure, will
make you happy."

The girl caught her breath quickly.

"That's the first kind word I've heard about him.
They called him 'fortune-hunter,' 'adventurer,' and
all such pleasant little names. I'll never forgive them
for it."

"Oh, yes, you will, when he has shown them what he
really is," Isabel said, kindly, her heart warm toward
Gilbert's friend.

Presently, when they were driving up through the
brightness, of the Champs Elysées, into the yellowing
avenues of the Bois, Isabel heard how Tommy, having

decided to follow her husband to South Africa, had
run over to Paris to say good-bye to an old aunt of
whom she was fond. She was going back the next
morning, to sail a week later.

"I do wish that I could see Meg before I go," she
said, sadly, "but she didn't write very nicely to me, and
her father is furious. You see, my brother being at the
War Office, would have made it a good affair for Jack,
only he, bless his honest heart, never saw it! And he
and Dick have come across each other out there, and
he's been awfully good to him. I wrote and told Meg
about it, and asked her to come to town and see me
before I went, but she just wrote back quite shortly
that her father didn't wish her to. And — have you
seen her at all lately?" she asked, anxiously.

"No." Isabel coloured as she answered. "She seems
to have some grievance against me in regard to Mr.
Clinch. Some one has evidently made mischief," was
her sad answer.

"She must be awfully changed," the little bride
agreed, "but what I mind the most are the queer
things people say about her and Lord Vernade."

"Surely they don't join her name with his?" Isabel
asked, aghast.

"I'm afraid so," the other acquiesced, and the two
women, who had each in their way loved Margaret,
were silent.

With the feeling of doing it for Gilbert, Isabel
bought a man's and a woman's diamond ring, and
took them to the Gare du Nord at the hour of
Tommy's departure.

"I shall be writing to Mr. Clinch," she said, bravely,

"and I shall tell him of your happiness."

"I wish that I might hear of yours," the little wife said, made wise through love, and with a warm embrace they parted.

Isabel never forgot the aspect of the Paris streets that morning, bright under a blue October sky, as she drove through them on her way back to Passy.

That drive was, in a way, an end to one chapter of her life, for when she reached home there on her writing-table lay a cablegram, which, as she opened it, she instinctively felt to be her order of release.

"Andrew Broderick died peacefully last night. No need immediate return," then came the signature of her man of business.

Such were the words that she read mechanically, passing on to sit down at an open window and stare intently at the brown leaves drifting down before a soft wind from a great lime-tree.

Last year's yellow leaves had seen her despair, the new spring ones had seen her revived courage, and now their passing was the passing of her long endurance of loneliness.

She made no effort to force her mind into pity for the dead man. She had pitied him living — she rejoiced for his sake that he was at rest, and for her own that the mockery of a tie was broken.

The spell of inactivity was broken and there was a lovely flush on her face as she reached for her gloves and stood, up. She had remembered her promise to Gilbert, and meant to keep it. There was a telegraph-office close at hand, and she would walk there, trusting no one else with the message.

"Wire date departure. Meet at Heathholm," she ended, and the clerk looked his admiration for the American lady who could thus lavish costly words.

The answer came that evening.

"Sail twenty-fifth."

She had thus a week to wait before leaving Paris, and it was an unsettled enough week. She could not work on the "Undine," which she knew would not be finished for the next Salon, though it might be ready for the New York spring shows.

She had inserted a notice of Andrew Broderick's death in Galignani and the London papers, and then closed her doors on the visits of condolence.

Edward Clarke was, however, in the habit of walking in the side door which led to the studio, and, one morning, when she was busy sorting out her portfolios, he appeared, taking in with a keen glance the preparations for departure.

"So the disturbing force has come," he said, gravely, as he took her hand. Then, as she merely bent her head, "Though I trust it may lead on into quiet paths of work?" he questioned.

"Eventually, I hope, but — there is likely to be delay now," and a deep blush told her secret.

She did not notice the old, tired look that came over his face.

"I see, I see," he said, gently. "Well, happiness and the 'warm hearthstone' are best. I trust life may not drive you back again among the toilers, but, if it does, come to me when you need help," and the words remained with her.

Chapter 43

A Forlorn Hope

It was on a morning as fine as summer that Isabel left Paris, the meaning of her plain black dress belied by the hope in her heart.

As she took her seat in the train, Elsa handed her the day's papers. To still that strange joy that almost frightened her, she opened one and glanced at it idly, the stab of a familiar name coming from the first column.

"Captain Eustace John Nugent-Barr killed trying to rally his men in a charge against the Boers."

There were only two kindly-looking old ladies in the carriage with her, and Isabel put her head down on her hands and sobbed for the honest, kindly blue-eyed boy who had loved her, for the sister who needed him so sorely. She was too sensible to blame herself, knowing well how seriously he had taken his profession, and that, happy or unhappy, he would have managed to be in the thick of it; but her heart ached for the futile waste that takes the best, leaving the feeble and useless. Not being an Englishwoman, she could not feel the proud national throb which comes as the first comfort for the loss. All that she knew was "the pity of it!" and the pity of it brooded over her for the rest of the day.

At Charing Cross there was the usual delay over luggage, and leaving Elsa to face the customs, Isabel went off to send a telegram.

Crossing near the platform where the Continental night mail was getting ready, she caught her breath at sight of a familiar figure. Margaret Nugent-Barr, in blue serge dress and a sailor hat with the bright band of her boating club, stood apparently waiting for some one near the open door of a saloon carriage.

Quickly Isabel's glance swept the neighbourhood. Yes, it was as she had guessed. Lord Vernade was giving directions to a man who was evidently his servant.

Conscious of nothing save the wave of womanly pity that bore her forward, Isabel hurried toward the lonely figure, that only as she reached it turned on her a face of startled aversion.

Such a heavy-eyed pallid face it was!

"Margaret, dear," she said, quickly, "I have been thinking of you all day, ever since I read it in the paper this morning. Oh, my heart aches for him, so brave, so young, so good! I am going home now; do come with me, and let me show you how I grieve for you."

Her hand was on Margaret's arm, but the latter shook it off as she answered, sombrely: "I am not going home, thank you. I am travelling with friends, so you need not worry about me."

"How can I help it, when I know how dear you were to Jack?"

"We will leave his name alone to-day, please. You ought to be satisfied in setting him against me. Until he knew you he was fond of me, proud of me, but after that, even to his very last letter, it was nothing but faultfinding. I never told him how I had seen through your coming to spy upon us for that man who is trying to rob us, but I think he guessed and was angry. And you think that I would let you take me home like a naughty child!"

The fierce words were poured out in an undertone that did not attract the attention of the passers-by. To Isabel they seemed the ravings of an over-wrought mind which she scarcely heeded.

"Oh, Meg," she pleaded, "if you were not so unhappy, I am sure that you would never think these cruel things of me. We used always to be such good friends. If you do not want to go home, come to my house, where we shall be all alone, and where you can rest and think about Jack."

Something like a moan broke from the girl's lips before she answered with the same subdued intensity:

"I mustn't rest. I mustn't think! I am going abroad to-night."

"Meg, I have known what it was not to dare to rest or think. Listen for a moment. You have felt that, believing in nothing, hoping for nothing, you had a right to do the thing you chose, and to let go your hold on all good. Yes, I knew all that when I saw my child lying dead under his mad father's grasp, but I managed to hold on to something, I hardly knew at first what it was, sense of duty, or personal pride, or what, but it kept me on my feet until I got back my reasoning powers. Ah, Meg, it can't be worse with you than it was with me then, and yet I lived it down. It's not too late to go back. Only have the courage to do so, and you will thank God all your life, Meg —"

The momentary flash of startled awe with which the girl had heard of so awful a tale was past, and Isabel knew that the fight was lost, and that she had laid bare her heart in vain, even before she heard the sullen words: "You have no right to torment me like this! You don't know. There is no going back possible. I have thrown in my lot with the only person who really cares for me, Ah, here he comes!" with a low laugh. "Are you going to make a scene, or will you go away now? When you write to him, tell him that he shall not get my money without a fight for it."

On the last contemptuous words she faltered, and a ghost of the old friendly light flickered in her eyes, as she whispered: "I think that perhaps you really meant to help me, but it's too late."

Heart-sick and trembling, Isabel was at that pass when a good woman forgets every personal thought in a passion of pity. She would have pleaded on, but that she saw that Lord Vernade had become aware of their interview, and was coming forward as though to interrupt it. Him she could not face, and so turned away with a sharp sob of pain for the unhappy girl.

Gradually her mind went back to her own personal happiness. Never before had she returned to Heathholm but with a shrinking from the lonely home-coming. How sweet and strange it was now to know that it was the destined meeting-place for her and Gilbert.

The gray autumn afternoon was already darkening when she drove up to the house, and she was tired out with the mental and physical strain of the day. But that strain was not destined to be ended yet, for the servant, who had known of her friendship with Margaret, met her with excited tales of the girl's disappearance the night before. It had been at first supposed that the shock of her brother's and grandmother's death had so disturbed her mind that she had taken the punt and gone either to suicide or an accidental death. They had been all the morning dragging for her body, when a lodge-keeper at Templemere had appeared on the scene with positive assurances that Miss Nugent-Barr had driven through the Park gates with Lord Vernade in the direction of Henley.

"And they do say at the house, mum, that she must have gone there in the punt last night, though how any mortal woman managed it against the current, with the water out —"

"That will do, thanks, Parsons. I must dress now," Isabel said, wearily, but the weariness went as she caught sight of a pile of letters and a telegram.

Yes, the latter was what she had been hoping for, a wire from Gilbert, sent ashore in Ireland, to say that he would be with her to-morrow. The sin and the sorrow that had so troubled her melted away to a distance, and a great peace soothed her.

But in the morning she did not find it so easy to be tranquil. To begin with, it went sorely against the grain to meet Gilbert in a black dress, but she was shy of doing otherwise before the servants.

"If only we had brought some flowers from town," she lamented to Elsa, as she stood before the glass.

She went out into the garden, basking in pale autumn sunshine, and her search was rewarded by a handful of late pale pink roses. Pressing their petals to her hot cheeks, she whispered:

"You used to comfort me last autumn, you dears, now you must be happy with me."

Then came the question of where she would welcome Gilbert, and that proved unexpectedly hard to settle. The studio was dismantled, the drawing-room was too formal, the garden too public. For a time she even debated driving down to meet him, but that was given up, and then things settled themselves unexpectedly, as they have a way of doing.

After lunch a good two hours before she could expect him, she lay down on the drawing-room sofa to rest, "just for ten minutes," but, tired out with yesterday's journey and agitation, she dropped into a deep sleep from which she only started to see a tall figure looking down at her, to hear a deep voice: "Isabel! At last!" and to find herself gathered, all confused and flushed with sleep, into his arms.

After a time, she said: "Let me have a look at you," and held him off with her hands.

Bronzed from the sea-voyage, and with hair a bit longer than usual, he had lost the air of a dweller in cities.

"You look like a wild man of the woods."

"That's just because my hair needs cutting. The ocean tan will soon wear off. But you," he said, tenderly, "you look tired, and there is an air about you that is almost sad. Surely, dearest, that has all passed now?"

"I am not sad now, but I was yesterday," she said, simply, laying her hand on his as he sat beside her.

"But how could you be sad, even then?" he protested.

"It was not sadness for myself, but for others. Oh, Gilbert, you know that I was fond of Meg and Jack?"

"Yes — well?"

And then she told the tale of the last twenty-four hours, breaking down into sobbing before she ended.

"What pains me most is the thought of that one small bit of softening at the last. It seems as though a little more effort might have saved her."

Gilbert soothed her "as a lover can."

"You did all you could," he said, decisively.

"Nothing could have saved her. She was doomed by temperament — the true fate. But that poor, true-hearted fellow, what a life to be flung away like that! Do you know, after he got out there, he wrote to me — such a simple, manly letter — saying that he wished to persuade his father to some compromise, and hoped we might some day become good friends. 'I feel sure,' he added, 'that when she is a bit wiser and older, my sister will see things more as I do.' I am so glad now to know that he had that feeling toward me," Gilbert ended, with a sigh.

"Yes, and it was all the finer," she said, eagerly, "because when he went he knew, he guessed, that it was you —" And she smiled up at him.

"And yet he could feel kindly toward me!" he said, in wondering admiration.

Gilbert had his own tale to tell of legal delays and difficulties.

"Though I can see no reason why I may not succeed in the end," he said.

To this Isabel seemed irresponsive, though she

roused quickly enough, when he said: "I wonder if you are really a brave woman."

"What do you mean?" she asked, startled.

"I mean a woman who is brave enough to set her own and another's happiness above any dread of public comment or criticism. Isabel, for more than a year Andrew Broderick has been dead to you. Will you marry me now without any further delay, and come home to begin our new life together?"

For a moment she sat silently watching the flickering firelight that now seemed to have possession of the room, while he looked intently into her face, then, she turned to him, laying her hand in his, that closed around it firmly, and said, gently: "Yes, Gilbert, I will do whatever you wish."

Chapter 44

"Homeward Bound"

And so it was settled that as soon as the reading of the bans was over they should be married in the little gray village church among the trees. Meanwhile, Gilbert was installed in his old lodgings. How much there was to tell of and talk over! Gilbert had been offered a splendid appointment in one of the foremost medical colleges of the day.

"How will you like being a professor's wife?" he asked.

"As long as it lets me be an artist, too. I could never face Edward Clarke again unless I finished my 'Undine.'"

"You shall finish it — after our honeymoon," he promised.

And then he had to hear of the love-affairs of Tommy and Brindle. The next morning he was help-ing Isabel to elaborate a scheme of hers for endowing a fund for the yearly purchase of six pictures by American artists, to be called the Andrew Broderick Fund, when a servant came in to say that an old woman wished especially to see Mrs. Broderick, and seemed distressed when told that she was engaged.

"It is some of my old cottage friends needing help,

perhaps. Show her in here," Isabel said. But the first sight of the woman, in careful new black clothes, and with tired face and tremulous aspect, told that this was a graver matter than some small charity.

"Sit down and rest. You are tired." Isabel said, kindly, but merely acknowledging the words with a polite "Thank you, ma'am," the old woman fixed her blue eyes intently on Gilbert.

"I took the liberty of coming to ask Mrs. Broderick if she could tell me where to find Mr. Gilbert Clinch," she began, "but, if I'm not mistook, this is him. I'm sure it couldn't be no one else. You are Susan Bauer's son, aren't you, sir?" and there was a touch of appeal under the assumed primness of her manner.

Gilbert's first surprise over, he knew at once that this must be Ellen Sievert, one of the witnesses to the disputed will, whose evidence was to count for much. Not wishing to startle her, he answered, pleasantly: "Yes, I am Susan Bauer's son, and you, I think, are Ellen Sievert. And why did you want to see me?"

The old woman turned her troubled eyes upon Isabel.

"If I might speak to you alone, sir," she hesitated.

"Mrs. Broderick knows all about my family," he reassured her. "She was living at the Moorings when Isaac Neisner told me about my grandfather, and she and I found the jewelled Virgin in the garret, the Virgin of Wrath."

At these last words the modest self-restraint of the old woman's best manners dropped from her like a veil, dropped as did the umbrella and bag from her hands.

"For the Lord's sake, sir! You found her at the Moorings? Well, I never! Then there was something true in what my old man used to mutter at night, when I thought it was just pork-chops or doughnuts. *He* saw *her* often enough at the last. Well, he's dead, and nearly every one else seems to be, excepting Isaac and me. But your mother, she's younger than me. She's not dead, is she?"

"No," was all Gilbert answered. He was leaving her to say her say in her own fashion.

"Well, I'm glad of that," Ellen Sievert conceded, in a more politely conversational tone. "We were always good friends when we went to school together. And you have a look of her" — with a critical inspection of Gilbert — "the honest, clean, Dutch look that she had. Tell you what, young man, you may thank the Lord that there's no drop in your veins of the blood of that old woman they buried to-day." With these last words her face had hardened with a tragic recollection.

"Why?" he asked, quietly.

"Because it's the snake's blood of a brown Martinique girl, and if you've never heard what that means, you've never sailed about the West Indies as I have, when my husband was master of a fine Lunenburg schooner."

She drew a deep breath, then, as the other two waited in silence, she went on: "Yes, a brown Martinique girl she was, and I've known it for years, and yet I came away with her and tended her faithfully when she got old and feeble, until that awful night when the Powers of Darkness called her in the storm. Lord sakes, I was near to crossing myself like a Papist in my fears of what might be around me! It was just at the end when the priest hadn't come, and she was shrieking out for him, that she told us how she had given the old master the stuff that killed him.

"We always knew, Isaac and I, that she had queer drugs and potions, and that was what frightened Isaac, and sent him off home after the master died. He was right, perhaps, but I was fond of the children, and stayed with my little Meg, and I always would have, too, if the finding out the old wickedness hadn't turned her brain and made her wicked, too."

At the sound of Meg's name, spoken with such simple pathos, Isabel caught her breath sharply and Gilbert's face grew sombre, but neither tried to speak, and the shrill voice of old age went on: "She was white and silent like a ghost, just crouching in corners that sorrowful day, after the news came of my poor boy's death. And she was frightened, too — Lord! She was down on the floor, hiding her poor pretty face, when the old lady screeched out that she had done it, and a tree crashed up against the house, just like long ago at home when the master died." Her voice had grown reminiscent, but she roused herself again to the present.

"And then, when it was quiet again — for the wind went when she went — didn't I hear my poor child a-begging her pa, by 'our two unburied dead,' she says, if there had been sin to do justice now.

"And when he got angry, as he does in that cold spiteful fashion of his, if any one breathes a word about his money, and told her to hold her tongue and go off to her bed, she just slipped away by herself to

her room while I was busy. And her ma was calling for
me, and, like an old idiot that I was, I fell asleep in her
room, being clean worn out, without ever going to see
that my pretty dear was all right. And in the morning,
when I thought to find her sleeping peaceful, she was-
n't there," and the two wrinkled hands dropped heavily upon her knees with a gesture of utter hopelessness.

"The Lord knows," she added, half to herself, "that
she must have been demented by trouble to go to that
lazy, smiling devil! And now," she went on, "her pa's
cursing her because she's got all her grandmother's
money. But I say as it's a good thing she has, or that
lord might be leaving her to starve when he's tired of
her, as he has others before now —"

At this, Isabel winced in intolerable pain, a movement which the old woman was quick to remark.

"Dear, dear," she said, with compunction, "it's a
dreadful thing to have a tongue that goes as mine
does. I ought to have minded that you were a friend
to her, ma'am, the poor lamb. But it comes of my feelings being so bottled up of late, for I knew well that
the poor, misguided child was meeting him about the
country, and yet, like the old fool I am, I did nothing.

"But I've given up the family now, and I'm going
back to end my days in the old place comfortably on
my savings. And that was why I wanted special, sir, to
find you out before I went. I had heard enough bits of
talk to know as you were trying to get your rights to
some of your grandpa's money, even before the letter
came asking me about being witness to that will as we
never heard no more on, and glad enough I'd be to

help you, for the sake of the days when your mother and I were girls together."

"Thank you," Gilbert said, quietly, though Isabel could see that his face was set in intense thought.

"Will you tell me what you remember about the will?" he went on, forbearing to prompt her.

"'Deed, and I remember everything about it, for many a time I've gone over it all in my mind, as I might have been reading it in a newspaper. It was the week before the old man died, and the mistress had gone out to church — it was some saint's day, I think — and I was ironing some of her laces when Isaac calls me up-stairs, and there was the master, propped up with pillows, a sort of writing-book before him, and a pen in his hand. Like the dead he looked, saving that his eyes were fierce and bright.

"'Watch me write my name, and then you two write yours after,' says he, short and sharp, in his old way, and we did it.

"'Now go,' says he, 'and don't ye speak of this to no one,' which we didn't, being used to obeying of him. And remembering it as though it were yesterday, I'm willing to testify in a court of justice, and I hope it may do you good, sir."

Her good-will was evident, and Gilbert answered, gratefully: "Thank you, Ellen. It may be of great help."

"And there's another thing as I made up my mind to tell you," she went on, "seeing that perhaps you never heard as there was a doubt whether the old master had ever married her when he brought her home?"

"No, I have not heard that," he put in.

"Well, you see, the sailors always had queer tales,

some of them saying as he won her at cards, the others, as he carried her off against her will.

"However it was, she hated him, and yet never tried any of her tricks with him. He had a grim way of chuckling at her, too, if ever she showed a spice of temper, as though he knew that he had the whip-hand of her. One way or another he generally did have the whip-hand. As he got feebler he seemed to feel the need to be cautious with her, doing things that more than once made me think he was afraid of poison. He mostly always managed that it was Isaac or me that took him his food. She thought the world and all of her son then, before she got tired of his meanness and dullness, and of his poor stupid wife; then she lost interest in all save Meg, who, I think, she did care for to the last — my poor little Meg whose soul she brought to the same ruin as she did her own." The old woman sighed deeply, and Isabel laid a kindly hand upon her wrinkled one in silent sympathy.

"God bless your good face," Ellen said, then, with an effort at briskness, "Well, I'm leaving the Grange in the morning, but if you'll write me a line, telling me what you want me to do when I get home, it will find me at 45 Culver Street, Islington, where I'm boarding for a week to buy some bits of duds, as are nowhere cheaper than in London. And if it's not a liberty, sir," rising as she spoke, "I'd like to shake hands and wish you good luck for the sake of Susan Bauer in old times."

"My good friend, yes," Gilbert said, "and thank you heartily for your kindliness. I shall write or see you before you sail, and" — turning to Isabel — "I am sure that this dear lady joins with me in saying that if ever you want a home or friends you will find them with us."

This first open linking of their names brought a wonderful glow to Isabel's face.

"Yes, indeed," she said, softly.

"'Deed and is that so?" crowed the old woman, jubilantly. "'Now may the Lord bless you and give you joy in each other,'" and the blessing sounded very sweet in their ears.

When Ellen Sievert had left them, the two stood together before the fire. Isabel was the first to break the silence.

"Gilbert," she began, in a low voice, "you heard what she said were Margaret's words — 'by our two unburied dead to-night, do justice'?"

"Yes."

"And you know what her brother wrote to you?"

"Yes," then suddenly turning and taking her two hands in his while his voice deepened with feeling: "And you have something to ask of me, and I cannot even have the joy of granting your first request, because I have already made up my mind that not one penny of that money shall follow us into our new life. I know that my uncle has no power to disinherit his daughter. Let it all go to make her dark way easier. A woman with ample independent means may be made unhappy enough, but she cannot be utterly crushed. My professor's pay is ample for my personal needs, but if I want more I can get it by writing."

Isabel looked mournful.

"But you won't refuse to share all that money of mine?" she protested.

"I won't refuse to share anything of yours, sweetheart, but you'll let me have my own little hoard for my private fads. And soon it will be "homeward bound," with the shadows all behind us. Only we must have a time to ourselves first: tell me, where shall it be spent, — on the Nile?" The Nile was agreed on, and it was the following March before Gilbert Clinch and his wife landed in New York.

Soon after, about the same time that the Andrew Broderick Artist Fund was made known to the public, there was an anonymous gift of fifty thousand dollars made to a home for old sailors, "being part of a fortune their toil had helped to accumulate."

Formac Fiction Treasures

ALSO IN THE SERIES

By Evelyn Eaton

Quietly My Captain Waits
This historical romance, set during the years of French-English struggle in
New France, draws two lovers out of the shadows of history — Louise de
Freneuse, married and widowed twice, and Pierre de Bonaventure, Fleet
Captain in the French navy. Their almost impossible relationship helps
them endure the day-to-day struggle in the fated settlement of Port Royal.
ISBN 0-88780-544-2

The Sea is So Wide
In the summer of 1755, Barbe Comeau offers her family home in the lush
farmland of the Annapolis Valley as overnight shelter to an English officer and his surly companion. The Comeaus are unaware of the treacherous plans to confiscate the Acadian farms and send them all into exile. A
few weeks later, they are crammed into the hold of a ship and sent south.
In Virginia she patiently rebuilds her life, never expecting that the friend
she believed had betrayed her and her family would search until he found
her. ISBN 0-88780-573-6

By W. Albert Hickman

The Sacrifice of the Shannon
In the heart of Frederick Ashburn, sea captain and sportsman, there glows
a secret fire of love for young Gertrude MacMichael. But her interests lie
with Ashburn's fellow adventurer, the dashing and slightly mysterious
Dave Wilson. From their hometown of Caribou (real-life Pictou) all three
set out on a perilous journey to the ice fields in the Gulf of St. Lawrence
to save a ship and its precious cargo — Gertrude's father. In almost constant danger, Wilson is willing to risk everything to bring the ship and
crew to safety. ISBN 0-88780-542-6

By Alice Jones (Alix John)

The Night Hawk
Set in Halifax during the American Civil War, a wealthy Southerner —
beautiful, poised, intelligent and divorced — poses as a refugee while

using her social success to work undercover. The conviviality of the town's social elite, especially the British garrison officers is more than just a diversion when there is a war to be won.

By Charles G.D. Roberts

The Heart That Knows
On her wedding day a young girl is suddenly abandoned. Standing on the Bay of Fundy shore she watches her husband's barquentine sail away without a word of explanation. Weeks follows days and she is left to face life as an outcast, scorned by her neighbours and family for being a mother, but not a wife. Over the years her son, like many sailors' children, grows up without a father. Confronted with the truth, the young man sets off to sea, determined not to return to his New Brunswick home until he seeks vengeance on the man who treated his mother so heartlessly. ISBN 0-88780-570-1

By Margaret Marshall Saunders

Beautiful Joe
Cruelly mutilated by his master, Beautiful Joe, a mongrel dog, is at death's door when he finds himself in the loving care of Laura Morris. A tale of tender devotion between dog and owner, this novel is the framework for the author's astute and timeless observations on farming methods, including animal care, and rural living. This Canadian classic, written by a woman once acclaimed as "Canada's Most Revered Writer," has been popular with readers, including young adults, for almost a century. ISBN 0-88780-540-X

Rose of Acadia
One hundred and fifty years have past since the Acadians were sent into exile; now, Vesper Nimmo, a Bostonian, sets out for Nova Scotia's French shore with the intention of carrying out his great-grandfather's wish to make amends to the descendants of Agapit LeNoir. Nimmo immerses himself in the struggles of the Acadians to preserve their culture and language while the lure of money and modern conveniences draws young people to the Boston states. He meets beautiful, angelic Rose à Charlitte, the innkeeper where he makes his temporary home. When he becomes ill she cares for him, but when he falls in love with her, she cannot marry him — not until she is freed from her past. ISBN 0-88780-571-X